FIRE CASTE

The lone alien stepped forward and dropped to its haunches, bringing its impassive crystal lenses level with his face. There was a crimson slash running along the spine of its helmet, identifying it as the leader, but Iverson was drawn to another mark – a deep crack running from its crown to the chin of its faceplate. The damage had been patched up, but the rippled scar of a chainsword was unmistakeable to a commissar.

'Your face,' he breathed. 'Show me.' The warrior tilted its head quizzically at the challenge. 'Or are you afraid?'

'Be watchful, shas'ui.' It was one of the traitors, his voice surprisingly crisp through his sealed helmet. 'This one is of the commissar caste. Even wounded this one will not yield.'

A WARHAMMER 40,000 NOVEL

FIRE CASTE

PETER FEHERVARI

BLACK LIBRARY

For my father, Professor Geza Fehervari, a passionate scholar, impeccable gentleman and the best of friends, who stepped into his Thunderground during the writing of this novel.
May you find your way through the storm.

A BLACK LIBRARY PUBLICATION

First published in Great Britain in 2013 by
Black Library,
Games Workshop Ltd.,
Willow Road, Nottingham,
NG7 2WS, UK.

10 9 8 7 6 5 4 3 2 1

Cover illustration by Hardy Fowler.

A CIP record for this book is available from the British Library.

UK ISBN: 978 1 84970 308 6
US ISBN: 978 1 84970 309 3

See Black Library on the internet at
www.blacklibrary.com

Find out more about Games Workshop
and the world of Warhammer 40,000 at
www.games-workshop.com

Printed and bound by CPI Group (UK) Ltd, Croydon, CR0 4YY

It is the 41st millennium. For more than a hundred centuries
the Emperor has sat immobile on the Golden Throne of Earth.
He is the master of mankind by the will of the gods, and master
of a million worlds by the might of his inexhaustible armies. He
is a rotting carcass writhing invisibly with power from the Dark
Age of Technology. He is the Carrion Lord of the Imperium for
whom a thousand souls are sacrificed every day, so that he may
never truly die.

Yet even in his deathless state, the Emperor continues his
eternal vigilance. Mighty battlefleets cross the daemon-infested
miasma of the warp, the only route between distant stars, their
way lit by the Astronomican, the psychic manifestation of the
Emperor's will. Vast armies give battle in His name on uncounted
worlds. Greatest amongst his soldiers are the Adeptus Astartes,
the Space Marines, bio-engineered super-warriors. Their comrades
in arms are legion: the Imperial Guard and countless Planetary
Defence Forces, the ever-vigilant Inquisition and the tech-priests of
the Adeptus Mechanicus to name only a few. But for all their
multitudes, they are barely enough to hold off the ever-present
threat from aliens, heretics, mutants - and worse.

To be a man in such times is to be one amongst untold
billions. It is to live in the cruellest and most bloody
regime imaginable. These are the tales of those times.
Forget the power of technology and science, for so much has
been forgotten, never to be re-learned. Forget the promise of
progress and understanding, for in the grim dark future
there is only war. There is no peace amongst the stars,
only an eternity of carnage and slaughter, and the
laughter of thirsting gods.

DRAMATIS PERSONAE

THE PHAEDRAN COMMISSARIAT

Holt Iverson	Veteran Commissar
Lomax	High Commissar
Ysabel Reve	Commissar Cadet

THE ARKAN CONFEDERATES

Ensor Cutler	Colonel, 1st Company
Skjoldis 'Lady Raven'	Sanctioned Psyker/ Norland Witch
'Mister Frost'	The Colour Bearer/ Norland *Weraldur*
Elias Waite	Major, 2nd Company
Jon Milton Machen	Captain, 3rd Company
Ambrose Templeton	Captain, 4th Company
Hardin Vendrake	Captain, Silverstorm Sentinel Cavalry
Pericles Quint	Lieutenant, Silverstorm Sentinel Cavalry
Beauregard Van Hal	Silverstorm Sentinel Cavalry
Willis Calhoun	Sergeant, Dustsnake Squad
Claiborne Roach	Greyback Trooper, Dustsnake Squad
Gordy Boone	Greyback Trooper, Dustsnake Squad
Kletus Modine	Greyback Trooper, Dustsnake Squad
Jakob Dix	Greyback Trooper, Dustsnake Squad
Obadiah Pope	Greyback Trooper, Dustsnake Squad

Audie Joyce	Greencap Rookie, Dustsnake Squad
Cort Toomy	Greyback Sniper, Dustsnake Squad
Jaques Valance	Scout, 3rd Company

THE LETHEAN PENITENTS

Yosiv Gurdjief	Penitent Confessor
Vyodor Karjalan	Admiral
Zemyon Rudyk	Penitent Commissar Cadet
Csanad Vaskó	Corsair Zabaton

THE 33RD VERZANTE SKYSHADOWS

| Jaime Hernandez Garrido | Pilot |
| Guido Gonzalo Ortega | Co-Pilot |

THE VERZANTE KONQUISTADORES

| Ricardo Alvarez | Corporal |
| Cristobal Olim | Aristocrat Officer |

THE UNQUIET DEAD

Nathaniel Bierce	Commissar, deceased
Detlef Niemand	Commissar, deceased
Number 27	Unknown Soldier, deceased

THE TAU

Shas'el Aabal	Fire Warrior Commander
Shas'ui Jhi'kaara	Pathfinder
Por'o Dal'yth Seishin	Water Caste Ambassador

PROLOGUE

Dolorosa Topaz – Thunderground?

And so we come to it. Well I'll tell you what I know, but be
warned that my mind may wander. The fever has a hold on
me once again and I'm freezing and burning up by turns.
As I write I can see my phantoms stalking from the emerald
shadows, staking their claim on the sins of my past. My
phantoms? Oh, there are three, standing shoulder to shoulder
in mute condemnation of my failings. To the right is Old
Man Bierce, inhumanly tall in his spotless black storm coat,
pinning me with that raptor's glare. To the left is Commissar
Niemand, pale and shrunken with the revelation of his own
eternally unravelling entrails, trapped forever in the moment
when I turned my back on him. And at the centre, always at
the centre, stands Number 27, her three immaculate, dead
eyes the greatest misery and mystery of them all.

Fever dreams or visions? I doubt it matters. Whatever
they are, they've come to bear witness when I walk my

Thunderground. No, don't concern yourself with the
expression. It's just an old myth from my home world.
We Arkan are a strange breed and there are some things
even the schola progenium couldn't drum out of me. The
Imperium took me away from my home long ago, but it
couldn't take my home away from me. Sometimes blood
runs deeper than faith.

But that's not what I wanted to tell you about. The
Thunderground has called to me and if I don't return, and it
falls to you to take my place, you'll need facts. You'll need to
understand the true nature of your enemy. Most importantly
you'll need to understand that you face a twofold beast.

First there's the foe you've travelled across the stars to
destroy: an unholy coalition of rebels and aliens who'll
butcher your men with anything from a bow to a burst
cannon. The tau are behind it all of course. You've read
the Tactica manuals so you'll already know how these
xenos operate. On this world they call their movement
'the Concordance', but don't dignify them with the
name. You'll find the same old pattern of infiltration and
corruption, so just call them blueskin bastards and purge
them as best you can.

Their leader calls himself Commander Wintertide – an
irony on a planet where winter is just a myth – but then
Wintertide himself sometimes seems little more than a
myth. He casts a long shadow, but you'll never actually
see him. Well, I plan to put his myth to the test. If it can be
done I'm going to find him and kill him.

But let me tell you about your other enemy, the spirit
killer who'll steal away your troops before they even face
the rebels. For men like you and I, pledged to put the steel

in their spines and the fire in their hearts, She's the true enemy here. Of course I'm talking of Phaedra Herself, this cesspit planet we've come to liberate or conquer or cleanse. Sometimes I forget which it is. It's been a long war.

Phaedra: too lazy to be a death world, too bitter to be anything else. While She can't muster the riot of murderous beasts or geological torments of a true death world, you mustn't underestimate Her. She'll do Her killing slowly – stealthy but steady. And yes, I do mean 'She'. All the troops know it, although High Command denies it. Survive long enough and you'll know it too. Just as you'll know She's corrupt to Her mouldering, waterlogged core, no matter what the Ecclesiarchy assessors say. You'll know it in the mist and the rain and the creeping damp that will be your constant companions here, but most of all you'll know it in Her jungles.

You see, you've come to a water world and found a grey-green hell like no other. The oceans of Phaedra are choked with islands and in turn the islands are overrun with a wildfire cancer of vegetation – a morass of stinking kelp, strangling vines and towering fungal cathedrals. Worse still, the islands themselves are alive. Just look beneath the waterline and you'll see them breathing and pulsing. The biologis tech-priests say it's some kind of coral – a minor, mindless blasphemy of xenos diversity. They say there's no taint to it, but I've heard the bitter blood music beating through this world and I say they're fools.

And so you've had your warning and my duty to you is done. Time is pressing and I must make my final preparations. Didn't I tell you there's a storm coming? It won't be one of Phaedra's killer typhoons, but it'll be a big

one all the same. I can taste it in the angry, electric air.
And they can taste it too, the rats hiding in the skins of
my charges and turning brave men sour. My charges? Oh,
they were called the Verzante Konquistadores back when
they were still a regiment unbroken by Phaedra's wiles.
Now they're little more than relics left to rot. Not unlike
myself. Perhaps that's why fate has led me to them. And
perhaps that's why I still care enough to try and save them.
They were never the finest troops in the Imperial Guard, but
they're not beyond redemption even now.

There are seven in particular whose struggles have been
piteous and an eighth beyond pity. I've watched them
teeter on the brink of heresy, held back by some last vestige
of honour or faith or perhaps simple fear. But now the storm
will kindle an unholy fire in their hearts and give them that
final push. I have to be there for them.

You are right – I have been weak. Doubtless my old
mentor Bierce would tell me an example was required long
ago, but I'm as broken as everything else in this meat-
grinder war. I've not had the courage to administer the
Emperor's Justice since the debacle of Indigo Gorge and
Number 27. Perhaps if I'd had Bierce's fire or Niemand's
ice and was a finer exemplar of our special brotherhood,
things would be different now and these Guardsmen
wouldn't have strayed so far, but Bierce and Niemand are
long dead and I'm the last one left to hold the line.

The traitors think I'm fever-blind, but I've caught their
sly whispers and know the truth of it. Tonight they'll run
and I'll be waiting.

Iverson's Journal

It was never truly dark in the Mire. By day the jealous canopy of the trees strangled the sunlight into a trickle, drowning the jungle in murk. By night the swarming fungi awoke, flooding the grottos and glades with bioluminescence, transforming the morass into a pungent wonderland. It was a world of rival twilights, but still the ghosts came out at night.

They bled from the tangled skein of the jungle and hovered furtively at the edge of the clearing. There were seven, every one an emaciated shadow in rotting fatigues. In the bilious light their khaki uniforms were a patchwork purple and their eyes seemed to glitter with indigo fire. Crouching at the tree line they scanned the clearing, battered lasrifles flitting about warily. With a flick of the wrist from the leader they dissolved into two teams and fanned out along the perimeter. Motionless, the leader kept watch on the ruin crouched at the centre of the glade.

The rain had turned hard and heavy, battering through the vault of the jungle and raising streamers of mist, but the pale dome of the temple glowed through the murk. It was typical of the indigenous architecture. Deprived of stone, the ancient Phaedrans had carved their buildings from coral, imbuing them with a globular, organic look that was repellent to Imperial eyes. The central cupola had collapsed and the walls were honeycombed with fissures, but there was no trace of the weeds or creeper vines that preyed on more wholesome relics. A circle of barren ground radiated from the temple, holding the jungle at bay for some ten metres or so. It was a pattern played out by a myriad dead temples across the planet. The mystery fascinated the Mechanicus priests, but to Ignatz Cabeza it was just another sign of this world's fundamental *wrongness*.

The sergeant was a wiry cadaver of a man, his features

moulded into a death mask by a paste of grey mud. His eyes gleamed in the hollows of the camouflage, the irises iridescent with the bloom of a Glory fugue, but Cabeza was no degenerate. He reviled most of Phaedra's fungal narcotics, but the Glory was different, its spores granting that razorwire sharpness a warrior sometimes found in the heat of battle. Of course the Glory was forbidden, but deep in the Mire, far from the vigilant eyes of the priests and commissars, a man made his own laws. Uneasily his thoughts drifted to Iverson, the wreck of a commissar who'd joined his regiment a month back. The man had presided over the remnants of the 6th Tempest like a carrion bird shadowing a dying man. And of course the 6th *was* dying.

The fall of Cabeza's regiment was a slow burning shame in his heart. They were Verzante, Konquistadores of the Galleon Meridian, Guardsmen of the God-Emperor and they had exulted in this campaign! Whipped into a fervour by Aguilla de Caravajal, the holy Water Dragon of the 6th Tempest, they had joined the crusade to Phaedra joyfully, eager to brand their name upon this heathen world. Instead they had drowned in its filth.

How long had it been? Three years? Four? Caravajal himself had fallen in the second year, raving and incontinent with blood, unravelled from within by a borefly infestation. Inevitably the regiment had unravelled in his wake, a thousand proud Konquistadores fading to a few hundred shadows. Tactically marginal, they had been shunted off to this worthless island crawling with xenos-tainted savages. Dolorosa Topaz – a backwater corner of the war where victory was as impossible as it was irrelevant. And here they were forgotten. *Almost.*

Long months after their exile began, an Imperial gunboat had appeared on the horizon. The Verzante gathered on the shore and Velasquez, the veteran capitán who'd held them together by sheer force of will, dared to make a show of hope, but the boat had carried neither reinforcements nor supplies, just a scarecrow in black.

There had been no mistaking the figure standing in the prow of the approaching boat. Strikingly tall and straight in his leather storm coat, his square-jawed face shadowed by a high peaked cap, he was a commissar cut in the classic mould. Watching him, Cabeza had shuddered. Though the 6th had lost both its disciplinary officers long ago, they'd left him with plenty of scars to remember them by. Not that he held it against them. He'd been a rowdy dog until the commissars had whipped him into shape. Luckily he'd been a quick learner, unlike his clan brother Greko, who'd wound up hanging by his heels in the parade ground as an example to the new recruits. After that they'd *all* been quick learners. And so Cabeza had wondered what this new tyrant would teach them.

But when the commissar stepped from the boat Cabeza had seen the truth of him. The newcomer's cap was tattered and his leather coat was more grey than black, its edges encrusted with a rime of mould. Up close he'd been pallid and unshaven, his grey hair hanging well below the shoulders. He was probably no more than forty-five, but already old with something that cut deeper than age. Worse still was the telltale lattice of a spidervine burn inscribed into his face. Only a blind man or a man too ignorant to see could have taken such a wound. Perhaps it had happened a lifetime ago, back in the commissar's first tour of the Mire, but to Cabeza the scar still marked him out as a fool.

Phaedra has no mercy for fools…

The newcomer's faded blue eyes had skimmed the Konquistadores briefly. Distant. Disinterested. 'Iverson', he'd said.

Then he'd stalked past them to claim a tent.

Commissar Iverson's tenure continued as it had begun. Aloof and indifferent, he had kept to his tent or wandered the jungle alone, scribbling away in his battered leather journal. Sometimes he talked to himself or to something in the shadows only he could see. Like a man possessed. And maybe he was. Cabeza had seen stranger things in his time. In any case Iverson had caught the fever in his second week and hadn't left his tent since. He was just another wreck among so many. An irrelevance... Cabeza had believed it until he'd glimpsed the commissar watching the camp from the shadows of his tent. And recently he'd caught Iverson's fever-bright eyes looking directly at him. *Almost as if he knew the treachery in Ignatz Cabeza's heart...*

Something battered through the foliage behind the sergeant. He scowled as the sour-sweet stench of zoma juice hit him. Zoma! Now there was a true high road to oblivion, exactly the kind of fool's glow that Cabeza despised. Almost as much as he despised the man who lumbered up alongside him. Cristobal Olim had rubbed the camouflage away from his pasty face, leaving it luminous in the fungal light.

'I told you to wait, señor,' Cabeza hissed.

'It's raining. The water was pooling in my boots,' there was a strident whine to Olim's voice that set Cabeza's teeth on edge. The few he still had left. 'Besides you've found our objective, sergeant!' Olim stepped forward and peered at the temple, his eyes bleary with zoma. 'Oh yes, you've most definitely found it. I knew my faith in you wasn't misplaced!'

Olim took another step forward and stumbled, his feet skittering on the rain-slick coral. Cabeza let him fall, keeping his attention on his comrades as they completed their sortie and converged across the clearing. Corporal Alvarez waved him the all clear – no threats on the periphery of the zone. That just left the temple itself. Cabeza signalled the advance.

Olim was still slithering about on the ground, whimpering as he tried to find purchase on the coral. Cabeza hauled him up with one hand, keeping his lasrifle steady with the other.

'On your feet, señor,' Cabeza said. 'I don't want to lose you.'

Olim clutched at his arm, his tone suddenly sly, 'No, you don't sergeant. You really don't. Because I'm the one they want, remember. I'm the officer here!'

Cabeza looked at him. The man's attempt at cunning was pathetic. Although the Mire had sucked the meat out of him Olim still looked fat. How was that even possible? Staring at that saggy sponge of a face, with its bulging eyes and deli-cate, zoma-stained lips, Cabeza felt an almost physical need for violence. He hated Olim. They all did. The fat aristo was responsible for the massacre of Capitán Velasquez and the other commanders. He'd been the duty officer on the night when a dead-eyed native had walked into camp with tales of a rebel supply dump. Hungry for approval, Olim had led the native straight to the command tent, where the infiltrator had triggered the melta bomb wired into his guts. Velasquez and the other officers had died instantly, but in a twist of fate Olim had escaped untouched. As the only surviving officer, he'd inherited command and carried the 6th Tempest into its final death spiral. The man was a travesty.

'Why… why are you looking at me like that, sergeant?' The wheedling tone was back and Cabeza turned away before it was too late. Olim was a degenerate, but he was the one who'd made contact with the rebels. How he'd managed it was anybody's guess, but he was Cabeza's ticket out of here. Lady Justice would have to wait a little longer. After all, she'd been in no hurry to claim Olim so far.

'Sergeant… what's wrong?' Olim stuttered.

'I was just thinking what a blind bitch she is, señor,' Cabeza said darkly as he stalked away.

The others were waiting outside the temple when Cabeza arrived with Olim at his heels. The fungal light faltered just inside the portico, but the sergeant was loath to break discipline and use a torch. He hesitated, sensing the same disquiet among his men. Not much unnerved Ignatz Cabeza anymore, but by the God-Emperor he didn't want to step inside that living dead shell. He'd swept enough of the ruins in his time and knew what was waiting in there: the passage would bifurcate endlessly, the arterial branches twisting and turning as they burrowed deep into the tainted flesh of the island. Many men had disappeared inside the bowels of these things.

'Where are the rebs?' Cabeza asked.

'Not far,' Olim said. 'There will be a beacon. They said it would be just inside the doorway.' Olim pointed at the leering portico. When none of the others moved he licked his lips, stepped forward and knelt by the threshold. Hesitantly his hands explored the broken coral under the lintel, finding nothing but dust.

'Here… they said… it would be… promised me…' Pinned between the darkness ahead and the hard eyes behind, Olim became agitated, then frantic, scrabbling through the detritus, reaching deeper until…

'Yes… Yes! Here it is!' Olim glanced over his shoulder, smiling with relief. Something bright was clutched in his podgy hand. Awoken by his touch it emitted a soft, rhythmic pulse.

And Cabeza looked up.

Maybe it was a subtle disturbance of the light that drew his eyes or maybe it was pure instinct. Either way, he saw the shape unfolding on the lintel high above. It was just a swathe of shadows against the pale dome, but it turned his guts to ice. Wired on the Glory, Cabeza hurled himself backwards, firing on full auto before his conscious mind had caught up. As his violet fire ripped skyward the thing reared up and leapt from its perch. The las-beams stitched contrails of steam through the rain as they chased the bat-like shape and clipped a ragged leather wing.

And then the beast was amongst them like a black whirlwind. Two men went down instantly, slammed into the ground by the force of its leap and cushioning its landing. The attacker teetered, almost losing its balance as it struck out again. There was a sharp crackle and a third man toppled and already the thing was spinning wildly towards Alvarez. Too close to fire, the Konquistadore swung out with the butt of his rifle, but something hard and unbending blocked the blow. Again that crackle and then Alvarez was roaring in agony, his rifle slipping from nerveless fingers. His scream was cut short by a brutal jab to the throat and he fell, jerking about in violent spasms. And the thing spun to its next victim…

Staggering backwards, Cabeza tried to get a bead on its jagged, graceless dance, but the attacker was woven too deeply among his men. He understood its game. Outnumbered and outgunned it had gambled on surprise and shock. *Shock…* Abruptly he saw through the mythic flush of his narcotic fugue and recognised the baton in the attacker's hand… then recognised the raw electric crackle as Estrada collapsed in a twitching heap. *Shock maul!* And when the whirlwind swung to face him, Cabeza finally recognised it.

'Iverson,' he said.

The commissar had lost his cap and there was a smouldering tear in his coat where Cabeza's las-fire had clipped his shoulder. He was swaying and breathless, the spidervine scars livid against his chalk white face. His eyes were burning with fever… and something more. Seeing the indigo fire in his pupils, Cabeza spat.

'What the hell kind of commissar are you anyway?' he yelled.

'The wrong kind,' Iverson said. He smiled bleakly, his scars twisting into a strange new geometry.

And then Cabeza was shouldering his lasrifle and Iverson was loping towards him, one leg twisted and trailing, probably messed up by the jump. And Cabeza's finger was tightening on the trigger… and Iverson was hurling the shock maul…

Time snapped back into shape and Cabeza's world exploded into pain. The shock maul smashed the rifle from his hands and a split second later Iverson barrelled into his chest and threw him from his feet. He landed hard and the commissar crashed down on top of him, grinding him into the sharp coral. Iverson's fists pummelled down as his mad eyes bored into Cabeza.

'She won't… have… your soul…' the commissar hissed through ragged breaths. 'I won't… let you… fall!'

Finally the deserter lay still and Iverson lurched to his feet, stumbling as he retrieved his shock maul. He could feel his stomach convulsing with the fungal filth he'd consumed, but there had been no other way to ride out the fever. It was just another small heresy to add to his growing tally. Old Bierce would be turning in his grave if he hadn't already clawed his way out to haunt his protégé.

But I've done my duty. I've hauled them back from the brink… I'll…

'Take you back… all of you…' Iverson mumbled as he counted up the scattered, semi-conscious bodies. He wasn't sure how he'd manage that part of his plan yet. Seven broken men to carry back to camp… *Seven?* Where was the eighth? He turned to the temple and saw Olim crouched at the threshold. The noble's eyes were wide with terror. Iverson felt bile rising in his throat at the sight of him. Yes, this was the eighth turncoat – *the worm*, the one who'd sown the seeds of corruption amongst the rest. For this one there could be no second chance. Iverson drew his laspistol and levelled it at the cowering noble.

You'll be Number 28, he realised. *Maybe your death will exorcise Number 27.*

Number 27? Iverson saw her then, standing in the shadowed portico behind the fat man, watching him intently with her three dead eyes. Waiting to see him kill again.

'For the Emperor,' Iverson told her, trying to conceal the edge in his voice.

Something darted from the trees behind him, buzzing like an angry insect. Iverson spun round firing, but the sleek white saucer streaking towards him zipped between his snapshots, skimming high above the ground on an anti-gravity field. The disc was only about a metre in diameter, but Iverson knew that a soulless intelligence guided the machine. It was only a drone, its artificial brain no more sophisticated than a jungle predator, but the very existence of such a thing was blasphemous.

Blueskin technology is a heresy upon the face of the galaxy!

Of more immediate concern were the twin pulse carbines mounted on the underside of the drone. As the disc whirled to dodge his fire those guns rotated independently to lock on him. He dived aside as they spat a stuttering enfilade of plasma. The dive slipped into a fall, saving him from a second burst as the machine whizzed by. He rolled over and fired after it, catching it with a couple of rounds as it banked into a turn, but his shots only mottled its carapace. Chattering angrily the drone soared back towards him.

A hail of las-bolts spattered the machine from the side, knocking it off kilter and exposing its vulnerable underbelly. Careening wildly through the air, the drone raked the ground with plasma, shredding two of the unconscious Konquistadores. Someone roared in fury and fresh las-fire ripped into the saucer's belly. One of its carbines exploded, taking the other with it and spinning the machine out of control. Gushing smoke and burbling in distress it retreated, losing altitude as it limped towards the trees, but Iverson was already on his feet and charging. Leaping, he swung the shock maul down on the drone, smashing it towards the ground. It tried to rise and he struck again and again, elevated by a hatred untainted by doubt.

The machine exploded.

Iverson was thrown from his feet. Falling for what felt like forever he watched a ragged arm spiralling towards the sky, its hand still clenching a shock maul. It was awful and absurd, but suddenly he was laughing and someone else was laughing along with him. He glanced across the clearing and saw Cabeza. The cadaverous Konquistadore was on his knees, cackling through a mask of mud and blood. His lasrifle was levelled at the wrecked drone.

Cabeza didn't know why he'd thrown in with the commissar at the end. He'd already turned his back on the Imperium to sign up with the enemy in the hope of a better deal. He wouldn't be the first Guardsman to do it, nor the last, so why make a bad move now? What could Iverson offer him except more pain and maybe a quick death? Even for a commissar the man was crazy! Just look at him, lying there with his arm torn off at the elbow and laughing like it was the best joke in the Imperium. *Crazy!*

Except Cabeza was laughing right along with him so maybe he was crazy too. And maybe that was all there was to it.

'For the bloody God-Emperor!' Cabeza cackled through the last of his broken teeth. Then a drone soared down behind him and his chest erupted in a superheated geyser of flesh and blood. Looking down at the sizzling cavity in his chest he frowned, thinking a full-grown mirewyrm could swim right through there. It was a miracle his torso was still holding things together.

But then it wasn't.

As Cabeza's corpse collapsed inwards like a slaughterhouse of cards the second drone flashed past, homing in on Iverson. Biting down on the sudden agony of his ruined arm, he rolled to his knees. His laspistol was gone, lost somewhere in the fall. It wouldn't have stopped the machine, but it would have given him a stand. Hadn't Bierce taught him that a stand was all that mattered in the final accounting?

But hadn't he stopped believing that long ago?

And if he'd stopped believing it, why was he still fighting? Maybe because Bierce was standing at the edge of the clearing, hands clasped behind his back in that parade ground rigor, watching and judging his pupil until the bitter end.

The drone swept past and began to circle him, chattering and chirping as two more descended to join its dance. The machines seemed to grow more alert and aware in numbers, almost as if they were parts of a collective mind coming together. Maybe it was just a delusion, but Iverson could have sworn there was real anger in that mind. He'd destroyed one of its components and it wanted revenge. And so the drones were playing with him, *enjoying* his hopeless, one-armed struggle against the coral, mocking his determination to die on his feet. He could almost taste their hatred. Wasn't that why the Imperium shunned such technology? Didn't the Ecclesiarchy preach that thinking machines loathed the living and would ultimately turn on their creators? Mankind had learned that hard truth to its cost long ago, but the blueskin race was still reckless with youth. Perhaps that would be its downfall. As the drones circled him Iverson took comfort in the thought.

The machine chatter rose to a higher pitch and he steeled himself for death, but abruptly the drones fell silent and drifted back a few paces. To Iverson's eyes they looked reluctant and sullen, like angry dogs leashed by their masters. And as the dogs withdrew, the masters emerged.

They crept from the trees in a low crouch, their stubby carbines sweeping from side to side as they advanced, hugging the coral with a bone-deep distrust of open ground. There were five, lightly armoured in mottled black breastplates and rubberised fatigues. Their long helmets arched over their shoulders, giving them a vaguely crustacean look, the strangeness heightened by the crystal sensors embedded in their otherwise blank faceplates. Iverson recognised them at once: pathfinders, the scouts of the tau race.

Despite their hunched postures the warriors were swift and graceful, fanning out to surround him with the perfect co-ordination of bonded hunters. Slipping on the coral yet again, Iverson abandoned dignity and faced them on his knees. He could see Bierce lurking at the periphery of his vision, demanding some final caustic rhetoric from his protégé, but Iverson had nothing to say. Glaring at the pathfinders, he noticed one of them was quite different to its companions – shorter and slighter of build, the set of its shoulders subtly wrong. The only one with hooves… Iverson's eyes narrowed as the truth hit him: the odd-one-out was the genuine article.

Under that loathsome xenos armour all the others are human!

The lone alien stepped forward and dropped to its haunches, bringing its impassive crystal lenses level with his face. There was a crimson slash running along the spine of its helmet, identifying it as the leader, but Iverson was drawn to another mark – a deep crack running from its crown to the chin of its faceplate. The damage had been patched up, but the rippled scar of a chainsword was unmistakeable to a commissar.

'Your face,' he breathed. 'Show me.' The warrior tilted its head quizzically at the challenge. 'Or are you afraid?'

'Be watchful, shas'ui.' It was one of the traitors, his voice surprisingly crisp through his sealed helmet. 'This one is of the commissar caste. Even wounded this one will not yield.'

The studied formality of the traitor's words disgusted Iverson, particularly the way he'd spoken that unclean xenos rank, *'shas'ui'*, with such reverence. These traitors weren't just mercenaries or cowards looking for a way out – they were true believers.

The shas'ui considered Iverson for a moment, then it began to unclip its helmet, its four-fingered hands nimble as they uncoupled the power feed and flicked an array of seals. Throughout the ritual its cluster of crystal eyes remained fixed on him, unwavering until the helmet was swept away and he saw the face of his enemy.

Even for an alien it was ugly. Its leathery blue-grey skin was tinged with yellow and pockmarked with insect bites. A rash of boils ran from its neck to cluster around a topknot of greasy black hair, but its most startling feature was the ruination left by the chainsword. A deep rift had been carved into the right side of its face, running from scalp to jaw, mirroring the crack in its helmet. It was an old wound, but still hideous. A bionic sensor glittered from the scabrous mess where its eye had been and the whole jaw had been replaced with a carved prosthetic. The remaining eye, black and lustreless, regarded the commissar inscrutably. For all its mutilated strangeness the creature was recognisably female. She was the first tau Iverson had seen up close and whatever he'd expected it wasn't this filthy, disfigured veteran.

You're even uglier than me. It was such an absurd, irrelevant thought that he almost laughed out loud.

'*Ko'miz'ar.*' The word sounded unfamiliar on the creature's lips, but he sensed it had faced his kind before... and had the scar to show for it. '*Ko'miz'ar...*' It was an accusation ripe with hatred.

'Once and forever,' Iverson answered, denying the lie and refusing to meet Bierce's gaze. The old raven was standing amongst the traitors now, his thirst for judgement blinding him to the irony. High above, the sky rumbled, pregnant with the storm... and Niemand's shade shuffled up beside Bierce, haggard with his curse. A moment later lightning lashed the canopy into emerald fire and there was a knife in the alien's hand, tearing towards Iverson's eye... *for an eye...* flashing... so bright and swift... *But don't the blueskins despise close combat?* Then a new pain as the blade impaled the hand he'd thrown up to ward off the blow... *Not this blueskin. It wants to taste my pain... Share its pain...* A stabbing agony as the blade punched through his palm and out the other side, the gleaming tip stopping just short of his eye... *Black xenos eye, glaring with a rage so like my own.*

Then they were at the eye of the storm, transfixed by a pure harmony of hate as the blueskin pushed on the knife and Iverson pushed back, neither of them willing to break the perfect ritual of the struggle. Iverson grinned savagely into that foul, ruined face and saw its eye widen... *grinning right back at me!*

And then Number 27 knelt down beside him, serene and oh so dead, and every moment bled into eternity as Iverson rose towards his Thunderground.

ACT 1
DESCENT

CHAPTER ONE

The Mire, unknown

The alien has cheated me of my Thunderground. One moment we were pinned in a deadlock of hate by its knife, the next… treachery! A twist of agony and then that blade was tearing up through my hand and slashing back down into my face. It took an eye for an eye and left a scar for a scar, but mocked me with my life.

I awoke on this little atoll, stranded Emperor knows where. The traitors had bandaged my wounds, pumped me full of xenos drugs and left me with a week's worth of supplies. They'd also left me the bloody relic of my severed arm, but the real insult was the pamphlet they'd stuffed into my pocket. 'Winter's Tide' it's called, named after the slippery tyrant who leads them on this world.

Yes, of course I read it. One must know one's enemy after all. Besides, it might have offered up some clue to Wintertide himself, but all I found was a diatribe extolling

31

the so-called Greater Good, the blasphemous philosophy that binds the blueskin empire together. The threat was implicit in every line, so polite it was almost an apology of malice: 'Join us, or else.'

Emperor damn them! They thought I was finished, but I'm not alone here. My trinity of ghosts is with me and together we will endure. There is such strength in hatred. But of course you already know that. We are of a kind are we not? That's why I've kept on writing with the wreck of a hand remaining to me. So you'll understand. So you'll be ready. But first we have to get out of the Mire...

Bleeding ectoplasm from the stump of an arm, Niemand gestures defiantly and tells me we'll be found soon, but sometimes it seems that this limbo has been forever and everything else was just a dream. Bierce always censured me for thinking too much, but out here there's nothing else to do. Besides, it's a flaw that runs blood deep, another shadow of my Arkan heritage that the schola couldn't exorcise.

You know, lately my thoughts keep turning back to Providence, the home I left so long ago. I think of the frozen Norland rifts and the blistering hell of the Badlands, the white marble colonnades of Capitol Bastion and the gabled mansions of Old Yethsemane. I think of the pioneers and the patricians, the machinists and the savages, all the clans and cartels and tribes, forever at each other's throats but forever Arkan. They came late to the Emperor's Light and they didn't come quietly.

Sometimes I wonder what became of them all...

Iverson's Journal

Following its ordeal in the warp, the transport ship was slumbering at low power, recovering its strength and resolve for the return journey. Its passage to Phaedra had almost ended in catastrophe and now there was hell to pay. While the ship's tech-priests worked frantically to salve its pain and the captain whipped his crew back into shape – and in one case into death – the passengers on Q-deck were left in ignorance. To the Navy men the Imperial Guard were little more than cattle with guns.

After the crisis a junior lieutenant had descended from the bridge to brief the regiment's officers, talking patronisingly of power outages and fluctuations in the Geller field – meaningless words that said nothing of the horror that had overtaken the eleven men billeted in Dorm 31 when the warp had seeped into the ship. Colonel Cutler had broken his nose and sent him blubbering back up to the bridge. After that the Guardsmen had heard no more.

All things considered, Major Elias Waite had to admit it was a bad start to the regiment's first campaign away from home. The 19th Arkan Confederates had travelled a long way from Providence, but they had a lot further to go in their hearts before this new life made any sense to them. Having passed his seventieth year, Waite doubted he'd be travelling the whole way with them. He was still technically their second-in-command, but he knew many of the officers regarded him as a spent force, and since the horror in Dorm 31 he'd begun to wonder if they were right. By the Emperor, he was tired of it all…

As he navigated the murky labyrinth of Q-deck, his lantern painting strange shadows across his path, he couldn't shake the feeling that the walls were just a thin line between life and the void. His path was carrying him along the skin of the ship, where the membrane seemed tense and fragile, ready to dissolve from one step to the next. His mind told him this wasn't so, but his blood told him otherwise and he was sure every man and woman in the regiment felt the same way. The Arkan simply weren't bred for deep space.

Well plenty of folks aren't, Waite chided himself, *but most learn to live with it. We'll just have to learn the trick along with the rest of them. We're true Guardsmen now and space is part of the job.*

The Imperium of man was a troubled giant and it was a Guardsman's lot to be shuffled back and forth across the galaxy as duty called. Besides, few Imperial forces had been as fortunate as the Arkan regiments, who'd fought all their wars at home for so long.

But were we really so lucky? Waite wondered.

Long ago, someone very wise and very bleak had remarked that civil wars were the worst kind. After the madness that had ravaged his home world, turning parish against parish and brother against brother, Waite wouldn't argue. The rebels had called it Independence, the brave old Union of Seven Stars reborn brighter and better than before. How the fools had rallied to their 'March of Freedom' – croppers and collarmen, hicks and gentry, even some of the savage tribes, banding together to throw off the shackles of Imperial tyranny.

Eleven years of blood and betrayal!

Suddenly Waite was breathing hard and there were tears in his eyes. It was the sheer waste of it all that hurt so much. What chance had the separatists ever had? Even if they'd won – and they'd come pretty damn close at Yethsemane Falls – well, what then? How could one planet have hoped to stand against the juggernaut of the Imperium? Fortunately it had never come to that. The price of victory had been high, but the Arkan faithful had put their own house in order before the wrath of the Imperium had come crashing down on their world.

'And now here we are, a billion leagues from home, come to

do it all over again to some other poor fools,' Waite told the darkness. 'emperor-damned rebels…'

There was to be no rest for the loyalists of Providence. With the civil war finally over, the surviving Arkan regiments had been thrown into the lottery of galactic deployment and scattered across space on the whims of some distant, inscrutable strategy. For the 19th Confederates that whim had led to a backwater subsector on the Eastern Fringe of the Imperium and a world called Phaedra.

Well, as the Emperor wills it, Waite decided wearily.

Realising he'd come to a standstill, he spat and got himself moving again. He wasn't usually a man prone to introspection. In his youth he'd been a traveller, wandering the high sierras and rift valleys of the frozen north, taking his chances as a trapper and a prospector, but always careful to play fair with the Norland tribes. They were a moody folk, not much inclined to trust a stranger (more inclined to spit and gut him if the truth be told), but he'd won them over. The fact was he'd always liked people and thirty years in the Guard hadn't changed that. True, he was old now, his face a brown leather walnut and his hair a fond memory of better days, but he'd kept his muscles and could still swing a sabre with the best of them. Damn, but he had to shake off this oppression. It was clinging to him like a leech…

Like the abomination Trooper Norliss had become in Dorm 31. Like the broken things they'd put to the sword in that blighted town back home. Like the tolling of the daemon bell hanging at the town's rotten heart. Waite had prayed never to hear those soul-jangling chimes again, but they had followed the regiment across the stars. Or maybe they had always been there, waiting in the warp for fools to listen. Whatever the truth of it, the daemon bell had tolled again inside Dorm 31.

Ringing in Trooper Norliss's changes…

But no, he mustn't go there. These were not memories to dwell upon at the best of times and certainly not in this gloomy mausoleum. Unconsciously Waite's fingers brushed the aquila symbol hanging from his neck. He was vaguely surprised to find that he had reached his destination. The viewing gallery was a grand atrium of fluted marble pillars and delicate murals, but in the dim emergency lighting it looked forbidding. He saw stars twinkling through the immense window in the outer wall, promising something brighter than this shadow-haunted concourse. Two figures were framed against the void, one very still, the other almost manic as it stalked back and forth, gesticulating with sharp, angry motions. Waite heard the murmur of their conversation, but the words escaped him. It was just as he'd expected: the colonel was with his witch again.

With a sigh Waite entered. Something loomed from behind a pillar and he leapt back, his hand reaching for his sabre before he recognised the giant. The man's face was pale against a cascade of ebony braids, his eyes canted above high cheekbones. He had a feral look that sat strangely with the smart cut of his grey Confederate uniform, almost like a wolf in man's clothing.

Waite cursed himself for a skittish fool. He should have expected the Norland giant. Wherever the witch went, her *weraldur* followed. The warrior had been ritually bonded to her when she'd first manifested the wyrd as a young child. As tradition demanded, he had waited patiently while his charge had made the long journey on the Black Ships to be tested for any trace of taint. If she had been found wanting and failed to return to Providence within a span of seven years that same tradition would have demanded his ritual suicide. Their fates were bound tightly in life, tighter still in death. He was her guardian and potential executioner. The double-headed axe strapped to his back was consecrated to grant the Mercy if his charge fell to the warp. Unsurprisingly the *weraldur* path was one of the few Norland traditions the Imperium had actively encouraged.

'The God-Emperor's blessings upon you, Mister Frost,' Waite said, feeling uncomfortable with the title. To call a strapping Norland warrior 'Mister' or one of their fierce, mysterious women 'Lady' was absurd, but after the war the Imperial witch hunters had come down hard on all the Outlander folk. Although many of the tribes had fought alongside the loyalists, the fanatics had campaigned to 'civilise' them all. The first things they'd stolen were their old tribal names. Take away a Norlander's name and you were halfway to owning his soul. It was the kind of logic that appealed to a witch hunter.

Waite tried a smile. 'Your vigilance commends you, *weraldur*, but I've words for the colonel.' He made to step past the giant, but the Norlander blocked him again. The major's expression turned hard and he raised his voice: 'I'm here on the God-Emperor's business, so step aside.'

He wasn't expecting a reply. The giant was a mute, his tongue removed during his bonding to the witch, but the confusion in his eyes was answer enough. Waite's brand of down-to-earth piety was well liked by the troops and since Preacher Hawthorne's death he'd served as the regiment's surrogate priest – which gave him a hold over this devout savage.

'Stand aside in His name, *weraldur*!' Waite boomed theatrically.

Frost frowned, trying to weigh up his divided loyalties. Suddenly he cocked his head, as if listening to a secret voice. The talk by the window had ceased and the silhouettes were watching them. Queasily Waite realised he'd been right about that secret voice. The witch was talking to her guardian, brushing his mind with hers. A moment later the giant stepped aside.

'Well now, I'll be damned if I recall asking for visitors,' a voice bellowed across the gallery, flush with anger and easy authority, 'but someone's here so I guess I must be damned or just plain stupid.'

'Never stupid, colonel!' Waite called back. 'And not damned yet if I've any say in it.'

Silence. Then laughter, deep and bitter and laced with something Waite didn't much care for.

'Get your scrawny arse over here, old man. There's something I want you to see.' Now there was genuine humour in the voice and Waite shook his head, already sure he wouldn't find the words to challenge his commander.

The witch drew back as Waite approached, hiding her face in the dark arch of her cowl. The colonel was still pacing across the stars, his back rigid with tension, his left hand clenching and unclenching ferociously, the right locked to the hilt of his sabre. His wide-brimmed hat was slung over his back, bouncing about as he stalked back and forth. He hadn't cleaned up since the horror in Dorm 31 and his rawhide jacket was still blotched with black stains. There was a gash in his right leg where a thorny tendril had whipped past his guard, but Waite knew it was useless telling him to see a medic. These days it was useless telling Ensor Cutler anything. These days he only had ears for the witch.

'Take a look outside, Elias,' Cutler said without breaking the fierce rhythm of his pacing.

Waite peered through the glass. The grey-green swathe of a planet curved away beneath them, looking mottled and moist, like a colossal fungal puffball. *Unclean.* A ship hung on the horizon, sharing their orbit. Waite could tell it was a behemoth and a warship, its prow blunt and pugnacious, its decks encrusted with gun turrets and sensor spikes. A welter of scars pitted the hull, culminating in a deep furrow carved across its midriff where something had almost sliced the ship in half. The fissure showed no signs of repair and Waite suspected any attempt to move the vessel would seal its destruction. The leviathan had taken a mortal wound and this planet would be its grave. If it weren't for the lights glittering in its portholes he'd have wagered the ship was already dead. He squinted, trying to decipher the faded tattoo of its name.

'The *Requiem of Virtue*,' Cutler said, as if reading his mind. 'Damn strange name for a warship.' Abruptly he stopped pacing and sized up the vessel. 'I don't trust it, Elias. And I trust that filthy planet even less.'

Waite hesitated, unsure whether the colonel expected an answer. He prided himself on reading the hearts of men, but Cutler had become increasingly mercurial over the last couple of years. Since Trinity and its bell. By Providence, that daemon-haunted town had cast a long shadow over the regiment.

'Zebasteyn. Estevano. Kircher.' Cutler chewed through the words one by one, evidently not much liking the taste.

'I don't follow your drift, colonel…'

'Another name I don't trust. Kircher's the Imperial Commander here – our lord and master until this war's done.' Cutler nodded towards the ship. 'Man runs the whole show from up there, hiding away in that floating hulk, keeping his boots squeaky clean while he throws good men after bad, pulling the strings and watching the chips fall. Calls himself the 'Sky Marshall', whatever the Hells that's supposed to mean! Is he army? Navy? Maybe even an Inquisition lackey…' He shook his head. 'I don't trust any of it. This war is *old*, Elias. It makes our little uprising look like a backyard tussle.'

When he got angry, Cutler always slipped into his Yethsemane

drawl. Like Waite, he wasn't a product of the aristocratic academies that churned out most of the Arkan officer class. He was a
patrician, but his family had been knee-deep in debt, so young
Ensor Cutler had signed up with the Dust Rangers, a rough-and-
ready cavalry outfit. While other officers had studied strategic
theory at Point Tempest, Cutler had made his name hunting
feral greenskins in the Badlands. The rawhide jacket he wore in
lieu of the regulation grey was a legacy of those wild days, its
tassels woven with greenskin tusks and finger bones. That coat
had raised a few eyebrows when Cutler had finally received his
commission from the Capitol, but he'd refused to discard it. It
was the kind of thing that made him who he was – the kind of
thing that got him into trouble. Inevitably the Old Guard had
clipped his wings, only granting him his colonel's stars when
the war was over and they could pack him off into space.

'It don't smell right, Elias,' Cutler was suddenly glaring at
Waite, his eyes bright, his lips drawn back into a snarl. Looking at that fierce, leonine face, with its shoulder-length mane
and tangled beard, Waite sensed this tarnished nobleman was
more savage than any Norland tribesman. But it was the *whiteness* that unnerved him the most.

Cutler wasn't yet fifty but his hair was dead white from scalp
to beard. Before Trinity there hadn't been a white hair on his
head. That town had changed so much about him, but the
whiteness was its most visible mark. Waite wondered if Cutler
knew his men had nicknamed him 'the Whitecrow'. And if he
knew, did he even care?

Suddenly Waite was sure time was running out for all of
them. He had to find the words to get through to this man
who'd once been his friend. He had to know what Cutler had
found inside the mouldering temple at Trinity's heart. Waite
had been by his side when they'd purged the town, but only

the witch and her guardian had faced the source of the cancer with him. Only they had *seen* the daemon bell.

Why did I let him talk me into staying behind? Why didn't I insist on going in there with him? But in his secret, guilty heart Elias Waite knew that nothing could have made him walk into that desecrated shrine.

'The bastards promised me a full sitrep once we made orbit,' Cutler stormed on. 'Campaign records and troop dispositions, field maps and recon reports… Some Emperor-damned orientation! And then they send me that!' He jabbed a finger at a crumpled sheet of parchment on the floor. 'One damn page!'

Waite bent to retrieve the document but Cutler waved him back. 'Leave it. You'll hear it all soon enough, but don't hold your breath.'

Suddenly Cutler frowned and glanced at the witch, his eyes narrowing as she whispered into his mind. The intimacy of it made Waite's skin crawl. Lady Raven, the men called her, and unlike her warden's childish name, hers felt *right*. His distrust for her came from the gut. She was a psyker, a mutant cursed with heightened psychic potential that made her a living, breathing time bomb of corruption. Yes, she had survived the tests that culled all but the strongest of her kind and been sanctioned to practise her craft in the Imperium's name, but you could never be sure with a witch. To Waite's mind a sanctioned psyker was just a rubber-stamped monster. How could Ensor allow her to touch his mind? And was there any truth to the whispers about them? She always kept her face hidden, as was the way of the Norland women, but it was rumoured that she was beautiful.

'Ensor…' Waite began, realising he hadn't used his comrade's first name in almost a year. Suddenly he was sure he had the words to get through to him. 'Ensor, we have to talk about

Trinity. How did that thing in Dorm 31 know...'

But the colonel waved him to silence, his attention on the witch. Finally he nodded and straightened up, rubbing his unruly beard.

'I have to go clean up, Elias. We'll be making planetfall in a couple of hours and the men deserve better than this. I'll see you at the assembly old man.' Cutler stalked away, trailed by the witch and her guardian. Alone in the dark, Elias Waite realised he had lost the words again.

'Word is Norliss went void crazy and chopped 'em up while they was sleeping. Chowed down on 'em too.' Kletus Modine licked his lips suggestively. In the dancing pilot light of his flamer he looked like a leering gargoyle. Not that the hulking, barrel-chested pyrotrooper was a pretty sight in any light. With his brutal potato head and bright red crest of hair, he was an archetypal Badlander and Dustsnake squad was his natural home.

The squad was hunkered down in a corner of the hangar bay, chewing over the fat as soldiers always did before deployment. There were near on eight hundred troops scattered around the cavernous chamber, clustered up in squads around their lanterns, creating pockets of light in the gloom. The emergency strips were running, but their thin red haze was somehow worse than the darkness. Everyone was jumpy after what had happened in Dorm 31 three days back, although nobody knew exactly what *had* happened. Nobody except the officers and they weren't talking. Sure, Verne Loomis had seen it too, but he wasn't doing much talking either these days.

'He ate 'em?' Boone's eyes were wide in his broad bumpkin's face.

'Down to the bone,' Modine affirmed. 'Colonel put a lid on them boys pretty quick too. Took a flamer in there and torched the lot of 'em. Didn't want us greyback grunts seeing what Norliss gone and done.'

'Figures.' Dix nodded sagely, always quick to back his hero. Another Badlander, he was a scrawny doppelganger of Modine, right down to the jutting crest of red hair.

'But that don't add up, brothers.' The voice came from beyond the lantern's pool of radiance, outside the Dustsnake inner circle.

'You say something back there, greencap?' Modine snarled over his shoulder.

'Just been thinking is all.' The speaker ambled into the light, seemingly oblivious to the hostility. He was almost painfully young, but taller than Modine by a head and built like a grox. His straw-blond hair was neatly cropped, his uniform pressed and pristine. The green trim of his flat-topped cap and tunic identified him as a raw recruit, just as the book of liturgies hanging from his belt marked him as a devoted student of the Imperial Gospel.

Audie Joyce was a misfit in this squad of veteran scum. He'd joined them just before they'd left Providence and Modine would have chewed him up and spat him out if the sarge hadn't been looking out for him. There was talk the old goat had had a thing going with Joyce's ma back home, might even be his pa, but not even Boone was stupid enough to ask bullethead Calhoun about something like that.

Frowning, Joyce continued, 'I mean it weren't just his squad. Norliss killed the commissar too. And *he* sure weren't sleeping.' Gravely the boy made the sign of the aquila. 'No, brothers, the commissar's chainsword was buzzing with the Emperor's own wrath when he walked into that chamber of iniquity. And he didn't go in alone neither.'

'The greencap's got a point, boys,' came another voice from the shadows, even further from the inner circle, mocking and low. 'Ain't no way one crazy man could've taken down the commissar, especially not with old Whitecrow along for the ride.'

It was true and they all knew it. Every one of them had been there when the horror had kicked off. It was the noise that had drawn them – a deep, irregular chiming that had run through the walls and shaken their teeth like a quake from hell. There had been no ignoring it so they'd gone looking and wound up outside Dorm 31 just as Verne Loomis had come crawling out. He'd slammed the hatch shut then folded in on himself like he was all broken up inside. The crazy look on his face had stopped their curiosity dead. Modine had hit the alarm. Nobody had gone for the door.

That was when the lights had died, leaving everyone standing around in the dark fiddling with their rifles as they listened to all the tearing and chewing and screaming going on behind that hatch. Maybe if the sarge had been with them it would have gone down differently, but he'd been up in the mess hall playing cards with the other NCOs. They'd all been kind of glad about that.

The colonel had arrived in double time, almost like he'd known what was going to happen. And maybe he had, because the witch and her watchdog had been with him and she'd probably seen it like she saw everything else. Then Major Waite and Commissar Brody had turned up and the five of them had gone inside, locking the hatch shut behind them. Five of the regiment's finest against one crazy man.

After that there'd been a lot more tearing and swearing, then a hellfire snarling that was more animal than man, but like no animal the Arkan had ever heard. And then the voices had started up and that had been the worst part. They oozed through the steel hatch, sounding like a whole chorus of corpses drowning in an ocean of maggots, laughing and gibbering as they sang the same words over and over, round and round: *'Trinity in embers… Trinity remembers…'*

Somewhere along the way they'd heard the commissar shrieking like no commissar was ever meant to. That had gone on forever and the greybacks had wondered how there could be so much screaming inside one man, but finally there'd been silence. After a while the hatch had opened and the slayers had come marching out. All except Commissar Brody. Every one of them was splattered with blood and some kind of black slime that reeked like a corpse pit. The witch had been shaking under her robe and Major Waite was watching her like a hawk, almost like he was afraid of her. And then the colonel had grabbed a flamer and gone right back inside. Afterwards he'd sealed the hatch shut and turned Dorm 31 into a tomb for nine men. Nine men and maybe something more than a man…

'It weren't no crazy greyback the Whitecrow torched,' the voice from the shadows continued. 'You gotta think bigger, man. Uglier.'

Modine snatched up a lantern and lumbered over to the speaker. The man was sitting cross-legged with his back against the wall, his eyes on the gnarled bone flute he was carving in the dark. The same flute he'd been carving every day of their journey through the warp.

'We talking uglier than you, *Mister* Roach?' Modine growled, angry that his safe little lie was unravelling. Scared of the truth.

Roach kept on carving, unmoved by the tired old insult. His hatchet face had the bloodless complexion of a Norlander, but his hair was bright red. 'Roach' had been his father's name – a solid Badlands moniker – but his mother had been a Norlander. It was a long story with a short, sharp end that had left him an outsider wherever he went. There'd been plenty of hurt and heartache, but after the war he'd decided he didn't much care either way.

'Ain't you heard?' Roach said. 'There's things in the warp just waiting to find a way inside a man's head and outside into the world.'

'We don't buy that Hellfire crap in the Badlands,' Modine sneered. 'All that spook talk's just to keep the Outlanders in their place! Course, a breed like you…'

'You saying you don't believe in daemons, Brother Modine?' Suddenly Joyce was standing beside Modine, his earnest face troubled. 'Or you saying you don't believe in the God-Emperor's Holy Gospel?'

'Now wait, that ain't what I meant…' Modine spluttered, not exactly sure what he *had* meant. He glanced at his comrades for support, but even Dix had looked away. Only Boone grinned back at him, too dumb to pick up on the tension. Modine could feel the intensity of the rookie's gaze, like he was some jumped up witch hunter angling for a burning. 'Look, I was just saying…'

'What Trooper Modine was saying is he's so dense the Emperor's light bends right on round him,' Willis Calhoun barked, marching out of the shadows.

The sergeant was a short, stocky veteran in his fifties whose bullet head seemed to shoot straight from his shoulders, hairless and almost pointed at the tip. Most men in the regiment towered over him, but there was a pent up ferocity in that compact frame that even the apes in Dustsnake wouldn't cross.

Calhoun strode over to the pyrotrooper and glared up into his face. 'See, Trooper Modine here is a piece of deep-fried grox crap, but he'd still lick the rust off the Emperor's holy throne. Ain't that right, Trooper Modine?'

'Every golden spot, sir!' Modine bellowed, staring into infinity.

'Damn straight!' Calhoun nodded. 'Right, playtime's over you righteous maggots. I've got our drop-ship designation, so haul your sorry arses!'

The sergeant sized up his nine charges as they grabbed their gear. They were rough scum all right – the troublemakers and meatheads who'd sunk to the underbelly of the regiment, picking up charges the way heroes chased after medals, but they were his scum and they could pack a helluva punch in a tussle.

Young Joyce was still frowning as he went past. The sergeant shook his head. The last thing he needed was for the boy to start acting like a greenhorn commissar. He'd told Maude the regiment was no place for him, but she'd argued and wailed until he'd sworn to take Audie under his wing. Willis Calhoun wasn't scared of any man, but Emperor's Blood, that woman could nag! If only the boy hadn't turned out so damn *holy*! He'd have to have a word with the young fool before he got himself killed. Teach him some basics. Faith wasn't optional in the Imperium, but some men believed a whole lot harder than others.

'You said you'd talk to him. You assured me he'd come to his senses.' As he spoke, Captain Hardin Vendrake kept his eyes on the Silverstorm Cavalry, alert to the slightest misstep amongst the mechanical steeds. So far his riders were keeping things together, guiding their walkers onto the waiting drop-ship with precise, elegant steps. Even Leonora was doing just fine and she was frankly the worst Sentinel rider Vendrake had ever known. He wouldn't have kept her on if her other talents hadn't been quite so exceptional…

Vendrake suppressed a smile as he addressed his fellow officer again. 'I admit I'm disappointed. Sir,' Vendrake finished pointedly.

'Don't question my judgement, captain,' Elias Waite said irritably. 'After Trinity, Ensor Cutler deserves our faith.'

'Does he?' Vendrake asked. 'Frankly I still don't know why we burned that old town to the ground.'

'Because it needed the burning!' Waite snarled. He knew Vendrake didn't like to talk about Trinity. The town had shaken the man up badly, but he was too proud to admit it. Or maybe it just didn't fit in with his neat little worldview. Seeing the unease on Vendrake's face, Waite calmed himself and tried again: 'By Providence, you were *there*, man! You saw the sickness with your own eyes.'

'Frankly I'm not sure what I saw,' Vendrake said, growing agitated, 'perhaps some kind of mass delusion… We were all half-starved and frozen when we stumbled on that place.' He waved the subject away. 'Besides, Trinity isn't the issue here.'

Waite shook his head in disgust. He despised true patricians like Hardin Vendrake, men bred with an unflappable faith in their own excellence. With his chiselled jaw and aquiline nose the captain had the look of a war poster hero, the kind of man who'd seen thousands of comrades die but never suffered anything worse than a tasteful scar. Vendrake actually had that scar, a tidy little line along his left cheek that had always gone down a storm with the ladies. But despite his rakish façade and wilful blindness, the man was no fool and Waite didn't need him for an enemy.

'Look, I'd trust Ensor Cutler with my soul,' Waite insisted, trying to believe it himself.

'And what about the witch?' Vendrake said, cutting to the chase. He smiled at the major's hesitation. 'Personally I don't give a damn who the old man cavorts with, but this is hurting the reputation of the 19th and I won't stand for that.'

'I'll talk to him after we make planetfall. You've got my word on it,' Waite said coldly and marched away.

'I'm just thinking of the regiment,' Vendrake called after him. He winced as Leonora's Sentinel slipped on the boarding ramp and she struggled to regain her balance, the clawed feet of her machine scrabbling on the metal. It looked like she was going to topple when Van Hal nosed his steed in and nudged her back to stability. Vendrake nodded his approval. A fine pilot and a gentleman was Beauregard Van Hal. A fellow made of the right stuff.

Still, he couldn't entirely blame Leonora for the error. He'd kept his riders on their toes but they'd only had a couple of months to play with the modified machines. Unfortunately there had been no choice about that. The colonel had warned him they would be fighting in swampland, where the Arkan-pattern 'hooves' of the Sentinels would be a liability. The heavy, flat pads were designed to race across the open plains and savannahs of Providence, but on Phaedra the design would mire the machines in no time, which would be fatal if they came under fire. Sentinels were light hunter-killers that relied on speed and agility to stalk their prey. While they might intimidate an infantryman, it didn't take much to penetrate their armour. Cutler had even hinted that Vendrake's force might have to sit this one out, but the captain was damned if he'd let that happen. The Silverstorm Cavalry was a bastion of nobility amongst the 19th and it would have its share of the glory!

Determined, Vendrake had sequestered the ship's forge and holed himself up with the regimental tech-priests to crack the problem. During the voyage they had replaced the Providence-pattern hooves with wide, splayed claws that distributed the weight of the machines more evenly and enabled a limited gripping action. Their research revealed that this was actually the prevalent model on many worlds of the Imperium. While extreme divergence from the sacred construction templates was deemed heretical by the Mechanicus priests, modest alterations were permitted, if not exactly encouraged.

Poring over reports of customisation throughout the Imperium, Vendrake had been drawn to the Drop Sentinels of the Elysian regiments. Fitted with grav-chutes, such machines were capable of diving directly into battle from airborne transports. Fired up by the tactical possibilities, he had resolved to win that capability for Silverstorm. At first the tech-priests had hesitated over such a radical deviation, but he had soon cajoled them into it. Under their soulless augmetics Arkan blood still ran through their veins and they hadn't lost the old thirst for invention. Lacking access to grav-tech they had opted for single-use jump packs and retro stabilisers, granting the Sentinels limited manoeuvrability during a drop.

Once the project had caught their imagination, the cogboys had pursued it with almost human passion. After that it had been a small matter to push them a little further with the modifications to his own steed, *Silver Bullet*. And over the months *a little further* had stretched the abilities of his Sentinel far beyond the norm. Bristling with directional thrusters and gyro-stabilisers, it was capable of swift contortions and great leaps that filled Vendrake with fierce joy whenever he trained in the hangar bay. The fact that some would have deemed his Sentinel a new *kind* of machine altogether – and likely denounced it as an abomination – cut no ice with the captain. He had lost himself wilfully in the challenge of forging the perfect steed. It was the kind of problem that made sense to him, unlike old Waite's obsession with that vile town...

No, he wouldn't think of that. The things he had seen there were impossible and impossible things could not be. He was a gentleman of Providence – a rational man. He wouldn't buy the propaganda the Imperium used to terrorise its ignorant rabble into submission.

Like many Arkan patricians Vendrake was no great believer in the Emperor's Light. After all, He hadn't shed much light on Old Providence. Just two centuries ago, blithely unaware of the approaching Imperium, Vendrake's ancestors had revelled in the new-found glories of steel and steam. It had been a time of unfettered innovation, with the Grand Machinists churning out new wonders every day. The Senate had declared the old gods dead and the Seven Hells mere fables. Men were free to explore a puzzle box universe where everything was possible and nothing was forbidden. Then the warships of the Imperium had arrived and crushed the dream, but the grand families had never forgotten their past.

Maybe that's why we keep on making the same mistakes, Vendrake mused. *Maybe that's why we keep on rebelling. The fools amongst us anyway...*

A klaxon buzzed and he saw the colonel stride into the hangar. Vendrake had to admit the old man had got his act together. His hair was tied back into a neat ponytail and he'd trimmed that scruffy beard. It looked like he'd finally washed too. The captain nodded approvingly, but then he caught sight of the witch trailing Cutler like a second shadow. Her giant watchdog was carrying the regimental banner, unfurled and resplendent. Vendrake's heart soared at the sight of the ram's skull and crossed sabres overlaid on the Seven Stars of the Confederation. It was good to see Old Fury awake again, even if it was in the hands of a savage.

The trio marched wordlessly through the silent ranks of the Arkan and stopped at the centre of the hangar. Suddenly Cutler let out a ferocious howl and leapt onto a crate, his agility belying his years. He held out a fist and the savage threw him the banner. The colonel caught it with a flourish and spun about, brandishing the flag above his troops as they gathered round.

'Seven Stars for Old Fury!' Cutler bellowed.

'Seven Furies for the Stars!' The men bellowed back.

'For Providence and Imperium!' Cutler roared, completing the regimental canticle. Then he led them through the litany again and again, binding them together with those glorious words, defying the horrors they'd come through and the ones still ahead. And despite himself, Hardin Vendrake shouted along with the rest of them, his heart soaring. This was the Ensor Cutler of old, the man whose audacity had won the day at Yethsemane Falls and turned him into a living legend! And then it was done and Cutler became the Whitecrow again. Vendrake could almost see the bitterness seeping back into the man as Trinity exerted its curse.

There is no curse, Vendrake told himself. *Cutler's intellect is weak. That's why the horror is eating him alive, but I won't fall for it.*

'I won't lie to you, Arkan.' Cutler's voice was flat with suppressed rage. 'And I won't dress things up nice and pretty either. You and me, we've come too far for that.' There were murmurs from the crowd, agreement and unease in equal measure.

Damn it all, Vendrake thought, *we're so far from home even the memories are stale. This isn't the time for truth. Give them some hope, man!*

'So I'm just going to tell you what I know,' Cutler continued, 'but frankly that's not a whole lot.' He touched a switch on his belt and a murky sphere flickered into life beside him. 'Gentlemen – and all you Badlander scum too – meet the Lady Phaedra.' The hologram was blocky and riddled with distortion, but the planet's essential ugliness still bled through.

I don't want to breathe Her air, Vendrake realised with sudden conviction. The intensity of the instinct disturbed him. It was entirely irrational.

'Pretty name for a rat's arse of a planet,' Cutler growled. 'She's got swamps, rain and a thousand dirty ways to kill you. Gentlemen, you're going to hate her like the Hells, but I've got something else you're going to hate even more.'

He threw another switch and the planet morphed into a disembodied alien head. Its skull was hairless save for a braided topknot that looked fibrous and fleshy. The face a flat wedge from brow to chin, bevelled with deeply recessed cheeks that gave it a vaguely cadaverous look. Its mouth was a lipless slit and there was nothing resembling a nose.

'What is it, sir?' asked Templeton, the quietly intense commander of the 4th Company as he peered at the hologram through thick round spectacles.

'That, Captain Templeton, is a tau,' Cutler said. 'Take a long, hard look because it's the reason you've been dragged halfway across the galaxy to this mud-ball. Seems these xenos have themselves a jumped-up little empire of their own and our Lady Phaedra is sat right between Them and Us. She's a worthless harlot, but we can't let her go and neither can the tau.' Cutler chuckled, the sound low and harsh. 'There's a whole subsector's worth of pain just waiting to happen if she falls. I guess the tau see it that way too.'

'These tau boys, what have we got on 'em, colonel?' Major Waite growled.

'I'm told they're big on guns and tech, but not so fond of getting up-close-and-personal.' Seeing that Waite expected more, Cutler shook his head ruefully. 'That's all I've got, Elias.'

'What about numbers? Mechanised divisions or air support?'

Under his bushy eyebrows Waite was frowning ferociously.

'I can give you rebels – a whole planet full of them. They call themselves the *Saathlaa*. As far as I can tell, Phaedra was a pre-Imperial colony much like home, but unlike us the Saathlaa were dead in the water by the time the Imperium came along. Whatever civilisation they ever had was long gone.'

'Savages,' Captain Machen sneered. The 3rd Company commander was notorious for his loathing of the Outland tribes back home. 'We cross half the hellfired galaxy and we still can't escape their stench!'

'Degenerates,' Cutler corrected, 'but that didn't stop them turning on the Imperium when the xenos came along. I'd guess these tau boys are sneakier than the greenskin vermin we're used to back home.'

'What's the game plan, colonel?' Waite again.

'Seems we'll be touching down on what's called a Poseidon-class battleship.' Cutler snorted. 'Which is a fancy way of saying a damn big boat. We're talking the old kind here – the kind that sails on water, not across the stars. From there we'll be joining up with a push on a chain of islands that go by the name of Dolorosa. Some kind of rebel stronghold...'

'How long, colonel?' Vendrake interjected. 'Exactly how long has this war been going on?'

'Sharp as ever, Captain Vendrake.' Cutler rubbed the bridge of his nose wearily. 'Like I said, I won't lie to you. Gentlemen, the Imperium and the Tau Empire have been fighting over Phaedra for near on fifty years.'

There was a long silence as the men thought it through. Then a murmur began, rising to a hubbub of disorder as the reality sank in. The explosive crack of a bolt pistol put a stop to it.

'Much obliged, Elias.' Cutler nodded appreciatively to Waite as the veteran holstered his sidearm. Vendrake could see the colonel gathering strength, dredging up every drop of his faded myth. Uncannily he seemed to be looking every man in the eye, talking to each soldier as if he were an old, personal comrade. 'Arkan, I expect better from you…'

Abruptly a klaxon began to wail. The main lights flickered on and Cutler glimpsed the hangar chief signalling to him. It was time to go, but he wasn't finished yet.

'In fact I expect the best!' Cutler shouted over the noise. 'It's what you've always given me and it's what you're going to give me now. Do that and I'll get you through this mess! Now move out and make Providence proud, Arkan!'

He knew they had no cheers left in them and he didn't much blame them, but at least they'd get on the drop-ships. Right now he couldn't ask for more.

CHAPTER TWO

The Sisyphus, Argonaut-class battle cruiser

A recon patrol found me wandering along the shallows of the Qalaqexi River, almost a hundred kilometres from the Verzante outpost on Dolorosa Topaz. The captain here tells me I was half-starved and delirious, raving about holy ghosts and unholy traitors. He also tells me I was carrying the maggot-riddled ruin of my own right arm, decayed beyond any hope of repair. Of course I had no such delusions, but I do not tell him this. I carried my arm out of the Mire because I refused to leave any part of myself to Her, but I do not tell him that either. Just as I do not tell him that I still see my ghosts, though I am no longer half-starved nor delirious. And I certainly do not tell him how holy they are. He would not understand these things. Such truths are only for you and me.

Instead I tell him about the traitors who are nothing but dead men running. I tell him about the fall of the Verzante

Konquistadores and the encroachment of the blueskins into Dolorosa Topaz. I tell him that I have been following Commander Wintertide's trail and must not falter now. I tell him that I am a commissar and he must offer me his every assistance.

Instead he contacts Lomax, who is the High Commissar of the Dolorosa Campaign and my direct superior. And of course Lomax recalls me to Antigone base. The captain tells me she has concerns.

Iverson's Journal

Abel... whispered the hollow voice.

'Abel...' she echoed, the name slithering from the immaterium onto her lips.

'Skjoldis?' It was the Whitecrow, urgent and angry, calling her back from the Whispersea. He was the only one amongst the blind folk who knew her true name. 'Skjoldis, snap out of it, woman!'

Abel seeks...

'...seeks the Counterweight,' she finished.

Her eyes flicked open and she saw the Whitecrow leaning over her, frowning ferociously. Over his shoulder she could see her *weraldur*, watching her with that special sharpness that always turned her blood to ice. The Mercy was still slung across his back, but his right hand was on the haft, poised to wrench the axe free in a heartbeat.

Is it my time? Am I poisoned?

Dispassionately she turned her gaze inwards and explored the secret hunting grounds of her soul, sifting through seething rift valleys of frustration and turning over spiny stones of despair, questing for the spoor of corruption. She had sensed no poison in the speaker called Abel, but the serpents could be so very sly–

'Raven!' The insult snapped her back into *annatta*, the shadow maze the blind ones called reality. In the maze she appeared to be lying on a cold marble surface under starlight that was even colder.

'Be still, Whitecrow.' Her voice was raw with the strain of the wyrd. 'There is no poison in me.' The tension in him subsided, but his stormy grey eyes continued to search her face.

My face? Open to the stars!

Her veil was gone, leaving her face vulnerable to the soul serpents waiting between the stars. Once they knew her face they could shape themselves into a mirror of her soul and seep inside. Her instincts screamed out against the violation and she reached for her hood, but the Whitecrow caught her wrist.

'Who in the Seven Hells is Abel?' he demanded.

It was the first time Cutler had seen her face in anything but the dim glow of an oil lamp. In the starlight he was struck anew by the mysterious confluence of her features. She certainly wasn't beautiful in any conventional sense. Her skin was like faded parchment stretched tight over a skull that was too narrow, accentuating her sharp cheekbones and lending her a carved, half-starved fragility. A gossamer tracery of tattoos wound from her temples to encircle her vivid green eyes before tapering into the bloodless bow of her lips.

Noticing Cutler's fascination she snapped her wrist free and pulled up the cowl, hiding her face in shadow... from shadows. Her eyes glared accusingly at him. 'You gave me your oath you would not touch the veil, Whitecrow.' The bitterness in her voice made him blanch.

'And I kept it,' he said. 'You took the thing off yourself, woman.'

Her eyes widened and she glanced at her *weraldur*. The giant nodded, a hint of hurt creeping into his flat eyes. She knew it was true; while there was life in him he would not allow anyone to violate the veil. Not even the Whitecrow.

What happened to me? Skjoldis wondered as she recognised the gloomy vault of the viewing gallery. She rose and the marble-clad window onto the void drew her gaze like a beacon. *Is it really a window… or a mirror?*

'What's going on, Skjoldis?' Cutler's voice had softened, but she didn't need to touch his mind to read the doubt in him. It stung like a betrayal.

'I am not *tainted*,' she said. It was the Imperium's word for the soul poisoning. 'Is that not enough for you, Whitecrow?'

'No, that's not enough.' He sounded tired as he scooped up her discarded veil and joined her. 'Even from you Skjoldis, that's not nearly enough.'

'Don't you mean, *especially* from me,' she said bitterly as she took the veil. If the soul serpents were watching it was already too late, but the garment was part of her identity. A truer friend than her own face could ever be.

Because my face is an open wound to my soul…

Cutler regarded the witch in silence as she covered her face. The wyrd had come over her in the hangar bay just after the second drop-ship had flown. He'd been chatting with Elias Waite when Skjoldis had started moaning. Feeling a sudden charge in the air he'd glanced round and seen her walking away with her watchdog at her heels. That had set Elias off, but Cutler hadn't let him make a fuss. He still felt guilty about the hurt on the old man's face when he'd ordered him to shut up and ship out.

I'll make it up to you, old friend, Cutler swore. We'll talk soon and I'll tell you whatever it is you need to know.

He'd left Waite and followed Skjoldis to the viewing gallery, a place that had always fascinated and repelled her. There she'd stood staring into space with her hands touching the glass, whispering nonsense and ignoring his entreaties. He'd sensed the wyrd gathering strength around her, creeping through the chamber like static electric frost and turning the air to ice. And suddenly she'd cast away her precious veil and pressed her face up against the glass, almost as if she'd been trying to push herself through into the void.

Can she hear the daemon bell? Cutler had wondered bleakly.

His hand had drifted to his sabre, compelled by a gut-deep dread of psychic corruption. The *weraldur* had mirrored the action, preparing to fulfil his most sacred duty. Had she fallen? Would she turn and leer at them with a grin that tore her face in two? Would she look like the thing Norliss had become in Dorm 31? Or would she be like the broken ghouls they'd slaughtered back home in that doomed town? *Would she be worse?*

But then the wyrd had receded and Skjoldis had fallen to the floor like a meat puppet whose strings had been cut. Drawing closer, Cutler had heard those last enigmatic words about 'Abel' and a 'counterweight'. Every instinct told him not to let the mystery go, but it would have to wait.

'We have to go, Skjoldis,' Cutler said, but she wasn't listening. Her eyes had slipped past the yellow crescent of the planet and fixed on the ancient corpse ship. And suddenly she remembered it all.

None of them noticed Hardin Vendrake watching from the shadows.

* * *

It was the stench that hit Roach first, a heady brew of the sea and the grave, like rotten fish vomited up by a corpse. A heartbeat later the heat came crowding in, thick and liquid, clinging to him like an oily second skin. He thought he'd beaten heat long ago, but this wasn't like the slow burn of the Badlands. The drop-ship hatch had only just opened and he was already drenched in sweat.

I'm never going to be clean again, he realised.

'Quit dreaming and shift your arse outta my way, breed!' Modine snarled over his shoulder. Roach glanced back at the men clustered in the drop-ship behind him. Their faces looked as grey as their fatigues. They could all smell the sickness waiting out there. All except Modine, who couldn't smell anything through the promethium tar clogging his nostrils. The ape didn't know how lucky he was.

'What you got, Snake Eyes?' Toomy asked, speaking for the whole squad. Roach might be a half-breed, but he was also their scout and they trusted his instincts. Probably because he *was* a half-breed…

They want something dark and wise from me, a touch of the Norland wyrd to ground their fears. And so I'm Snake Eyes now, the squad's totem against the unknown, but later on, when they're all sat around the fire together, I'll just be the breed again. At least Modine always says it like it is. Well to the Hells with 'em all!

Without a word Roach turned back to the hatch. The exit ramp had lowered then stuck midway, but it was only a couple of metres to the ground so he swung himself over the lip and jumped. He landed with catlike grace on the deck below, but almost slipped on the slime coating the corroded plates.

In this heat maybe even metal has to sweat, he thought with disgust.

He heard Modine swearing above him and smiled coldly.

Getting off was going to be a bitch for the pyrotrooper with that bulky flamer strapped to his back. Still, Roach was the squad's eyes and he didn't want any of them breaking their necks on his watch, not even Modine, so he called back a warning as he scanned the terrain.

True to the colonel's words, the drop-ship had touched down on the deck of a ship, but Cutler's 'damn big boat' didn't come close to the reality. Roach had served on his share of steamboats back home, but this monster was nothing like those brave old vessels. It defied belief that anything so vast could even float. He guessed the landing strip alone was some thousand metres long and maybe five hundred across, the space sliced into a grid of landing pads and fuelling stations, all connected by a web of pipes and cables. Ugly barnacles of machinery clung to the deck and a crane sprouted from the starboard side like a gallows for giants. He squinted at its outstretched arm. By the Seven Hells, there *were* bodies hanging up there! Not giants, just ordinary men – dozens of them. It was hard to be sure at this distance, but it looked like they'd been skinned.

Uneasily Roach tore his eyes away from the crane and took in the rest of the ship. Sternwards the deck erupted into a sprawl of metal blocks and conning towers that loomed over the strip like a cast-iron fortress. The keep had been daubed with a crude rendition of the Imperial aquila, the double-headed eagle snarling savagely. The bow was dominated by the ship's main gun, a mounted cannon that looked big enough to punch a hole in a starship. The monster was bolted to the deck by rivets the size of a man and tended by a whole squad of scarlet-uniformed troops. Psalms from the Imperial canticles ran the length of the barrel, the white paint livid against the black metal. Along the port and starboard sides smaller emplacements jutted from the battlements, manned by more men in scarlet. The troops were too far away for Roach to get a good look at them, but he sensed they were ignoring the newcomers.

The clarion call of a bugle drew his attention to another drop-ship further along the deck. He guessed it had touched down a few minutes earlier because its passengers were already disembarked and standing to attention. They were Captain Templeton's 4th Company and he could see the man himself strutting back and forth like he was on the parade ground. The captain's dress uniform was sagging in the wet heat, making him look like a drowned peacock, but Roach had to give him credit for trying. Templeton wasn't nearly as stupid as he looked and he wasn't a total bastard like 'Ironbones' Machen, Roach's own company commander.

The Dustsnakes had once been part of the 10th Company, but that was back in the days before Yethsemane Falls, when the regiment still had almost two thousand men to its name. After that carnage the Dustsnakes were the *only* part of the 10th Company. It had been a similar story throughout the regiment and Cutler had been forced to reshuffle the survivors into four functional units, each numbering around two hundred men. Unfortunately the Dustsnakes had wound up at the arse end of the reformed 3rd, under Jon Milton Machen, a man who believed Norlanders and Badlanders were just two strains of the same plague. It was yet another piece in the cosmic puzzle that proved life, the immaterium and the Emperor all had it in for Mister Claiborne Roach.

'Fire from the sky!' Modine roared and slammed down beside him with a meaty thud. He had all the grace of a dead grox, but to Roach's surprise the pyrotrooper didn't stumble.

'Almost squashed you under my boots like a 'roach, Roach!' Modine said with a sneer that was oddly half-hearted.

'Make some space down there you brain-dead sons o' bitches!'

Sergeant Calhoun bellowed from above. As the two greybacks obeyed, more hatches clanged open along the ship and the rest of 3rd Company began to disembark. Sourly Roach noted that *their* exit ramps hadn't jammed.

He saw Captain Machen stomping onto the deck at the head of his command squad. In his Thundersuit the man looked like a vast iron crab that had reared up to walk on its hind legs. Under its elegantly moulded carapace the suit was an industrial masterwork of spinning cogs and pistons that clattered and hissed in perfect harmony, almost drowning out the stirring chords of 'Providence Endures' booming from its brass shoulder speakers. A heavy stubber was fixed to one ironclad paw, the ammo belt coiling into a fluted dispenser on the back, while the other ended in a massive drill inscribed with the 'Testament of the Founding Fathers'. The captain's crew-cut head was visible through the thick glass porthole of his baroque helmet. He was still wearing his wide-brimmed officer's hat and there was a fat cigarillo rammed between his jaws, but even he wasn't quite crazy enough to light it in there.

Roach wasn't impressed by the spectacle. The antique fighting suit was a legacy of Old Providence, a cherished heirloom passed down generations of the captain's blueblood family. Sure, there was no denying its toughness – after all, the thing was closer to a tank than a suit of regular power armour – but it was unpredictable and hideously difficult to maintain – not to mention noisy as all the Hells! To the scout's way of thinking such relics were more effective as status symbols than practical tools of war.

Which probably suits that son-of-a-bitch Machen just fine...

Jon Milton Machen was the spiritual father of the Steamblood Zouaves, a cross-company brotherhood of mechanised nobles who revered the Emperor in His aspect as the Machine

God. There were eighteen of them in the regiment, all patricians with the wealth to maintain a fighting suit. They saw themselves as questing knights, free to align themselves with whichever unit had the most need. Each Zouave possessed a unique, customised suit, but they were mostly variants of the smaller Stormsuit template and none of them possessed anything like Machen's monstrosity. Modine had once joked that the captain was compensating for inadequacies elsewhere. It was the only time Roach had laughed along with the pyrotrooper.

He glanced across at Modine, surprised the big man was sticking alongside him. In the green light the Badlander's face looked bestial, but his eyes were filled with wonder as they took in this ugly new world.

'You still with us, Snakeburn?' Roach asked.

'The sky's full of blood,' Modine muttered. Roach saw he was right: there was nothing like a natural cloud in the blotchy canopy, but it was woven with threads that looked just like the thin blue vessels in a man's arm. Or like that stinking cheese the aristos liked so much – the kind that was all wormy with fungus. As he looked at them, those threads seemed to twitch and it began to rain – a sticky, slow motion drizzle that clung like glue.

It's more dribble than drizzle, Roach thought. *Like the sky is drooling over us.*

'It ain't natural.' Modine seemed mesmerised by the rainfall.

'Different world, different rules,' Roach said, unsure of the Badlander's mood. 'We just got to learn how it works, man.'

Modine looked at him, frowning. Then he spat in disgust and found safe ground. 'Yeah, like you'd know shit about it, breed.'

'Aw no, don't you be doing that!' Dix yelped behind them.

They turned just in time to see young Audie Joyce standing in the hatch, heaving up his guts over the scrawny Badlander below.

'You greencap rookie piece of crap! You total frakwit!' Dix shrieked as he fumbled for his lasrifle. Modine stalked back and swung him round.

'Easy, Jakob,' the pyrotrooper said. 'Boy didn't mean nothing by it.'

'The greencap trash gone and puked over me, Klete!' Dix yelled. With the vomit dripping down his long nose, his scraggy face would have been funny if wasn't burning with hate. 'I'm gonna…'

'You want Calhoun to put you down like a crazy rhinehorn bull?'

'But he *puked* on me Klete,' Dix whined, sounding petulant now. When all was said and done, Jakob Dix had always been yellow.

Roach had lost interest in the argument, his attention diverted by the strange party emerging from the battleship's metal fortress. Three of them were dressed in the distinctive storm coats of commissars while two others wore the red robes of tech-priests. They were flanked by a contingent of troops armoured in glossy crimson plate and tall, conical helmets. He didn't recognise the bulky guns the soldiers were carrying, but each was linked to a shoulder-slung power core and he guessed they'd pack more punch than a regular lasrifle. Trailing along behind the rest was a whole procession of Ecclesiarchy types. He counted six zealots with wild hair and jutting beards. All wore filthy rags and vests of chainmail that must have been hell in the heat. Several dozen flagellants loped along beside them, their scarred bodies almost naked below their peaked hoods. The whole troop was chanting and wailing something high and mighty from the Imperial Gospel. To Roach they looked even crazier than the puritans back home.

That's one heck of a welcoming party, he thought uneasily.

A glint from one of the conning towers caught his eye. There was someone up there. The figure was silhouetted against the sky and Roach couldn't make out any details, but he was sure it was watching them – any scout worth his salt would recognise the flash of magnocular glasses in an instant. He was reaching for his hunting scope when the company bugler blared the assembly and Calhoun yelled at him to get into formation. It was only as he rushed to obey that he realised why the watcher had unsettled him so much: something about its shape had been *wrong*...

'Have you prayed for me, Gurdjief?' The voice fluttered fitfully, little more than a dry rattle. The speaker lowered his magnoculars as the sharp-eyed newblood on the deck below hurried back to his squad. There were so many of them this time. Surely some would serve.

'I always pray for you, my lord.' The confessor's rich baritone was a stark contrast to the watcher's brittle rasp, but then everything about Yosiv Gurdjief was a world away from the blighted creature he revered. Despite his shabby robes the priest looked like a heroic statue given life, a sculpture of coiled steel turned to muscle through the alchemy of faith. His black hair fell below his waist and obscured his face behind a filthy curtain, yet for all his wildness his features had the arrogant cast of a noble. Taller than most men, Gurdjief towered over his stunted master.

'Then why is there no end to this pain?' the ruined man asked.

'Pain is a blessing. Through suffering we share in His eternal sacrifice and draw closer to the light of His wrath.'

A withered claw shot out and clasped Gurdjief's wrist.

'Then why do you not share this blessing, priest?' the wreck snarled.

Gurdjief could feel the spiny nodules in the man's palm digging into his skin, but he was unmoved. This was an old ritual between them and they both knew he was immune to the fungal leprosy. Most men were. Phaedra was a world of a thousand blights, yet Her foulest pestilence was also Her most selective, capable of infecting less than one in a thousand. In Gurdjief's eyes Admiral Vyodor Karjalan had been exalted.

'I am unworthy, Vyodor,' Gurdjief breathed, twisting his wrist to grasp that ruined claw, just as he twisted his words to grasp the admiral's name and seal their friendship. 'But you have served Him for almost two centuries across countless worlds. You have earned this benediction.'

'And what of Bihari and Javorkai and all the other peasants who were *blessed* with this filth?' The admiral sneered, recalling the dozen mariners who had shared his curse. 'What of Natalja? She was just a girl. How did *she* earn your precious gift, priest?'

'Do not question Him, Vyodor.' Gurdjief's mournful eyes were suddenly bright with wrath and compassion. 'We cannot know what secret heroisms our brothers and sisters performed in His name. Their glory is lost…'

'Their lives are lost!' The screech tore a cloud of spores from the admiral's desiccated throat, triggering a spasm that sent him reeling against the balcony. Gurdjief breathed deeply of the blight as he watched his master's rapture. The man's misery was truly inspiring. Under his misshapen greatcoat every inch of Vyodor's flesh was covered in fungal swellings. Some had ripened to calloused spines that threatened to tear through the fabric, while others clustered in bloated, pulsating reefs. The infestation had rooted itself deep in the man's bones, contorting his skeleton into a new shape. Without the regular blood transfusions devised by the ship's tech-priests his joints would calcify and render him immobile. Gradually the transformation would accelerate, the fungus reshaping its host's flesh while nurturing and preserving the brain with hideous intimacy. Gurdjief knew this to be true for he had catalogued the process in other hosts. Indeed he had witnessed the final, magnificent torment…

'Natalja… is dead,' the admiral wheezed, drained by his rage. The priest grasped his hands, willing him the strength to rejoice in his suffering.

'She died a saint in the Emperor's eyes,' Gurdjief insisted, glossing over the lie. He had not granted Vyodor's daughter the Emperor's Mercy as he'd promised, but he had not allowed her the transfusions either. Despite her screams and curses he had forced the girl to face her destiny, even consecrating a chapel to her in the bowels of the ship. They had been secret lovers once and he had felt an obligation to enlighten her. Over the years she had bloated and blossomed to fill the chamber like a sacred cancer until she *was* the chapel. Whenever Gurdjief felt doubt rising in him, whispering that his faith might have taken a dark twist, he would descend to Natalja's sanctum and steady himself with the purity of her torment. Her eyes were still so very beautiful…

'Then perhaps I should die too,' the admiral taunted. 'Perhaps I should make a clean end of it.' He stared down at the vertiginous drop from the tower. 'I could do it now.' But they both knew it was a lie. Admiral Vyodor Karjalan had lived too long to embrace death, no matter how hideous life had become.

There was a rumble overhead and they looked up as a third

drop-ship swooped over the tower and descended towards the landing strip.

'What if none of them have the right blood, Yosiv?' Karjalan asked. Only those who were susceptible to the blight were viable for the transfusions and the admiral's supply was running perilously low.

'It will be as the Emperor wills it, Vyodor,' the confessor said. 'But now I must join my brethren for the consecration of the newbloods.'

'Indeed, priest.' The admiral's twisted form seemed to straighten at the call of duty. 'I have received word from General Oleaus at Dolorosa Breach. The 81st Encinerada have been routed and the Iwujii Jungle Sharks are pinned down a league into the Mire. The push is faltering.'

The confessor nodded, unsurprised. The push was *always* faltering. The Imperial drive to subjugate the Dolorosa continent was the oldest, most bitter campaign on Phaedra and the cost in lives was immeasurable. The region was a vast tangle of islands riddled with waterways and infested by some of the worst jungles on the planet. It was also the heartland of countless Saathlaa guerrillas and their xenos puppet masters. It was even rumoured that Wintertide, the tau commander, lurked somewhere at the heart of the continent.

'Oleaus needs more men in the Mire. We cannot lose momentum now.' Karjalan's eyes were bright points of passion in the dark morass of his face.

Sometimes Gurdjief pitied his friend's petty dreams of victory, but perhaps they were a mercy. If they gave Vyodor the strength to endure then so be it. For the confessor there were no mercies left. He had ventured too deep into the Mire and seen too much to deny the truth of things. By any sane reckoning the archipelago was the worst kind of no-man's-land imaginable, but Gurdjief had abandoned sanity long ago and seen the horror behind the horror. Unlike his master he understood that the Emperor had not cast them into this hell to find victory.

The Lethean Mariners had come to Phaedra fresh from the glorious Purgation of Sylphsea, where Vyodor Karjalan had prosecuted a masterful campaign against the Aoi brood armada. It had been a magnificent triumph marred only by the loss of the Imperial Governor's son, a young hothead who had sailed his cruiser into the jaws of a brood submaniple. There had been no saving him so Karjalan had fired the main gun on the lot of them, making the boy's death count for something. Unfortunately the Governor hadn't seen it that way and their next posting had been this dead-end war. Despite the insult, Karjalan had been confident of breaking the Dolorosa stalemate and winning absolution. Back then he was still an unbreakable commander of men who had never known defeat. Back then Gurdjief was still a naïve young soldier with no thoughts of entering the priesthood.

Back then was more than a decade ago.

'I want these Arkan dandies on the transport boats within the hour, priest,' Karjalan said. 'They have the look of toy soldiers, but perhaps there is fire in their hearts.'

'As you say, my lord.' Gurdjief bowed and turned away.

'But save me the true bloods,' Karjalan whispered, watching the troops on the deck with bleak, hungry eyes.

The drop-ship shuddered as it dipped into the viscous soup of the planet's atmosphere. Strapped into flight couches along the cramped tunnel of the cabin, the Arkan avoided each other's eyes. Most of them were Burning Eagles, the elite 1st Company of the regiment. Unlike the regular Confederates they wore navy blue jumpsuits padded with dark leather. The standard flat-topped foraging caps were replaced with fluted bronze helmets, their visors sculpted into the visage of a ferocious raptor. The imagery was more than a conceit: the Eagles were paratroopers, trained to fight as they rappelled or dived from the sky, but they weren't riding an Arkan steam dirigible now and their disquiet hung in the air like a psychic smog. Captain Vendrake wondered if the witch could taste it more keenly than the rest of them.

He was watching her out of the corner of his eye. She was sitting further along the cabin, squeezed between her watchdog and the colonel, unreadable in the swathes of her midnight blue robe. Behind her veil she might be grinning at their naiveté. Or changing...

Just like the damned of Trinity.

Angrily he thrust the thought aside. He hadn't been able to shake the memory of that confounded town since his argument with Waite. If he didn't get a grip he'd end up as mad as the Whitecrow. He had to put the past and its daemons – real or otherwise – behind him and focus on the clear and present danger amongst them. The witch was the issue here! The sight of her face in the viewing gallery had unnerved him. He'd seen no beauty or grace there, only a bitter weariness that wasn't quite human. Perhaps she had a place in the regiment as a weapon, but if so she was the kind of weapon that could backfire on its wielder like an overloaded plasma gun. Certainly she had no place as the consort to the regimental commander. He stared at the colonel sitting so arrogantly beside his pet hag. How could such a soldier fall so far?

'We're all behind you, Hardin,' Lieutenant Quint whispered into his ear. 'Just say the word and we'll back you to the blasted hilt.'

'Back me how exactly?' Vendrake asked, turning to the man sitting beside him. Quint's earnest expression sagged with hurt. Silverstorm's second officer had once been considered quite dashing, but he'd let himself run to fat.

'Oh come now, Hardin,' Quint wheedled. 'We've all seen you scheming away with old Waite.'

Vendrake shook his head sourly. Pericles Quint was a vaguely competent rider, but he was also a total idiot. Like most of Silverstorm he was a patrician, but his lineage was on a different order of magnitude. Hailing from one of the Founding Families, he was the wealthiest man in the regiment, with a dozen titles to either side of his name. The only mystery about him was why he hadn't jumped ship back on Providence.

'Scheming is a vulgar sort of word, lieutenant,' Vendrake said. 'Not the sort of word a gentleman of Providence would care to associate himself with.'

Quint began to bluster, but Vendrake had already turned back to Cutler. He knew that Silverstorm would back him if he moved against the colonel, but the key players would be the company commanders. If they stood with him the whole regiment would fall into step. The Norland-hater Machen was already champing at the bit about the witch so he'd play along for sure, but Templeton was a strange bird and Waite was still fiercely loyal to his old friend.

Unexpectedly Cutler looked up and met Vendrake's gaze, his expression stony. The captain's mouth went dry. Had the witch sensed him spying in the viewing gallery? Had she plucked the treason from his mind and informed on him? How could he defend against something so insidious?

Suddenly the colonel's attention snapped to his vox-operator. The elderly greyback was sat opposite Cutler, too far away for Vendrake to hear over the rumble of the engines, but he saw the man fiddling with his vox-set, growing frantic as Cutler harangued him. Others in the cabin began to notice the commotion.

What in the Seven Hells is going on? Vendrake wondered.

Then Cutler howled. It was a sustained bellow of rage that made Vendrake's hackles rise. No sane man would make a sound like that…

The colonel's face was twisted with wrath and his muscles bulged against his harness, fighting straps he could have simply unbuckled. With a final effort he broke free and surged to his feet. Convinced his commander had finally snapped, Vendrake reached for his sidearm.

He's like a man possessed!

Then Cutler reeled to an abrupt standstill and swung round to stare at the witch. Long moments passed, then Vendrake saw his face twitch as the mania drained out of him, leaving a residue of cold fury.

She's leashed him in like a mad dog. Vendrake was repelled by the insight.

The colonel breathed deeply and seemed to grow taller as he glared around the cabin. 'Confederates, I've just received word from the ground.' Cutler paused, playing his old trick, addressing them all, yet seeming to speak to every man individually. 'Major Waite is dead and we have all been played for fools.'

With that the colonel drew his pistol and stalked towards the cockpit.

The boat crested an angry wave, tilting almost vertically as it crashed back down into the churning ocean. Sour spray cascaded over the gunwales and splashed the men huddled on the metal benches within. The water looked like curdled milk, yellow and blotchy with a glutinous algal scum that reeked of sewage. The stench had been bad enough up on the battleship, but down in the seething cesspit sea it was almost unbearable.

Another wave wrenched the boat and Toomy lolled senselessly against Roach's shoulder. The man's head looked like one enormous bruise above his vomit-encrusted beard. Absently the scout pushed the unconscious sniper aside and continued carving his bone flute, seemingly oblivious to the angry sea. Sat across from him, Dix gagged and threw up again, not even bothering to target the greencap this time. Wedged beside him, gripping the safety rail so hard it hurt, Audie Joyce felt his own guts heaving in sympathy, but he was all out of puke. Most of the men in the boat were. Over the last hour almost everyone had added to the rancid soup swimming around the bottom of the boat, even Sergeant Calhoun.

It had scared the Hells out of Joyce seeing Uncle Sergeant Calhoun retching like that. He'd always thought the old man was a rock – immovable and invulnerable, but he'd been the first to pay his dues to the sea. Only the half-breed had managed to hold it all in, but Joyce figured that must be down to his Norland blood. The savages were tainted so maybe they liked keeping the puke inside them. That made sense, didn't it? He clung onto the thought because nothing else made much sense anymore…

Major Waite was dead. Joyce had seen it happen and he still didn't believe it. The Confederates had been lined up for inspection when the major's drop-ship had touched down with the 2nd Company. Everyone had watched proudly as the Old Man had marched over to meet the welcoming party from the battleship. But then there'd been a lot of arguing and another holy man had come down from the iron castle and joined in. Joyce could tell the newcomer was *really* important because he was taller than anybody he'd ever seen in his life.

At first the boy had wondered if the man might even be a Space Marine, but he wasn't wearing the sacred armour he'd seen in all the paintings so Joyce had decided he was probably a saint instead. Later he'd heard the sailors call the man Confessor Gurdy-Jeff, which sounded like a pretty holy name to him.

As a child Joyce had once seen Deacon Jericho give a sermon and thought him the holiest man alive, but Confessor Gurdy-Jeff made Providence's senior witch hunter look like a common street preacher. Despite the stink of this heathen world Joyce had felt his heart soar at the thought of fighting alongside a hero like that, but for some reason Major Waite had kept arguing with the saint, shaking his head and waving angrily, like he'd been told to jump into a fire or something. Joyce hadn't understood him at all – if Confessor Gurdy-Jeff had asked *him* to jump into a fire he'd have leapt without a second thought, content in the knowledge that he was doing the God-Emperor's work.

Worried that Major Waite would make the Arkan look like heretics to these holy folk, Joyce had grown angry. The saint must have been angry too, because suddenly he'd quit talking and jabbed a hand into the major's face, the fingers straight and pointed as knives. Some of the others weren't sure what had happened, but Joyce had seen the major's eyes pop. The Old Man had fallen to his knees with blood running through his hands. He'd squealed like a stuck hog until the saint had brought that holy fist chopping down onto his neck so hard that Joyce swore he'd heard the snap. Sergeant Hickox, who'd been with the major forever, had tried to pull a gun then, but the three commissars from the battleship had been faster and he'd gone down in a storm of las-bolts. Then Lieutenant Pettifer had tried to step in and they'd just shot him too. They hadn't stopped shooting until all three bodies were sizzling and smoking like boomerfish on a griddle.

After that everybody had gone real quiet, just standing there like the sky was raining frogs, the way that Deacon Jericho always said it would if folk didn't do right by the God-Emperor. Then some of the others had gone for their guns, but Captain Machen had shouted them down and across the deck Captain Templeton had done the same. That was when Joyce had noticed how the gun turrets on both sides of the deck had spun right round to cover the Confederates. If it had come to a scrap those big guns would have minced them up in no time.

Joyce wasn't too sure about what had happened next, but Captain Templeton had gone over to the saint and started gabbing away, all nice and peaceable like. Joyce hadn't caught any words but he figured they must have straightened things out because suddenly the priests in chainmail had been everywhere, rushing around and blessing the Arkan with some mighty fine words. Their cog priests had followed, sticking needles into folk, taking blood and checking it in a machine that one had growing right out of his gut.

Cog priests had always made Joyce queasy. With their strange machine bits and messed up metal faces no two were ever the same, but all were as ugly as sin, even the pair who served the regiment. The Arkan called their cog priests 'professors' because that's what their kind had been called before the Imperium came to Providence, but the name didn't make them any better. Professor Mordecai's face looked like a steam engine had tunnelled through it and got stuck halfway, but Professor Chaney was even worse. Under his hood there was nothing but a windmill of mirrors that reflected a man's face right back at him in a thousand different shapes and sizes, all spinning and whirling like a silver twister. They both made Joyce's skin crawl, but since they were *priests* he guessed they must be all right. He still hadn't got that part of the Imperial Gospel figured out...

'Why do we call them priests?' Joyce wondered out loud. 'The professors I mean, how come they're priests too?'

Everyone in the stinking, heaving boat looked at him like he was snakebite crazy. He remembered that his brothers didn't worry about the Gospel as much as he did, which was kind of sad and probably bad too.

'Only thing I want to know about those coghogs is why they took Klete,' Dix said, wiping the puke from his lips. There was a dazed look in his eyes that had nothing to do with his messed up guts. Joyce guessed he must be missing his friend and knew he'd feel the same way if the cog priests had taken Uncle Sergeant Calhoun instead of Brother Modine. Something bad had shown up in Modine's blood and the priests had said he'd need 'noculating' against the sickness in the jungle. They'd promised to give him back but none of the others had really believed it and Brother Modine had looked real scared. For a while Joyce had thought he might even put up a fight, but in the end he'd just chucked down his flamer, told them to find her a good home and gone quietly. The cog priests had marched him off, along with a couple of boys from the 2nd Company.

'Why'd they have to go and pick Klete?' Dix moaned again.

'Maybe those sailor boys were running short of fresh meat,' Roach taunted. 'Plenty of meat on good old Klete...'

'Shut your trap, breed,' Dix snarled. The snarl turned into another gut heaving retch as the boat bucked violently. Toomy lolled against Roach again and blood oozed from his broken mouth as he groaned wetly.

'I'm just saying...' Roach shoved Toomy away. 'If you wanted meat for your larder you could do a lot worse than Kletus Modine.'

'Knock it off, both you maggots!' Calhoun snapped, but there was no fire in it. Joyce had never seen the sergeant looking so tired, but then he'd never seen the sergeant looking tired at all. Hunched down on the metal bench with Modine's flamer cradled in his lap like a lost dog, Willis Calhoun looked *old*.

Although he was only a greencap and this was his first time in the fire, Joyce was pretty sure wars didn't usually go like this. He wasn't sure about much else though – like why they were on this boat and where it was taking them. Things had happened so fast after the cog priests had done their tests. The sailors in red had herded them onto the boats hanging alongside the battleship like big metal boxes, corralling them fifty to a boat like cattle in a stockade. One wall of each box had been tilted down into a gangway, waiting for them to get on board, then snapping shut like a trap afterwards.

There'd been a sailor waiting inside, sitting up front in a little cabin while everyone else was left out in the rain. He'd turned and welcomed them with a grin like a hungry landshark, but there was an aquila branded into his forehead so Joyce guessed he must be all right. Speaking with a voice like broken glass, the sailor had ordered them to sit with their backs straight and grip the safety rails, warning them to keep their jaws shut unless they wanted to bite off their tongues. The man had laughed at that last part like it was the greatest joke ever told and Joyce had decided maybe he wasn't all right after all.

One of the Steamblood Zouaves had boarded the boat alongside them, clanking onto the deck like a clockwork god. He was too big for the benches and too proud to listen to the grubby sailor anyhow, so he just stood in the aisle, looking grand. Joyce wasn't sure if the Steambloods were *properly* holy, but they did look mighty fine and he was glad to have one along for the ride.

And then the sailor had pulled a lever and sent the boat plunging down into the sea. Joyce's guts had rushed up into his mouth and his butt had surged off the bench. Scared half to death, he'd gripped the safety rail and forced himself back down, fighting for his life against the freefall. Just then the Zouave had come careening down the aisle, all out of control. He caught Toomy's head with an iron boot as he flew past and it was a miracle he hadn't kicked it clean off! There were no miracles left for the knight though. Joyce had seen his eyes through his visor as he flew past and they were wide with a surprise that was bigger than fear. And then he was gone, tumbling over the stern gunwale like a scrap metal bird. They'd heard him splash into the ocean a heartbeat behind the boat, but nobody had tried to do anything. Even a greencap like Joyce knew the iron man must have sunk like a stone. Only the sailor had reacted, giggling hysterically like he'd played a fantastic joke on the new boys.

Nope, nothing made sense anymore.

Bobbing about in a puke-filled box on a sea of sewage, Joyce remembered the knight's eyes and wondered if everyone looked that way when they were about to die. The thought made him uneasy so he prayed instead. He prayed for the soul of the lost knight who'd died without honour or glory. He prayed for poor Brother Toomy who was looking really bad right now and he prayed for Brother Modine who'd looked so scared when the cog priests had taken him away. But most of all he prayed that doing the God-Emperor's work was going to get a whole lot more glorious than this. And somewhere along the way it seemed to him that the God-Emperor answered.

CHAPTER
THREE

Imperial Seabase Antigone, the Sargaatha Sea

I've been on this creaking, ocean-straddling base for over
a month now, healing up while I wait on High Commissar
Lomax. She's never liked me and I doubt my unauthorised
sojourn in the wilderness will have improved her opinion
much. She'll want answers, but where do I begin? How can
I explain the path that led me to those Verzante deserters
when I don't understand it myself? How can I make her
believe I was on the trail of Commander Wintertide when
I'm not sure I believe it myself? Perhaps she'll have me shot.
Or more likely she'll just do it herself.

But no, I've been given a new eye and a new arm so
execution won't be on her agenda. Did I say 'new'? In truth
both the augmetics are ancient, doubtless salvaged from
one corpse after another. The hand is a tarnished metal
gauntlet that grinds whenever I flex the fingers and locks up
unless I keep it lubricated, but the optic is worse. It's like an

iron spike rammed into my eye socket – a hollow iron spike with an angry wasp trapped inside it. Not that I'd give a damn if it worked properly, but sometimes things flicker or flare and suddenly I'll see the world through a hash of snow or broken down into a crude mosaic of reality. And sometimes I'll see things that aren't there at all. It's just as well I've learned to recognise true ghosts.

Take Niemand for example. He has stood vigil at the foot of my bed throughout my time in the infirmary, invisible to the medics and orderlies, but occasionally glimpsed by the worst of the wounded. A few days ago they wheeled in a man who looked like a heap of raw meat and I saw him staring at my revenant in abject terror. Doubtless the dying man thought the shade had come for his soul. He could not know that Niemand cares only for me.

Detlef Niemand is the least of my three ghosts, yet his hate runs the deepest. He was always a cold bastard, the kind of man who brought nothing but malice to the Commissariat. I once believed that our kind were exemplars of the Imperium, unflinching in the face of death and faithful to a fault. How else could we be trusted with the power of life and death over our charges?

'We have to be the best of the best, Iverson,' my mentor Bierce used to say, knowing full well that few of us ever were. Even so, Niemand was amongst the worst of the worst. He was assigned to me on my first tour of the Mire and although he was just a cadet back then, I could see the darkness hiding behind his pale, colourless eyes. He was morbidly proud of the six executions he'd already made and took every opportunity to regale me with the details. I loathed him from the start and never understood why he was so reverent of me, a twenty-year veteran with a paltry ten executions to my name. When he finally earned the scarlet and took his own commission his departure was like a shadow lifting from my soul.

The next time our paths crossed we were equals: joint commissars serving with the 12th Galantai Ghurkas in the kroot-infested tributaries of Dolorosa Magenta. By then Niemand had tallied almost two hundred executions, taking a life for even the slightest misdemeanour amongst his charges.

'Iverson, you think too much,' he chided whenever I confronted him, echoing Bierce's old admonitions. 'You and I are engines of the God-Emperor's will, unshackled from the doubts and passions that enslave lesser men. Hesitation can be our only crime!'

That icy façade never fooled me for an instant. I could see how much he enjoyed the killing. That was why I left him to the kroot. How did it happen? We were lost deep in the Mire when he took a wound to the gut – a solid slug that tore him right open. He pleaded with me to carry him out or make a clean end of it. Instead I shot off both his hands so he couldn't do it himself. As I walked away I remember him begging and cursing and then finally screaming when the xenos found him. You see the kroot are particularly foul lapdogs of the blueskins. They are avian carnivores that delight in tearing their enemies apart and eating their flesh. And not always in that order...

I suppose Niemand's return was inevitable, but I underestimated his poison. One way or another he damned me. After he came back I grew increasingly careless with the final resort, almost trebling my executions in the space *of two years and thinking nothing of it. Thinking nothing much at all in fact, until Indigo Gorge and Number 27, the girl with the eyes of a saint. After that everything changed.*

Iverson's Journal

'But you can't come in here!' the young drop-ship pilot blustered, his eyes agog at the antique autopistol in the intruder's hand. 'The shipboard regulations are quite unequivocal about–'

'Nothing's ever unequivocal son, except the man pointing a gun in your face,' said the white-haired madman who had burst into the cockpit. 'And maybe the Emperor's word, though I'm none too sure about that one right now.'

'Besides, the man is already here, Jaime,' the co-pilot observed languidly. 'And I'd wager he'll not be going away any time soon.'

Colonel Cutler turned from the youth in the pilot's chair to the much older man lounging in the seat beside him. The co-pilot's thinning grey hair was tied back into a drooping ponytail, giving him the air of a faded rake. His mahogany skin was deeply seamed and the bags under his eyes mirrored the sagging sack of his gut. Cutler guessed he was well past sixty and looked every day of it.

'Your name, sir?' the colonel asked, unable to decipher the letters on the rogue's crumpled jumpsuit.

'That would be Ortega, señor.' The co-pilot's cadence was almost theatrical, the voice of a man who enjoyed talk for talk's own sake. 'Guido Gonzalo Ortega, pilot third class and falling, 33rd Verzante Skyshadows, indentured unto the glorious 6th Tempest in service to his Holiness the esteemed Water Dragon Aguilla de Carajaval, may his exalted bones bless this pestilential snake pit unto eternity.'

'That is heresy, Ortega!' his comrade protested stridently. 'The Water Dragon is doing the Emperor's work in the Mire, cleansing the savage and purging the xenos.'

'The Water Dragon drowned in his own blood and vomit years ago, boy.' There was an unexpected bitterness in Ortega's tone. 'Along with every one of the poor fools he dragged into the Mire with him. No, we Skyshadows are the last of the 6th Tempest, Jaime.'

'You will address me by my full rank, sub-pilot Ortega!'

'Son, why don't you just fly the ship and leave the talking to us oldsters,' Cutler said, waving his pistol at Jaime.

Indignantly the pilot returned his attention to the helm and swore at the blinking red light that indicated yet another clogged engine filter. The drop-ship was submerged in the effluvium of the Strangle Zone, Phaedra's miserable excuse for a cloud layer. Flying through the dense strata of floating fungal detritus was dirty work, but dropping below the smog was far more dangerous. The fleet had lost countless birds to enemy 'sky snipers' – high altitude drones armed with lethal rail guns.

With expert fingers the pilot flicked a sequence of switches and flushed the filter. The red light winked out and he sighed with relief. It was Ortega's job to supervise the filters, but the fool couldn't be trusted with anything these days. Jaime had reported his laxity many times, but the Sky Corps was so short of airmen that Ortega had escaped with a demotion. More importantly the report had earned Jaime Hernandez Garrido the silver badge of the Skywatch, an honour awarded only to men of impeccable loyalty. Garrido wore the winged eye on his lapel with pride, relishing Ortega's dislike of it. Unfortunately the old goat's retribution had been a vigorous campaign of flatulence that had turned the cockpit into a toxic no-man's-land to rival the smog outside. With any luck Ortega's luck would run out soon and Jaime would be assigned someone younger and more devoted. It was the natural order of things. There was no room for broken relics in a holy war.

The metal gangway crashed down onto the shore and Ambrose Templeton, captain of the 4th Company, lurched from the boat. Still reeling from the boiling embrace of the sea he stood blinking on the ramp, trying to make sense of the chaos that was the beach. Searching for words...

Blind, bound and broken heartless, dancing eyeless to a symphony of sorrows.

Templeton had written those words on the killing fields of Yethsemane Falls, scrawling them feverishly into a notebook with blood-slick hands, diverting the horror to the page before it could drown his sanity. Beneath his gaudy finery the captain was a grey man, sallow faced and balding, but beneath the grey he was a riot of restless words. Before the Providence uprisings he'd been an assiduous historian of warfare, poring over the strategies of the past to inform the tactics of the future. The discipline had served him well during the conflict and the scholar had become a fine officer. And in time the fine officer had become a fair poet. After Yethsemane, Templeton had come to see the materiel cost of war as material for his own epic, his 'Canticle of Crows'...

Carrion hawks, circling in strident contemplation of man's fathomless loss...

Lieutenant Thone staggered from the boat behind Templeton and slipped, sending them both tumbling to the beach. The captain thrust his hands out to catch his fall and felt them punch through something soft and brittle that exploded into a cloud of liquid fetor. Choking and spluttering, he found himself straddling a fleshy fungus that looked like a crude parody of a man. Then he saw the dull eyes staring up at him from the violet balloon of its face... Saw the distended jaws rammed open by the gnarled toadstool erupting from within... Saw the gleaming dog tags engraved into its bloated neck. By a small miracle his spectacles hadn't slipped loose and he could even read the name of the fungus: *Falmer, C.A., Corporal*. Templeton squinted in confusion, trying to make sense of it, hunting for a metaphor...

...Like bittersweet flowers of boundary, the dead shall bloom and the blossoms shall devour those that linger at the threshold...

And then he saw Falmer's skin rippling and quaking and he felt something nipping at his hands inside the ribcage. Nearby Thone was screaming and Templeton felt an echo welling up inside himself. If he let that scream out he knew it would never end, so he tried to drown it with more...

...words to snare and bury and deny all the sins that...

'On your feet Kapitan Bloodbait!' The voice was guttural and thick with the accent of the battleship crew. Lethean, Templeton recalled through his rising panic.

The speaker grabbed him by the collar and hauled him to his feet, tearing his hands free of the corpse in an eruption that spattered his glasses with ichor. He tried to wipe the slime away, but his hands were knocked aside and someone began to brush him down urgently. Through a liquid haze he could see dozens of pale, coin-sized grubs being swept from his sleeves. The vermin were all shells and pincers and thorny tendrils, something between a crab and a jellyfish. Several clung stubbornly to his hands, fighting to burrow into his flesh, but his rescuer tore them off with practised efficiency.

'The dead, they are full with the skrabs.' The Lethean laughed harshly. 'Mostly they only bite, but is not good to be bleeding inside a meatbag!'

Behind the voice Templeton could hear his men cursing as they deployed to the beach. Lieutenant Thone was still shrieking like a madman and Sergeant Brennan was bawling at him to stand still. Lubin, his vox-operator was praying in a breathless staccato rhythm. Behind the familiar voices he could hear distant shouts and cries punctuated by the clatter of Steambloods and a shrill blare of whistles.

'Is done,' said the Lethean. 'Welcome to the Dolorosa Breach, Kapitan Bloodbait.'

Wiping the slime from his glasses, Templeton peered at his saviour and groaned inside. Another damnable commissar! This planet was crawling with them!

Under a quagmire of scars and sores the fellow looked too young for the role, but there was no mistaking his black storm coat and high-peaked cap, though both were threadbare. Like the commissars on the battleship he'd woven razorwire into the blue band of his cap and epaulettes, ornamenting his faith with the promise of pain. Pinned to his lapel alongside the traditional Imperial aquila was an unusual silver icon: a diamond-shaped eye framed with angular wings. Templeton had never seen anything like it, but every regiment had its own traditions and the ram's skull of the 19th probably looked equally peculiar to this commissar.

'I am the Commissar Cadet Zemyon Rudyk of the Lethean mariner corps,' the youth announced, gesticulating fiercely to punctuate his words. The brass whistle hanging from his cap bobbed about in accompaniment.

Before Templeton could answer, Thone lurched towards him, clutching at his coat with beseeching hands. The lieutenant was still screaming and Templeton caught a glimpse of his eyes glittering through a writhing crustacean carpet. To his horror Templeton realised the man was covered in the creeping, clawing skrabs. Instinctively he reached out to help, but Rudyk shoved him aside and launched a brutal kick at Thone, sending the hapless officer reeling to the ground. A moment later the commissar's autopistol barked and silenced the screams.

'Was too late for that one, yes?' Rudyk grinned at Templeton, exposing blackened teeth that had been filed to sharp points. 'And the Emperor, he condemns.'

Templeton recognised the phrase from the Lethean battle-ship. The savage confessor had uttered the same words after he'd murdered poor Elias Waite. That injustice was still burn-ing a hole in Templeton's heart, but the recriminations would have to wait. Back there on the battleship capitulation had been their only option. It had been a crisis for all of them, but only Templeton had grasped the extent of the confessor's mad-ness and seen his regiment's peril. Just like the hellfire puritans back home, the Letheans had turned the sharp, cleansing blade of the Imperial Gospel into something twisted. There could be no reasoning with such men.

Once again, Templeton thanked Providence he'd been able to vox a warning to the colonel during their sea crossing. What Cutler would do with the warning was anybody's guess, but at least he wouldn't be coming in blind. Even so, Templeton sensed that nothing could prepare a newcomer for this world. There was a sickness here that ran deeper than the stench and the vermin, a malaise that could rot away a man's very soul. But there was also inspiration here. Gazing across the open graveyard of the beach, Templeton felt his soul ignite with imagery for his dark saga. Where the sea of sewage ended, the sea of decay began, drowning the shore in a swathe of death. Corpses were strewn everywhere...

...*deposited in geological sediments of corruption, the bleached skeletons of the first wave buried beneath the suppurating efflorescence of the last...*

'Kapitan Bloodbait!' The commissar snapped at him, misreading Templeton's awe for fear. 'The Emperor, He demands the courage!'

Templeton turned to him, the wonder in his eyes magnified by his thick glasses. 'Or else the Emperor condemns?'

'Is so, yes,' Rudyk agreed. 'Now get your newbloods off beach before the skrabs eats them all!' He gave Templeton a comradely slap on the shoulder and jerked the whistle to his lips.

Sergeant Calhoun heard another shrill whistle blast and yelled at his squad to shift their arses. There were at least three of the snakebite commissars prowling the shore, pouncing on the new arrivals as they spilled from the boats, bawling and cussing at the muddled men. He'd already seen two greybacks and an officer gunned down and he was damned if he'd lose anyone to the bloodthirsty blackcoats. Boone lumbered past with Toomy slung over his broad shoulders. Catching a glimpse of the broken man's bloody scalp, Calhoun swore viciously. It was a helluva thing to lose their sniper before the bullets had even started to fly.

'It just gets better and better don't it, sarge?' called Roach as he sped past, dancing nimbly between the corpses.

Calhoun shook his head, taking it all in. The beach was a screwed up hellhole, but when all was said and done things could have been much worse. It looked like the 19th had arrived on the tail end of the *really* bad stuff, after the fighting had already moved inland. This coastline had already been captured and the corpses choking its shores had paid the price. There was no telling how long it had taken and how many waves of men it had cost. For all he knew the beach might have been won and lost over and over again across the course of this decades old war. That grim thought turned his mind back to the boy. Why had he let Maude talk him into bringing young Audie along? And where was he anyway?

Everyone was off the boats now and racing towards the distant tree line, but he hadn't seen the greencap go past. Stubbornly he refused to acknowledge his anxiety. Despite what Maude had said he wasn't convinced the boy was his. The kid seemed too creed-struck to be a genuine Calhoun. Even so, he couldn't deny his relief when Joyce emerged from the boat. The boy paused on the ramp, gazing at the shore with a faraway look.

'What in the Seven Hells are you doing back there, greencap?' Calhoun hollered.

Joyce turned his distant eyes on him and Calhoun saw something almost furtive in his expression. Then the boy leapt to the shore and saluted smartly. 'Just checking something out, Sergeant Calhoun, sir,' he said.

Calhoun was about to question him further when Dix started shrieking.

'Looks like Brother Dix is in need of salvation, sir.' Joyce pointed further up the beach and Calhoun grimaced. Too damn right Brother Dix was in need of salvation! The rangy Badlander was struggling frantically to free his foot from the clinging carcass he'd trodden in. Cursing, Calhoun stalked over and hauled the idiot out of the rotten mire.

'Get it together, greyback!' Calhoun bellowed. 'I'm not pulling your grox feet out of every meatbag on this beach!'

'It ain't right sarge!' Dix wailed. 'It ain't right to just leave 'em here like trash. Thousands of 'em gone to feed the 'shrooms and the grubs like meat candy and...' The words bubbled out in a manic stream that told Calhoun the man was heading for the edge.

'I'll feed you to 'em right now if you don't can it!' Calhoun slapped Dix across the face. Hard. The greyback stared at him stupidly and Calhoun slapped him again, catching him as he stumbled. 'Are we done here, Trooper Dix?'

Dix nodded uncertainly, still snivelling. Calhoun snorted and thrust Modine's flamer towards him, but the Badlander jerked away as if he was being offered a venomous snake.

'He'd want you to have it,' Calhoun said stiffly. 'You going to dishonour the man, trooper?'

'No sarge, you got it all wrong.' There was a pleading look in Dix's eyes. 'See Klete, he'll be back real soon, just like them cogboys promised. I ain't touching his girl!'

'I'll take her, sergeant,' Joyce said, startling Calhoun. He hadn't seen the boy come up alongside him. 'I did some practising with burners in basic and they told me I got a gift for it. I always loved the sacred burnings back home. There's a holiness in fire you can't get from a bolt or a bullet.'

That serene glaze was back in the boy's eyes and Calhoun found himself feeling oddly uneasy. 'You still with us, boy?' he asked gruffly, feeling awkward.

'I'm just fine, sergeant.' Joyce reached for the flamer and Calhoun found himself handing it over. The greencap slung the bulky fuel canister over his shoulder and smiled happily. 'And Lady Hellfire's going to be just fine too.'

Captain Jon Milton Machen loped up the beach, the pistons of his colossal Thundersuit bellowing and wheezing furiously in the heat. The machine armour was a cantankerous old monster, but he knew it would never fail him. Like Machen himself, it was too full of bile and spite to lie down and die. Too hungry for war!

Prentiss and Wade kept pace with him on either flank, leaping over the corpses in their lighter Stormsuits while Machen simply waded through them, pounding the dead into pulp beneath his iron boots. He'd lost contact with Gledhill and Ashe but the rest of the Zouaves had signed in on the intra-suit vox. They were scattered along the beach, supporting the Arkan infantry like hard points in a tapestry of soft meat. His iron knights!

He surged past the blackened husk of a tank, catching sight of the yawning cavity in its hull. It was just one of countless broken hulks littering the beach. He'd clocked dozens of Chimera transports and Hellhound tanks, even a couple of heavier machines he didn't recognise, all shredded into scrap metal in mute testament to the power of the enemy munitions. There was no clue to the identity of the tank killers, but he knew that even a glancing shot from one of those mystery guns would obliterate his armour in an instant. The thought made him uncomfortable and he suddenly felt vulnerable out on the open coral. He didn't fear death, but he wouldn't welcome a fool's end!

Finally he saw the jungle looming over the coral dunes. The tangled wall of foliage looked like it had been dredged up from the sea bed and left to rot in the sun. Wherever he looked he saw stems and stalks and bladders and tendrils, puffed up with a fleshy, unclean vitality that sickened him and urged him to burn and burn. Lovingly he stroked the trigger of his flamer…

And a screaming torrent of fire lanced up from behind the dunes, immolating a cluster of cancerous trees. A moment later a second stream leapt up alongside the first, then another and another, uniting into a blazing, cleansing wave that surged through the jungle. It was as if the Emperor himself had granted Machen's desire to burn.

Puzzled, the captain crested a final dune and saw the base. The

Letheans had only offered a cursory briefing on the battleship, but they'd mentioned Dolorosa Breach. It was the only Imperial base on the southern archipelago, a rag tag camp manned by the remnants of several decimated regiments. There were at least twenty Hellhound tanks down there, stretched out along the tree line, their inferno cannons shrouded in steam as they cooled down. Scattered among the flame tanks were dozens of Chimeras and a pair of Leman Russ Vanquishers. Machen scowled at their slipshod formations: they were spaced almost randomly and some weren't even facing the jungle. Behind the mechanised perimeter things looked even worse.

The outpost was a sprawling shanty town of tents and makeshift huts that had obviously grown without any central or defensive planning. There were at least a thousand men bustling about the camp, but there was no cohesion or discipline to them. The troops were clustered up in their original regiments, still bound – and doubtless divided – by their old allegiances. Their uniforms spanned countless traditions, ranging from simple khaki fatigues to faded velvet finery to rusting suits of armour. Machen even spotted a gaggle of dark-skinned warriors galloping along the perimeter on horseback, whooping manically as they raced each other between the flames. To the captain's rigorous eye it was absolute bloody chaos.

By the Golden Throne, the Dustsnakes will fit right in with this rabble! Machen thought grimly.

'Do we go in, sir?' Wade voxed, his disgust mirroring Machen's own.

The captain had stopped on the dune and the rest of his company were catching up and fanning out on either side of him, awaiting his orders. Further along he saw young Lieutenant Grayburn leading the 2nd Company towards the outpost, while that dreamer Templeton lagged halfway up the beach with the 4th. And there was still no word from the colonel and his vaunted Burning Eagles. Doubtless the old man was still fooling around with his Norlander witch while his regiment was thrown to the wolves, leaving Jon Milton Machen to pick up the pieces.

The Hellhounds roared again and their stubby inferno cannons doused the jungle in a fresh wave of fire. Watching that filthy tangle burn, Machen grinned and boosted the output of his shoulder speakers, assaulting the dunes with a riot of martial chords. This war was a mess, but it would offer countless opportunities for a man who cared only for vengeance.

'Of course we're going in!' Machen bellowed. 'We didn't cross the damned stars to rust away on this Throne-forsaken hill!'

'No colonel, what you must understand about Phaedra is that there are countless spiders caught in Her web alongside the flies like us,' the portly co-pilot, Guido Ortega, observed sagely. 'They've been weaving their own little traps within the greater trap for decades, building petty fiefdoms in hell. For instance, take this Admiral Karjalan – the Sea Spider we call him…'

Keeping his eyes on the control panel, Jaime Garrido frowned. Ortega was still gabbling away to the crazed Guard officer as if they were old comrades reunited across a gulf of lost years, waxing lyrical about his conspiracy theories and picking holes in their sacred crusade. With mounting fury Garrido touched the silver icon on his lapel, praying for guidance. The shuttle was coasting through a relatively clean pocket of air right now and the turbulence had died down. With the Emperor's grace the ship's machine spirit could be trusted to coast along untended for a minute or so. If Garrido moved swiftly…

'Diseased you say?' the colonel was asking.

'So the rumours go,' Ortega paused for effect. 'Naturally the admiral keeps himself locked away in the high towers of his accursed warship, hiding away like one of those bloodsucking monsters from the old myths. Nobody has actually seen the man in years save for his priests. Ah, but they're a grim crowd! The Lethean Penitents they call themselves. I tell you señor, those bastards will crucify you as soon as look at you!'

'Would I be right in thinking you're not a devout man, Guido Ortega?' Cutler asked.

'On the contrary señor, I would cast my soul into the warpsea for the God-Emperor!' Ortega protested. 'But these Penitents are a perversion of the Imperial creed. They have made a virtue of malice, a sanctity of suffering…'

'And what about the Sky Marshall?' Cutler cut through the man's increasingly purple rhetoric. 'Seems to me he's sleeping on the job up there in orbit…'

'Sky Marshall Zebasteyn Kircher is a hero of the Imperium!' Garrido snarled, spinning to face them. There was a stubby service pistol in his hand. Cutler dived aside as the youth fired. A round whizzed past his face and another tore through the shoulder of his jacket, but the third was completely off. As the bullets ricocheted wildly around the confined space a distant, coldly professional part of the colonel's mind observed that Garrido was an appalling shot. Then Cutler was on his knees, levelling his own pistol, but Guido Ortega was already on top of the young pilot, wrestling for the weapon like an angry old bear. Garrido was spitting and snarling furiously, but like his aim, his muscles weren't much to speak of and he couldn't shift Ortega's bulk. The co-pilot smacked the youth's trigger hand against the control panel, mashing it against the sharp edges until the gun slipped free. As Garrido howled in pain Ortega head-butted him full in the face. Once. Twice. After the third crack the youth slumped senselessly into his chair.

The burst of strength drained out of the co-pilot and he slumped against the helm, breathing hard. His sweaty face was spattered with blood from his comrade's pulverised nose. Slowly at first, then with increasing violence, the ship began to shake.

'Ortega!' Cutler growled.

The Verzante threw him a dazed look as the shuttle groaned and the cockpit canted sharply downward. Ortega swore and crashed down into his seat. His hands darted over the controls like birds of prey as he struggled to rein in the vessel's neglected machine spirit.

'Padre de Imperios...' Ortega breathed as the turbulence finally subsided and the world steadied around them. His eyes were fixed rigidly ahead.

'You still with me, flyboy?' Cutler asked.

'That was... a very long time coming,' Ortega said through harsh gasps.

'Feels good, doesn't it?'

'And what exactly is it that I'm feeling so good about?'

Cutler stared at him for a long moment, suddenly unsure himself. Then he sighed, dredging up a soul-deep weariness that made him seem much older than Ortega. Instead of answering he hauled the unconscious pilot to the floor and sank into his place, gazing at the nebulous fog swirling past the windows and seeing nothing. Ortega lost himself in the old, trusted task of steering the ship while he waited for an answer. His rasping breaths had slowed by the time Cutler replied.

'Tell me Guido Ortega, would you have the balls to fly this tug into a hot zone?'

'I might say that I could do it with my eyes closed and my hands bound,' Ortega said. 'But that would be a manifest exaggeration.'

'I guess I'm going to take that as a yes,' Cutler said. 'Which is just as well, because we won't be stopping off on the Spider Admiral's boat.'

'I'm not sure that I follow you, señor.'

'Does a place called Dolorosa Breach mean anything to you?' Cutler was watching him with bright, angry eyes.

'Nothing that I like,' Ortega said carefully.

'Well that makes two of us, sir.' Cutler nodded. 'But I'm not asking you to like it. I'm just telling you to take me there.'

Keeping his eyes on their guide, Captain Templeton slashed a path through another snarl of creepers with his sabre and swatted hopelessly at the swarming flies. The vermin had hit the Arkan in a furious, biting wall the moment they had entered the jungle, then harried them every step of the way like tiny winged daemons. Nothing seemed to deter them and some of the men had already given up the fight, but their sly bites made the captain's skin crawl and he kept slapping at them stubbornly. The Phaedran veterans probably had some kind of repellent for the vermin, but if so they hadn't offered it to the newcomers. They hadn't offered much of *anything* except a rapid passage into the Hells.

There had been little respite at the ramshackle base called Dolorosa Breach. Templeton's company had been met by a patrol of slovenly sentries and waved on to the tree line where a craggy-faced officer had been overseeing all the new arrivals. The crew-cut ogre had ridiculed their tardy landing and 'dandy boy' uniforms, gloating that they wouldn't last a day in the Mire, but he'd soon grown bored, almost as if the newcomers weren't worthy of his wit. Without bothering to offer his name or rank, the brute had launched into a mission profile that was so thin on detail it would snap from a sharp glance. In short – and there was no long – their orders were to reinforce a push on an ancient temple complex some three kilometres inland. Designated 'the Shell', the necropolis was thought to serve as the primary rebel base for the region. The attack had begun three days ago and there were at least two other Imperial forces involved, but the composition, disposition and current status of those forces was unknown. Intelligence on the enemy seemed equally threadbare to Templeton: they would be facing a small contingent of tau, probably a few xenos mercenaries and a whole heap of 'fish'.

'Fish?' Templeton had asked, trying to ignore the furious itching in his left hand where the skrabs had bitten him.

'Yeah, Fish. The indigenous scum.' The officer had pointed to a band of gangly figures in grey jumpsuits slouched by the perimeter. Templeton had assumed they were simply bedraggled Guardsmen, but that mistake hadn't stood up to closer scrutiny. The Phaedrans – or Saathlaa as Cutler had called them in his briefing – were clearly of human stock, but their degeneracy was obvious. There was nothing overtly wrong about them, but nothing that was quite *right* either. All were at least a head shorter than an average man, but their stature was further diminished by their spindly bowlegs and hunched posture. Their faces were uniformly broad, flat and brutish, with widely spaced goggle eyes and fat, rubbery lips.

'Fish. You see it, right?' The officer had grinned and Templeton had reluctantly agreed that yes, he did indeed see it. In fact the degeneracy had unsettled him deeply.

Is the human bloodline really so open to corruption? Templeton had wondered. *And if so, might our entire race not sink back into the primordial slime with the passing of ignorant aeons?*

'Webbed fingers too,' the brutish officer had continued. 'Personally I'd cleanse the lot of 'em, but apparently they just about pass muster for human. Well, they're ugly scum, but they've got their uses. The ones who didn't rebel are almost pitifully loyal, probably because they know the rest will skin 'em alive if we lose the war. And they make damn fine guides.' He pointed to the gang by the trees again. 'These boys call themselves *askari*. I guess that means "scout" in Fishspeak.'

After three hours trekking through the Mire, Templeton had come to share the officer's faith in the *askaris'* jungle craft. The native assigned to his platoon had led them through the jungle with swift, knowing steps, steering them around impenetrable clusters of vegetation and creeper infested fissures. They were travelling a clotted, broken land that conjured up visions of a vast weed-choked regicide board where the light and dark squares corresponded to vitality and decay. Aware that one misstep in this tangled disharmony of life and death could prove fatal, the captain found himself growing more grateful for their guide the deeper they went. For all his degeneracy the native was their lifeline in this maze.

Occasionally the *askari* would bring them to a halt with a raised hand and drop to his haunches, sniffing suspiciously at the ground like an animal, then nod and scurry on. Often he would stop to peer at a glistening fungal tree or a swarming curtain of creepers, keeping his distance as he searched for some obscure telltale clue. Then he would either hurry past or urge his charges back with sharp gestures. On one occasion he had fled from something on the path ahead, frantically shooing the platoon away. As he retreated, Templeton had caught a glimpse of a titanic violet bloom leering at him from the clearing ahead and shuddered at its gently undulating mantle of tendrils, both fascinated and repelled. He hoped the other platoons had been gifted equally talented guides.

Their force was spread out, advancing through the jungle in

a loose wedge of twelve platoons, each numbering around fifty men. The platoons of the 2nd Company had taken the centre, while those of the 3rd and 4th had fanned out on either flank. They had entered the jungle in a much tighter formation, but the labyrinth of trees had played havoc with that plan and the teams had soon lost sight of each other. Although they maintained vox contact, nobody really knew where they were anymore and Templeton could only pray that they were all going in the same direction.

The wiry *askari* guide raised his hand and the greybacks of Dustsnake and Hawksbill squads crowded up alongside him, peering into the murk. A few paces ahead the ground dipped sharply and the jungle dissolved into a mist-wreathed swamp. The water was strangled by a tangle of mangrove-like trees, but those weren't the only things choking the swamp. There were bodies everywhere, floating languidly with their limbs splayed like broken dolls. Some were so riddled with arrows that they looked like human pincushions, while others were shockingly charred and sundered, evidently the victims of powerful energy weapons. Although the corpses were crawling with flies and leeches, they were obviously still fresh.

'Must be at least a hundred of 'em down there.' Sergeant Calhoun had to raise his voice over the buzzing feeding frenzy of the vermin. 'Looks like the poor bastards never even saw it coming.'

'The Jungle Sharks,' Lieutenant Sandefur said sombrely. The tall, square-jawed veteran had been given overall command of the two squads and Calhoun figured that was just fine. Sandefur might be an academy boy with a pole rammed up his backside but he was actually a half-decent soldier. By Willis Calhoun's reckoning that was a pretty good result for an officer.

'Aren't those the boys we're meant to be linking up with?' Calhoun asked.

'Indeed, but let's not be in a rush to link up with them now, eh sergeant,' Sandefur said with grim humour. He shot a questioning look at their guide and the Saathlaa nodded, indicating that their path lay through the corpse-choked swamp.

'Well now, don't the Emperor just love his greybacks today,' Roach muttered, drawing a frown from the lieutenant.

'It isn't a question of love, Dustsnake,' Sandefur said. Then he spotted the scout's tassels hanging from Roach's cap and smiled. 'Care to take point with our swampy friend, scout?'

'And here I was thinking you'd never ask, lieutenant.' Roach tipped his cap and grinned sourly at their *askari* guide. 'You and me, we're going make a fine team, *Mister* Fish.'

To his surprise the native grinned right back at him.

'Do you smell that?' Valance asked. The black-bearded scout had stopped, sniffing suspiciously at the smog rising from the marshland.

Machen couldn't smell anything through his sealed helmet, but he trusted the ex-trapper's instincts. Unusually for a scout, Jaques Valance was a barrel-chested bear of man, but he could move as silently as any Norland tracker. Rumour had it he'd learned his craft smuggling skins past the feral ork tribes.

'What do you have, scout?' the captain growled, scanning the skeletal trees for a target. The damnable mist was filtering everything into a soft focus blur.

'Don't know captain, but it's something new.' Valance was frowning as he tried to make sense of the odour. 'Smells like milk that's turned sour... and something else, something sharp. Maybe blackroot or...'

'We've lost the Fish!' someone shouted from up ahead.

'Prentiss, Wade, with me,' Machen called on the intra-suit vox. He tore his iron boots free of the clinging sludge and clanked towards the unseen speaker with his brother Zouaves on either flank. For the last hour or so his platoon had been up to their ankles in mud and over their heads in smog. The stuff rose from the ground in thick streamers, transforming the vegetation into a ghostly graveyard parody of the jungle. Everything looked withered and desiccated here.

Even by the standards of this arsewipe planet this region is ugly! Machen reflected gloomily.

'Hill and Baukham are gone too!' There was an edge of panic in the point man's voice as the Zouaves stomped up alongside him with Valance at their heels.

'They were there a moment ago!' The greyback pointed ahead. 'Just past those trees…'

Machen signalled to Valance and the scout advanced cautiously. He stopped by the suspect cluster of trees, his sharp eyes picking out a residue of black slime splattered across the trunks. Gingerly he sniffed the stuff and gagged at the stench. Catching a glint of metal, he dropped to his knees and ran his fingers over the bark, wincing as something drew blood. Squinting, he saw the trunk was riddled with a web of tiny, razor sharp metal filaments.

'I've found…' A soft hiss came from the smog ahead and Valance froze. A moment later the hiss was followed by a low, wet rattle. The scout rose and backed away, his eyes never straying from the mist ahead.

'There's something out there,' he breathed. 'Something more than an animal.'

'Form up around me, greybacks,' Machen commanded, stoking up the old fury in his gut like a loyal friend. If the Hells were going to break loose then Jon Milton Machen was ready to oblige them.

Templeton had lost his bearings hours ago, but their guide clearly knew his business so he had immersed himself in the nightmare trek, hoping to embrace the living dead phantasmagoria of the jungle. It offered such a wealth of allusions to a refined spirit, such potential for metaphor and wordplay... Yet try as he might the words eluded him, lost in the smog of pain that had slowly seeped across his mind. It was the bites of course, some infection he'd caught from those damnable corpse crabs back on the beach. His left hand had been throbbing for hours now, summoning up a fever that was turning his thoughts to sludge.

The captain paused to catch his breath, letting the others march past as he unwound his makeshift bandage and inspected the wounds. His whole hand had swollen up and he could see a tracery of purple lines weaving up his wrist. Once again he cursed himself for letting the bites go untended at the outpost, but they'd seemed so trivial back then. Besides, he hadn't wanted to look weak in front of Machen. His fellow captain already had precious little respect for him.

Something whirred by overhead with a sonorous, buzzing drone. Templeton glanced up and caught a shape flitting between the treetops, dark and jagged against the emerald canopy. It was gone in the blink of an eye, but he was left with the impression of something thorny and misshapen, like a huge insect...

The Lord of Flies, chitinous monarch of sickening skies.

'One helluva big bug that, eh sir?' Sergeant Brennan said, disturbing Templeton's vague inspiration. Brennan was a cheery, pragmatic bruiser who might have been the captain's polar opposite. 'Seen half a dozen of 'em fly past in the last hour. Don't much like the look of 'em.'

'The Mire is full with the xenos filth, yes,' Commissar Cadet Rudyk interjected as he came up alongside them. Much to Templeton's irritation the youth had fastened onto his squad. 'Here all animal and all plant is tainted. One day we burn them all, but it is not today.'

Rudyk marched past and Templeton saw that the back of his storm coat was riddled with bullet holes. The young cadet wasn't the first man to wear that coat and probably wouldn't be the last. In all likelihood commissars didn't last very long on Phaedra.

Another of the giant insects flittered by overhead, punctuating its flight with a rhythmic medley of twitters and chirps. Its strange song drew a chorus of replies from a dozen unseen companions. Through his growing delirium Templeton felt something nagging at him. Something about that song…

'You all right, sir?' Brennan asked, peering at the captain's pallid, glistening face.

'Just a touch of heatstroke, sergeant.' Templeton smiled weakly, unsure why he was hiding the truth. 'Best get on. We don't want to fall behind in this maze.'

But as they went deeper into the Mire, Templeton found his eyes returning to the canopy, watching the treetops for a flash of chitin.

CHAPTER FOUR

Imperial Seabase Antigone, the Sargaatha Sea

I was discharged from the infirmary two weeks ago,
yet High Commissar Lomax still hasn't summoned me.
Doubtless she's engaged with more pressing matters than an
errant commissar, but sometimes I can't help thinking she's
playing games. I have occupied my reprieve by exploring
the abandoned lower tiers of this rusting old sea platform,
delving through the flooded under-chambers as I try
to straighten out my story. Any lie will do, so long as it
convinces Lomax of the one truth that matters: I am going
to kill Commander Wintertide.

Number 27 accompanies me on my wanderings, a mute
reminder of Indigo Gorge, where my quest began nine
months and an eternity ago. Indigo Gorge. In twenty years
of soldiering across more worlds than I care to recall I've
never seen the likes of that killing ground. We were dying
in droves, wading upriver through the red corpse paste

of our fallen as the flickering lances of the blueskin guns sliced down from the escarpments high above. They had the cover, the range and the elevation. What good was faith against that? And what possible purpose did my twenty-seventh execution serve? If that murder had somehow turned the rout, well what then? Another thousand lost, probably more, yet we'd have been no closer to victory. But Niemand's shade was with me that day, filling my heart with ice, so when the charge faltered and my charges fled, I didn't hesitate to take the shot. There was no calculation in my choice – the sacrifice was just another fleeing shape amongst so many. A coward. Expendable. Execrable.

I'd still believe it if I hadn't seen her eyes, but as she fell she rolled over and I caught her gaze. Her features were made strange by the distorting waters, stranger still by the perfect geometry of the third eye my bullet had punched through her skull. She couldn't have been more than eighteen, a plain girl already haggard with the rigours of life in the Guard, but as she slipped into the water and out of life she looked right at me and I caught the last flicker of something that I can only call holy.

And so Number 27 became the third member of my shadow triumvirate, but while Bierce and Niemand despise me, her gaze burns with a terrible pity that is so much worse. It is for her that I will kill Wintertide and end this meat grinder war.

Iverson's Journal

The men of Dustsnake were wading waist deep through the curdled soup of the swamp, their rifles held over their heads to keep out the muck and their mouths shut to keep out the flies. Together with the Hawksbill greybacks they followed their guide through the morass with silent determination. All except Boone.

The burly Badlander was cussing and splashing about, angrily chewing up insects as he tried to dislodge the razor-toothed thing that had latched onto his boot. Toomy was still slung across his shoulders, a dead weight that sometimes burbled and groaned, but showed no other sign of recovery. A couple of the others had offered to take a stint carrying him, but Boone had refused. The sniper had always been good to him, never calling him a groxbrain and even letting him win a few hands of cards now and again. Sergeant Calhoun had wanted to leave the injured man behind at the outpost, but Boone hadn't liked the looks of that place and eventually old bullet-head had backed off. The big man had it all worked out. Even if Toomy didn't get better, it would be fine because then Boone wouldn't be the dumbest greyback in the squad anymore. This was probably the deepest insight of his life and it had made him intensely happy. Despite the heat and the flies he'd carried his burden with a big smile, sure that life was finally on the up. And then the eel thing had started biting at his boots. It spoiled the last few minutes of Gordy Boone's vague life.

When the end came Calhoun was shouting at him to shut the Hells up and Roach was turning to offer a gem of sarcastic wisdom. And then something slapped Boone right in the eye. For a moment he was angry and then he was hurt and then he wasn't anything anymore except a slab of dead meat toppling into the water. Toomy splashed down beside him, groaning reflexively at the shock.

Roach grinned, thinking the big groxbrain had slipped. And then he saw the black spine sticking out of Boone's right eye as he sank below the scum. Something whickered past Roach's ear and a Hawksbill greyback gurgled, clutching at the arrow sprouting from his throat. In another heartbeat the air was alive with a hail of arrows and men were screaming and falling all around him. Their native guide dived below the water and Roach followed, screwing his eyes shut against the filth. Above him the surface popped with impacts and he felt something scrape his shoulder. Desperately he forced himself down to the silt bed and swam, blindly hunting for cover.

'Get into the mangroves!' Calhoun yelled, ignoring the arrow jutting from his shoulder as he surged through the mire towards a clump of trees. Cully and Pope splashed along beside him, firing wild volleys of las-fire at the shadows dancing in the mist. They could see Lieutenant Sandefur leading a gaggle of Hawksbill men to a mound of fallen trees, his sabre raised and his pistol flaring, sending heroic, hopeless bursts into the mist.

The three men crashed down into cover and found Dix already there, struggling to jam his wiry frame into the cavern of gnarled roots. To Calhoun's disgust he was whimpering Kletus Modine's name over and over like a child begging for its mother.

'They're coming at us from all sides,' one-eyed Cully snarled, frantically trying to train his lasrifle everywhere at once as the Saathlaa guerrillas tightened their circle. The naked warriors dissolved out of the mist like hunched ghosts, fired their arrows with guttural whoops and then faded away to reload.

'Get in as deep as you can!' Calhoun shouted, his eyes hunting for the boy as he snapped the shaft in his shoulder and crawled into the tangle. He breathed a sigh of relief as he caught sight of Joyce crouched in the hollow bole of a tree across from him. This was the greencap's first real tussle but he didn't look scared. In fact there was a big grin on his face that made Calhoun proud and uneasy at the same time.

Dix squealed as a huge spider flopped down onto his face from the rotten hollows of the mangrove. It gripped his head like a pair of skeletal hands, all bony legs and hard ridges and far too many eyes. Calhoun ripped it away and threw it aside. It took Dix's nose with it, leaving a gushing crater in the middle of his face. Swearing in disgust, Calhoun pumped the scrabbling spider full of las-bolts and turned to the others.

'We've got to start dishing the pain back at 'em!' Calhoun yelled, trying to blot out Dix's screeching. 'They can't get at us under here, but we've got to hold 'em back!'

One of the giant insects swooped low, hooked its clawed feet into a man's back and tore him shrieking from the ground. Surging back into the treetops it let go, turning its victim into a shrieking, flailing manikin. Captain Templeton leapt back as the man crashed into the mulch at his feet, broken but still breathing. Blood gurgled from the wreck's ruptured throat as it tried to beg for help and Templeton fell to his knees, his hands fluttering helplessly over the broken pile as it gasped for words that wouldn't come. Templeton understood. The words wouldn't come for him either.

Commissar Cadet Rudyk charged past him, leafing frenetically through a battered Tactica manual with one hand as he snapped off shots with the other. Somewhere nearby Sergeant Brennan was shouting and the vox-operator was screaming into his crackling set and a Steamblood Zouave had triggered his shoulder speakers, flooding the glade with bombastic music. And men were swearing and fighting and dying all around Ambrose Templeton.

The captain shook his head and slapped himself hard in the

face, trying to dislodge the clouds in his skull. The attack had come so suddenly. His platoon had just entered a wide forest glade when a battle had flared up somewhere in the distance. In that moment the insects had surged down from above, almost as if they were obeying a prearranged signal...

And damn it all, they were! And I knew it was coming all along! I knew they were talking to each other!

Yet again Captain Machen heard the ghost rattle from the mist. Then again on their left flank... their right... from behind...

'Whatever it is, there's more than one,' Valance whispered.

'Let's flush the craven scum out,' Wade said over the intra-suit vox, his patrician tones filled with contempt.

'Wait. Let them come to us,' Machen hissed. 'They're hungry for it.'

He had the platoon formed up in a tight phalanx that bristled with lasrifles on every front, reinforced by the three armoured Zouaves and their heavy stubbers at equidistant points. It was a textbook defence that Machen had favoured against feral greenskins and Outlanders back home on Providence, but his patience was wearing thin. They could all hear the muffled sounds of distant las-fire as the other platoons engaged the enemy, winning glory while Jon Milton Machen just sat here.

Suddenly something clacked and whirred in the fog, like a machine slowly winding up. Two more machines chugged alive in response.

'Sir, might I suggest...' Prentiss began, but his voice was disintegrated in a screeching cacophony as a storm of metal erupted from the mist, tearing into the phalanx from three sides.

* * *

Sergeant Calhoun grinned as another primeval guerrilla leapt from the mist – right into the sights of his lasrifle. Before the Saathlaa could loose his arrow the sergeant lanced him through the eye and flicked the barrel across to another savage. Cully and Pope were wedged between the roots on either side of him, backing him up with short, sharp bursts, but he'd given up on Dix. The injured Badlander had huddled up into a foetal ball, whimpering pitifully as he clutched at his ruined face.

The ambush had cost them nearly half their number, but the survivors were pulling things back. Lieutenant Sandefur had set up a decent firing perimeter with half a dozen greybacks, targeting the rebels with precise, disciplined volleys.

These savages have spirit and cunning, but bows and arrows are no match for Arkan fire! Calhoun thought fiercely.

A bolt of energy streaked from the mist and tore through a tree sheltering a lone greyback, sundering his chest into charred chunks of meat. Calhoun's confident grin faded.

'What in the Hells was that?' Pope hissed.

'That was us fragged,' Cully answered as a second killing bolt sizzled out of the jungle. And Calhoun had to admit he was probably right.

Something buzzed behind Templeton. He lurched round and stared blearily into a face out of nightmares. It looked like an insane three-tiered pyramid of compound eyes built on a plinth of mandibles. Long, tapering antennae flared out from either side of the conical head, tilted sharply towards its prey as it closed in.

Despite his peril, Templeton was fascinated by the monstrous warrior, almost hypnotised by the quicksilver blur of its wings. The thing was craggily bipedal, but any resemblance to humanity ended there. Its double-jointed legs ended in massive talons and its body was a patchwork exoskeleton of hard plates and vicious barbs. Strangest of all, the insect was carrying a gun. As it levelled the weapon he saw the blur of its wings flitter and oscillate, modulating their rhythm. The crystalline prong in the gun barrel shimmered, resonating in harmony with the droning, almost as if the wing case was calibrating the gun and…

Sergeant Brennan bowled into Templeton and threw him aside. Spinning, he sent a volley of las-fire into the insect's face, incinerating two tiers of eyes. The creature chittered in pain and pulled away, its wings beating furiously as it soared towards the canopy. Brennan spun after it, tracking its path with a stream of las-fire that flared off its tough exoskeleton. With icy calm he adjusted his aim and ripped through the delicate web of its wings. Twittering furiously the thing crashed headlong into a tree and plunged to the ground. A band of baying, vengeful greybacks were on it in seconds, hacking and stabbing with their bayonets.

'We have to find cover!' Brennan yelled, hauling Templeton to his feet.

A ripple of energy pulsed down from above and struck the sergeant, unravelling his atoms in a frothing crimson spiral. A moment later, all that remained of Brennan was the hand gripping Templeton's greatcoat. The captain glanced up as Brennan's killer streaked towards him with outstretched talons. He ducked frantically and the insect swept over his head, whipping him with a trailing claw that shredded his hat and sent him reeling. Off balance, he sent a salvo of wild las-rounds after it and drew his sabre, hunting the sky.

Watch the skies, the fangs of their eyes, weeping chittering chitin rain…

* * *

Only the three Zouaves had weathered the razor blade storm. Wave after wave of metal filaments had bombarded Machen's phalanx, the tiny threads shredding flesh and bone but only scratching the solid Steamblood carapaces. The attack left them standing over the mangled wreckage of their comrades like knights in an abattoir. Incredibly a few of the butchered carcasses were still alive, moaning and wailing as they bled out from a thousand cuts.

'Both of you stand absolutely still,' Machen whispered over the vox.

'I don't understand…' Wade voxed back.

'Quietly!' Machen hissed. 'We're sealed up tight but let's not play with fire. Now just do as I say unless you want to die!'

'By your command,' Wade whispered formally.

'Prentiss?' Machen said. 'Prentiss, did you get that?'

There was no reply from the third Zouave, but Machen couldn't risk checking on him. He had to ignore the wounded too. They were probably beyond help, but that didn't make it any easier.

'Sir, what in the Hells just happened to us?' Wade's voice sounded strained and Machen guessed some of the filaments had got through his armour, probably slipping in at the joints.

'Loxatl,' Machen said bleakly. The moment the attack had come he'd recognised the weapon and realised the folly of bunching his men up.

'What are those lizard trash doing here?' Wade hissed incredulously.

'What they're always doing – killing for pay. It seems these tau bastards like to hide behind mercenaries.'

I've travelled so far only to find the same old vermin waiting for me, Machen thought bitterly. *And why should I be surprised when that has always been the way of things?*

Long ago an old preacher had thrown him a scrap of wisdom that hit him with the force of absolute truth: 'Wherever you go, there you are.' It was a bleak truth, because wherever Machen went, horror went too. Why would Phaedra be any different? Besides, the loxatl were naturals for this filthy planet and its filthier war: amphibians and mercenaries who fought for the highest bidder, just as they'd fought for the rebels back on Providence.

'I can't see anything out there,' Wade said. 'What are we going to do?'

'We'll wait.'

'But they'll tear us apart!'

'I've faced these scum before. They're virtually blind on land. They rely on smell and taste to find their prey.'

There was a long pause as Wade considered this.

'Our armour...'

'Exactly. We're sealed. If we stand perfectly still the bastards won't even know we're here.'

'Sir... I'm bleeding. Rather badly as it happens.'

'And so are fifty other souls, lieutenant. Just stand still and the lox won't sniff you out from the crowd.'

'But the wounded...'

'Will draw the lox out. These scum may kill for pay, but they *like* the killing.'

'You want to use the wounded as bait?' Wade sounded appalled.

'I want to give them vengeance, man!' Machen struggled to keep his voice down as the fury welled up. He crushed it with an effort. 'The lox won't leave anyone alive, but they'll want to enjoy the killing. If we wait they'll come to us...'

* * *

Another bolt of superheated energy sizzled across the swamp, tearing a chunk out of Lieutenant Sandefur's cover, but Calhoun's eyes were on his boy. Joyce had slipped quietly into the water and lay floating on the surface, playing dead. Calhoun had seen him emptying some of the promethium from his flamer's fuel canister and wondered what he'd been playing at. Well it was obvious now, but Calhoun didn't like it any better. The air in the tank was keeping Joyce buoyant as he paddled slowly towards one of the lethal snipers. To a careless observer he would pass for another floating corpse, but it was a hell of a risk. Calhoun ground his teeth in frustration.

As he bobbed towards the Emperor's foes Audie Joyce was thinking of the saint from the battleship. How proud that wonderful, terrible giant would be of him now! Like the saint, he had passed beyond fear and doubt. The epiphany had come to him during the terrible sea crossing, born from the fate of the Zouave knight who'd been thrown overboard. Joyce hadn't been able to shake the look of surprise in the knight's eyes and the more he'd thought about it the angrier he'd become at the sailor who'd doomed him. That was why he'd crept back to the cabin after the boat had landed. The sailor had grinned impudently, but he'd soon stopped grinning when Audie had put his big hands round his throat. He'd watched the man's eyes goggle with shock as he squeezed and squeezed, confirming his intuition that men were always surprised when death came for them.

That vengeance had felt pure. *Holy*. Like the saint, Audie Joyce had done the Emperor's work with his bare hands, but now he had a flamer and there was more work ahead.

* * *

'Aim for their wings!' Templeton yelled, trying to make sense of the chaos around him. His greybacks were dashing about, firing frantically into the air or diving to avoid the deadly beams. Several of them had fallen to their knees, risking death for a better shot at their speeding tormentors. Their remaining Steamblood knight had locked his armoured legs, transforming himself into a sturdy firing platform. His massive heavy stubber was blazing away, raking the canopy with a steady stream of high velocity rounds and spilling out a cascade of spent shells. Martial music blared from his shoulder speakers in accompaniment to his amplified bellowing. The man's comrade had fallen in the first flyby, atomised by a concentrated lattice of beams, and the surviving knight wanted payback.

As Templeton watched, the Zouave snagged a flier from the air and the greybacks yelled triumphantly. Like a mob, they charged towards the tumbling ruin of chitin and Templeton charged with them, suddenly eager for blood. Commissar Cadet Rudyk got there first, yelping with hatred as he rammed the barrel of his pistol between the creature's twitching mandibles and emptied his clip on full auto. His eyes were bright as he looked up at Templeton and grinned. He shook open the Tactica manual clutched in his other hand, revealing the page he'd marked with a finger. Templeton glimpsed a crude sketch of the insect warriors.

'Is the *vespid* we face, yes! Ves-pid Sting-wing!' The youth explained, brandishing the manual triumphantly. 'Is vassal race for the tau, you see? For scout and assault. Is very quick and is very agile.'

'We have to… find cover…' Templeton muttered blearily, seeing two grinning cadet commissars.

'Maybe we find the kroot here too!' Rudyk said, licking his lips at the prospect.

* * *

The loxatl slithered from the mist with sly, sinuous movements, crawling with its belly to the ground on four clawed legs. It paused and sniffed at the air with flaring nostrils, sifting through the scent of carnage for a threat.

Watching the beast from the corner of his eye, Machen's finger caressed the trigger of his heavy stubber. The loxatl aroused an almost primal revulsion in him, its serpentine form somehow embodying the worst aspects of *otherness*. Its head was a flat, snake-like torpedo that bristled with teeth under the slits of pale, almost sightless eyes. Black saliva drooled from its maw as it flicked its snout back and forth, tasting the air with a questing tongue. Its languid movements were mirrored by the stubby flechette blaster attached to its back. Mounted inside a synapse-linked augmetic cradle, the gun responded directly to the creature's thoughts, allowing it to track prey without encumbering its claws. Machen heard the weapon clack and whirr as it spun about, lingering on the men who still breathed amongst the pile of bodies.

'Sir, one of the bastards has just crawled right into my sights,' Wade voxed from somewhere behind him. 'Request permission to open fire.'

'Wait. That's only two. There's still one more out there,' Machen said.

'Sir, I'm bleeding…'

'I said wait. We'll only get one chance at this.'

Motionless, Machen kept his eyes on his own loxatl. He couldn't see the one approaching Wade or risk looking around for the third, but he sensed it watching and waiting. It was more cautious than its brethren, probably the brood leader, old and canny with the wisdom of countless hunts. Even so, once its packmates started killing the wounded it wouldn't be able to hold back…

* * *

Roach felt a gentle tug at his shoulder. Gasping for breath, he surfaced amongst a bed of tall reeds. The Saathlaa scout was waiting for him, crouched low with only his neck showing above the waterline. Instinctively Roach followed his lead. The *askari* had guided him through their desperate underwater flight with occasional prods or tugs, always signalling when it was safe to come up for air. Apparently the native had no problems seeing in the murky water with those big, fish-like eyes of his. The greyback guessed he was lucky his guide had taken a liking to him, but the native's impulsive loyalty made him uncomfortable. Claiborne Roach wasn't much used to anyone looking out for him.

He heard an electronic burble as something scudded over the water towards their position. With an urgent wave the *askari* dived again. As Roach followed he saw the shadow of a disc flitting by overhead. He heard several more of the things whiz past, their machine chattering dampened by the water.

It felt like an age before the native pulled him back to the surface. The cacophony of battle raging across the swamp had intensified with the arrival of the flying discs. Peering cautiously through the reeds, Roach saw them whirling around his embattled comrades, sometimes skimming low over the water, sometimes flitting amongst the treetops. They were only about a metre in diameter and looked kind of ridiculous to Roach, but the twin guns fixed to their undersides were no joke. Fortunately their aim was poor when they were on the move, only stabilising when they came to a hovering halt. Each time one of the discs attempted that, the Arkan defenders tore it apart with concentrated fire, but it was a dangerous game.

And then there were the snipers. Roach had counted three of them, scattered about the swamp, hidden deep in the mist. Their rate of fire was slow, but the power of their weapons far exceeded anything the Arkan infantry carried, slicing through flesh or solid bark with equal ease. The sneaky bastards had already picked off four greybacks. Unless something was done about them this skirmish was going to end badly.

'We're running out of time,' Roach whispered to the *askari*.

Keeping low in the water, the native gestured to a clump of mangroves some twenty metres away. Roach waited and a moment later a bolt of energy whooshed from the hideout.

'Nice work, Mister Fish,' Roach smiled, winning a lopsided grin from the *askari*. 'Okay, let's take him down.'

They dived again.

'Tell the colonel… tell him we've been thrown to the wolves,' Templeton rasped through a raw tunnel of pain.

'I'll do my best, sir,' Lubin muttered as he fiddled with his vox-set, 'but I can't promise you anything.'

The pessimism was an old ritual between them, but the skinny little man was the best vox-operator in the regiment and Templeton had personally financed his long-range comms set. It was the kind of foresight that had served him well in the past.

'Kapitan Bloodbait, we must advance, yes!' Rudyk snapped at him. 'A Guardsman, he must go forward always! The Emperor, he…'

'He condemns. Yes… I do recall…' Templeton said, quite sure that the Emperor had already condemned *him*. His infected hand had swollen monstrously under the bandages, pumping the skrab poison through his whole body, but mercifully his head had cleared a little. He scanned the jungle uncertainly, trying to work things through. His platoon was sheltering under the drooping canopy of a huge toadstool, crouched behind a bed of smaller fungi. The stingwings had broken off their attack, but there were other enemies out there.

'We need… to regroup… find the others…'

'And together we go forward, yes!' Rudyk said, slapping his hands.

'Yes,' said Templeton, thinking no.

Machen was staring at the scouting loxatl, willing it to signal the 'all clear' to its wary brood leader.

'Sir, I've got a clean shot!' Wade's voice buzzed eagerly over the vox.

Abruptly Machen's loxatl reared up onto its hind legs and cocked its head, gurgling that liquid rattle deep in its throat. Somewhere behind the captain its companion responded. Machen cursed Wade, sure the beasts had detected the muffled vibrations of his voice.

'Sir, don't you think–'

'Keep quiet you fool.'

Suddenly the loxatl leapt, streaking through the air almost too fast for the eye to follow. It landed on Machen's towering Thundersuit with a wet thud. One of its claws scrabbled against his domed helmet and a milky white eye peered blindly through the porthole of his visor. He froze.

Perhaps it thinks I'm a tree. A strange tree to be sure, but then this Emperor forsaken jungle is full of strange trees. If Wade can just keep his mouth shut for…

'It's almost on top of me!' Wade buzzed.

The dead eye widened and the loxatl hissed. As it tried to spring away the captain's iron-clad arms shot out and caught it in a vice-like grip, crushing its flechette harness like matchwood. Its claws raked desperately against his armour and its jaws snapped at his faceplate, but it couldn't penetrate the carapace. He squeezed hard, grinding the beast against his cuirass until its attack turned to a frantic escape attempt. Behind him he heard Wade open fire on his own lizard, but he had no attention to spare. The lox in his grasp was writhing and contorting like a snake, its oily skin so slick he could barely hang on to it. But he did hold on, grimly tightening his grip as he paid back the horror eating him up from inside.

The horror that could never be paid back...

Machen had once thought he'd lost the capacity for horror on the killing fields of Yethsemane, but he had been wrong. Returning home after the war he'd found horror waiting for him like an old friend in the smouldering ruins of his estate. Valens Parish was far behind the loyalist lines, but horror had rushed ahead of his homecoming to give him a hero's welcome in the charred bodies of his wife and daughters. One of the estate's slaves had seen it happen: the killers had been stragglers heading back home, leaderless and drunk on victory. Badlanders. Loyalists.

The captain had strung up the slave for surviving when his family had died, then tracked down and executed the murderers with the same fussy precision he directed towards troop movements and munitions supplies. Afterwards he'd screamed until he had nothing left inside but hate. Then, with nowhere else to go he'd returned to the 19th. His family had been avenged, but vengeance was greedy.

And vengeance wasn't choosy...

Something snapped in the loxatl's back and a froth of mucous erupted from its jaws, spattering Machen's faceplate. For a moment the beast jerked about spasmodically, then fell still. With a triumphant howl the captain cast the broken carcass aside.

There was an angry hiss from the mist and a hail of flechettes sliced towards him and clattered harmlessly across his armour.

Snarling, he returned the gesture with a burst from his heavy stubber, raking the fog as his unseen attacker bounded away.

'Wade, did you kill yours?' Machen shouted into the vox.

'I hit it!' Wade replied excitedly.

'Did you *kill* it, man?'

'I… I'm not sure. It was so damnably fast, sir.'

Machen swore and stomped over to the Zouave, who was tracking his weapon uncertainly across the smog.

'I did hit it! It's bleeding out all over the place!' Wade pointed to a trail of black slime that disappeared into the mist. From somewhere beyond they heard a ragged growl as something dragged itself through the mulch.

'You have to hound a killer down and finish him!' Machen snarled, storming into the mist after the blood trail.

He found the second loxatl crawling painfully towards a stagnant pool. It swung on him with a defiant hiss, its mangled flechette blaster clicking impotently. The creature's left forearm and half its face had been torn away by Wade's salvo, but it still lunged at him, snapping feebly with its shattered jaws. He batted it to the ground and crushed its skull beneath an iron boot.

Just one more and this game is over, Machen thought hungrily.

Roach and his guide surfaced quietly some ten metres behind the sniper's hideout. There were three guerrillas hunkered down in the bushes. To his surprise the sniper himself was a native, almost naked under a thick paste of grey mud. Incongruously the Saathlaa's head was encased in a sleek, backswept helmet fitted with a crystalline optical sensor. The warrior was a bizarre amalgam of the primeval and the hi-tech, but there was no mistaking his skill with the oversized rifle he cradled. He handled the heretical weapon with a tenderness that bordered on worship, whispering to it and stroking the barrel each time he took a shot.

In a way, the other two guerrillas were even more surprising. Both were true humans and undoubtedly professional soldiers. They wore open-faced helmets and loose black fatigues augmented with cuirasses and shoulder pads. The armour looked like it was moulded from some kind of hard plastek and had a rounded, alien aesthetic.

Alien. Yes, it was the xenos that Roach had expected to find here. The *true* enemy, not more savages and these human traitors. Some part of him had wanted to bring pain to the tau themselves, to get some payback for poor dumb Boone and the others. From somewhere across the swamp he heard the unmistakable whoosh of a flamer and the three guerrillas began to argue furiously, the humans harassing their Saathlaa sniper to switch targets fast.

Well, whoever they are, they're still the enemy, Roach decided.

Signalling to the *askari* beside him, he sighted along his rifle and took the shot. The gun fizzled impotently, something inside it wrecked by the drenching it had taken. He grimaced as the native sniper cocked his head at the sound and began to turn. The *askari* leapt up and flicked something from his hand. A dagger-like thorn slapped into the sniper's chest and sent him crashing back into the mesh of creepers he'd been lurking in.

The two human traitors swung round and Roach dived forward, ducking under their first snapshots. Desperately he jabbed the barrel of his rifle into one man's eye and sent him reeling, but the other smashed the butt of his own weapon into Roach's face. Stumbling drunkenly he saw the *askari* cannoning into his attacker and heard the splash as they hit the water hard. The first soldier was lurching about, clutching at his ruined eye with one hand and trying to level his rifle with the other. Fighting the concussion, Roach lurched along with him and saw the dead sniper entangled in the creepers. He snatched the big thorn from the corpse's chest and staggered into the half-blind solider, batting away the man's rifle and ramming the makeshift dagger into his remaining eye.

And then it was all too much and the world spun out from under his feet and came crashing down.

Audie Joyce felt the Emperor's wrath pulsing through his veins as he incinerated the xenos-loving heretics. Their hideout was a blistering wire-frame inferno and he could see the rebels flailing about in there like charcoal skeletons. One of them dived into the water in a cascade of steam, but Audie could tell it was too late for him. A couple of savages leapt out of the jungle to his right and he swung the cleansing stream of fire over to greet them, grinning as they flared up.

Everything had gone to plan, just as he knew it would. Even the heathen discs had missed him as he paddled towards the sniper's nest. When he had leapt up and unleashed the holy fire he'd caught a flash of surprised eyes in the foliage and smiled at his growing wisdom.

'Get into cover you greencap idiot!'

Joyce swung round at that familiar voice and saw Uncle Sergeant Calhoun charging towards him in slow motion, struggling through the treacle of the swamp. His lasrifle was spitting fire as he advanced, chasing the discs that were racing ahead of him towards Joyce. He caught one and sent it spinning and smoking into the water. The others chattered furiously and whipped round, soaring back towards the veteran. Roaring like a madman, Calhoun emptied his clip at the advancing discs, standing his ground as return fire from a dozen guns stitched the water around him into steam.

As Joyce stormed back towards his hero he saw other grey-backs leap out of cover to support Calhoun and draw some of the heat. Everyone was shooting and dashing about now, all caution thrown to the wind as the Arkan chased the Thunderground in their souls. Three of the discs went down in flames, three others swept past leaving a couple of Arkan dead. The surviving sniper claimed another victim, but several greybacks clocked his position and raced towards him, heedless of the risk.

Joyce heard the clamour of martial music as a Steamblood knight waded in from their left flank at the head of another Arkan squad, its heavy stubber blazing away at the rebels fleeing before it. Arrows pinged off his armour from all sides and the beleaguered Arkan cheered mightily. As if in retaliation, a kind of madness seemed to wash over the Saathlaa and they charged out of the mist, whooping wildly as they cast aside their bows and bore down on the Arkan with coral-tipped spears and clubs.

'Engage the savages!' Lieutenant Sandefur shouted, his sabre flashing through the putrid gloom as he surged towards the guerrillas.

Joyce heard someone hollering angrily at the Saathlaa to stay put and cursing them for brainless savages. Guessing he was hearing the enemy leader, he veered off towards the voice. A guerrilla leapt at him, jabbing with a spear and spitting like a venomous toad. He blocked with his flamer and answered with a burst of purifying fire. One of the machine discs whipped past, coming so close it almost knocked him off balance. He sent a stream of flames after it and turned it into a fireball. It flittered about blindly and splashed a couple of rebels with burning promethium before crashing into a tree. Joyce howled along with the savages.

This was glory!

* * *

Machen was creaking about and firing randomly into the mist, acting as bait while Wade watched over him silently. If the final loxatl went for the captain it would offer him a brief target. It wasn't a bad plan, but the brood leader was cunning and Wade was nowhere near silent enough. The creature had already figured out that it faced two enemies, so it ignored the obvious lure and homed in on the muted clicks and whirrs from the smaller metal warrior.

It was crawling stealthily through the heap of fallen Arkan, intent on Wade's back when one of the bodies surged up from below and ripped open its belly. The creature squealed in pain and peppered Wade's carapace with flechettes as Valance tore his hunting knife up through its body. Desperate to throw off its attacker, the creature flipped over onto its back, but the scout hung on, driving the knife in again and again. Driven by the loxatl's pain reflexes, the blaster strapped to its back continued to fire, shredding its hide before exploding in a hail of white-hot shards. It was over, but Valance continued to hack into the corpse until Machen pulled him away. The scout's eyes were glazed with hatred as he wiped his knife clean. He was panting hard, exhausted by the struggle.

'I ducked down... behind you... when they hit us,' Valance gasped.

'It was well done, scout. I shall put you forward for a commendation,' Machen said, entirely serious.

Six other greybacks had survived the loxatl ambush, but two of those were beyond help. Solemnly Machen gave them the Emperor's Mercy. As he'd suspected, the third Zouave was also dead. There must have been a flaw in Prentiss's faceplate because the flechettes had shattered the reinforced glass. Inside the confines of his helmet the man's skull had been liquefied, but his rigid exoskeleton had kept him standing. The suit would probably remain that way for decades after Phaedra had devoured the soft flesh inside its shell. Machen wasn't sure how he felt about that.

'What's the game plan, sir?' Wade asked. The edge of pain in his voice was more pronounced now and Machen guessed he was bleeding badly. Unless he got the man to a medic soon he would lose both his wingmen today.

'We find the others,' Machen said and looked at Valance. 'Can you do it, scout?'

Sheathing his knife, Valance surveyed the fogbound jungle. Somewhere in the distance he could still hear the sounds of gunfire.

'This place hasn't got anything on the Methuselah Swamplands back home,' Valance lied. 'Sure I can do it, sir.'

'Then lead the way man,' Machen growled. 'There's Arkan blood being spilt out there!'

Joyce saw Willis Calhoun die. It was a bad death, clumsy and pointless. The sergeant took a spear in the groin from a dying guerrilla floundering in the water beside him and reeled backwards, right into the fire of a passing disc. It tore him clean in two.

The boy went cold as part of him died with his unspoken guardian. He wasn't exactly sure what he'd lost, but he thought it might have been the *best* part of him. Then he heard the guerrilla leader shouting again, still hidden but very close now. Like a drowning man grasping for a line, Joyce gripped the barrel of his flamer and gritted his teeth as the red-hot metal stoked up his rage. Then he was on the move again, fighting through the rebel scum like a man possessed.

He heard the leader snapping at someone who replied in calm, oddly accented tones. Something about that second voice made his hackles rise and he snarled as he fought his way towards the unseen pair. He found them lurking behind a curtain of fronds, hunched down over one of the killer discs. The saucer was hovering at waist height, its casing bristling with sensor spikes and blocky modules of alien machinery. Joyce guessed it was carrying some kind of comms array, maybe even the control device for all the other discs. A warrior in strange armour had his head down in the array while a burly man in combat fatigues watched impatiently. Going by their bickering Joyce was sure they were officers.

Grinning like a skull, he tore through the fronds and levelled his flamer. The rebels looked up and Joyce felt a thrill of horror as he recognised the flat wedge of the machine operator's face – *black eyes, no pupils and no nose*. He'd seen the holo-pict of a tau but it hadn't prepared him for the unclean reality of the xenos.

He froze up.

Watching Joyce with steady brown eyes, the human officer raised a placatory hand and spoke. 'Son, you don't want to do this.' There was a tired wisdom in the man's voice that reminded Joyce of Uncle Sergeant Calhoun. 'Whatever they've been telling you, it's all lies,' the officer continued. 'You don't have to throw your life away for–'

Joyce squeezed the trigger hard and lit them both up like greasy candles. The traitor stopped talking and started screaming. The screaming didn't last long but Joyce kept on burning until the flamer had run dry. He was sweating with something that had nothing to do with heat and everything to do with hate.

'You're both insane!' Jaime Garrido wailed through broken teeth. The young pilot was kicking about on the cockpit floor, struggling against the cords that bound him. 'Ortega, you know the regulations! We don't fly over enemy territory!'

Cutler and the co-pilot ignored him. Ortega's attention was riveted to the controls as he made his descent. Moments later the ship dropped out of the Strangle Zone and the dense smog outside the window segued into the grey-green blur of the Mire rushing by below.

'If there are any sky snipers up here we're dead,' Ortega breathed.

'There won't be,' Cutler said. 'If I've read them right, the tau won't waste that kind of tech where it's doing no good.'

'And how, precisely, would shooting down an Imperial drop-ship do the tau no good?' Ortega asked with a raised eyebrow.

'You say nobody's flown over this stretch in years, right?'

'Indeed, the Dolorosa archipelago is a no-fly zone, by direct order of the Sky Marshall himself.'

'You ever wonder why the man would give an order like that?' Cutler asked with a frown, sensing yet another mystery. He put it aside, filing it away with all the other unanswered questions for the moment. 'Anyway, the tau will have shifted the snipers somewhere useful.'

'With respect, you are guessing, señor.'

'Call it tactical gambling, friend.'

Cutler's personal vox-bead buzzed and Vendrake's voice piped into his ear.

'The Silverstorm Cavalry is locked and loaded, colonel.' The Sentinel officer sounded strained.

'We'll be going in hot, captain. If any of your riders aren't up to the job I want them to sit it out. That blonde gal of yours…'

'We're all good to go,' Vendrake snapped and signed off.

Cutler frowned, knowing there was going to be trouble from that quarter sooner or later. Probably sooner.

'We'll be over the Shell any minute now,' Ortega said, sweating profusely. 'That whelp Garrido is right, señor. This is utter madness.'

'Maybe so, but that's just the way I like it.'

With a shudder Ortega noticed the colonel was grinning like a white wolf.

The Shell was an apt name for the rebel base. It was a hollow, twisted city of temples dedicated to forgotten gods who had stopped listening eons ago. Presiding over a vast swathe of barren ground, the necropolis spiralled out in a coral web of melted ziggurats and globular rotundas. It was a gestalt leviathan, every structure bound to the whole by arterial, rubble-clogged colonnades and soaring, flanged walkways. Age clung to the dead city like a veneer of dust, mocking the alien vehicle gliding gracefully through its streets.

The sleek hover tank was a creature of the future, arrogant with youth. The smooth contours of its glossy black carapace shrugged off the dirt and the rain, defying any blemish to its dignity. Its dorsal engine nacelles were massive, but they propelled the tank along in near silence, keeping it suspended just above the street. The prow curved gently towards the ground, splaying out into broad fins on either side, each one emblazoned with the mark of Commander Wintertide: a white circle containing a geometric black snowflake. Mounted alongside each mark was the distinctive disc of a dormant drone, but the tank's main weapon was the fearsome rotary cannon protruding from beneath its nose. Commissar Cadet Rudyk would have identified the vehicle as a Devilfish, the primary troop transport of the tau race.

The tank halted as a deep rumble rolled over the necropolis, approaching like distant thunder. The twin drones rose from their mounts and spun about, burbling uncertainly as they assessed the disturbance. Somewhere an alarm began to chime. Moments later the warning was echoed throughout the city. And then the alarms were drowned out by a thunderous roar as an Imperial drop-ship swept in low over the rooftops, shaking the coral structures. The ship was gone in seconds, storming towards the heart of the necropolis. Chattering furiously the drones zipped back to the tank and it accelerated away in pursuit.

Squads of Concordance soldiers were racing through the streets, some on foot, others crammed into open-topped hover transports. There were no native guerrillas amongst them. These troops were all professional soldiers equipped with moulded flak-plate and stocky pulse carbines. They were gue'vesa janissaries, humans who had forsworn their old vows and pledged allegiance to the Tau Empire. They were something more than mercenaries, something less than respected allies.

The Devilfish overtook the transports, negotiating the twists and turns of the streets with breathtaking precision. A couple of T-shaped skimmers flipped out of a side street and buzzed past like enraged hornets. The open-topped Piranhas were rapid response scouting vehicles, each carrying a pair of tau Fire Warriors. The helmets of their hunched riders blended into the contours of their vehicles, melding tau and machine into a single blur as they surged ahead.

The Devilfish caught up with its speedier brethren as it swung into a wide plaza and braked to a frictionless halt. A circular hatch slid open and a slender tau warrior in rubberised grey fatigues and black plate slipped from the interior. Her head was enclosed in a battered helmet, the matt black scored with the twin honours of the crimson stripe and an old chainsword scar. As her gue'vesa neophytes fanned out behind her, the veteran watched the invading drop-ship from behind a veil of sensor lenses.

A hail of ordnance raked the intruder from all sides as it dipped towards the plaza. Angry drones flittered around it, peppering its hull with small-arms fire while janissaries scorched it with heavy weapons from distant rooftop emplacements. The pilot fought to keep his vessel steady amidst the firestorm, hovering some fifty metres above the ground. There was a collective hiss and hatches swung open along the length of the ship, spewing out guide ropes. A moment later soldiers in bronze helmets rappelled towards the ground, firing lasrifles one-handed at the janissaries who rushed to meet them. Both the Piranhas raced into the fray, but the scarred veteran held her pathfinders back, unwilling to commit.

With a pneumatic shriek the ship's cargo hatch burst open and a wingless metal bird leapt towards the plaza. The jump pack fitted to its casing burned brightly, fighting to cushion the bird's fall. Even so, the invader's claws hit the ground with a crash that cracked open the brittle coral, but its reverse-jointed legs absorbed the impact. With barely a pause the machine hopped forwards, racing to intercept the Piranhas as a second walker made the jump. The tau skimmers spat fire and the bird replied with a storm of bullets from its rotary autocannon. One of the Piranhas was shredded but the other strafed away in a blur of speed.

Sentinels. The veteran scowled behind her faceplate, recognising the invading machines. Her anger grew as the drop-ship hovered about with surprising agility, deploying men and machines across the plaza. One of the Sentinels landed badly and lost a leg in a tremendous snap of metal. Crippled, the bird hopped about frantically, then toppled over, pulverising a couple of invaders. The gue'vesa neophytes cheered, then cheered again as a pair of solid projectiles lanced into the drop-ship from across the plaza. The missiles struck with such force that the ship was sent spinning, pitching a waiting Sentinel into an explosive nosedive and sending several invaders tumbling from their ropes.

Recognising the devastating power of a rail gun, the veteran squinted, triggering her optics to zoom in on the armoured giant lumbering into the fray. Like all tau battlesuits it was an elegant construct of interlocking plates and modular, geodesic blocks mounted on massive piston-like legs. Its boxy, lens-encrusted helmet looked small in proportion to its body, but the veteran knew the 'head' was just a sculpted housing for the suit's sensor array. The tau pilot was safely encased within the heavily armoured chest cavity, linked to the machine by a neural interface that afforded an intimacy the crude gue'la technology could never match.

Amongst the warrior caste of the Tau Empire it was considered a great honour to command a battlesuit. The veteran had earned the right long ago, but she had chosen to remain a pathfinder. She knew that many of her Fire Warrior comrades thought her disfigurement had made her insane, but they were wrong. The injury had defined her place in the *Tau'va* and made her whole. Had she not found her true name through her scars?

Jhi'kaara – the broken mirror.

The others found her choice unsettling, just as they found her fascination with knives repellent. Perhaps that was why she had been left to rot in this remote enclave.

'What are your orders shas'ui?' one of her neophytes asked, calling her by her caste and rank. It was the proper form of address from a gue'vesa janissary.

Intent upon the battle, she did not answer. The battlesuit was tracking the drop-ship with the twin-linked rail guns mounted on its broad shoulders. The angular cannons jutted out like blunt tusks, projecting so far it seemed a miracle they didn't imbalance the machine. Of course Jhi'kaara knew the real miracles were the anti-gravity stabilisers supporting the cannons, and like every miracle of her people they were not really miracles at all, but the fruits of vigorous technology. Unlike the stunted, superstitious gue'la, the tau exulted in innovation. Insane or not, she was certain that the future belonged to her race.

But not this city. Not today.

Even as the Broadside battlesuit fired again she knew it was too late and this battle was lost. Most of their force was deployed in the jungle, leaving only a token garrison within the city – no more than twenty Fire Warriors and two hundred gue'vesa janissaries. The Broadside was their only battlesuit, her Devilfish their only tank. It would have been enough if the silk-tongued Water Caste had been true to their word, but despite their assurances the invaders had attacked from the sky.

The second Piranha burst into flames and Jhi'kaara felt the rage building inside her, but beneath the rage there was a fierce joy. *Today everything has changed,* she realised. The Imperials had violated the Invisible Accord so painstakingly arranged by the Water Caste. Once word of this treachery spread amongst the Fire Caste all the talk of 'shadow treaties' and 'long games' would end and the warriors would be free to fight this war unfettered. Once again Jhi'kaara saw her path on the *Tau'va*. She would be the one to carry the good news to her comrades.

With a flick of the hand she ordered her neophytes back on board the Devilfish. As she followed, she glanced over shoulder and saw the lone battlesuit torn apart by a trio of Sentinels.

'Your sacrifice will further the Greater Good,' she promised. 'I swear it.'

CHAPTER FIVE

Imperial Seabase Antigone, the Sargaatha Sea

High Commissar Lomax has finally summoned me, but I still have no answers for her. I cannot explain, excuse or justify my actions with anything but results. Only Wintertide's death will exonerate my desertion.

And there you have it. I've finally accepted the word that is anathema to our kind. Desertion. Old Bierce glares at me as I make the confession at last, but you must understand that it wasn't fear or faithlessness that drove me into the wilderness after the massacre at Indigo Gorge. I swear to you that it was duty.

Unfortunately Bierce will never accept that. His suffering is on my hands and words will never sway him. He has been my judge for too long, watching and hating and waiting for my fall with the bitterness of the betrayed...

What? No, of course I didn't kill him! I loved the old man as a father, albeit a harsh and humourless father who never had a kind word to say. He raised me to terrorise and take the lives of lesser men, but I understood his calling – our calling – and I was always loyal. Yes, even when I betrayed him.

It was complicated. You see I'd just completed my apprenticeship and earned the scarlet. I was impatient to escape the old man's shadow and make my own name, but he insisted that I accompany him on one final campaign. It was an inglorious affair – yet another petty uprising, yet another wretched world too angry to know better. Fool that I was, I thought I'd seen it all before.

Well, we crushed the rebels soon enough, but the pacification dragged on forever and I grew restless, eager for enemies worthy of the name. My arrogance blinded me to the assassin. Oh, I saw him all right – a ragged little bag of bones shambling towards Bierce – but all I saw was a filthy street urchin hunting for scraps, not a child soldier chasing martyrdom. I certainly didn't see the needle gun concealed under his rags. None of us ever figured out how such vermin came by so rare and precious a weapon. Maybe one of the rebel leaders kitted him out in a last ditch bid for revenge or maybe he found it in the ruins of the aristo palace. Either way he was true to the whims of hate. He died in a hail of fire a heartbeat after he struck, but that was a heartbeat too late.

My second betrayal came a week later. Bierce wouldn't die you see. The neurotoxin in his bloodstream was cruel, twisting him into a mute, misshapen tangle of pain, but taking its time with the killing. The medicus warned me he might last for months. Emperor forgive me, I just couldn't abide it.

I remember retching at the stench when I walked into the old man's room. He looked like a living corpse. As I drew my pistol he stared at me, silently urging me on. I pointed the gun right into his face… and froze. His eyes hardened with contempt, dismissing my struggle, already certain that I lacked the courage to pull the trigger. Because of that contempt I'll never know if it was love or hate that stayed my hand. Perhaps I've never really known the difference and maybe that's a mercy in a galaxy where there can only be war.

And so I fled Bierce and that nameless world, but his shade came after me, following me across the stars. Over the decades I did my duty in one dead-end war after another, fiercely proclaiming the Emperor's glory but feeling nothing inside. And eventually the spiral ended on Phaedra. After that there was nowhere left to run and the old man finally caught up with me.

My first shadow has never talked. His contempt has no need of words. Well, I must trust that Wintertide's death will satisfy him and lay all three of my ghosts to rest. Until then I dare not die.

But now I must answer the High Commissar's summons.

Iverson's Journal

Night crept furtively through the jungle. As the sunlight slithered away an unseen orchestra struck up a symphony to greet the fungal dawn. Listening to the croaking, chirping cacophony, Ambrose Templeton thought the transformation both hideous and beautiful. He was in a strangely mellow mood. With nightfall, his fever had subsided to a rhythmic pounding deep inside his head…

Like a seismic migraine seething in my psyche, teething through the tectonic plates of my skull…

He cast the words aside and tried to focus on the task at hand, knowing the reprieve wouldn't last long. What was it he had to do? Ah yes… the perimeter. He was going to do the rounds one last time.

Keeping his head low, the captain crawled painfully along the inner rim of the caldera where his forces had dug in. The depression was almost two metres deep and totally devoid of vegetation, a paradoxical dead zone in the jungle. Templeton suspected the atrophy had something to do with the strange building coiled up like an alabaster snake at the heart of the crater. There was a brooding, expectant quality about the ruin that called to him, promising answers to questions he'd never thought to ask and wasn't sure he even understood…

Beckoning with the secret wisdom of murder-tainted aeons, tempting saints and sinners alike to enter the eye of the needle-storm that unstitched time…

'Care for some recaff, sir?' Templeton jumped at the voice, blinking rapidly as he tried to make sense of the steaming mug in the speaker's hand.

'What?' he managed vaguely.

'There's a dram of firewater in there too.' The man's uniform was caked in dried mud. 'No disrespect to you captain, but you look like you could use it,' the greyback continued. 'We've only the one small keg between us, but I figured you'd earned it, seeing as you pulled us out of that swamp and all.'

Unsure whether the fellow was being impudent or genuinely hospitable, Templeton mustered a wan smile and accepted the drink. He'd never been adept at bantering with the rank and file.

'My thanks, trooper…'

'Roach, sir.'

'Quite so,' Templeton muttered. 'My thanks to you, Trooper Roach.'

Sipping the drink, Templeton regarded the men hunkered down around Roach. They were a peculiar bunch of ruffians to be sure. One was a boy with the eyes of a zealot who cradled his flamer like a holy relic. Another just sat staring into space from a face that was one big bruise. A third was rubbing obsessively at the raw crater where his nose had been. Strangest of all was the native guide wearing a flat-topped Confederate cap. Seeing Templeton's quizzical look, Roach nodded towards the savage.

'Mister Fish here saved my skin, so I figured I'd sign him up to the squad for keeps,' Roach said. 'It's not like there's many of us left.'

'Quite so,' Templeton repeated, unsure what else to say.

'Strange sort of nights they got round here, don't you think, captain?'

'Indeed. One would venture to speculate that the indigenous fungi are equipped with a metabolic…' Seeing the blank look on the greyback's face, Templeton trailed off. 'Yes, a strange sort of night indeed,' he finished lamely.

After that they drank their laced recaff in awkward silence. Templeton found the brew unpalatably bitter, but he finished it gamely, thinking it was the right thing to do. He had no idea what else to say so he just handed back the mug and moved on with his inspection.

The greybacks were crouched below the rim of the caldera, manning the improvised battlements against the jungle. There were almost two hundred men in the crater, including nine armoured Zouaves. Templeton hoped there were more survivors out there, but these were all his search had turned up.

After the vespid stingwings had retreated he had set about consolidating the scattered greybacks, methodically tracking down the other platoons. It had been a desperate, embattled search, but his force had grown steadily. Despite the savagery of the ambush the Confederates had given a decent account of themselves and weathered the storm. The Saathlaa guerrillas were numerous and slippery, but they were a poorly armed rabble, prone to panicked routs and suicidal charges. Templeton suspected they were afflicted by a racial insanity that made them unstable in the heat of battle. Doubtless it was a consequence of their degeneracy.

Unfortunately there were other, more dangerous foes in the jungle. The vespid stingwings had continued to harass his forces, but they had become cautious, keeping to the treetops and picking off stragglers with sneaky hit-and-run attacks. Reading aloud from his Tactica manual, the late Commissar Cadet Rudyk had explained that the stingwings were considered elite shock troops, prized by the tau for their mobility and speed. Thankfully there hadn't been very many of them in this benighted region.

The squadrons of flying discs – gun drones, Rudyk had called them – were much more numerous. Worryingly, the Tactica manual implied that the drones were just the tip of the tau war machine. The young morale officer had shown Templeton sketches of outlandish battlesuits and hover tanks, chattering on about 'Crisis Suits' and 'Broadsides' and 'Hammerheads' with a morbid enthusiasm that had done very little for the captain's morale. He prayed that his men wouldn't encounter anything like that after he was gone.

The fever was resurfacing with renewed vigour now, threatening a skull-bursting eruption and Templeton pushed on before it was too late. He was exhausted by the time he reached

Machen's position. The Zouave captain stood watch like a crude iron statue, unable to crouch down in his massive carapace. His head and shoulders were out in the open, making him an easy target for one of the lethal guerrilla snipers, but he'd refused to remove his armour.

The man is stubborn to his miserable core, Templeton thought. *He hasn't even bothered to clean the blood off his gauntlet. Commissar Cadet Rudyk's blood...*

'Captain Machen,' he began uncertainly.

'It had to be done,' Machen snapped. 'The murderous runt was going to kill you. And after you, how many more until he got his way?'

Templeton knew he was right. There had been no alternative. Once the Arkan had regrouped in the caldera, Rudyk had railed at them to push on with the attack, growing furious when Templeton had tried to argue. Finally the cadet had drawn his gun. The captain had hoped it wouldn't come to that, all the time knowing it would. Even so, he couldn't help feeling sorry for the boy. Despite his black storm coat, Rudyk was just a brutalised youth with too much responsibility and too little sense. Templeton had wanted to try reasoning with him again, but Machen had simply stomped in, bearing down on the cadet like a tank on legs. The boy had opened fire instantly, backing away with wide eyes as the auto rounds ricocheted off the heavy carapace. He'd tried for Machen's visor, but couldn't crack the reinforced glass. Then he'd tripped. Scrabbling backwards he'd yelled for assistance, but the greybacks had stood by with stony faces, remembering what Rudyk's comrades had done to Major Waite. Then Machen had reached down and grasped the cadet's head in a massive gauntlet.

'The Emperor con–' Rudyk had begun as Machen squeezed.

Templeton didn't want to remember the sound Rudyk's head

had made. Instead he addressed the sombre giant: 'I wanted to thank you, Machen. For saving my life.' *Even if you've only delayed matters…*

'Enough Arkan blood has been spilled today.' Machen's voice sounded hollow inside the cavern of his helmet. Templeton realised his faceplate was open. Did the man have a death wish? Well, perhaps he did… He recalled that Machen's platoon had been hit hard in the ambush. A man like Machen would take that personally.

'I really must speak with you, Machen.'

'Later. I am standing vigil for my men.'

'It's my arm you see…'

'Go away, Templeton.'

Well, I believe I shall. And I'll probably be gone for quite some time.

Templeton hesitated a moment longer, but suddenly getting through to Machen didn't seem so important anymore. Gingerly he rubbed at his wounded arm and felt something slithering wetly under the bandages. It took him a moment to realise the movement was actually under his *skin*. He sighed, too tired for disgust and too wise to the inevitable to care any longer. He had done his duty by his men as best he could. Machen would have to take up the mantle now. His only regret was that he'd never complete his beloved 'Canticle of Crows'. Through the rising fever he could hear the spectral ruin calling to him again, whispering of veiled paths between the stars…

…winding like glistening ribbons of misbegotten hope through the hearts and minds of dead dreamers, hastening their flight as they sleep down the slope of nightmare…

Tentatively at first, then with growing conviction, Templeton crept towards the waiting ruin.

* * *

Much later, Machen saw the tip of a fungal tower topple as something tore a path through the jungle beyond the caldera.

'What do you think it is?' the greyback beside him whispered nervously.

Machen ignored him, intent on the unseen metal beast trampling through the jungle. There was something familiar about that grinding, clanking rhythm. On an impulse he flicked his shoulder speakers into life, flooding the night with the bombast of Providence. The man beside him almost jumped out of his skin. Moments later everyone in the caldera was dashing about frantically. Someone hammered on his armour, pleading with him to shut the noise down, but he paid no heed.

It didn't take long for the machine to find them. Machen allowed himself a cheerless smile as the Arkan Sentinel burst through the trees. It prowled restlessly around the caldera, dazzling the men with a questing searchlight, then skittered back to face the Zouave captain. There was a hiss of pneumatic pistons as the walker powered down and sank back onto its haunches. A moment later the cockpit swung open and the pilot leaned out.

'Well met, Captain Machen!' Lieutenant Quint hollered, his fat face beaming with delight at his discovery. 'Would you and your men care to join us for a spot of dinner at the Shell?'

It was only when they abandoned the caldera that Machen realised Templeton was missing. A hurried search uncovered the man's prized notebook by the entrance of the ruined temple. The dusty steps of the portico were scuffed with footprints, but the trail petered out just beyond the inner threshold. They called for him, but there was no answer from the dark chamber. It was almost as if Captain Ambrose Phillips Templeton had walked right out of the world.

* * *

Skjoldis saw her *weraldur* drop into a rigid fighting stance. She froze, watching his silhouette through the canvas of the tent, but a moment later he relaxed and resumed his vigil outside her quarters. She knew he was nervous in this tainted place. Her guardian didn't possess the wyrd, but any Norlander could sense the wrongness of the ancient city slumbering around them. She had warned the Whitecrow against camping within its precincts, but he had been stubborn. His men had bled hard to capture the city and he wouldn't abandon it so quickly.

With a sigh Skjoldis returned to her divination. Kneeling on the raw coral she muttered the Emperor's name and cast the sacred whisperbones, watching as they scattered in the thrall of gravity, then leapt up and danced in the name of something even older. Her eyes narrowed as the carved fragments flipped and spun about, clacking restlessly like dead men's teeth in a hollow skull, unable to find peace.

'So what do your trinkets have to say, Raven?' Cutler sneered from the recesses of the habtent.

Intent on her reading, Skjoldis ignored the insult. The Whitecrow always used her mock-name when she cast the whisperbones – the Emperor's Bones they were called these days. It was his way of dealing with the elder traditions of her wyrd. Besides, he'd been drinking, swigging down his precious firewater like their supply was endless.

'Raven, I asked you…'

'The whisperbones say everything and so they tell me nothing,' she snapped, troubled by the fretful runes.

'Are you finally admitting you're a charlatan, woman?' Cutler chuckled.

She scooped up the bones and looked at him with distaste. He was slumped on a trestle bed, staring up into the darkness with his arms crossed behind his head. His jacket lay crumpled on the ground, alongside several empty bottles. When he was like this, drunk on firewater and self-pity, she almost despised him.

But he has just lost his closest friend, she chided herself. Although Elias Waite had always distrusted her, the old man had been like a brother to the Whitecrow. Ashamed of her impatience she tried to explain.

'The bones sail the whispertides of a world, but where there are no words, they can find no harbour.'

'Or maybe this world's just talking crap!'

'Yes, that is also a possibility.'

'Or just talking too fast for your old bones to keep up.'

'I am serious Whitecrow. There is something very wrong here.'

'Are you going to tell me this is a *bad* place, Raven?' Suddenly the drunken slur was gone and he was razor sharp with sarcasm. 'Because I already figured that out for myself.'

'I am telling you that this world is poisonous.'

He laughed bitterly in the darkness. 'Every world is poisonous, woman. You just have to peel back the skin and you'll find the teeth waiting for you.'

She knew he was thinking of Trinity again, the backwater hovel that had gone to the Hells while nobody was watching. It had made him hers, but only because it had broken something in his soul.

'On some worlds the poison can be rooted out and bled dry,' she said. 'On others it has run too deep and spread too far. Here it has become one with the weave and weft of the world.'

'High Command says there's no taint here.'

'They say whatever suits their purpose.'

'And what do you think that is?' He turned towards her, his eyes gleaming yellow in the shadows. 'Because I sure don't see it. All I see is waste and plain murder. You know, I think those bastards *wanted* to throw my men away today.'

She understood his anger, but she had no answers for him.

'Your plan worked,' she said instead.

It was true. His bold assault on the rebel base had been a magnificent success. Once the battle in the plaza was won the enemy resistance had crumbled rapidly. The Whitecrow himself had cornered the rebel commander on the steps of a towering ziggurat. It had been an unsettling encounter. Countless years in the waterlogged jungle had shrivelled the rebel officer, making him look ancient inside his glossy xenos-forged armour. His head had protruded from the plastek gorget like a shrunken prune, yet his eyes had been clear and strangely placid as the Arkan surrounded him. When the Whitecrow had demanded his surrender he had simply smiled and tapped the snowflake tattoo on his forehead. Then he'd raised his rifle and died, falling to a hail of Arkan fire that never touched his smile. The serenity on his dead face still intrigued Skjoldis. What truth had carried him so far beyond fear?

'My plan worked because they didn't expect any trouble from above,' Cutler said, breaking her train of thought. 'I knew it in my gut, but why in the Hells would the tau be so sure of it?'

'Does it matter?'

He stared at her as if she were a fool. Before she could say anything more he leapt to his feet and began to pace, running his hands through his unruly white mane.

'They mothballed us you know,' he growled, 'those armchair generals back home. All that fine talk of sending us to the stars to win glory for Providence – that was all poison honey. They just wanted us gone!' He paused, thinking it through. 'They wanted *me* gone. It was never about the 19th. It was always about me.'

'Whitecrow, this is empty talk…'

'They sent my men to the Hells for my sins. Because of that damned town.'

Skjoldis wondered how much longer she could hold the fractures inside him together. Would this world finish what Trinity had begun?

'Back in space,' Cutler murmured, 'that thing from the warp that took Norliss in Dorm 31… How did it know me?'

Skjoldis sighed, knowing this conversation had been inevitable. 'The Whispersea, which you call the warp, flows through all things, Whitecrow. It reflects time and space in an infinity of shadow consequences and dim possibilities. Most of them are too tenuous and misshapen to prosper, but no whisper is ever lost and sometimes a predator will listen. The serpents – the daemons – thrive on our doubts and desires. It is their way into our world.'

She saw him struggling to understand, a plain-speaking man whose world of absolutes had been swept away by something impossible yet undeniable. He was too stubborn to accept the truth, but too honest to deny it. Such men often drowned in the Whispersea. It was why he needed her.

'That doesn't explain it,' he insisted. 'That thing in Dorm 31 looked right at me and laughed! It *recognised* me.'

'And then we killed it. That is our purpose.'

'I can feel it watching me all the time, you know. Like it's looking for a way inside. Just like it got into Norliss and all those poor damned fools at Trinity.' He sounded brittle now. 'Am I cursed, Skjoldis?'

She laughed. It was a hoarse, broken cackle that set her own teeth on edge.

'Of course you are cursed, Whitecrow!' Seeing his bleak expression she stifled the laugh. 'You are cursed and that is why you must not fail in your duty.'

'And what exactly is my duty on this sewer world?'

She regarded him thoughtfully, weighing up his mood.

'What is it, woman?' he pressed.

'Do you recall my… trance… in the chamber of stars?'

'Too damn right I recall it.' His eyes narrowed suspiciously.

'Then perhaps it is time that I told you of Abel.'

Captain Hardin Vendrake was bone weary, but sleep wouldn't come so he just kept on riding, haunting the coral avenues of the necropolis like a lost soul. At each junction he would pivot his Sentinel at the waist and pierce the gloomy side streets with his searchlight, weighing up its prospects on a whim. Sometimes he would whip past and sometimes he would take the new branch, navigating the maze as the mood took him. He'd told his men he was going out on patrol, but they'd all known it was a lie. He was riding to stay ahead of the guilt.

Leonora was dead. The leap from the drop-ship had proven beyond her limited abilities and she'd snapped her Sentinel's leg clean off. He hadn't seen her fall, but he'd heard her terrified cries over the vox as she fought for balance. She'd been calling for him, but he'd been too busy chasing a tau skimmer to pay any attention.

Too angry with her for screwing up again...

He'd found her in the mangled cockpit of her walker. Under those long blonde tresses her head had been twisted right round, dangling from a neck turned to jelly. There were two men dead under her machine, crushed and broken by her fall. Pericles Quint had played the bleeding heart card, sucking up to him as always, but the rest of Silverstorm had kept quiet and avoided his eyes. They all knew it was his fault. Leonora had never been cavalry material, but he'd kept her on anyway.

She'd been terrified of the jump, but too proud to back out. And he'd let her go ahead and try.

Knowing all along she wouldn't make it…

Havardy was dead too, his steed blasted right out of the drop-ship by the tau battlesuit. His blood wasn't on Vendrake's hands, but he'd been a talented rider and his loss weakened Silverstorm. There were only ten of them left now. But despite the lost Sentinels, Vendrake had to admit that Cutler's gamble had paid off. The drop-ship had taken a beating, but the pilot had made a remarkable crash landing, saving all hands on board. Afterwards the 1st Company had taken the city with surprisingly few casualties. Unfortunately the same couldn't be said for the rest of the regiment.

With the city secured, Cutler had tasked Silverstorm with tracking down their missing comrades. Determined to cover as much ground as possible before nightfall, Vendrake had scattered his Sentinels through the jungle. At first they'd only found stragglers – men so exhausted they could barely walk. The survivors told of ambushes and xenos abominations. One battered Zouave knight, almost delirious with terror, raved about a swarm of avian monsters that had hounded his platoon from the trees, pouncing on men and tearing them to shreds. He swore the beasts had devoured the flesh of the slain. But despite the grim evidence of slaughter, Silverstorm had met no opposition. It was as if the enemy had melted away when their city fell.

The Sentinels had drifted back to the city one by one, bearing too many horror stories and too few survivors. To Vendrake's surprise, Pericles Quint had been the last to return, sauntering back to camp in his gaudily decorated machine long after nightfall. Behind him was a train of weary survivors, including an unusually subdued Captain Machen. By the sorry standards of the day it was a triumph and Quint had preened in the glow of Cutler's praise. The look on his fat face had–

Vendrake jumped as something clanged against the canopy of his Sentinel. Uneasily he swung about and angled backwards, raking the rooftops with his searchlight. Fat drops of water swarmed down the bright beam, clattering angrily against his windshield. Just moments ago he'd have sworn the rain was little more than a faint drizzle. Cursing, he flicked on his wipers and leaned forward, trying to pierce the murk. The rain-blurred buildings seemed to shrink back from his beam, recoiling from the light like startled creatures of the deep sea. Of course it was only a trick of light and shadow.

Get a grip man. It was just a splinter of debris that hit you. This place has probably been falling down forever. The rebels have fled. There's nothing alive in this tomb but us. Somehow the thought didn't reassure him.

His vox crackled, breaking the almost hypnotic drumming of the rain.

'Vendrake,' he acknowledged.

The only response was a babble of static. He tried again with the same result. Growing irritated he killed the noise and got moving. The downpour had taken the edge off the heat, turning his cabin cold and clammy. Suddenly he was eager to get back to camp, but the poor visibility restricted him to a cautious crawl. At this rate he wouldn't be back before dawn.

The vox hissed again. He scowled and snapped it to send: 'Vendrake here. Who in the Seven bloody Hells is this?' More static. 'Quint, is that you? Look, I'm in no mood for games.'

There was a barely audible sigh, like something washed up on a tide of white noise. He leaned towards the vox, frowning in concentration as he strained to filter out the static. It sounded like someone was breathing on the other end, harsh and irregular. As if they'd forgotten how…

'Who is this?' he whispered.

'*Belle du Morte* signing in.' The voice was as brittle as dry leaves in the wind, so fragile he might almost have imagined it.

But I didn't imagine it.

Suddenly Vendrake was racing away at breakneck speed, all thoughts of caution crushed by the need to escape those haunted streets.

'*Belle du Morte*' had been Leonora's call sign.

As a bobbing trio of will-o'-the-wisps approached through the downpour, Audie Joyce pushed himself deeper into the shadows of the colonnade, holding his breath until the lanterns had faded away. He wasn't sure why he was hiding from the patrol, but he figured they'd start asking him questions – like what he was doing out here in the rain when he could be huddled up inside a habtent. He didn't want to answer questions right now. He just wanted to be left alone with the Emperor.

Screwing his eyes shut he carried on talking to Him, praying hard and fast. It was the only way to stop the tears. If he let them fall they'd drown him and he couldn't let that happen, not when the Emperor was counting on him. Uncle Sergeant Calhoun was gone and Audie's ma would be mad at him for letting that happen. She'd never understand that the old man was with the Emperor now, fighting dead heretics forever and watching over Audie to make sure he kept sending them his way. That was how things worked: the living and the dead were all part of one big justice grinder, with the Emperor right up there as the Chief Grinder. Audie still wasn't sure if *He* was living or dead, but guessed He might be both. The Emperor was complicated like that.

The greencap heard laughter from the habtent nearby and grimaced. How could the Dustsnakes be celebrating when they'd just lost their sergeant? Audie had expected the squad to pray together through the night, but after they'd reached the heathen city the men had started up with the drinking and the cards, acting like nothing bad had happened. Roach had even tried to rope him into it...

'We're just paying our respects to the sarge and blowing off steam,' the half-breed had said. 'If you don't roll with the punches they'll break you in half, boy.'

For a moment Audie had almost believed him, but then the native freak who'd become so pally with Roach had offered him a drink – some kind of filthy local brew that would probably turn him into a 'shroom. Seeing that moony, fish-eyed face grinning at him from under a decent Arkan cap, Audie had exploded. Snarling like a prairie lizard, he'd shoved the mutie right off his feet and stormed out of the tent.

Listening to their laughter, he decided the Dustsnakes were too stupid to know they were finished. There were only seven of them left and that included Toomy, who was worse than useless. The medics didn't think the sniper would ever recover from the head injury he'd taken in the boat. It made Audie mad that a brainwreck like that had survived the ambush when Uncle Sergeant Calhoun had died. He'd felt sorry for Toomy once, but now he hated him. Just like he hated all the Dustsnakes – hated them for their easy laughter and dirty jokes and all their little blasphemies. He was pretty sure Saint Gurdy-Jeff would call them heretics. Suddenly he wondered how the saint was doing.

Confessor Yosiv Gurdjief entered the Shell at dawn. The rain had finally subsided, leaving the ruins swathed in a halo of mist that writhed around his chugging gunboat. He had sailed up the great Qalaqexi River and entered the city via its central canal. Standing in the armoured prow of the boat he watched the ruins seep past like titanic, fossilised anemones, rising then falling back into the smog. This was his first visit to the dead city, but he remembered the river well, for he had travelled its treacherous paths long ago.

It was said that a man could cross the entire continent along the Qalaqexi, but Gurdjief doubted many men would complete such a journey, for deeper inland the river frayed into a tangle of tributaries that could lead a traveller in circles forever. They called that labyrinth the Dolorosa Coil. Gurdjief had once entered the Coil and returned, but he often wondered if he had ever truly escaped.

Sailing through the mist-shrouded dawn, his mind drifted back to that delirious voyage. It had been the Letheans' first year on Phaedra and Admiral Karjalan had requested volunteers to reconnoitre the wilderness behind enemy lines. It was dangerous work, but Gurdjief had been a fresh-faced lieutenant eager to make his mark. Posing as a lone pilgrim in search of enlightenment he had ingratiated himself amongst a tribe of nomads called the Nirrhoda. Even by the standards of Phaedra they had been degenerates, but they had embraced his lies and allowed him to join their wanderings along the Qalaqexi. And in time his cover story had become a perfect truth, for deep in the Coil all thoughts of spying and war had sloughed away like fading dreams until nothing had mattered but his quest for the God-Emperor's Truth.

Time flowed strangely in that grey-green limbo. He recalled years of soul-grinding despair punctuated by fleeting moments of ecstasy. He had explored lost valleys haunted by colossal, primordial beasts and wandered the sunken ruins of pre-human civilisations that made the Shell seem a modern metropolis. Deep in the coral heart of the planet he had duelled and debated with daemons, never quite knowing whether they were real or delusions and not even sure there was a difference.

Strangest of all, he had once encountered a lone tau warrior wandering the jungle in a hulking battlesuit. Judging by the cracks riddling its tarnished ceramic plates the armour had seen better days, but it was easily capable of annihilating Gurdjief, so he had offered no hostility. Instead he had tried to make sense of the mystery. The suit was painted a mottled crimson, a colour at odds with Wintertide's stark whites and midnight blacks. Gurdjief had no idea what faction the alien belonged to, but the five-flanged sunburst adorning its breastplate looked like personal heraldry, identifying its wearer as a warrior of distinction.

They had talked like fellow pilgrims, sharing tales and striving to map the impossible geometries of the Coil. The xenos was a soldier like himself, lost in time and place but still true to the mission that had led him into the wilderness. He had been vague about that mission, but so far as Gurdjief could make out he was hunting a band of traitors he called 'The Canker Eaters'.

'The savages turned on us and slaughtered my comrades,' the warrior said. 'They devoured our flesh.'

'Yet you survived?'

'I… Yes… I survived. It must be so,' but the xenos had seemed uncertain.

When Gurdjief had politely enquired about his caste, already knowing he must be a Fire Warrior, the tau had become confused. Finally he had answered 'Smoke'. Gurdjief had sensed no lie even though he knew the tau only had five castes and 'Smoke' was not one of them. They had parted without incident, neither friends nor foes, which had been a mystery in itself. Afterwards he realised that the enigmatic warrior had offered neither his name nor his rank.

Decades later, Gurdjief had returned from the Coil and found he'd been away less than a year. He could offer Admiral Karjalan neither maps nor news of the enemy. Instead he bore the seeds of revelation, together with other, stranger seeds that soon took root in the admiral's own flesh – voracious fungal spores he had carried unwittingly from the heart of the Coil. When Gurdjief's beloved Natalja also ripened with the blight he had first despaired, then rejoiced at her suffering. And so his creed had gradually taken shape. Mankind was born damned and redemption could only be achieved through divine suffering in the God-Emperor's name.

'The renegades, they are watching us,' said the commissar beside Gurdjief, drawing him back to the present. 'I have seen them spying from the ruins and scurrying away like rats.'

'They know they have strayed and must face the Emperor's judgement,' the confessor said sadly.

'The Emperor, He condemns,' the commissar offered devoutly.

Yes He does, Gurdjief agreed. *And today He will condemn this rogue colonel – this Ensor Cutler.*

The Arkan commander had spurned the *Puissance* and cheated its admiral of precious donors, sending poor Vyodor into an apoplexy of rage. That insult had been injury enough, but Cutler's victory at the Shell had sent ripples of discord all the way up to the Sky Marshall himself. In truth Gurdjief cared nothing for the Marshall's arcane schemes, but he had threatened Vyodor with removal unless the Arkan were brought to heel. That was something Gurdjief would not tolerate. Nothing must interfere with his master's sacred pilgrimage of torment.

An example will have to be made of this heretic, Cutler. Something particularly enduring...

As the canal wound into a rubble-strewn plaza a spectral army dissolved out of the mist: Arkan, hundreds of them, lined up along the banks like lost souls waiting for passage out of limbo. Most were haggard, pale-faced ghosts in grey, but a few wore those ridiculous clockwork suits that Vyodor had laughed at. Gurdjief also counted several Sentinel walkers towering over the crowd, tracking his boat with an array of heavy weapons.

'I do not like the look of these heathens,' murmured the commissar. 'Have a care my lord confessor. I have only fifty men with me.'

Gurdjief ignored him. His eyes had fixed upon a tall officer standing in the front ranks. The man's white mane lent him an ancient yet paradoxically ageless quality, a duality of faded dignity and savage vigour. He could almost taste the hatred pent up inside that apparition. A sane man would have sailed away, but Confessor Yosiv Gurdjief simply smiled, knowing he had found his quarry.

Cutler waited in silence as the robed giant leapt ashore and stalked towards him, smiling like a shark behind a morass of black hair. A skeletal commissar followed, flanked by a squad of soldiers in crimson flak-plate. Though the Letheans were heavily outnumbered and outgunned he saw no trace of fear on their vicious, tattooed faces.

'That's the maniac who did for Elias,' Machen hissed. The armoured Zouave stood behind the colonel, reined in like a thunderstorm in an iron cage. By Providence, Cutler knew how the man felt!

Whitecrow, we walk a narrow path! You must cloak your heart in ice–

Angrily Cutler shoved Skjoldis out of his mind and saw her flinch beside him. He had no patience for the witch woman's anxieties now, not with Elias's murderer standing right in front of him.

'You are Colonel Ensor Cutler.' It wasn't a question and the priest didn't wait for an answer. 'I am Confessor Yosiv Gurdjief, First Herald of the Emperor's Justice for the Dolorosa continent. You will come with me.'

'Where are my men?' Cutler asked.

Gurdjief looked at him blankly. He obviously had no idea what Cutler was talking about.

'Elroy Griffin, Grayson Hawtin and Kletus Modine,' Cutler snapped. 'Your cog priests took them away. I want them back.'

The confessor was taken aback. This fool had lost almost half his regiment, yet he was concerned about three peasants.

'They are dead, colonel,' he lied. Gurdjief expected some kind of outburst, but Cutler said nothing, almost as if he had expected the answer. 'Regrettably they succumbed to Phaedra's pestilence,' Gurdjief continued smoothly. 'As you have doubtless witnessed, this is a blighted world.'

'That it is, sir.'

Gurdjief waited, but Cutler said nothing more. Determined to seize control of the encounter, the confessor spread his hands in a gesture of openness.

'Colonel, your recent actions have caused some… consternation. Nevertheless you have won a great victory here. If you will accompany me back to the *Puissance* I can assure you a fair penitence.'

'I see.'

Another long silence. Gurdjief felt his patience fraying and he hardened his voice. 'Surely your men have suffered enough, colonel.'

'Elias Waite,' Cutler said. His eyes looked cold and dead.

'I don't follow you...'

Cutler moved like a whirlwind, wrenching his sabre from its scabbard and lunging forward in one fluid motion that tore Gurdjief's confusion into bright agony. The confessor looked down and saw the blade buried in his abdomen. Fascinated, he watched as his robes blossomed crimson around the wound.

'For Elias Waite,' Cutler said, plunging the sabre deeper. 'And all the others.'

Gurdjief gasped as the blade ripped through his back, bringing him closer to the white-haired renegade until their faces were only inches apart. He saw that the colonel's eyes were no longer cold and dead. In fact they seemed to be on fire, blazing from the man's skull like twin suns. Abruptly the confessor wondered if this was another delirium. The pain seemed so real, but perhaps he was still lost in the grey-green eternity of the Coil.

How could I hope She would ever let me go?

The sudden cacophony of battle exploded around him, but it seemed muffled and distant. Unimportant. The world had narrowed to the scope of the terrible, agonising blade that bound him to the monstrous colonel.

'Is this a dream?' Gurdjief asked.

The apparition appeared to give it some thought.

'I guess you'll know if you ever wake up,' it replied.

Then Cutler thrust the priest away, ripping his sabre free in a welter of blood. Gurdjief tottered backwards, mouthing wordlessly as he tried to break out of the nightmare before it killed him.

It cannot end here. I have walked the tainted heart of this world and wrestled with daemons and seen the secret clockwork bones of reality.

But perhaps all those raptures had been mere delusions and he himself nothing more than a madman. His feet stumbled on empty air and he toppled over into the canal. As he sank into the fecund embrace of the Qalaqexi, Yosiv Gurdjief wondered if he would indeed wake up.

The skirmish was almost over when Vendrake's Sentinel raced into the plaza, but the insanity was still burning fiercely. The captain clattered to a halt as he saw the last couple of Lethean soldiers die, blasted from the deck of their gunboat by a barrage of high velocity rounds from Silverstorm. Swarming along the banks of the canal, the greybacks roared and fired a victorious salvo into the air.

With an oath, Vendrake swung open the canopy of his machine and leapt to the ground. His legs almost buckled under him, rebelling after long hours in the cramped cockpit. His hellish journey through the city streets had lasted all night. The web of ruins had seemed to close in around him, every junction leading onto another and another, but never offering a way out. And somewhere in that maze he'd heard another Sentinel behind him, racing at a speed that should have been impossible for something so battered and broken.

Nothing is impossible or inviolable, Vendrake realised as he watched the chaos on the shore. *There are no rules and there never were. There is no sense or sanity to any of it. Waite was right. I just didn't see it until I came here. I wouldn't see it...*

A black-bearded ruffian crashed into him, howling like a savage. The captain threw him aside and pushed his way through the throng like a man fighting to reach his own execution. All around him, greybacks rushed about, whooping and jeering, some of them spraying dead Letheans with las-fire, scattering and burning the corpses like ragdolls. Vendrake heard himself railing at them, but his own words were lost to him, stifled by the shadows of the past.

It's like Trinity all over again, Vendrake realised as long-buried memories came flooding back. *The sickness in our souls rising up to make monsters of us all…*

He saw Cutler and Machen through the riot. They were standing over a broken commissar who was struggling feebly, trying to rise to feet that were no longer there. Cutler was leering down at the man with a bestial grin that turned Vendrake's blood to ice. Machen was little better; through his open faceplate the Zouave's jaws were frozen in a rictus of hate, transforming his face into a grinning skull. Only the witch seemed troubled by the madness, fluttering desperately around Cutler while her giant *weraldur* loomed over her, shielding her from the crowd. Unexpectedly her green eyes locked onto Vendrake's and she screamed into his mind: *You have to stop this!*

He was stung by the insult as much as the invasion. Of course he had to stop it! *I can't stop it. There's no turning back.* Forcing down the doubts, he barrelled his way through to the officers.

'Enough!' Vendrake yelled, shoving Cutler away from the commissar. 'By Providence, that's enough! We're Arkan, not warp-tainted animals!'

Not like the damned souls of Trinity!

Cutler swung to face him, snarling as he raised his sabre. Vendrake recoiled from the fury in the colonel's eyes, but stood his ground over the injured man and glared back, willing the madman to back down. And then a stronger will than Vendrake's joined the struggle and Cutler faltered, his face contorting as he wrestled against the invader. This time Vendrake was grateful for the witch woman's intervention, but it was a hard-fought battle. He could see her physically quaking with the effort to calm her charge. As she tightened her grip the humidity in the air froze around them and fell in a sprinkling of ice crystals. And then Cutler's sabre clattered to the ground and he looked at Vendrake with dazed eyes, like a man waking from a nightmare.

'Seven Furies for the Stars…' Cutler murmured.

Move! The witch lashed Vendrake's mind, throwing him aside as a las-bolt streaked towards him from the ground. He spun round and saw the mutilated commissar aiming a laspistol at him.

'The Emperor con–' Machen cut the Lethean commissar short with a merciless stomp.

'That's becoming a habit,' he said balefully.

As the skirmish died down, Roach felt Audie Joyce sagging in his grip. He nodded to Mister Fish and they released the greencap. The boy fell to his knees, crying like a big, broken child. *Which is pretty much what he is*, Roach figured. Still, Joyce was old enough to get himself killed if he didn't get his act together. The kid had gone wild when Cutler had gutted the crazy priest, screaming about heresy and murder. It had taken two of them to hold him down.

'Glory Days!' Dix yelled. Roach grimaced as the rangy Bad-lander sauntered back from the riverbank, grinning like an idiot. 'Reckon I just got me a piece of my Thunderground, boys!'

Roach spat in disgust. The skirmish had been a massacre – fifty men torn apart by nearly five hundred, including nine Sentinels! The Letheans hadn't lasted a minute. Roach had no love for the murderous bastards, but he hadn't wanted any part of it.

'What you looking at me like that for, breed?' Dix growled.

'I ain't looking at you no-how, Dixie. You ain't never been a pretty sight and I sure don't have the stomach for the new you.'

He turned his back on the mutilated Badlander.

'Don't you walk away from me, breed!' Dix pulled a knife and charged, just as Roach knew he would. The scout spun, catching Dix full in the face with a kick that sent him lurching backwards. If he'd still had a nose, it would be a ruin now.

'You really want to walk your Thunderground, man?' Roach snarled as he waded into the stunned Badlander with a flurry of punches. 'Then you got to look a whole lot harder. You got to *bleed* for your Thunderground, Dixie!'

The rest of Dustsnake looked on impassively as Roach battered the man, throwing all of the horror and pain of the past day into it. When Dix went down the scout waited, then kicked him as he tried to get up. He turned away, then thought better of it and kicked him some more, just to be sure. He noticed Mister Fish staring at him with wide, troubled eyes and felt oddly ashamed.

'Hey don't worry about it,' he said. 'Me and Dixie there, we go way back.'

'There is no going back,' Machen said with finality.

'But that priest murdered Major Waite!' Lieutenant Quint insisted. 'Surely if we were to explain what really happened…'

'What happened is we killed a ranking member of the Ecclesiarchy and his entourage,' Machen said. 'This is the Imperium, not the Capitol judiciary back home. Justice is irrelevant.'

'You sound almost happy about that, Jon,' Vendrake said, knowing that Machen loathed being called by his first name.

'I am merely stating the facts, *Hardin*,' Machen spat back.

'Or maybe the life of a renegade sounds just dandy to you…'

'We are not renegades!' Cutler shouted, his voice echoing hollowly around the amphitheatre. The meeting had been running for almost an hour, but it was the first time he had spoken. Now he eyed the seven men gathered around him, sizing each of them up in turn. They were standing in a loose circle, debating on their feet in the old Arkan manner: the last surviving officers of the 19th Confederates.

'The men we fought in this city, *they* were renegades,' Cutler went on, 'or more precisely, turncoats. They were Guard gone bad, gentlemen.'

'But do we know that for sure, sir?' Quint asked. 'What I mean is, these tau chaps seem to have quite the propensity for mercenaries.'

'We found meat tags on the bodies – regimental insignia,' Lieutenant Hood interjected. He was a Burning Eagle, curt and efficient to a fault. 'According to the tags every one of those men belonged to the 77th Oberai Redeemers.'

'And they still fought as a functioning unit,' Cutler said. 'The whole sorry regiment's probably deserted to the enemy.'

'If they got the kind of reception we did, I wouldn't blame them!' Lieutenant Grayburn blurted out.

'Wouldn't you, lieutenant?' Cutler looked at the young officer who had stepped up to fill Waite's shoes. 'Well that's worth knowing, because personally I despise them.'

Grayburn reddened and began to bluster, but Cutler waved away his protests.

'No, Grayburn, I'm not gunning for you. You did a fine job out there with the 2nd and I know you're mad after what happened to the major, but mad won't get us through this mess.'

Vendrake tried to reconcile this scrupulous, charismatic leader with the savage he'd seen scant hours earlier. It was almost as if the rage had purged Cutler, leaving him stronger and sharper than before.

Maybe that's how he deals with the truth, Vendrake thought uneasily. On the back of that intuition came another, more disquieting one. *I'm going to need a solution of my own for that particular problem, because I won't be able to bury Trinity again. Leonora won't let me...*

'Gentlemen, something stinks to High Terra about this set-up,' the colonel was saying. He had begun to pace, as if chasing an idea that wouldn't quite crystallise. 'I don't know what the Sky Marshall's game is, but it has cost us near on three hundred men and I'm done playing.' He stopped at the centre of the circle and looked up sharply. 'But we are not the 77th Oberai. We are the 19th Arkan and the 19th Arkan are not and never will be renegades nor traitors.'

Impulsively Vendrake decided to test the man: 'I doubt the Imperium would agree with you, *Whitecrow.*'

Cutler froze at his words. The assembled officers eyed each other uneasily. None of them had ever used the colonel's mock-name to his face. But when he looked at Vendrake, Cutler's expression was calm, even faintly amused.

'I fear you're likely right,' he said. 'And that's why we're going to have to play this the hard way.'

Jakob Dix drifted away from the bustle in the plaza, looking for some space before the regiment moved out. Night had fallen and the greybacks were almost done breaking camp. They'd loaded up the captured Lethean gunboat, along with some transport ships left behind by the rebels. It was going to be a squeeze, but the colonel figured they had enough boats to float everyone upriver. Dix didn't know *why* they were going upriver and he didn't much care, which was pretty much how he felt about most things. So long as there was drink and cards and maybe some gals along the way, Jakob Dix just did what he was told, but he sure did miss old Klete Modine. Things had taken a nosedive since his buddy had gone – 'Bullethead' Calhoun had bought the farm, Dix had lost his nose and now the breed had all the Dustsnakes ganging up on him. Worst of all, the squad was almost out of firewater.

Dix stopped as he saw Joyce mooning about on the banks of the canal. The big greencap was sitting on his haunches and staring into the water like it was full of gold dust. The Badlander grinned, seeing an opportunity for a little fun. If he just crept up quietly and shoved…

'Don't worry, Brother Dix, you'll get your payback,' Joyce said without turning. Dix stopped a couple of feet away, caught off guard by the strangeness in the greencap's voice.

'I weren't going to do nothing,' he said guiltily, not sure why he was making excuses to a lousy rookie.

'But you will,' Joyce said fervently. 'If you embrace His light you'll do great things, brother. Down among the Dustsnakes, you and me, we're like candles in the wind. That's why they hate us. That's why the breed beat up on you.'

'Well that weren't hate exactly,' Dix said, confused by the way this was all going. 'We just do things rough in the Dustsnakes is all.'

'*It were hate!*' Joyce snapped and turned to look at him. The boy's eyes seemed to glitter in the darkness. 'They hate you because you tried to do what's right.'

'I… did…' Dix said uncertainly.

'You and me, we were the only ones who tried to save the saint when the heathens turned on him,' Joyce said bitterly.

'We did?' It slowly dawned on Dix that Joyce had got things mixed up. The kid thought he'd run into the skirmish to fight *for* the crazy confessor, not shoot up dead Letheans. A dim instinct told Dix it was probably best to let things be.

'The heretics held me down and you had to fight for the saint alone,' the boy's voice quavered with emotion. He rose to his feet and grasped the Badlander's hands.

'You couldn't save him, Brother Dix, but don't you be despairing none. The Emperor, He don't let His chosen die easy.' Joyce nodded at the canal. 'The saint, he's only sleeping down there. I been talking to him and I tell you he's going to come back some day. And he won't forget what you done.'

'He won't?' Dix licked his lips, peering uneasily at the murky waters.

'Ain't nothing ever lost in the Emperor's eyes, but until that day comes, lesser men got to carry the burden.' Joyce was staring at the Badlander with the intensity of a hunting cobrahawk. 'You and me, Brother Dix, we got to be like Space Marines among the sheep.'

'Space Marines,' Dix said with wonder, imagining himself in the awesome armour of the Emperor's finest. Even with his face all messed up he reckoned that would win him plenty of gals. Real Space Marines probably had to fight the ladies off every night!

'That's right, brother,' Joyce urged. 'It's going to be a long, dark road out of the Hells, but we got to lead our folk true, 'coz if we don't...' He paused and Dix found himself hanging onto his words, mesmerised by the boy's intensity. 'Well, the Emperor condemns, Brother Dix. He sure does condemn.'

ACT 2
COIL

CHAPTER
SIX

Imperial Seabase Antigone, the Sargaatha Sea

There are Arkan on Phaedra! They have been here nearly seven months and I never knew – an entire regiment of my kinfolk, or whatever's left of them, lost in the hell of the Dolorosa Coil. And they have gone rogue… But no, you are right. I am getting ahead of myself.

From the beginning then…

My meeting with High Commissar Lomax was perplexing and I am still trying to weigh up the implications as I prepare for my departure. The news about the Arkan was the most surprising part of it, but everything about our encounter was unexpected. Except for her dislike of me of course. Some things never change. But her contempt aside, Lomax had changed. She was already old when she arrived on Phaedra, but she had always carried the years with a grim ferocity that seemed to elevate her into something ageless. Like my mentor Bierce, this compact, dark-skinned woman with the close-cropped iron hair had once seemed the epitome of our unbreakable kind, but Phaedra had finally worn her down...

Iverson's Journal

The haggard ghost who met Iverson in the windswept watchtower of the Antigone was not yet broken, but she was close. Lomax had shed so much weight that her greatcoat hung loosely from her bony shoulders, dragging across the floor like a sloughed skin as she prowled the confines of the tower. The whole time they talked she kept moving, flitting from corner to corner like a condemned prisoner looking for a way out. But if there was fear in her, Iverson sensed it was the fear of dying before her work was done. Even at the end, Lomax was a creature of duty.

She never questioned him about his desertion. It was almost as if she knew that pursuing the matter would oblige her to take his life. He didn't understand her mercy until he realised it was no mercy at all, but necessity. Despite her long-standing dislike, Lomax trusted him.

'You and I are relics, Holt Iverson,' she said. 'Between the two of us we've given more years to the Emperor than any ten of Phaedra's so-called commissars taken together, and I'm not talking about the snot-nosed cadets the Sky Marshall sends me these days! He chooses them himself, you know – draws them from the regiments he favours and orders me to train them up. Oh they're brutal enough, but it takes more than muscle and spite to wear the black. These idiots get themselves killed almost as fast as I can send them into the field! I haven't had a genuine graduate of the schola progenium in years. You're a bloody mess, Holt Iverson, and you brood like a Space Marine on downtime, but you're the closest thing I've got to a real commissar on this side of the planet. On Phaedra we're a dying breed.'

That was one reason why she had chosen him for the task ahead. The other was his heritage. Although he had been little more than a child when Bierce took him from Providence, Holt Iverson was still Arkan and the High Commissar's problem was with his kinfolk. And so he listened as she told him the story of a wayward regiment who had been thrown to the wolves and lived through it to become the wolves in turn.

Naturally she didn't put it quite like that – she was a High Commissar after all – but she made it easy for him to read between the lines. Besides, they both knew the reputation of Admiral Vyodor Karjalan and his hellish battleship. The admiral wasn't nicknamed the Sea Spider for nothing, but like so much else on Phaedra, his rot had been allowed to fester and spread. By the Seven Hells, Iverson was proud of the way his kinfolk had escaped the Spider's web!

'Their commander is called Ensor Cutler,' Lomax explained. 'He's the kind of man some would call a maverick hero. I don't share that view. As you know, I have little patience with... unpredictability.' She threw him a pointed glance. 'However, neither am I inclined to trust that old monster Karjalan at his word.'

Iverson was surprised by her frankness. Karjalan was a favourite of the Sky Marshall, a paragon of his stagnant regime and not a man to cross lightly. On other worlds, under other overlords, a High Commissar would have removed a cancer like Karjalan long ago, but this was Phaedra and the Sky Marshall's word was the only law. It seemed Lomax was growing reckless in her twilight.

'Colonel Cutler has led his men into the Dolorosa Coil,' she said. 'They're operating deep inside enemy territory, well beyond our advance...'

'Our advance?' Iverson snapped. 'There's been no advance into Dolorosa for years. All we do is shuffle back and forth along the same lines, winning and losing the same beaches, pushing just so far upriver before being pushed back. The whole campaign is a travesty!'

Lomax looked at him sharply and Iverson thought he'd gone too far, but her eyes were sly and calculating. Suddenly he realised she agreed with every word he'd said. She was quietly crossing a line of her own, which was why they were meeting in this remote tower rather than the confines of her office. Nothing about this encounter was quite what it seemed.

'The intelligence I've received has been sketchy at best,' she went on, 'but it seems that Cutler has spent the last seven months turning his regiment into a Titan-sized thorn in the enemy's backside. His renegades have been waylaying rebel patrols and supply convoys, sabotaging comms relays, even raiding small outposts.'

'He's loyal,' Iverson said firmly. 'Despite whatever those degenerates on the *Puissance* did to his regiment, the man is still fighting for us.'

'Or for himself,' Lomax said. 'Either way, he's stirred up a vespid's nest amongst High Command. They say the Sky Marshall has come down on Karjalan like a virus bomb, even threatened to sink his little empire unless he ends Cutler's spree.'

'Ends it? The first real incursion we've made into Dolorosa since this Emperor-forsaken war started and the Marshall wants to end it? That's insanity.'

Again Lomax threw him that sly look: 'Sky Marshall Kircher is not insane, Iverson.' There was something telling about the way she said it, almost as if the denial was a condemnation, but she moved on before he could dwell on it.

'As you'd expect, Karjalan has sent kill teams after Cutler, but the Letheans are little more than sledgehammer zealots. I doubt any of them got anywhere near the renegades. Certainly none of them ever made it out of the Coil. The Sky Marshall has demanded another approach. We need something with more finesse.'

'Surely you're not signing up to this debacle, Lomax?'

'*High. Commissar. Lomax.* As always, you forget yourself, Iverson. It's a failing that may do worse than kill you one day. And no, I am not signing up to any debacle. I am however, tasking you with tracking down our rogue colonel.'

'You want me to kill Cutler because he's actually hurting the enemy?' Iverson was aghast.

'I want you to test Colonel Ensor Cutler before the Emperor's Justice,' Lomax said, emphasising the words with steely precision. 'And then I expect you to do your duty.'

Mission Log – Day 1 – The Sargaatha Sea: Beginning an End?

Finally I am away, bound for Dolorosa Vermillion, the western archipelago where my errant kinsmen made their landfall seven months ago. There's no telling how deep into the Mire they've travelled, especially if they're following the tangle of the Qalaqexi River, but it's my best starting point. I'll follow in their footsteps and trust in the Emperor's providence. I have to believe that such a thing still exists.

Regardless, it's good to be out on the open sea again, even if that sea is more like an open sewer than a sane ocean. It'll be a long crawl in this transport tug – a rusty crate that's as worn as the war itself – but at least I'm free of the Antigone. There's a slow doom creeping up on the old sea base that's drawn closer during my absence. Or maybe it was just Lomax getting to me. That brittle, sly-eyed raven was like a harbinger of my own doom. You see, at the end she entrusted me with more than the fate of a rogue regiment...

'There's something else,' she told me.

And then she gave me a dossier sealed with a scarlet ribbon. She offered no explanations or instructions, but as I took it I understood that she was passing on a curse. Can one more really make any difference to me? How many times can a man be damned?

Day 2 – The Sargaatha Sea: The Fall of the 19th?

No, I've not touched the scarlet dossier. There are other, more prosaic documents that require my attention first. I have a whole heap of reports on the Arkan 19th and their role in the civil war back home. I never knew there'd been another Arkan uprising, but I won't say I'm surprised. We're a reckless, restless folk and this Ensor Cutler reads like the worst of us – an arrogant glory hunter who leads his men on little more than a wing and a prayer. It's no wonder that his record is such a patchwork mess of distinction and notoriety. The deepest mystery here is why he fought for the Imperium instead of the rebels. But no, that's not entirely true. There is another mystery – something that doesn't quite fit with his fast and loose, yet always heroic exploits: the massacre of a backwater town called Trinity. I haven't found the details yet, but my gut tells me it matters. I must dig deeper. Lomax's scarlet dossier will have to wait.

Day 3 - The Sargaatha Sea: A Fourth Shadow

Lomax didn't warn me about my shadow. No, I'm not talking about my dead shadows — my ghosts appear to have taken their leave of me for the present — but the living, breathing spy who has attached herself to me. Commissar Cadet Ysabel Reve caught up with us this morning, ferried in by a speeding sea skimmer. The first thing I noticed about the girl was her height. She can't have been much past twenty, but she was almost a head taller than me and I'm taller than most. Everything about her was hard and brutally efficient, from her lean, muscle-plated build to her square-jawed face and shaven scalp. Her storm coat and boots glistened with polish, complementing the bright silver pin of the Sky Marshall's chosen. By Providence, the girl was even carrying a gold-plated autopistol!

I didn't believe any of it for a moment…

Iverson's Journal

'Yes, I'm sure you're a first-class shot, Reve, but that won't be nearly enough in the Mire.' Iverson shook his head. 'This isn't going to be a routine patrol. I won't be able to look out for you, girl.'

And I don't want to be looking over my shoulder for *you.*

'I have done three stints on Dolorosa Azure,' the girl said in a clipped, guttural accent he couldn't quite place. 'I will pull my weight, sir.'

Iverson didn't doubt it. The band of her cap might be blue, but this woman was no raw cadet. He wasn't even convinced she was a commissar. That pristine storm coat and fancy autopistol were a façade to lull him into thinking she was green, but he'd learnt never to trust the obvious. A person's story was written in their eyes and Ysabel Reve's were flat and cold. They told an assassin's tale.

She's not here to learn from me or watch my back. She's here to finish the job if I can't. Or stab me in the back if I won't. But who sent her?

'Look, does Lomax know about this?' Iverson said.

'Indeed yes, the High Commissar approved my appointment personally, sir.'

'I see. Well, we're only three days out of Antigone,' Iverson said with a shrug. 'I'll get her on the vox to confirm that. For your sake, you understand.'

'I am sorry, sir. Did you not receive the news?'

'I have no idea what you're talking about, cadet.'

'Sir, High Commissar Lomax is dead.'

Iverson stared at her.

'She died the day after you sailed, sir. I assumed you knew.'

'How did she die?' he asked flatly.

'She fell from the watchtower, sir. The medicae believe she died instantly.' Reve lowered her eyes. 'I am sorry. I know that you and she were friends.'

'Friends…'

'Yes, the High Commissar always spoke highly of you, sir. In the training sessions.'

Did she really? Somehow I doubt that, Reve.

'They say it was suicide.' The girl hesitated and Iverson could see she was thinking, weighing him up. 'I am sorry, sir,' she repeated finally.

Once again, Reve, I rather doubt that.

Day 4 – The Sargaatha Sea: The Scarlet Testament

I am troubled by Lomax's death. We were never friends but she was a constant in this changing-changeless morass.

She was true to her vows to the Emperor and utterly unswerving in her duty. And at the end she chose to trust me.

I must make the time to study the papers she passed into my care… But no, that is sheer prevarication! Time has nothing to do with it! This damnably slow tug has given me all the time I could possibly need, but I cannot bring myself to break the scarlet seal of that dossier. I can feel it bulging with documents and picts, almost certainly hiding the truths that killed her. I know my duty, yet I hesitate. Why?

Where are my ghosts when I need their counsel?

Day 7 – The Sargaatha Sea: Shadowplays

We are due to rendezvous with the Puissance tomorrow. Her reputation precedes her, but this will be the first time I actually set foot on that grim old battleship. Apparently Admiral Karjalan wants to brief me personally. I suspect I'm his last hope of staving off the Sky Marshall's displeasure so he'll offer me the best he has. That will be a gunboat and a platoon of his finest men, probably the infamous Penitent Corsairs. From what I've heard about those zealots they're just about the last troops I'd want along on a mission like this. I have enough to worry about with Cadet Ysabel bloody Reve looking over my shoulder all the time. That girl's playing a sharper game than I first gave her credit for…

Iverson's Journal

'Commissar Iverson, may I speak with you? Off the record?'

'You're a commissar, Reve.' *Aren't you?* 'You know nothing's ever off the record.' He glared at her. 'Especially something you want off the record. Out with it.'

'Very well,' she steeled herself visibly. *Overacting again…* 'I do not believe the High Commissar killed herself, sir.'

'You don't?' Iverson was surprised.

'Sir, High Commissar Lomax was a true hero of the Imperium,' Reve said passionately. Iverson was impressed – the girl sounded genuinely upset. 'She had too much steel in her soul to take the easy way out.'

'What are you getting at, cadet?'

Reve hesitated before looking him straight in the eye.

'Sir, I believe she had enemies amongst High Command. I believe she might have discovered something. Something damaging.'

'That's a very serious allegation, Cadet Reve,' Iverson said, watching her closely. 'What do you think she was on to?'

'I was hoping…' She paused, returning his intense scrutiny – *Testing me as I am testing her* – 'I was hoping that she might have told you, sir.'

He had to admit she was good. If she hadn't overplayed her hand with that spotless uniform and ridiculous sidearm he might even have believed her.

'Why would you think that, Cadet Reve?'

'Because she trusted you, sir.'

'Perhaps not as much as you think,' Iverson said. 'Look, I've got nothing for you, cadet. Lomax was old and worn to the soul with this filthy planet. Maybe it was just plain suicide.' He turned away from her. 'Despite what you've been led to believe, none of us are unbreakable. Sometimes things are simply what they seem.'

But not you, Ysabel Reve, most definitely not you…

* * *

Day 8 – The Puissance: Death Ship

If ever a ship was tainted, it is this ancient Lethean ironclad. I'm no damned psyker but I sensed it the moment I saw her on the horizon, rising like an iron canker on a sea of sludge, vast and dark and spiteful as the Seven Hells. They say the Puissance hasn't moved in over a decade – not since old Karjalan took ill and disappeared from sight – and I have no reason to doubt that.

The water around the ship was encrusted with a rime of glutinous algal scum. Thick tendrils of the stuff had climbed the hull, twining round the corroded battlements and binding the vessel to its floating grave. The morbid tribulation continued on the deck, where corpses hung from the ship's crane, some of them still fresh, others little more than skeletons. And wherever we wandered I saw the metal glistening with a patina of slime, something excreted rather than acquired, almost as if the iron marrow of the vessel itself was polluted.

By Providence, even the Mire feels pure beside the Puissance! It appals me to tarry here, but Karjalan was unable to see us until after nightfall due to a shipboard crisis. It seems that a prisoner broke free of the brig shortly after our arrival. I wonder at the man who could manage it and cause the Letheans such vexation. And I admit that I wish him well in his flight from this charnel ship. Whoever he is and whatever he has done, his crime cannot be greater than Karjalan's own.

As I prepare to meet the admiral, one thought gnaws at me: if the web is so foul, then how much worse the Spider?

Iverson's Journal

'Forgive the theatrics, Commissar Iverson, but I fear I am not the man I used to be,' the voice warbled from the darkness, sounding desiccated and damp in the same breath. 'But despite Her depredations, Phaedra has not yet worn away my vanity.'

Iverson peered across the chamber, trying to pierce the gloom, but the speaker hadn't put his trust in shadows alone. A silk screen had been drawn across the furthest recesses of the room, turning the man into a vague silhouette. He could make out little more than a hunched shape swaddled in heavy blankets. Occasionally its arms would wave about loosely, stick thin and oddly frayed, but it was impossible to gauge its height or build. For all he could tell, Admiral Vyodor Karjalan looked exactly as he sounded: a mummified corpse bloated on congealed blood.

Shaking off the unwelcome image, Iverson tried to focus on the admiral's words, but his thoughts came slow and muddy. The humidity in Karjalan's chamber was worse than anything he'd experienced in the Mire, almost like a hydroponic hothouse. The air was hazy with the bittersweet reek of incense, but the smoke couldn't quite disguise a deeper stench – the promise of something ripe with decay.

The soporific effect was heightened by the rhythmic gurgle-hiss of an arcane life support array in the far corner. Two Lethean priests attended the machine while a Penitent Corsair in scarlet plate stood watch. A muddle of pipes sprouted from the array like questing, industrial creepers. Some trailed away behind the admiral's screen, while others coiled around a body lying on a pallet nearby, its waxy flesh pierced by a lattice of needles. Iverson could see the victim's blood being siphoned away into that greedy snarl of pipes.

'I trust my medication does not disturb you?' Karjalan wheezed, seeming to read the commissar's mind.

'I'm long past being troubled by anything I see,' Iverson lied. He couldn't help taking some satisfaction in Cadet Reve's pallor. Perhaps the assassin wasn't quite as cold as he'd first imagined.

'Nevertheless, I am grateful for your indulgence, commissar.' The admiral chuckled and his silhouette jerked fitfully. 'I occasionally toy with making an end of things, but my service to the Emperor prohibits it. And my beloved Letheans would be lost without me. Indeed, they vie with one another to offer up their blood that I may live.'

'Admiral, I am hoping to set out at first light,' Iverson said, struggling to pull his thoughts into order. 'I'll be needing a gunboat and...'

'Do you find my conversation so tiresome, commissar?' Karjalan hissed. 'Are you bored with me so soon, *Arkan*?'

Iverson ignored Reve's sidelong warning glance and forged on.

'Admiral, I'm here on the Emperor's business...'

'As am I! Have you not heard of the Lethean Revelation, commissar?'

'I've given it little thought.'

'Ah, but you must! You see the Emperor condemns!' Karjalan cackled wetly. 'And I am holy! So damnably holy it hurts!' Abruptly his humour dried up. 'Your kinfolk have done me a grave insult and a graver injury, Holt Iverson. Tell me; are all the men of Arkan such savages?'

Iverson hesitated, taken aback by the insult. To his surprise Reve spoke up: 'My Lord Admiral, Commissar Iverson has often told me of the shame he feels over the conduct of the Arkan 19th. His blood ties have made the matter personal for him.'

'The matter is *personal* for me also,' Karjalan said. 'These

Arkan scum slaughtered fifty of my Letheans in cold blood, together with a man who was like a brother to me!'

'Confessor Yosiv Gurdjief,' Reve said with a nod. 'His murder was a heinous crime against the Ecclesiarchy…'

'It was a crime against *me*!' Karjalan shrieked, splattering the screen with ichor.

'Sir, I assure you that Commissar Iverson takes this matter…'

'Be silent you soulless bitch! Does your precious master have no voice of his own? Where's your tongue now, eh, Iverson? Won't you speak up for your backwater brothers? Don't you have the courage to–'

There was a wet pop and Karjalan's voice disintegrated into a ragged cough. His form heaved and something raked the curtain spasmodically. One of his attendant priests flitted urgently behind the screen.

'My Blessed Lord, you must not excite yourself so–'

The priest's admonishment was choked off as something lashed out and seized him by the throat. Horrified, Iverson and Reve watched the priest's silhouette shudder to its knees, twitching frantically. The other two attendants watched the mayhem with something like rapture on their faces.

'This is monstrous,' Reve whispered, beginning to rise.

Iverson caught her wrist, then her eyes, holding both in an iron grip.

'This is Phaedra,' he said.

They heard something rip violently behind the curtain and more fluid splattered the fabric. This time it was dark and viscous.

Day 9 – The Sargaatha Sea: Penance and Pain

We sailed from the Puissance at dawn, but my relief at escaping that tainted ship is tempered by shame. The

reality of the Sea Spider proved to be much worse than
the darkest rumours: Karjalan is an abomination in body
and soul. Duty demands that I take his life, yet duty also
demands that I keep my own for now. Duty delights in
making a man dance on hot coals! But I digress...

Once Karjalan was done with feasting his reason returned
and he remembered that I was his last hope of tracking
down the rogues. With ill grace he granted my request for a
Triton-pattern transport – an amphibious gunboat capable
of negotiating both land and water. They are fine vessels
and woefully rare on Phaedra. If we had more such vehicles
we might have won this war long ago. I am beginning to
wonder if that is why we have so few...

In typical Lethean fashion my craft is called the Penance
and Pain. I won't deny that it is a fitting name.

Iverson's Journal

'I do not trust them,' Reve growled, indicating the troops in
scarlet plate prowling the deck below. 'They are the creatures
of a debased heretic.'

'A heretic who thinks he's a martyr to the Emperor,' Iverson said. 'Look, it's not a question of trust, cadet. This ship is
Lethean. I had to take her crew. Besides, we couldn't sail her
alone.'

They were standing together on the upper deck, watching
the Penitent Corsairs lumber about their duties with brutish
determination. There were eight of the hulking zealots on
board, every one a tattooed, shaven-headed thug bristling with
devotional charms and totems. To Iverson they looked more
like steroid-boosted hive gangers than professional soldiers,
but their equipment belied it. All of them wore sculpted body

armour with jagged shoulder plates and conical helmets that flanged into fins at the sides, giving them a distinctly marine look. In place of regular issue lasguns they sported high-powered hellguns connected to fluted, shell-like backpacks.

In a more sober regiment Iverson guessed the Corsairs would be classed as storm troopers, but these elites had a propensity for fevered prayer and self-flagellation. Fortunately they went about the business of war as if the Emperor Himself was breathing down their backs, never slacking on patrol and manning the gun emplacements to port and starboard as if they were holy shrines.

The more mundane matters of sailing and maintaining the craft fell to the lowly Penitent Mariners. Iverson wasn't sure how many of the scraggy ratings they had on board, but he guessed there must be at least twenty. They were all filthy, tangle-haired ruffians who revered the Corsairs as holy knights. In turn those worthies treated them as slaves, regularly brutalising and beating them. It was a tried and tested dynamic that Iverson had seen countless times over. It could be as strong as folded steel or as brittle as rotten timber.

'How can they believe that abomination serves the God-Emperor?' Reve sneered.

'Karjalan believes it himself,' Iverson said, regarding her curiously. 'Besides, he's a creature of the Sky Marshall. Isn't that enough for you?'

Reve looked at him sharply: 'It is not, sir.'

'That mark you're wearing says otherwise.'

'This?' She jabbed at the silver icon on her lapel, understanding dawning on her face. 'This is why you do not trust me?'

'I didn't say that, Cadet Reve.'

'You did not have to,' she glared at him with what looked like real bitterness. 'The Skywatch is nothing to me, but with respect sir, you are a *starblood*.'

'What in the Seven Hells are you talking about, cadet?'

'Commissar, you were sent to Phaedra from… from somewhere else,' Reve gestured vaguely towards the sky. 'You arrived with rank and honours, but I was born in the mud and blood of this war – just another Guard brat among thousands. This is the only world I have known. There is no schola progenium here, only the Skywatch Academies. They are the only path to advancement for my kind.'

'But you trained under Lomax?'

'Only because I am of the Skywatch!' With a snort she ripped the badge from her lapel. 'But if they murdered the High Commissar I want no part of them.'

'Be careful, Reve.'

'I am done being careful.' She flipped the badge overboard with an indifferent flick and stalked away, leaving Iverson frowning at her back.

You almost had me there, but you overcooked it again at the end, girl.

His frown turned to a sour smile as he noticed Bierce standing vigil at the prow of the ship. The old revenant had his back to Iverson, intent on the dismal coastline of Dolorosa Vermillion rising on the horizon. Seven long months ago the Arkan 19th had landed on those shores and disappeared into Hell.

And wherever you've gone, brothers, be sure that I'll follow.

Iverson's grin faded as he realised his augmetic hand had jammed up, locking his grip to the railing.

Day 10 – Vermillion Sound: The Broken Man

I have returned to the Mire and my ghosts have returned to me, creeping back one by one, as I always knew they would. It is only right and proper, for Commander Wintertide still lives and my penance is not yet done.

Fortunately their restoration has blessed me with a strange clarity. I am now certain that this hunt for my rogue kinsmen is part of my greater quest. It cannot be coincidence that our threads have crossed the stars to interweave in the Dolorosa Coil. Somehow Ensor Cutler will be the key to my salvation. Somehow he will open the door to Wintertide.

Yet despite my conviction I cannot put Lomax's death – her murder – from my mind. I believe the High Commissar knew her enemies were closing in and the scarlet dossier is her last testament against them. If I don't accept it she may yet rise and make my trio of ghosts into four. I have welcomed my shades back, but I will not countenance another on my conscience. No, it's time to face her will.

I have the dossier beside me, but I cannot seem to rally my thoughts. With nightfall the mouldy reek of the Mire has become almost overpowering in the confines of my cabin...

Iverson's Journal

Iverson paused, his pen hovering over the page as he listened for the sound. A moment later it came again – a low, ragged rasp, like a man struggling for breath. He turned slowly, his hand slipping towards his holster as he squinted into the murk of the cabin. The lantern perched on his desk cast a flickering aura that merely taunted the gloom. Iverson rose to his feet and raised the lamp over his head, trying to throw back the crowding shadows. There was something lurking at the threshold to his small washroom.

'You ain't got no call for the shooter,' the intruder said. Its voice was little more than a hoarse croak, but the accent was unmistakeable, even though Iverson hadn't heard that thick burr in decades. *Arkan.*

'Show yourself,' Iverson demanded.

'Not a problem, but I got to warn you, I ain't a pretty sight, brother.' The shape shook with something between a chuckle and cough, sounding uncannily like the infested admiral. Suddenly Iverson recognised the rancid ordure wafting from the shape – it was the same stench that had permeated Karjalan's chambers.

'You're no brother to me,' Iverson said.

'I heard you talking up on deck,' the shape drawled wetly. 'I can tell you've been gone a while, but you ain't lost your Providence twang. You're Arkan. In this hellhole that makes us brothers.' With that the speaker stepped from the shadows. He was a massive, craggy-faced brute, naked save for a filthy medical smock. His mottled skin hung from his bones in sagging wattles, as if his flesh had been sucked dry.

'The name's Modine, Private third class, 19th Arkan Confederates,' the intruder said. 'And I could sure use a drink if you've got anything going.'

Day 11 – The Shell and Dolorosa Breach: The Sleeping Front

We sailed through the Shell at dawn. The coral maze was deserted, long abandoned by the Imperial forces that had followed in Cutler's footsteps. The men of Dolorosa Breach had occupied the necropolis for less than a week before evacuating to the saner, safer horrors of the Mire. We found them a couple of leagues upriver, entrenched in a sprawling tract of burned jungle. Cadet Reve was dismayed by the chaos, but the ragtag army was no worse than I'd expected. Thanks to Cutler's efforts our advance has staggered a little further inland, only to falter into stagnation once more. I suspect they haven't moved in months.

We stopped off for supplies and I took the opportunity to requisition fatigues and a flamer for the fugitive who crept into my quarters last night. I'm not entirely sure what to make of Private Kletus Modine and his escape from the Puissance, but he was right about one thing – we are both Arkan and I cannot surrender him to the Sea Spider. Besides, after the horrors I witnessed on board that death ship I have no reason to doubt his story.

For the record, Modine told me he was the last survivor of three troopers taken by force and bled dry to curb the admiral's disease. I won't elaborate on the lurid details of his torment and escape, but it seems he got wind of our arrival and made a break for it, surprising the captors who thought him comatose. He's brazen to the point of insubordination and tests my patience relentlessly, almost as if he's daring me to shoot him, but I won't do it. There's more to Kletus Modine than meets the eye and he may yet prove to be my only ally on this journey. I have claimed a storage berth alongside my cabin for the stowaway. For the time being he will remain my secret.

Oh yes, there was one more thing: a prisoner waiting for us at the Breach...

Iverson's Journal

'Please, you have to get me back to my squadron,' the haggard youth in the tattered jumpsuit pleaded. 'I'm a pilot, you see. And a member of the Skywatch!'

'I understand, Airman Garrido,' Iverson said coldly, 'but

you'll have to give me something on the renegades if you want my help.'

'But I've told you everything I know! The scum hijacked my ship and flew us into the Shell. I swear I fought them, but that old heretic Ortega betrayed me! And then they all turned on the Letheans…'

'And you're quite certain that Cutler killed the confessor personally?'

'I saw it myself. That white-haired savage is insane. He was like a man possessed, but they were all bloody barbarians! Now please, you can't let me rot down here…'

Iverson dismissed the pilot, already convinced he knew nothing more. Jaime Garrido had been found hiding out in the Shell, abandoned when the renegades fled upriver. The commissars of the Breach had kept him locked away in anticipation of this fleeting, fruitless interrogation.

The pilot was still pleading when Iverson walked away. For Jaime Hernandez Garrido it was the end of the road.

Day 13 – The Qalaqexi River: Modine's Blasphemy

Tonight I returned to my quarters and found Modine trawling through Lomax's testament. The scarlet ribbon lay on the floor and her precious secrets were scattered about my desk: classified troop and munitions reports, officer psych assessments, tactical maps and surveillance picts and Emperor knows what else, all passing through the grubby hands of a diseased greyback. He met my shock with a cheerful leer…

Iverson's Journal

'You needed a push,' Modine said. 'I seen you staring at this thing like it was a ticking bomb. You was too scared to open it, but too hungry to back off. Well you've been good to me, so I figured I'd lend a hand, chief.'

The insolence washed over Iverson as he approached the muddle of papers. Now that the secrets were out their call was hypnotic, reducing Modine to a faintly irritating irrelevance.

'Of course, I ain't never been too sharp with my letters,' Modine went on, 'so I ain't got too far...'

'Leave,' Iverson interrupted, his eyes never straying from the documents.

'Aw, come on, Holt...'

Iverson spun round and Modine found himself staring down the barrel of an autopistol. The commissar's surviving eye bored into him, an open window to somewhere glacial and unforgiving. To the greyback it looked less human than its augmetic partner. Modine raised his hands slowly. 'Hey, no worries, brother.'

Iverson's face twitched with an involuntary spasm. 'Out,' he said.

Keeping his eyes on the gun, Modine nodded and backed out of the cabin. Iverson's ghosts took his place, drifting from the shadows to encircle their beacon as he sank into a chair and began to read.

Day 16 – The Qalaqexi River: The Wages of Truth

I haven't stirred from my cabin since the night Lomax's plague of truths was loosed, but there's still so much to digest. It will take weeks to sift through her catalogue of errors and inconsistencies and accounts of sheer stupidity and bloody-minded madness, but one thing is already certain: we have all been betrayed.

Iverson's Journal

Reve was pounding at his cabin door again.

'I'm busy,' Iverson growled, rubbing at his surviving eye. The augmetic one was buzzing furiously, threatening to gnaw a hole through the back of his skull.

'Sir, you have not been on deck in days,' Reve called from behind the locked door. 'The Letheans are beginning to ask questions.'

They should be asking questions, Reve. We should all have been asking questions long ago.

Day 17 – The Qalaqexi River: Seven Stars

We are sailing through no-man's-land. The sleeping ghosts of the Shell and the Dolorosa Breach are far behind us. The hungry ghosts of the Qalaqexi Coil lie ahead. There are no Imperial forces past this point save for a few scattered jungle fighters working deep recon. We're on our own and if we run into a significant rebel detachment we'll soon be dead. But that's unlikely to happen once the great river narrows and frays into the Coil.

I've never been this far inland, but I know the stories of the infamous labyrinth. There are dozens of paths to the heart of the continent and many more to nowhere at all. If we go slow and silent and the Emperor's Grace goes with us, we might stay undetected for months. Of course logic dictates that this is a double-edged sword, for how will we in turn find our quarry? Well, my friend, this is where we must abandon logic and cleave to faith, or whatever else it is that guides us. You see, despite the odds I know that we shall find them. Or they shall find us...

Iverson's Journal

'I want this hoisted,' Iverson said, unravelling the heavy banner. The Seven Stars of Providence glittered against its deep blue fabric, looking impossibly bright in the murky dawn light. The Lethean Mariners shuffled about, casting uneasy glances at their armoured overlords. One of the Corsairs stalked over and inspected the flag with unbridled disgust.

'The Penitents, we do not sail under false idols,' he growled.

'You're talking about the Seven Stars, the flag of my home world; a world that has stood by the God-Emperor for ten thousand years,' Iverson lied, quite certain these ignorant zealots wouldn't know any better.

'But is Lethean ship…'

'No, it's the Emperor's ship and I am His appointed servant on this holy mission. Do you question His word?'

The Corsair glared pure hatred at him, but Iverson paid him no heed. 'Hoist it,' he snapped at the Mariners. 'Now!'

As the seadogs scurried to obey, Cadet Reve raised a quizzical eyebrow.

'Before you ask, I had it commissioned back on the Antigone,' Iverson said. 'As to why, Cadet Reve… Why don't you tell me?'

'Obviously you are hoping to draw the renegades out,' she answered without hesitation. 'That was not my question, sir.'

'Then enlighten me, cadet.'

'If they do come, what will you say to them?'

'What do *you* think I should say?'

She hesitated. The game between them was growing more treacherous by the day. Finally she made a cautious move: 'That is not for me to say, sir.'

'A good answer, Reve,' Iverson said and turned his back on her.

* * *

Day 19 – The Qalaqexi River: The Mouth of the Coil

We entered the Coil at dusk. The jungle seemed to darken and close in around us as we slipped into the embrace of that primal morass. Even the Lethean thugs were unnerved by the change and I suspect there will be no end to their coarse prayers tonight. Dead Niemand, who approves of their ways, has urged me to share their worship, but I no longer believe the God–Emperor cares for such prattling. Like the Coil, my own faith has unravelled into something dark and tangled, yet I sense His hand pulling at the threads, urging me forward. I can only hope that He isn't laughing.

Iverson's Journal

It was raining again, the heavy drops punching through the dense canopy to spatter the leather-coated commissars standing watch on the upper deck. Iverson ignored it, so Reve ignored it too, their intransigence an unspoken bond.

'What do you think we'll find in here?' she asked, eying the grey-green walls of the Mire seeping past on either side.

Vengeance, Niemand gloated.

Justice, Bierce glared.

Redemption, Number 27 beseeched.

'All or nothing,' Iverson said. *My Thunderground,* he thought.

CHAPTER SEVEN

**PROVIDENCE MILITARY ARCHIVES,
CAPITOL HALL
REPORT:** GF060526
STATUS: *CLASSIFIED*
FROM: Major Ranulph C. Kharter, Investigating Officer (Internal Affairs)
ATT: General Thaddeus Blackwood, Director (Internal Affairs)
REF: War Crimes – 19th Arkan – Trinity Township, Vyrmont
SUM: As per orders I have undertaken an investigation of the frontier township designated *Trinity*. Preliminary evidence supports claims the town was razed with maximum prejudice. All structures have been burned. A mass grave was discovered on the town perimeter (speculate intent of concealment) containing several hundred corpses. Despite advanced decomposition the bodies

were clearly burned, but the cause of death appears to be various and violent. No evidence of significant rebel affiliations apparent.

CON: Further investigation recommended.

Note: What in the Hells did Cutler do to these poor bastards?

The bell tolled again, booming somewhere deep inside the prisoner's gut. He moaned as he felt himself slipping back into the hungry old nightmare. Awakening again...

It was long after sunset, but the blizzard had stained the night white, transforming the old town into a blur of crooked silhouettes lost in static. The gale whistled through the narrow avenues like a forlorn ghost, stirring up the snow around the intruders as they pressed on toward the town square. Every man in the squad was half-frozen and bone-weary, but if there was any welcome to be had in this backwater burg it would surely be there.

We'll find no welcome here. None that we'll be glad of anyways...

Major Ensor Cutler thrust the gloomy thought aside, irritated by the dark mood hanging over him. It was strange that victory had left him feeling so hollow, but word of the rebels' final surrender had reached the 19th late, catching the regiment deep in the Vyrmont rifts with the first frost of winter already in the air. They had been hounding Colonel Cadey's infamous Liberty Brigade and the old warhawk had led them a wild chase, fighting to the last man despite Cutler's entreaties that the war was already over. It was a shabby epitaph to a shabby war. Cadey had been a courageous foe and hunting him down like a mad dog had left Cutler feeling dispirited and dishonoured. More importantly it had left the 19th battered, exhausted and lost in the middle of nowhere with the Big Freeze bearing down on them. Hoping to outrun the winter they had marched south, but the snow had caught up within days, tormenting them like Cadey's vengeful spirit. When men began to die, Cutler had scattered the Sentinels into the wilderness to scout for shelter. He hadn't held out much hope, but two days later *Muse in Iron* had called in a discovery.

'Major, I've gone and found you a town,' Lieutenant Nevin 'Kiljak' Jaxon had voxed, his smugness loud and clear through the distortion. 'It's not much to look at, but this far north... Well, I'd say it's a miracle it's here at all.'

Cutler hadn't argued. Taking a squad of volunteers, he had forged ahead to reconnoitre the town while the regiment trailed behind with the wounded, but hope had soon turned to bitter disappointment. Their sanctuary was a ghost town. His hails had gone unanswered and the creaking timber houses they'd checked out had proven stone cold and empty. They'd found no victuals or anything else of use either.

What they had found was a bizarre, almost clinical mayhem: garments shredded to thin strips and furniture smashed to matchwood, even utensils bent out of shape. No object had escaped intact. Strangest of all, the detritus had been arranged into neat, geometrically perfect piles, forming shapes and structures that seemed redolent with meaning yet at the same time totally senseless. The junk sculptures had lured the eye and reeled in the mind with the need to *understand*. Even the memory of those deranged symbols made Cutler's head pound. And then there were the pervasive messages scrawled across the walls of every hovel, sometimes painted, sometimes carved, but always the same:

'THE BELL TOLLS, THE WORLD UNFOLDS'

'These hicks sure must've loved this damn bell of theirs,' Captain Waite had observed gruffly, but Cutler had wondered. Was it love or something darker that had inspired such devotion?

As they pushed on towards the square, his thoughts kept returning to that enigmatic bell, chewing over the mystery with growing disquiet. And then he heard it. A discordant note rumbling under the wind, so deep it was almost subliminal.

The echo of a drowned bell...

For a moment the snow whirled apart and he caught sight of a tall shadow in a wide-brimmed hat standing in the street ahead. He couldn't make out its face, but some instinct told him it was looking directly at him.

'Who goes there?' Cutler hollered over the squall, but the snow had already swept the wraith away. He strained, listening for another chime, looking for the stranger, but both were gone.

If they were ever there at all...

'What's up?' Elias Waite yelled beside him, his voice muffled by the woollen scarf wrapped around his face. Clearly the old captain hadn't noticed anything untoward. Nor had any other member of the squad for that matter.

Cutler peered warily at the shuttered windows on either side of the narrow street. They were just dark blurs through the swirling whiteness, but he imagined furtive eyes behind every one of them, watching the intruders with growing malice.

'Ensor?' Waite urged.

'Quinney,' Cutler called to the squad's vox-operator, 'any word from *Muse in Iron* yet?'

'Been trying to raise him every couple of minutes, sir,' the skinny greyback answered. He was hunched miserably under the bulky vox-set strapped to his back. 'Ain't got nothing since before sunset. Could be the storm fragging with the comms of course,' he finished doubtfully.

Cutler frowned, wondering if Jaxon had run into trouble. He had ordered the cavalryman to meet them at the edge of town, but like most Sentinel riders, 'Kiljak' was a cocksure chancer who couldn't sit still to save his hide. Besides, what did a Sentinel have to fear from a bunch of stir crazy inbreeds?

'It don't feel right, does it?' Waite said, sensing Cutler's mood. 'You know, I'm thinking maybe we ought to pass on this hand, Ensor.'

'We've a killing cold at our backs, old man,' Cutler said. 'Even if this town's dead we can hole up and wait out the storm here.'

'And what if it ain't dead, just dying?'

'I'm not losing another man to the snow, Elias.'

Although it might be a cleaner way to die than all the filthy fates waiting for us here...

Uneasily Cutler waved his squad onwards.

The prisoner stirred, his body fighting unconsciously against the restraints that bound him as his mind fought against the hooks dragging him inexorably deeper into horror...

They found *Muse in Iron* standing forlornly in the town plaza. The walker's canopy was thrown wide open but there was no sign of Jaxon. Cutler halted the squad at the edge of the square, hanging back in the cover of the street. His instincts were jangling like alarm bells and his muscles were taut with a tension he couldn't explain.

Why do I feel like I'm trussed up like a steer in a slaughterhouse?

'I see a light,' Waite said, tapping his shoulder. Cutler followed his pointing finger to a tall building that loomed over the rest like a hunchbacked giant. It was a crude edifice built from timber and brick, but it had probably pushed the ambition of this stunted town to the limit. The light was seeping through a huge, lopsided window above the portico. Something, probably the glass, had stained the glow into a polychromatic chaos that writhed like a living thing in the white noise of snow.

'Now that has to be the sorriest excuse for a temple I've ever seen,' Waite growled. Cutler saw him touch the aquila pendant hanging from his neck. Warding off evil. In his rough-and-ready way, the captain had always been a true believer.

But it didn't save you, Elias…

An inexplicable pang of sadness hit Cutler as he looked at his old friend. He was suddenly sure that Elias Waite was long dead.

'Why you looking at me like that, Ensor?' Waite asked, but Cutler had no answer for him.

That was when someone stepped from the temple. For a moment the newcomer stood silhouetted against the rainbow light, swaying gently as if unsure of its balance, then it began to walk towards them, homing in on their position with unerring accuracy. The squad tensed up around Cutler like a gestalt animal, raising lasguns and bayonets like defensive spines to ward of a predator. Then the stranger emerged from the varicoloured haze and they recognised him.

'Jaxon!' Cutler called out.

The tall cavalryman stopped a few metres away. His finely chiselled features looked flat and lifeless without their characteristic smirk, but it was his dead white hair that turned Cutler's blood to ice. When Jaxon had departed the regiment two days ago his hair had been a deep brown.

'Lieutenant, what happened here?' Cutler pressed. 'Why did you abandon your Sentinel?'

Jaxon looked at him with eyes like painted eggs – false eyes only pretending at life. 'They gave me a choice sir,' he said in a flat monotone, every word flowing into the next without texture or inflection. 'Many choices actually so many there was really no choice at all sir.'

'Who gave you a choice?' Cutler stepped forward, wanting to shake the man, but instinctively unwilling to touch him. 'Are you talking about the townsfolk, lieutenant?'

'No the townsfolk are all gone sir.'

'Gone where? Are you saying they're all dead?'

'No not dead they're still here just gone sir.'

'You're not making any sense, man.'

'That's as it should be if you just look between the lines they'll show you how it really is sir.'

'Who are *they*?' Cutler said, taking another step towards him.

'Oh you'll see them soon sir they already see you.' Jaxon's hand came up holding a bright dagger. 'They say I have to go now.'

'Easy son, we're here to help you,' Waite said steadily.

'There is no help.' The ghost of a smile haunted Jaxon's face as he put the dagger to his own throat. 'And all the choices are lies.'

'Wait!' Cutler shouted, but it was too late. The cavalryman jerked the dagger convulsively and bright arterial blood sprayed into the blizzard. For a moment he just stood there watching his life drain away, then he looked at Cutler and his lips moved as if he wanted to say something more, but his vocal chords were gone so he just sighed and toppled. His corpse hit the snow with a sonorous clang that reverberated across the square.

Cutler stared at the corpse in confusion, unable to link that concussion of sound with the sight. Then the boom came again and he glanced up at the temple, suddenly understanding. It was the bell tolling. Calling to the damned…

And the damned came by the dozen, bursting from shadowed

doorways and windows like starved rats. They were the citizens of the blighted town, broken ghouls eager to share their curse. Despite the cold, most were stripped to the waist and their flesh shone blue with the frigid kiss of hypothermia. A few carried antique firearms, but most made do with the makeshift weapons of home and hearth. They laughed and wailed in an ecstasy of misery as they bore down on the greybacks.

'Fire at will!' Cutler roared without hesitation, but the townsfolk were already on top of the squad, hacking and slashing with wild abandon.

Cutler rammed his sabre between the tines of a jabbing pitchfork and twisted, tearing the weapon from his attacker's numbed hands. The peasant glared at him, one eye burning with fury, the other brimming with merriment. His cadaverous face was a bipolar caricature, the left side twisted into a rictus of joy, the right into a snarl of hate. It reminded Cutler of the grotesque carved masks he'd seen back in the Capitol playhouses.

'Stand down!' Cutler shouted at the disarmed man.

With a sob of joy the maniac leapt forward and impaled himself on Cutler's blade, then thrust onwards, rapturously disembowelling himself as he groped for his killer. Horrified, Cutler rammed his autopistol under the man's jaw and blew away that insane flesh mask. As he struggled to withdraw his sabre an axe came chopping in from the right. Desperately he swung the impaled corpse round and caught the blow. The axe man ululated furiously, his distended face rippling like melting wax as he struck again and again, trying to break through Cutler's meat shield.

The bell tolls and the world unfolds…

Cutler caught snatches of his beleaguered squad through the chaos. He heard the boom of Waite's antique bolt pistol and the throaty roar of Sergeant Hickox's chainsword revving up. To his right he saw a burly greyback thrashing about with his bayoneted lasrifle, holding back the crazies while another knelt beside him, snapping off wild rounds into the teeming horde. To his left he saw Belknap go down, his face split wide open by a meat cleaver. His killer, a mountainous matron with a bone-white mane, waved her weapon about and howled triumphantly. Cutler put two bullets into her skull and she toppled like a felled tree.

'Give no quarter!' Cutler bellowed.

Something tugged at his arm from below, sending his pistol tumbling away. He glanced down and saw a scrawny girl child latched onto his wrist, trying to gnaw through the heavy fabric of his greatcoat. She had the face of a shrivelled crone and her eyes were sewn shut. With a cry of revulsion he pulled his arm away, but the urchin clung on and came with it, her feet kicking the air as he tried to shake her loose. The meat shield pinned to his sabre was coming apart under the axe man's blows so he let the sword go, sidestepping as the madman toppled forward under his own momentum. With his free hand he wrenched the child loose and threw her through a broken window. Then Waite was at his side, tearing into the horde with explosive bolt-rounds. It bought Cutler a moment to retrieve his sabre.

'Form up around me, Arkan!' Cutler yelled, beheading the axe man as he clambered to his knees. 'Fall back in good order!' Three men had gone down in the first onslaught, but the survivors held their nerve admirably, pulling together into a tight phalanx and covering every approach as they backed away down the street. Hickox cleared their path with his buzzing chainsword while the others kept the horde at bay with pistols and bayonets.

'What's got into these wretches?' Waite shouted as he ejected a spent clip, but the revulsion in his voice told Cutler he had already guessed the truth. While civil war had raged across their world, another, more insidious madness had taken root in this forsaken town. The soul taint had come to Providence.

A cadaverous hag leapt from a window overhead in a shatter of glass. Screeching manically she landed on Trooper Dawson's back and clung on with her scrawny legs. He thrashed about frantically as she clawed at his face, sending the man beside him skidding to the ground. Seeing an opening, the horde rushed in like wolves, leaping over their dead in a frenzy of blissful bloodlust. A pitchfork nailed the fallen greyback through the back of the neck, pinning him to the snow. Another trooper hurried to fill the gap and caught a barbed pole in the gut. Dropping his weapon he clutched at the spear, his face frozen in shock. A moment later he was gone, tugged from the phalanx by his unseen assailant.

'I'm through 'em!' Hickox called from the back.

Cutler glanced round and saw the sergeant standing over a heap of slaughtered degenerates. With visibility down to a few metres there was no telling what lay in the street beyond, but it was their best chance. The defensive phalanx was disintegrating under the sheer weight of the horde and once the crazies got in amongst them it would be over.

'Disengage!' Cutler bellowed. 'Withdraw at speed!'

Run... It was a bitter order to give, but the alternative was suicide and they had to live through this. The cancer they had stumbled upon here must not be allowed to spread.

'Move yourselves!' Cutler slashed about in a wide arc as the surviving greybacks raced past Hickox. Waite was still at his side, firing two-handed to control the violent bucking of his bolt pistol.

'Just like Yethsemane Falls, eh Ensor!' Waite growled,

knowing full well this was nothing like that honest bloodbath. Fearing it might be something infinitely worse.

'Get clear!' Sergeant Hickox yelled behind them as he threw a grenade over their heads. Cutler saw it fall among the throng and felt the concussion at his back as he spun and ran, pushing Waite along in front of him. The frag grenade tore through the close-packed townsfolk like a shredding wind, throwing mangled bodies into the air and bowling others from their feet. It didn't stem the tide for more than a few heartbeats, but it was enough for the battered platoon to vanish into the blizzard.

As they raced through the streets, Cutler heard the frustrated howls of the cheated ghouls loping after them. Trooper Dawson was just ahead with the hag still clinging to his shoulders like a crazed jockey. He kept flailing at her as he ran, protecting his bleeding face but unable to dislodge her. Cutler caught up with him and swept away her head with a surgical slash of his sabre, but her legs remained locked tight. Abruptly Dawson giggled and threw him a broken look. One of his eyes had been gouged out and the other was wide with madness. Then the big greyback whirled around and ran back the way they had come, ignoring Cutler's shouts. He made to follow, but Waite pulled him back.

'He's gone, Ensor!'

A shutter flew open alongside the squad and a shotgun flared in the darkness beyond. The vox-set on Quinney's back exploded, sending him sprawling into the snow. Waite put a burst of fire through the window while Cutler stooped to haul the injured man over his shoulders. Then they were running again, storming through the town gates with hell on their heels. A wooden sign flashed past. It was wormy with rot, but the crudely carved words were still legible:

'WELCOME TO TRINITY – Pop. 487'

Not any more, Cutler thought grimly.
Not on either count.

The prisoner awoke to the sound of his own ragged laughter. Blinded by the sudden brightness he felt himself falling again. This time he held on, pushing away oblivion as he struggled with the straps binding him to the high-backed chair. Finally the glare resolved itself into a padded cell and he remembered that he was still…

…dreaming.

There was an alien staring at him through a shimmering force barrier. Its face was a wizened wedge of faded blue, unmistakably ancient, but its eyes were bright with fascination.

'Welcome, Colonel Ensor Cutler,' the xenos said in perfect Gothic. 'I am Por'o Dal'yth Seishin of the Wintertide Concordance and it is my sincere aspiration that you and I shall walk in friendship.'

CHAPTER EIGHT

Day 44 – The Coil: Adrift
Reve is right. We are completely lost.

Iverson's Journal

'If you do not know your place in the Tau'va, you do not know yourself. And if you do not know yourself you have no place at all.'

Winter's Tide

Claiborne Roach battered his way through another wall of clinging fronds and burst into the clearing beyond. His breath came in short, ragged gasps now, trying to keep time with his hammering heart. The rain thundered down in an angry barrage, churning the soil into treacherous mulch, but he didn't dare slow his breakneck pace. His pursuers were too close. He could hear them crashing through the foliage and calling to each other, no more than thirty paces at his back. He'd cut the chase fine, but sometimes a man had to play for all or nothing.

With a whine of displaced air a tau drone shot by overhead and spun to scope him. He threw the hovering disc a grin as he raced forward, flashing past the coral corpse at the centre of the clearing. The ruin was little more than a broken stub, but it was enough to sterilise almost twenty square metres of jungle. And it was more than enough for his plan.

He heard a triumphant shout as the first of the Concordance janissaries broke into the clearing and spotted him. Fine beams of markerlight lanced around him as he hurtled towards the trees ahead. Dredging up a last burst of speed he dived for cover, ducking under the lattice of violet fire that swept after him. Rolling to his knees, he tore his carbine free and swung round, but it was already over.

As the janissaries raced past the ruin, Roach's comrades rose from behind the coral and unleashed an enfilade of their own markerlight into their backs. The hunters' weapons deactivated in a bleeping tide of mock kills, taking them out of the game in quick succession. Their leader swore and threw down his dead carbine as Roach ambled back from the foliage to join his victorious cluster. Mister Fish met him with a grin and they slapped hands like old gang buddies. And truth to tell, the Saathlaa guide *was* the closest thing Roach had had to a friend in years. The *askari* had told him his real name once, but 'Mister Fish' had already stuck and the native didn't seem to mind it. Life would be a whole heap easier if more folk just went with the flow like the Fish, Roach reckoned.

'That was well done, Friend Roach,' Ricardo Alvarez, the leader of their cluster declared. 'Your skill in the field almost compensates for your doubts about the *Tau'va*.'

'Doubts keep a man sharp,' Roach quipped.

'*Kauyon*,' someone said behind them, speaking in an

inflectionless electronic monotone. They turned and Roach squinted, hunting for their hidden observer. He nodded in satisfaction as he spotted a vaguely humanoid shimmer lurking at the edge of the clearing. The translucent shape looked like it had been sculpted out of thin air by the rain; in other conditions the tau stealth suit would have been almost invisible.

'You honour us, Shas'ui Jhi'kaara,' Alvarez said with a bow, acknowledging the tau's compliment. *Kauyon*, which loosely translated as 'the Patient Hunter' was one of the two fundamental philosophies of the tau art of war. It was an approach dedicated to stealth and cunning, stressing the use of a lure to entrap the enemy.

'It was a passable execution of the principle, but you risked much,' the rain-shadow continued. 'If your foe had fielded pathfinders the ruse would have failed.'

'They were cocky,' Roach said. 'I knew they'd fall for it.'

The shape flickered then blurred into solidity, revealing a compact black battlesuit with a hefty burst cannon attached to its right arm. To Roach the xenos looked like a bulkier, better armoured Fire Warrior rather than a stealth operative, but as with all things tau its advantage lay with techno-wizardry. Although there was no arguing with the effectiveness of the suit's integrated distortion field, Roach didn't regard it as *real* scout-craft.

'And you, Janissary Roach,' the tau said, 'were you not equally… *cocky*?'

Recalling the grin he'd flashed the observer drone, Roach shrugged affably. 'Like I said, I know my business, *shaz-wee*,' he answered, stumbling over the alien honorific.

'You are gifted with spirit, but crippled by arrogance,' the tau observed.

'It's not like that,' Roach said, surprised he cared enough to argue.

Staring into that inscrutable, crystal-studded faceplate, he found himself wondering what Jhi'kaara actually looked like. Alvarez had said their officer was female, but that angular armour and toneless vox-coder gave nothing away. Nevertheless something about the alien's manner told Roach that Jhi'kaara was indeed a she. She could sure be bitchy as hell when the mood took her, which was all too often. Whatever else she might be under all that plate, the lady was certainly one angry xenos.

'You will either live long or die quickly, Janissary Roach,' Jhi'kaara concluded before amplifying her voice to address the rival clusters. 'This exercise is ended. We will return to the Diadem.'

And then she was gone.

Alvarez slapped Roach on the back and grinned, 'I think our shas'ui likes you, Friend Roach!'

The Cuttlefish troop transport nosed its way through the clinging smog, skimming just above the surface of the lake. Its whirring anti-grav rotors barely stirred the turgid expanse of water.

Dead water, Roach thought. Mister Fish had told him the place was called *Amrythaa*, which meant 'Wellspring of Life', but Roach guessed things must have changed a whole lot since the ancient Saathlaa had done their naming. The great lake was virtually an inland ocean, but its size didn't make it any less dead. Or any less rank…

Roach hawked and spat over the side of the vessel, adding a dram of black saliva to the ooze. The stench rising from the water was bad enough, but what really got to him was the smog. It hung over the entire valley, dusting the vegetation with soot and congealing into thick scum on the water's surface. The stuff got everywhere, making skin itch and throats burn, but there was no escaping it during the crossing. The tau had issued them all with rebreathers, but the cheap masks clogged up fast, making them worse than useless. Only the real arse-kissers persevered with them, always keen to suck up to their alien masters.

Of course those masters don't share our misery, Roach observed sourly, glancing at the armoured xenos standing at the prow of the skimmer. Doubtless Jhi'kaara's helmet was equipped with a proper filtration system, unlike the mass-produced junk doled out to the human grunts. Still, at least she showed her charges a little respect, unlike the rest of the blueskins on the Diadem.

The Diadem. Now there was another screwed-up, high-faluting name for a place. Guido Ortega had explained that 'diadem' was a fancy word for 'crown', but there was nothing regal about the Mechanicus monument that crowned the dead lake. In fact the massive refinery was just about the ugliest thing Roach had ever set eyes on. Hidden deep within the Coil, the rig dated back to Phaedra's first pacification, making it almost a thousand years old.

And it sure as the Hells looks its age…

Roach could see the relic looming out of the smog now, towering over the lake on a frame of stilts and pipes like a colossal jellyfish cast in iron and rockrete. Its mantle was a puzzle-box of manufactories and hab-tenements that bristled with chimney stacks and coolant towers, all bound together in a web of pipes and catwalks. The visible section was as big as a town, but Roach knew the monster's tendrils ran deep beneath the water, piercing the silt lakebed and burrowing into the living coral like an industrial vampire. Down there they were busily sucking the blood out of the planet and pumping it back up to the distilleries to be sifted and refined into promethium. In return the engine threw out waste on an epic scale, flooding the valley with toxic slag and smoke.

No wonder Lady Phaedra hates us so much, Roach thought. *We've been ripping out Her guts for centuries. Compared to us the tau are just gnats. Even if they have stolen our thunder here...*

As they drew closer to the monster he heard its heart pounding – a deep, hungry beat that rippled through his blood and set his teeth chattering. Like the smoke, the rhythm was at its most painful out in the open where there was no cover. Soon enough the vomiting began, running through the janissaries like a tide of nausea, with poor Ortega suffering the worst of it. Roach saw the elderly Verzante hugging the side of the boat, looking shockingly grey and drawn. The once portly pilot had slimmed down and toughened up since he'd thrown in with the Arkan, but he was just too old for this kind of punishment. Roach decided he'd talk to Alvarez about letting him sit out Jhi'kaara's endless games. Rumour had it she was looking to recruit a batch of trainee pathfinders, but Ortega was never going to make the grade, so why push him? Besides, if the old man's heart gave out Roach's own plans would be well and truly fragged.

Suddenly a wave of dazzling light cut through the smog, casting the world into a negative image of itself. The janissaries shielded their eyes, but the beam passed by in seconds, swept away as the titanic lamp continued its steady rotation. Mounted in the apex of the Diadem, the great beacon was like a tireless eye that watched over the lake for approaching enemies. Uneasily Roach wondered if the sentinel could see right through him. As if to confirm his anxieties, the transport was swathed in light again as the floodlights of a Devilfish punched through the mist. Roach found himself holding his breath as the hover tank pulled up alongside them and disgorged an inquisitive drone. Jhi'kaara's own drone rose to greet it with a burst of machine chatter and the guardian slinked away satisfied.

It's just routine, Roach chided himself. *I should be used to it by now.*

He had been at the Diadem nearly a month now and was no stranger to this journey, but it still unsettled him. He'd counted at least six Devilfish prowling the lake, their patrol intersected by darting Piranha skimmers and twittering squadrons of gun drones. A heavier tank lurked by the feet of the rig, tracking their approach with a massive turret-mounted ion cannon. Alvarez had told him the Hammerhead was a tank killer, a variant on the standard Devilfish that sacrificed transport capacity to pack more punch. Eyeing that big gun, Roach guessed even a glancing hit would take out a Sentinel. The xenos were taking no chances here.

I've never seen so many blueskins in one place, he mused. *Maybe it's just the promethium they're after or maybe it's something more, but this old rig is important to them. It might even be their HQ in the Coil…*

The transport glided into the nest of piers splayed around the refinery like lazy tentacles and nosed its way towards an empty berth. Hulking, heavily armoured combat servitors patrolled the promenade, gliding back and forth on elegantly moulded anti-gravity skirts. Their heads were little more than nubs of dead meat protruding from iron torsos, hanging between their massive shoulder pads like dried fruit. Roach shuddered at the sight of their sightless, milk-white eyes. By any yardstick that counted, servitors were dead men, mind-wiped and melded with machines to serve as soulless thralls to the Imperium.

Except these walking corpses aren't even walking and they sure don't serve the Imperium no more...

While all servitors were mongrels of man and machine, these creatures were tri-part hybrids, twisted a notch further away from humanity by the touch of xenos-tech. The smooth contours of their anti-gravity skirts betrayed their alien origin, along with the burst cannons welded to their right arms and the drone antennae jutting from their skulls. Those high-tech plumes linked the dead men into the Diadem's security array, granting them an eerie sharpness that sickened Roach more than all the other violations heaped upon them. Sometimes he'd swear there was real hatred burning behind those cataract-encrusted eyes...

If the tau are so bloody enlightened, why didn't they scrap these poor bastards when they set up shop here instead of joining in with the fun?

But Roach already knew the answer to that one. His time among the Concordance had taught him plenty about the tau mindset. While many races fastened onto grand notions like honour, glory or righteous hate, the tau simply got on with the job of winning. For all their fine talk of the Greater Good they were hard-nosed pragmatists: a race of materialists who saw the world as an ornery, but essentially logical, place that could be chipped, whittled and sometimes just plain hammered into shape. More to the point, they hated waste and loved tinkering, hence the fate of the augmented zombies they'd 'inherited' at the Diadem.

Although technically the zombies don't belong to the tau, Roach reflected. *I guess the cogboys are still pulling their strings.*

The servitors weren't the only relics on the rig. There were a whole bunch of Mechanicus priests here, including a full-blown magos, backed up by an army of tech-guard – Alvarez called them *'skitarii'*. These augmented heavies were the rig's permanent garrison, as opposed to the janissary clusters who just passed through for training. At first Roach had been surprised to find the skitarii were all drawn from native Saathlaa stock, but given the age of the Diadem it made perfect sense. The original off-world soldiers would have died out long ago, forcing the priests to recruit – or more likely enslave – replacements locally.

Of course the priests themselves were a different matter. Such men had the knowledge to make themselves virtually immortal, although the price they paid might make them unrecognisable as men. After centuries of augmetic butchery there was no telling what Magos Kaul and his cronies were hiding under their flowing red robes, but Roach doubted it would be anything he'd call human.

I still don't know what the deal is with this place. What have the cogboys been doing here for all these centuries? Were they stranded after the first pacification lost steam or did they want *to stay? And what about now? Are they working alongside the tau or are they just glorified slaves like the rest of us?*

As he hauled himself up onto the pier, Roach realised he was still a long way off cracking the Diadem's secret. Probably he never would.

'Subject 11 persists in obfuscating my endeavours to establish a rapport, habitually retreating behind a barrier of atavistic hostility.' Por'o Dal'yth Seishin paused to gather his thoughts, steepling his fingers in an oddly human gesture. 'He presents a most perplexing, yet compelling paradox.'

Perched cross-legged on the padded dome of a floating throne drone, the tau Water Caste ambassador had the look of a mystic immersed in some profound meditation. His emaciated body was swathed in an azure robe of shimmering silk that flared into a rigid, high-backed collar to frame his hairless skull. Although his face was little more than a wedge of bone wrapped in grey parchment, his black eyes shone with vigour. At eighty-three he was an ancient, his lifespan extended well beyond the natural limits of his species thanks to Magos Kaul's juvenat techniques. Doubtless some of his more orthodox colleagues would disapprove of such artificial longevity, but O'Seishin knew it was all for the Greater Good. He had entered the Fi'drash conundrum at its inception and would see the matter through to its logical conclusion. However, if everything proceeded according to plan that would be a very long time coming.

'As I have posited previously, the gue'la are afflicted by a racial predilection towards extreme psychoses,' he continued. 'I would further postulate that the fungal pathogens contaminating this planet's atmosphere might induce a psychotropic response in emotionally charged individuals...'

There was a chime at the chamber door and O'Seishin sighed. 'Suspend recording,' he ordered his attendant data drone. 'Come.'

The scarred warrior who entered offered only the hint of a bow. It was a slight from one of her rank; she was a veteran of the Fire Caste, but he had attained the pinnacle of his own. While tau society attached no stigma to those of lower rank, experience was to be respected and obeyed. In the absence of a ranking Fire Warrior he was her superior.

'You summoned me, O'Seishin,' Jhi'kaara said, using his personal name with impudent familiarity.

'That is so, shas'ui,' O'Seishin answered, countering her disrespect with perfect courtesy. 'Regrettably your request for reassignment to front line service has been denied. It seems your most excellent mentoring of the gue'vesa neophytes precludes it. Your talents are too valuable to place in jeopardy.'

And you are best placed precisely where I can see you, he thought.

'I am a warrior,' she said bitterly. 'I was born to fight.'

'Correction: you were born to fight for the Greater Good,' O'Seishin said smoothly. 'And for the time being the Greater Good requires you to forge capable janissaries.' His nostrils flared in the tau approximation of a smile. 'I do however have some good news for you. Your achievements here have been recognised by the shas'el and he has approved your promotion to the rank of shas'vre.'

'What of my request to meet with the shas'el?' There wasn't a trace of gratitude in her tone. O'Seishin frowned, finally becoming exasperated by her insolence.

'It is in process,' he said, 'but the acting commander is burdened by manifold and onerous responsibilities. Be assured that he will summon you in due course.'

'It has been many *rotaa* since I reported the gue'la's treachery at the Shell,' Jhi'kaara urged. 'I swore an oath of consequence to my comrades when they died.'

'Shas'el Aabal has been informed of your concerns. In the meantime I have requested an XV8 battlesuit for you, shas'vre.'

'That is unnecessary–' she began.

'*It is necessary*,' he snapped. 'According to the records you are battlesuit trained and you are now the ranking Fire Warrior here. You must be prepared for any eventuality.' He glanced at the chronolog on his data drone: his session with Subject 11 was due shortly. 'Regrettably I must excuse myself, shas'vre. I am also burdened with multifarious responsibilities in service of the Greater Good.'

* * *

'No, friend Roach, you're still not getting it. The Greater Good, it don't work that way,' Alvarez urged. 'It's something new, man. Something better than the lies the aristos and the padres been telling us since forever.'

'I see that, but grunts like you and me, we still don't matter none,' Roach said. 'Sure, these tau boys treat us decent enough – a whole lot better than the patricians did back home – but that don't mean they *care* about us.'

'They gave me back my voice, Friend.' Alvarez tapped his scarred neck. It was an old wound and a favourite parable of the Verzante deserter. 'I told you how that crazy commissar busted me up real bad, right? So why did the tau put me back together if I don't matter?'

There were murmurs of agreement from the other Concordance janissaries gathered in the dormitory. Mister Fish looked uneasy and Ortega threw Roach a warning glance, but he ignored them both, too irritated to back down.

'They fixed you up because you're a good soldier,' he insisted. 'You're *useful* to them, but you're still just a cog in the Big Machine, just like you was back in the Imperium.'

'No, we're talking a whole different *kind* of machine here, Friend Roach,' Alvarez said. 'Sure I'm a cog, but so are the Fire Warriors and the Water Speakers – even the Ethereals themselves. See, we're all in this together, everyone doing their bit for the Greater Good. And we're in it because we believe, not because some crazy *pendejo* in black leather is holding a gun to our heads.'

'And they don't judge a man by his blood,' Estrada piped up, nodding meaningfully at an obese Verzante slumped on a bunk. 'Else fat Olim over there would still be calling all the shots.'

'That's right!' Alvarez was nodding furiously. 'The tau reward a man by what he can do, not the clan he's born into.'

'But that don't go for the tau themselves,' Roach said triumphantly. Seeing their blank faces he pressed on. 'I mean for *them* it all comes down to how they're born, right? A tau that's born a warrior won't get to build anything and one that's born a builder won't get to fight, no matter how angry he gets. Every caste is a prison they can't ever escape.'

'Why would a warrior want to build anything?' Estrada seemed genuinely confused.

'The newcomer is implying that your logic is flawed, Señor Estrada,' the pariah, Olim observed languidly. 'He is actually rather bright for a peasant.'

'You say something back there, aristo?' Estrada snarled, rounding on the fallen nobleman. Olim cringed, instinctively shielding the bruised potato of his face.

'Be easy, Friend Estrada,' Alvarez restrained his comrade. 'Friend Olim already knows his place in the *Tau'va*.' He flashed a benign smile at the cowering noble. 'The latrines will need cleaning before you start your shift in the comms tower. Don't disappoint me now, Friend Olim.'

Olim scurried away like a plump mouse, keeping his distance from the others as Alvarez turned his smile on Roach: 'As for you, Friend Roach, you're still new to our cluster and have a way to go, but you got to open up your mind…'

'That's what I keep telling him,' Ortega said, ambling over with a conciliatory smile. 'But will he listen?' He gave Roach a pointed glare and the scout shrugged helplessly. Ortega had indeed warned him repeatedly against baiting their fellow janissaries, but Roach still kept walking into the same old arguments. The crazy thing was he *liked* Alvarez and the rest of them. Sometimes he even caught himself thinking there might actually be something to their whole Greater Good deal.

'We must make allowances,' Ortega continued. 'I fear these Arkan churls don't have the wit and wisdom of Verzante Seabloods like you or I, Friend Alvarez.'

'That's no excuse, Friend Ortega. Just look at his kinsman over there.' Alvarez indicated another neophyte whose face was buried in a laminated copy of *Winter's Tide*. 'He's picking up the path real quick. Isn't that so, Friend?'

The reader looked up and his disfigured face broke into a gap-toothed grin: 'For the Greater Good,' Jakob Dix drawled. 'Damn straight.'

'It ain't right,' Audie Joyce growled over the inter-suit vox. 'We've been watching these xenos-loving heretics near on a month now, but we're still skulking in the hills like jackals. This ain't what the God-Emperor forged us for!'

There was a crackling chorus of assent from the other Zouave knights hidden along the ridge. They were spread out in a loose line overlooking the smog-choked lake far below, keeping watch on the activity around the rebel base. All they could see of the refinery itself was the slow gyration of its beacon light, but their vantage point took in the connecting waterways, revealing a restless flow of ships back and forth between the lake and the rest of the Coil.

'We've found the heart of the cancer, brothers!' Joyce went on fervently. 'How long must we wait to burn it out?'

Captain Machen frowned, once again regretting the arrogant greencap's promotion to the Zouave brotherhood. 'We'll wait as long as it takes, boy,' he said. 'The colonel will send word when it's time.'

'No disrespect intended sir, but he's probably skrabmeat by now,' Joyce said.

'Ensor Cutler is alive. If he was dead *she* would know.'

'And you'd trust the word of a Norland witch, captain?' Machen blanched at the scorn in the youth's voice. 'emperor's Blood, she might even be working for the blueskins!'

Once again the Zouaves lent Joyce their support and Machen gritted his teeth, biting clean through his unlit cigar. The boy had only been among the Steamblood Brotherhood five months, yet the old guard was rallying around him as if he was some kind of hero. Joyce's meteoric rise had exceeded Machen's worst fears about opening up the brotherhood to commoners, but there had been no choice.

During their first weeks on Phaedra the Arkan had been hit hard by the planet's more insidious taints. Fever and fungal infections had swept through their ranks like wildfire, laying almost everyone low. Thirty-three men had never recovered, including two of Machen's Zouaves, leaving him with eleven warsuits and just nine nobles to wear them. Forced to recruit from the common greybacks, he had been determined to find the best.

Unfortunately the *very* best had proven to be a rookie from Dustsnake squad whose passion for the Imperial creed bordered on stupidity. His comrades had taken to calling Joyce 'the Preacher' and most were only half-joking. The youth's brand of hellfire rhetoric was backed up by true grit, winning him plenty of admirers, while his apparent immunity to Phaedra's ailments had sealed his status as a rising regimental legend. Machen, who still suffered from a dozen disorders, detested him with the malice of a fading alpha wolf. If the boy hadn't been so damnably talented he would have weeded him out long ago, but his instinct for the iron was uncanny. Within weeks of his initiation Joyce had been throwing his armour around like a veteran. A month later he'd surpassed the lesser knights. After that it had been too late to expel him.

'The Emperor has blessed our flesh with iron and our hearts with fire,' Joyce was ranting. 'I won't hang my fate on the ravings of a barbarian witch!'

'That's enough, boy!' Machen snapped, furious to be defending the woman, who he personally despised. 'The colonel trusts her and she's led us true so far. We've no cause to doubt her now.' He could almost taste the friction on the vox-band, but Joyce had just enough sense to shut up. Wrestling down his irritation Machen levelled his voice. 'We're the steel backbone of the 19th, not a pack of greencap hotheads fired up by the Gospel. We've got our orders and we'll stand by them. If we throw that away we're nothing but renegades.'

'He's back,' Valance's voice crackled into his ear over a secure channel. 'Just got into camp this minute, captain.'

Machen acknowledged the scout and stalked away, leaving Wade in command. His old wingman was the only Zouave who hadn't bought into the boy preacher's mystique – the only one who was still loyal to the old order. Stomping down the other side of the ridge he wondered how things had become so hellfired complicated. How had he ended up backing Ensor bloody Cutler and speaking up for his Norland whore? The Machen of old would have been champing at the bit to turn the tables on them both and make a play for command. In truth he'd have shared the boy's eagerness to take the battle into the valley. What had changed?

Ringing in the changes, like a cawing, clawing canticle of crows heralding damnation valley, where dead men come to cast the die…

Machen snorted at the words that had slithered into his head like leeches. The Seven Hells take Ambrose Templeton and his confounded ramblings! Machen supposed it was guilt that had prompted him to keep the notebook left behind by the vanished captain. They had never been friends – far from it in fact

– but there was no denying that Templeton had proved to be an able leader on their first day in this hell, yet Machen had turned his back on him.

Go away, he'd said when the man had asked for help. And Templeton had. That was why Machen had begun to read his notebook and somehow never stopped. He always got lost somewhere around the halfway mark, where the tale turned slippery, its meaning contorting upon itself and forcing him to go back and reread from the start. Over and over again...

Am I haunted by a dead man's unfinished tale?

The thought made him shudder inside his carapace. Whatever the truth of it, Templeton's doomed epic had wormed its way into his soul, leaving him riddled with doubt. These days his thoughts kept drifting back to his lost wife and daughters, dragging him down to a horror that rage alone could no longer tame. Once again he swore to burn the treacherous book, knowing full well he never would.

'The risk is too great,' the witch insisted, her eyes boring into Vendrake like viridian suns. 'The forces arrayed against us at the Diadem are many and grievous. We cannot squander the Sentinels on this venture of yours.'

Exasperated, Vendrake threw himself down onto the stool opposite her. Skjoldis saw that his hand shook as he wiped the sweat from his sallow, stubble-smeared face. It was sweltering hot in the cramped cabin, but the Sentinel captain was used to such things.

What he isn't used to is being on the wrong side, she reflected. *Even if he understands that the wrong side is actually the right side.*

The regiment's self-imposed exile had been difficult on all of them, but Hardin Vendrake had taken it harder than most. For all his rakish posturing he was an idealist and idealists had further to fall. Certainly the ragged apparition slumped across from her was a far cry from the dashing patrician officer of old. With his unruly hair strangled up in a red bandana he looked more like a feral jungle fighter than a graduate of the Capitol Academy.

Especially with that indigo stain in his eyes…

'Captain, I have asked you to abstain from the Glory,' she said. 'The fungus carries a taint.'

'And I've told *you* the Glory keeps me sharp,' he shot back with a sickly grin. The tension between them had eased after she saved his life back at the Shell. Sometimes she even felt they were drifting towards a brittle friendship, but he still didn't trust her.

And why should he when the Whitecrow and I have kept our secrets so close? We should have told him about Abel long ago. He deserves the truth.

'When did you last sleep?' Skjoldis asked.

'Look, I'm touched by your concern witch, but that's not why I came to see you.' Vendrake leaned forward, glaring right into her face. 'We have to bail this commissar out.'

'If you save him he will almost certainly turn on you,' Skjoldis said with a sigh. 'Such men are not renowned for their forbearance, captain.'

'But he's flying the Seven Stars. And he has the look of an Arkan. I think he wants to talk.'

'Or he plans to trick you.'

'It's a chance we have to take,' Vendrake urged. 'We've been playing Cutler's game almost nine months now, wandering around the Coil like pawns on a regicide board, chasing after a redemption only the two of you seem to understand…'

'And I have promised you that the endgame is in sight.'

'That's not enough anymore!' he snarled, showing stained

teeth. Drawn by the captain's anger, Mister Frost loomed out of the shadows behind him. Skjoldis shook her head and her hulking guardian faded away, but Vendrake had caught the movement. Since their exile he had grown almost preternaturally sensitive to the slightest movement at his back, almost as if he were afraid something was creeping up on him. Or *galloping* up on him, she sensed in a frisson of psychic empathy.

He still blames himself for the death of his protégé.

'You must calm yourself, captain,' Skjoldis said with a peculiar sense of déjà vu. Did a streak of madness run through every Arkan officer? Was it her doom to play nursemaid to one tortured patrician after another?

'The men are running out of hope, witch.'

'And you believe that a commissar can give them hope?'

'I believe he can give them *legitimacy*,' Vendrake hissed. Seeing her scorn he slumped back and closed his eyes, hovering at the edge of exhaustion.

She waited.

'Beauregard Van Hal,' he said in a whisper. 'You won't know the name because he keeps himself to himself, but he's probably my finest rider. Might not have a whole lot going on up there,' Vendrake tapped his temple, 'but he's loyal to a fault and born to the cavalry.'

'I do not follow your meaning.'

He silenced her with a weary hand. 'The other day Van Hal asked me why we were fighting the rebels when it was the Imperium who wanted our hides. He was wondering why we didn't just sign up with the tau like all the other sorry dregs who've been screwed over in this mess. You know what I said?' He opened his eyes and looked at her with a terrible blankness. 'I didn't say a damn thing.'

'Vendrake, you need to be patient. The Diadem is what we've

been searching for. Once the colonel sends word...'

'It'll be too late,' he shook his head. 'No, woman, we need something *now*. Maybe you're right and this commissar will prove to be another bloody zealot, but he's the only shot we have.'

Still brooding, Machen strode back into camp. Brushing off the sentries' half-hearted calls for a password he wove through the sprawl of habtents, making for the flotilla of ships moored along the riverbank. They were a miserable sight: most of the stolen gunboats and transports were little more than rust-bitten shells on their last legs. Much like the regiment itself, he mused grimly. There were some three hundred and fifty men gathered here, virtually all that remained of the eight hundred who had left Providence a lifetime ago. These Arkan were survivors, but they were also ghosts...

Crooked shadows lost on the crow road from Despair to Delirium...

Angrily Machen shook Templeton out of his skull, struggling to focus on the facts, but tone and texture kept slipping back in, hinting at meanings he didn't need – or want – to see. Every one of the greybacks was lean to the point of starvation, with bloodshot eyes that either blinked too much or didn't blink at all...

Facing oblivion with a twitch or a stare, souls laid bare to the empty one-way mirrors of fate and fortune squandered...

Most were suffering from multiple afflictions – foot rot or gutrot, mire fever or swamp burn, greyscale rash or splinter-skin... The roll call of Phaedra's petty torments was as endless as the windings of the Coil, but misery was the only constant amongst the troops. Only the proud Burning Eagles of the 1st Company still had the look of a coherent unit. Their bronze raptor helms and para-armour had withstood the rigours of the Mire while the uniforms of the common soldiers had sloughed away, forcing each man to improvise his apparel as best he could. Many had scavenged synthetic fatigues or flak armour from dead janissaries, stubbornly scrubbing away the rebel insignia. A few had gone further and salvaged fragments of tau armour. Although the xenos breastplates were too small for a man, the pauldrons and tessellated greaves were serviceable. Even the helmets could be made to fit with a little work. Cully, the one-eyed rogue from Dustsnake squad, appeared to be on a mission to rebuild himself as a patchwork Fire Warrior. The veteran had a knack for tech and had even got some of the targeting optics in his pilfered helmet working. Many such opportunists had also adopted the lighter, punchier carbines of the janissaries, with Cully sporting a prized rail rifle.

The more devout men shunned such heretical gear and stuck with their sturdy Providence-pattern lasrifles. Following the example of their *askari* guides they had woven rough garments from animal skins and vines that made them look wilder than the savages back home. But despite the tangle of xenos and native junk, every man wore scraps of his Arkan heritage: a threadbare jacket here, crimson-striped breeches there... polished rhineskin belts and harnesses... flat-topped kepi caps bearing the ram's skull icon of the Confederacy, carved from bone as was the regimental custom...

Pirates! We look like Throne-forsaken pirates, Machen reflected miserably.

'He's with the witch,' Valance said, interrupting the captain's reverie. Machen snorted, irritated that the scout had crept up on him. It was uncanny how such a big man could move so quietly. Nevertheless, the scout was one of the few greybacks he still trusted.

'Stormed into camp in an all-fired hurry,' Valance continued.

'Went straight to her. It ain't seemly, especially with her being the colonel's lady and all.'

Machen nodded inside his helmet, recognising the Sentinel standing beside Cutler's command boat. Vendrake had been gone nearly two days, shadowing the idiot commissar who had followed them into the Coil. He didn't understand his fellow captain's obsession with their pursuer and he didn't much care, but it was intolerable that he'd gone gallivanting off into the jungle when so much was at stake. They had put their differences aside in Cutler's absence, working together to keep the regiment afloat, but Vendrake's vices had eaten away his brains. It was time to have things out with the degenerate.

As Despair sows Delirium so Delirium sows Discord...

'Shut the Hells up you dead bastard!' Machen snarled. Ignoring Valance's quizzical look he marched towards the command boat.

'Our plan hangs on a knife edge of synchronicity,' Skjoldis insisted. 'What if he calls and your Sentinels are not here, Vendrake?'

'So ask him,' the captain said. 'I know you can do it. It's how you've coordinated things since they took him.'

'It is not so simple. He is no psyker. At this distance it is difficult to touch his mind – and painful for him. We have agreed times...'

'Well, that's too bad because the commissar's time is running out. The man is sailing right into the bloody Meatlocker,' Vendrake hissed. 'Do you have any idea what's waiting for him there?'

'I–'

'Vendrake!' Machen bawled from the shore. 'Vendrake, get your fungus-addled arse off that boat! We need to talk!'

Skjoldis glanced towards the cabin door, but Vendrake gripped her wrist urgently.

'Ask him!'

Subject 11 groaned and began to shudder, struggling against the restraints that bound him to the chair. His eyes were screwed tight shut in a face wracked by an agony of concentration. Alarmed by the seizure, Por'o Dal'yth Seishin skimmed backwards on his throne drone. Although a force barrier separated him from his prisoner, the ambassador had not lived so long without exalting prudence.

'*Do it...*' the prisoner hissed. A crimson trickle oozed from his right nostril. 'Go get him.' Suddenly his head snapped backwards and he looked directly at O'Seishin, his eyes gleaming with sly malice.

'Trinity remembers!' he roared in a savage croak. Then he slumped lifelessly in his chair. O'Seishin watched the man uncertainly, but he didn't stir. Cautiously the ambassador hovered back to the barrier.

'Do you require medical assistance?' the tau asked. The prisoner's eyes flicked open and gazed at him through a tangle of white hair. 'Your meaning eluded me,' O'Seishin pressed, debating whether to retreat again. 'Who was it you wished me to get?'

'I was just thinking out loud,' the exhausted man wheezed, straightening up with an effort. 'Us humans, we do that sometimes. Especially the crazy ones.'

'Our assessments would indicate that your cognitive faculties are unimpaired,' O'Seishin said. 'You do however exhibit symptoms of severe personality disorder, perhaps even latent schizophrenia...'

'Glad to know it,' the prisoner snorted.

'Indeed, knowing oneself is the first and final step to enlightenment, my friend.'

'I'm no friend to you, blueskin.'

'I concede that this is so, yet I aspire to overcome our differences, Ensor Cutler,' O'Seishin said.

'You know, you talk real fancy for a xenos pen-pusher, Si.'

'My thanks, it is the calling I was born to.'

Cutler chuckled, the sound low and mocking.

'You believe I do not understand sarcasm, Ensor Cutler?' The tau's nostrils flared in amusement. 'You are mistaken. I am of the Water Caste and as I have previously stated, communication is my calling.' O'Seishin paused, then finished more haltingly: 'You-son-of-a-bitch.'

This time Cutler's laugh was genuine.

'But you...' the tau said, leaning forward on his floating perch. 'You choose to communicate in the manner of an obtuse barbarian, which you most assuredly are not. Why do you persist in this fabrication?'

'Full of questions today aren't we, Si?'

'It is–'

'Your calling! Yeah I already got that part,' Cutler said. 'Look, why don't you just send in the *bad* xenos and get started on the needles and shockwires or whatever it is you blueskins use to get answers, because I've got nothing to say to you.'

'There are no bad agents of the Greater Good,' O'Seishin replied primly. 'Such would be a contradiction.'

'Well, what about Wintertide then?' Cutler suggested. 'Why don't you send in the big chief and maybe I'll talk to him, one soldier to another.'

'Perhaps I am Commander Wintertide.'

'And I'm the Sky Marshall.' Abruptly Cutler cast off his brash mask and was all business. 'Why are we talking, Por'o Dal'yth Seishin?'

The tau considered the question. This was his eleventh interview with the renegade commander, yet they were no closer to a rapport. He reviewed the facts once again: Cutler had been captured almost a month ago, betrayed by a squad of his own men who had grown weary of their piratical existence. For nearly two weeks he had raved in his cell like a savage, throwing himself against the force barrier and refusing food until O'Seishin had indeed doubted his sanity. Then, seemingly from one moment to the next, he had become deadly calm. After that O'Seishin had begun the interviews and the duel for Cutler's mind had begun.

'Look, I don't know where my men are or what they're up to,' Cutler said. 'And I if did, I sure as Hells wouldn't pass it on to you.'

'Your comrades are irrelevant,' the tau murmured, still lost in thought. 'Since your capture they have caused us no tribulation. We have concluded that their spirit is broken.'

'Then you're fools.'

You'll need strong men who haven't forgotten how to think, O'Seishin recalled the Sky Marshall telling him. Forget the zealots who'll die before they dream a new thought, or the fickle rabble who'll follow anything that promises change, then hanker after another change and another, until they've got nowhere left to go. Such folk are the fodder of humanity and all you'll build with them is a paper castle. But win the heart and mind of a man like Ensor Cutler and you'll have a true hero by your side. And where such men lead others will follow.

'What do you want from me, xenos?' Cutler urged.

O'Seishin's nostrils twitched in a wry smile. 'I want you to do what is right, Ensor Cutler.'

* * *

Skjoldis frowned as she watched Vendrake's taskforce depart. The regiment could ill afford to lose any of the precious machines. Despite the devotion of the tech-priests the Sentinels were dying, worn down by the Mire. The remaining eight were running on little more than cannibalised parts and prayer. Risking them on this fool's errand was insane, yet she couldn't find it in herself to blame Vendrake.

Tell me the truth about Trinity, the cavalry captain had urged once again. Tell me what really happened there?

The doubts eating him alive had been seeded long ago, but they had lain dormant, waiting for the right catalyst. Skjoldis didn't know if that catalyst had been his lost protégé or Phaedra Herself, but Vendrake was on the brink of madness. He deserved the truth – about Trinity and about Abel. She would have relented if Machen hadn't started hammering at the door, demanding his own answers.

The Zouave captain was still storming about the camp now, angry at Vendrake's snub and frightened by something else. Skjoldis supposed she should talk to him, but she was too weary. Weary and terribly afraid for the Whitecrow...

He has been alone with his daemons too long.

Her telepathic contact had taken the colonel by surprise and for a few brief moments his soul had been unguarded. In those moments she had looked below the surface and his daemons had looked right back and grinned.

Cutler was awoken by an ungodly shriek. Alarmed, he reached for his sabre, then realised the sound was only the wind whistling through the eves of the rickety old barn. The blizzard was still raging, threatening to tear down the shack where the platoon's survivors had gone to ground after their flight. They were on the outskirts of the tainted town, watching the road for the trailing bulk of the regiment and praying the crazed citizens wouldn't show up first. The tension in the draft-riddled shack was electric: every one of the greybacks here would have chosen the sane perils of wind and snow over the horrors just a stone's throw away, but Cutler had ordered them to sit tight.

'What's up, Ensor?' Waite asked. The seams in his walnut face were etched deeper by concern. 'For a moment there it looked like you weren't at home.'

'I was just thinking,' Cutler murmured.

Of doing what's right…

'We have to go back,' he said, his voice growing stronger as reality firmed up around him. 'We can't let this stand.'

'Ensor, that town is warp-touched,' the captain protested. 'Listen, Fort Garriot can't be much more than three days march from here. We can call this mess in from there and let the witch hunters deal with these degenerates. It's what they're trained for.'

'Providence can't carry this kind of shame, especially not after the uprisings,' Cutler said. 'We're in the Inquisition's bad books already.'

'You really think they'd get involved?'

'Make no mistake about it, those planet-murdering bastards are watching us like hawks.' Cutler shook his head grimly. 'They've let us put our own house in order so far, but if word gets out that we're not just ornery, but *tainted* with it…'

'But this is just one misbegotten slum in the boondocks!'

'Maybe that's how the fall always starts.' Cutler sighed. 'We can't take the chance, Elias. It was providence that led us here and it's for Providence that we'll return.'

'I see 'em!' Sergeant Hickox called from the upper floor. 'Our boys is coming up the road now!' There were brittle cheers from the other survivors gathered in the barn.

'I need to talk to the witch,' Cutler said, running a hand through his glossy black hair. 'Maybe she can give us an angle on this mess. Then we have to go back.' He squeezed his comrade's shoulder. 'It ends here, old friend. With us.'

CHAPTER NINE

Day 63 – The Coil: The Scarlet Dossier

Are we nearing the heart of the Coil or just sailing in circles? It is impossible to tell when nothing changes from one day to the next save the diminishing measure of our supplies. The only certainty is this grey-green limbo and the river running through it. That and the black joke the Sky Marshall has worked on us all.

I've finished studying Lomax's Scarlet Dossier and it's all there, the whole sorry debacle of this war mapped out in a damning geometry of incompetence, negligence and sheer madness. Every shred of evidence was annotated with the High Commissar's spidery scrawl and focussed into a sharp truth. Taken individually each folly might be dismissed as mere misfortune, but seen together they spelled out nothing less than wilful betrayal.

Consider the High Command of the Phaedran War Group. We are cursed with witless tyrants like General

'Ironfoot' Mroffel, who convinced himself that tanks could float and sent an armoured battalion to a watery grave; or aristocratic buffoons like Count Ghilles de Zhegal, who dallies with war like a colour-blind regicide player, confusing blueskins with greenskins and gunboats for gunships. And then there are the madmen like Vyodor Karjalan and Ao-Oleaus (who is known as the Clockwork Butcher for the obsessive timing of his doomed sallies). Of course the Imperium harbours many such fools and monsters in its darker corners, but here they have been nurtured to strangle any hope of victory stillborn.

And then there is the record of perverse strategic decisions that range from the anomalous to the outrageous. Why the blanket embargos on long-range shelling and flights across enemy territory? Why the preferred requisitioning of tanks over amphibious vehicles? And why was the offer of a brigade of Catachan Jungle Fighters turned down when such men were surely born to tame the Mire? Why... why... why? Question upon question, error upon error and every one of them spiralling back up to the Sky Marshall himself.

For years Lomax had been surreptitiously collating and cross-referencing Zebasteyn Kircher's follies, building a case she knew she'd never live to make. That's why she passed the torch on to me, the only person on Phaedra she still trusted. And that's why she sent me into the Mire after my kinfolk. They were never meant to be my quarry. They were meant to be my allies.

Iverson's Journal

'You know your problem, Holt? You think too fragging much,' Modine pronounced sagely. He laughed at the baleful glare

Iverson threw him. 'What? You got that look again, like you seen a spook or something?'

'Just answer my question, greyback,' Iverson said, trying not to gag on the stench wafting from the diseased man. Modine's condition had worsened steadily over the weeks and his make-shift cabin reeked of decay. In the gloom his face had the look of a crude coral sculpture and his fatigues bulged with something that wasn't quite muscle anymore.

'You saying you don't like hanging out with old Klete no more?' Modine said with feigned hurt. 'You ain't stopped by to see me in days, Holt.'

'I need to know if Cutler will hear me out,' Iverson pressed.

'Well it ain't like I ever knew the colonel personal like,' Modine said. 'The big boys never hung out with grunts like me.'

'But is he an honourable man?'

'From what I seen of him I reckon *he'd* say so.' Modine shrugged. 'Look, if he thinks you're straight up he'll likely back you, especially if you can clear his name.' He peered at Iverson suspiciously. 'Are you on the level about that part, Holt? You really going to wipe the slate clean for the 19th?'

'I have that authority,' Iverson said, the lies coming easily these days, 'but redemption has a price.'

'And what about me?' Modine said with sudden vehemence. 'Are you going to yank that sick frak Karjalan outta his web and haul him over the coals for what he done to me?'

'It's complicated…'

'Yeah, that's what I figured,' Modine spat.

'It's complicated, but yes. You have my word on it,' Iverson said, determined that this would be no lie. 'Vyodor Karjalan is a heretic and I'll see that he faces the Emperor's Justice for his crimes.'

Along with all the other monsters that have stalled this war and wasted so many Imperial lives.

Modine held his gaze for a long moment. Finally he nodded. 'Well then, me and Lady Hellfire's sweet daughter over there...' he pointed at the flamer Iverson had requisitioned for him, 'we've got your back all the way.'

Day 65 – The Coil: Modine's Folly

Despite my warnings Modine got careless this morning. I was on the upper deck with Cadet Reve when a commotion broke out down below. Recognising the stowaway's furious shouts I guessed what must have happened, but it was too late to stop it. We arrived just as he was dragged up top by a mob of Letheans. He was putting up one hell of a fight, kicking and punching like a cornered beast, but there were too many of them. They must have taken him by surprise, catching him before he'd been able to go for his flamer.

I watched as the Letheans threw him to the deck and surrounded him like jackals, jeering and taunting and cursing him for a mutant freak. In the emerald light he certainly looked the part: his gnarled skin had a reptilian cast and his body seemed to seethe and contort beneath their blows. I admit I almost let them finish their work, but then I caught Modine's tormented eyes and I knew.

If I stood by he would come back...

Iverson's Journal

'That's enough,' Iverson said. He yanked a Mariner aside and stepped inside the vicious circle. 'I said enough! This man works for me!'

Almost as one, the Letheans went quiet, fixing him with hostile stares that ranged from the sullen to the outraged. Cadet Reve looked as angry as the rest.

'What is this you say?' Csanad Vaskó demanded. The

shaven-headed brute was the Lethean's 'zabaton', a warrior priest they revered and feared in equal measure. He was also the man who had confronted Iverson over the matter of the Arkan flag, an affront he had never forgiven. His rage was a palpable, poisonous charge in the air.

'Private Modine is a specialist assigned to me for this mission,' Iverson said. 'Due to his affliction I requested that he remain in isolation until we reach our target.'

'He is touched by the hand of Kaosz,' Vaskó growled. 'Must be burned.'

'You are mistaken,' Iverson said, wondering at the fanatic's blindness to his own leader. Then again, Karjalan kept himself hidden from all but his most dedicated servants. Vaskó and his crew probably had no idea that they served a monster.

'Perhaps the zabaton has a point,' Reve spoke up. 'This individual is evidently tainted, sir.'

'Is so. The Emperor condemns!' Vaskó insisted.

'And don't He just love doing it,' Modine wheezed from the floor. His cackle turned to a cry as the zabaton sent him reeling with a kick to the ribs.

Iverson drew his autopistol slowly, letting them taste the ritual as he levelled it at Vaskó. 'I have already cautioned you once against obstructing the Emperor's will,' he said. There were angry murmurs from the gathered Letheans, but the zabaton himself didn't even blink. 'This will be my final warning.'

Don't make me shoot you. Your dogs will tear me apart if I do it.

'A good death bring a man closer to God-Emperor,' Vaskó said coldly.

'And is this such a good death?' Iverson asked.

'Better than the one you get if you kill me.'

'Sir, this is not a sound tactical…' Reve's words were shredded by a terrified scream from above. She whirled to stare at the upper deck, along with most of the Letheans. Only Iverson and Vaskó remained frozen, each man tacitly challenging the other to break first.

'Janosz!' One of the Mariners yelled as the scream was cut short. He headed for the stairway, but Reve shoved him aside and took the steps by twos. Iverson whirled away from the standoff and stalked after her.

'To your stations, seadogs!' Vaskó bellowed as he followed with a pair of Corsairs. 'The Emperor calls!'

They found a broken lasrifle by the ladder to the crow's nest, but the lookout was gone. Muttering angrily in his native tongue Vaskó started to climb, but Iverson yanked him down. The zabaton snarled at him, baring black teeth. The commissar didn't remove his hand.

'Whatever took him could still be up there,' Iverson said levelly, nodding at the arboreal snarl overhead. Some of the fronds were trailing right through the crow's nest as the ship drifted along. The zabaton shook him off and glared at the canopy.

'You think was plant took him?' Vaskó asked.

'It could have been anything. There's no telling in the Coil, but the crow's nest is off limits for now. And we need a team up here day and night. At least one Corsair among them.'

Vaskó nodded and headed for the steps, but Iverson called after him: 'Private Modine falls under my authority, zabaton.' The man froze. 'Is that understood?'

Vaskó turned and appraised Iverson with a frown.

'Very well, is so,' he answered softly, 'but understand this, commissar. If you prove false, I make new flag from your hide.'

Day 66 – The Coil: Canker Eaters

Sometimes I think I'm dead to horror, but then some new

abomination steps up to the challenge and shoves the truth down my throat: horror can never be sated and no man will ever be allowed his fill. There is always more and worse to come.

Iverson's Journal

The ship bucked violently and Iverson staggered, almost losing his grip on the iron handrail. With a curse he hauled himself along the cramped corridors of the lower deck, reeling about like a drunk as the world tossed and turned around him. Water was gushing through the ceiling and swilling around the floor, almost ankle deep. He threw open the hatch to the main deck and a volley of hard rain hit him like gunfire. Still drowsy with sleep, he tried to make sense of the chaos.

Are we under attack?

It was long after nightfall, but there was no trace of the jungle's pervasive bioluminescence. In the dim glow of the emergency lights he saw Mariners scurrying about with torches and buckets, harried by their Corsair overlords. Beyond the gunwales there was nothing but inky blackness.

'Why are the engines dead?' Iverson yelled over the gale.

'Seems the river's jammed up just ahead,' Modine called back. He was slouching beneath an awning by the steps, nursing his flamer protectively. 'And this fraggin' squall sure ain't helping none!'

'I told you to keep out of sight.'

'Hey, I'm just keeping an eye on things for you, Holt.'

A flash of lightning lit the deck and Iverson caught sight of Vaskó up in the wheelhouse. The zealot was cracking his ritual whip and bellowing orders. Old Bierce stood beside him with his hands clasped behind his back, brooding over the may-hem. He caught Iverson's eye and shook his head.

I don't like it any better than you do, old man, Iverson thought as he struggled across the heaving deck. The spray coming over the sides was flooding the ship almost as fast as the Letheans could bail it out. Why in the Hells weren't the pumps working? He hadn't come this far to drown in the Qalaqexi...

Iverson froze on the steps to the wheelhouse as he caught sight of the threatening shapes surrounding the ship. They loomed out of the gloom like spongy, malformed giants. Then a searchlight flashed across them and he relaxed, recognising the lumpy Saathlaa igloos. Like the natives themselves, the buildings were degenerate and slovenly, just simple timber frames caked in dried mud and thatched with broad leaves. These primitive hovels were an order of magnitude removed from the coral edifices of the ancient Phaedrans.

'Is Fish village,' Vaskó called from the wheelhouse. 'River runs through it, but there is wall ahead!'

Iverson joined him and peered through the rain-smeared glass of the cabin. Following the wide beam of the ship's forward searchlight he saw a dam straddling the river about twenty metres ahead. Although crudely woven from timber and creepers, the thing was at least three metres thick and twice that in height. One of the ship's scout boats bobbed about in the churning river alongside the dam, crewed by a gang of Letheans. The Corsair leading the party kept watch while his Mariners hacked away at the barrier with machetes and axes. It was a brave, but futile endeavour, especially in the storm.

'Can't you just punch through it with the main gun?' Iverson asked, indicating the lascannon at the prow.

'Can,' Vaskó said, 'but power cells very low. Only six, maybe seven shots left. Do not want waste, no?'

'Seven shots?' Iverson was outraged. 'But we haven't even fired the bloody thing! Why would the cells be drained?'

'Is Phaedra,' Vaskó said with a shrug, as if that explained everything. Unfortunately Iverson knew it did.

'We should back up and take another branch,' a voice said at his shoulder. He turned and saw Reve standing beside him, frowning at the barrier. To his surprise he realised he had almost missed his fourth shadow. 'This smells like a trap.'

'But this place just stinking Fish nest!' Vaskó bridled. 'Is nothing here my Corsairs cannot kill dead, girl.'

'Maybe so, but Cadet Reve is right,' Iverson said. 'We can take another path.' *After all, we're not really going anywhere.* 'Get those men back on board, zabaton.'

'We only need to weaken wall, then we push through it easy!' Vaskó insisted, unwilling to back down yet again.

'Zabaton…'

Something whipped out of the storm and shattered the forward searchlight, plunging the men by the barrier into sudden darkness. Down in the prow the Mariners operating the light yelled and scrabbled about for a replacement.

'Bring more lights!' Vaskó shouted into the ship's loudhailer.

A shrill howl ululated through the gale. Out by the barrier a Mariner lit up a torch. Iverson saw him perched atop the dam, frantically chasing shadows with his beam while his comrades fumbled about for their own lights.

'Pull them back,' Iverson ordered.

'Is just Fish!' Vaskó said stubbornly.

A rangy shadow leapt from the gloom and swept the light-bearing Mariner from his perch. As he splashed into the water the night rushed back in like a hungry ghost and the screams began. They were riddled with bestial snarls and strange, warbling cries that made Iverson's hackles rise. He had hoped never to hear those sounds again.

'Those aren't Fish,' Iverson hissed.

Crimson laser light slashed through the darkness as the stranded Corsair opened up with his hellgun, then a flash of lightning threw the tableau into stark relief, revealing stooped, predatory shapes slinking amongst the Letheans. A heartbeat later it was pitch dark again and the Corsair stopped firing.

'Forward!' Vaskó shouted to the helmsman. 'To battle stations, seadogs!' he yelled into the loudhailer.

The Mariners reacted with swift discipline, casting aside buckets and unslinging lasguns as they rushed to their posts. The Corsairs stalked among them like armoured gods of war, chanting prayers as they powered up their hellguns. The forward searchlight flared back into life and pinned the dam in bright light, but the work team was gone.

'The engine awakens, my zabaton,' the helmsman said.

As the ship chugged forward something slammed down onto the cabin roof. They glanced up as clawed feet scrabbled about for purchase. Vaskó fired without hesitation, his superheated hellbolts punching through the metal ceiling as if it were paper. The unseen boarder yelped and a tangle of bony legs toppled past the window.

'Zabaton, turn this tug around now!' Iverson ordered.

And then the predators were everywhere. Propelled by powerful, reverse-jointed legs they bounded from the rooftops of the village and soared over the gunwales. One landed by the wheelhouse steps. It came down on all fours and skittered off balance on the rain-slick metal. Although its sleekly muscled form was canine its rapid, jerky movements suggested an avian metabolism. Its grey flesh was leathery and hairless, but a ruff of sharp quills jutted from the back of its neck.

'Is that a dog?' Reve breathed from the doorway.

At the sound of her voice the creature's head snapped round on a sinuous neck. They caught a glimpse of slanted eyes above a curved, razor blade beak evolved for rending and tearing. The thing hooted – a strange sound somewhere between a bark and a squawk – and pounced straight for the wheelhouse.

Iverson shouldered Reve aside and thrust out his augmetic arm. The hound's jaws clamped shut on the metal, but its momentum sent him crashing back into the petrified helmsman and they both went down under its bulk.

'*Ördög kutja!*' Vaskó cursed in his native tongue, unslinging his hellgun.

As the beast's claws tore at his coat Iverson clenched his trapped hand around its tongue and squeezed. The hound tossed its head about furiously, spattering him with drool as it tried to get at the soft flesh beyond his augmetic. The carrion stench wafting from its maw made him dizzy with nausea, but he held on, tightening his grip. Up close he could see the monster's flesh was covered in suppurating lesions and tangled fungal nodules. Phaedra had claimed the beast as Her own.

'Kill it!' Iverson roared at the others.

Vaskó was at his side first. The zealot jammed his rifle up against the monster's midriff and opened fire. It squawked in agony and sent him flying with a flailing claw, but the hellgun had virtually torn it in half and its strength was fading fast. A carefully placed shot from Reve punctured an eye. A second tore open its skull and it lay still.

'The Emperor condemns!' Vaskó bellowed as he raced out into the storm, eager to spill more blood in his god's name.

'By the Throne, what are they?' Reve asked as Iverson pulled himself up.

'Kroot hounds,' the commissar said bleakly. 'And where there are hounds the handlers won't be far away. We have to get out of here.'

Down on the storm-lashed deck Modine stood with his legs splayed wide for balance. His flamer coughed as he gunned it into life. He spun as one of the dog-things leapt for him, its beak slick with gore from a butchered Mariner. He batted it aside with the bulky weapon and sent it crashing against the guardrail in a snapping, snarling tangle. It was on its feet again in an instant, howling with raw malice. Modine howled right back and torched it. The monster's challenge turned to a squeal and the pyrotrooper cackled, revelling in the mayhem. He was being eaten alive by some kind of mutie mushroom and everyone he'd ever known was probably dead, but by the Hells life could still be good!

He saw a Corsair crawling along with a hound straddling his back. Its jaws were locked around the man's head, trying to crack his helmet like an iron egg. Whistling softly, Modine bathed its quills in a delicate wash of flames and it let go with a yowl of pain. As it spun to face him he rammed his flamer between its jaws and cooked its brains. Breathing in the scent of burning flesh, he looked around the deck eagerly, but all the hounds were dead and the fight was done.

It seemed the Corsairs had enjoyed the tussle as much as he had. They were all chanting some kind of hallelujah to the God-Emperor with big, cheesy grins on their faces. Even the idiot who'd nearly had his head chewed off was singing along. The Corsairs might be Throne junkies, but Modine had to admit they weren't short of guts. The Mariners had guts too, but mostly they were the wrong kind – red and raw and littered about the deck like off-cuts in a slaughterhouse. Nope, things hadn't gone down well for the deck monkeys. Without the hellguns and armour of their masters they'd been easy meat for the dogs and Modine guessed more than half were done for. Well, the runts had been just as quick to beat up on him as the heavies so he wasn't going to shed any tears for them.

'You fight well for mutant scum,' said the Corsair he had saved.

'That wasn't no fight,' Modine drawled. 'That was just playing around.'

Mangled Helmet grinned, flashing teeth studded with shiny gemstones.

Someone wailed in the wind, long and lost and full of pain. Everyone on the deck heard it, but it was the zabaton who spoke: 'Is Zsolt. The Fish scum have taken him.' The zealot's tattooed face was a devil mask of fury. 'They mock us, brothers!'

'It's not the Fish who took your man,' Iverson said from the wheelhouse steps. 'There's something far worse out there.' He indicated the shantytown stretched out along the river. 'Something we don't want to tangle with right now.'

'I will not abandon a brother Corsair,' Vaskó said coldly.

'He's already dead…' The cry came again, putting the lie to Iverson's words. 'It's a trap,' he urged, but the zabaton was already turning away, shouting orders at his surviving comrades.

'Zabaton, the mission comes first!'

The zealot whirled on Iverson. 'Then you must shoot me, Holt Iverson,' he snarled, 'because this time I will not yield.'

Seeing his hate-glazed eyes, Iverson didn't doubt it for a moment.

'But I should go with you, sir,' Reve insisted. 'You will need backup out there.'

'That's Modine's job,' Iverson said. They were talking up in the wheelhouse while Vaskó prepped his search party on the deck below. 'Besides, I'll need backup right here. Our zaba-ton insists on taking all the Corsairs with him. Someone needs to watch the fort while we're gone. If we lose the ship we're finished.'

'Are you saying you trust me, commissar?'

'Are you saying I shouldn't, cadet?'

She gave him a wintry smile and he almost returned it. Their cat-and-mouse game was almost playing itself these days.

'Anyway, if I'm right and there's a kroot war band waiting for us in that village...' He gave her a pointed look. 'Well, let's just say this would be a very bad time to let me down, cadet.'

'So what's the deal with you and the ice maiden?' Modine whispered as they crept amongst the huddle of Saathlaa igloos.

'I don't believe I take your meaning, greyback,' Iverson said, his eyes dancing over the huts. They were dilapidated and mangy with rot, their walls puckered like the skin of spoiled fruit. Decay hung over the shantytown like a mantle.

'Aw, come on Holt. You can't fool an old dog like Klete Mod-ine,' the pyrotrooper said with a leer. 'I seen the way you two is always gabbing away together.'

'Are you telling me you're jealous, Modine?' Iverson said. 'I remember what they used to say back home: never trust a Bad-lander at your back.'

Modine sniggered. 'Did you just crack a joke on me, Holt? You know, back in...' His words trailed off as the missing Cor-sair cried out again.

Vaskó called a halt, trying to get a bearing on the sound. It was much closer now, but between the darkness and the storm the settlement was proving a nightmare to navigate. The zabaton was growing increasingly agitated, but to his credit he hadn't suggested splitting the search party up.

We're already too few, Iverson thought, glancing over his comrades. *Seven bloody-minded zealots, four terrified seadogs, one degenerate Badlander and a faded commissar. Not exactly the stuff that legends are made of.*

'It came from that way,' Modine said, jabbing a stubby finger to his left.

Vaskó scowled at him. 'You think I do not know this?'

'So what's the hold-up then, boss?'

'There is no path, fool!'

'Sure there is,' Modine said, obviously enjoying himself. 'You just got to think creative is all.' With that he kicked out at a neighbouring igloo. His foot went through the wall as if it were matchwood, shaking the entire structure. Another couple of kicks brought the barrier tumbling down. They saw that the splintered wooden frame was riddled with ropey grey fibres that glistened like maggots in the rain. Iverson was repelled: the igloo was just a husk, sucked dry by the insidious fungus. The entire village was probably infested with the filthy stuff. Suddenly he was glad of the hard rain. In any other conditions the air would be ripe with spores.

'See, us Badlander boys, we like to make our own way in the world,' Modine said with a grin.

After that any attempt at stealth seemed irrelevant and the pyrotrooper led the way, whistling cheerily as he bulldozed a path towards the siren cries. While the others stepped over the tainted debris gingerly, he seemed to revel in it. Iverson guessed that infection wasn't a big worry for Kletus Modine anymore…

He's already halfway to being Phaedra's, even if he doesn't know it yet. Then again, maybe he knows it perfectly well and this little rampage is a kind of payback.

They found their quarry in a big roundhouse that was built to a grander scale than the igloos. The place might have been a chieftain's hall in better days, but those days were long gone. As they crowded inside their torches sliced the shadows into flickering wedges of horror.

'Hellfire…' Modine breathed, his cockiness draining out of him like lifeblood.

The lost Corsair was dangling from the ceiling by his feet, swaying gently back and forth. The other missing Letheans were hanging beside him, along with Janosz, the Mariner who had been snatched from the crow's nest the day before. Janosz was already bloated with decay, but while the others were fresher they were just as dead, including the Corsair. Every one of them had a ragged red tear in his chest where his heart had been ripped out.

'I'd say this jaunt is looking like a really bad idea right about now,' Modine growled.

The roundhouse was an ossuary. The floor was littered with the relics of death – cracked skulls, yawning ribcages and an unrecognisable muddle of lesser bones, all heaped together in casual desecration. A fur of grey mould shrouded everything, clinging to the walls and hanging from the ceiling in thick cob-webs. Tendrils of the fungus wove through the chamber like shrivelled snakes, coiling around the bones and insinuating themselves into eye sockets.

There are enough pieces here to build a hundred skeletons, Iverson estimated grimly. *And enough skeletons to repopulate a whole village with the dead…*

There were other bones caught up in the foetid skein: smaller, more delicate and darker of hue. The xenos skulls were devoid of the gaping nostrils and grinning teeth that gave humanity its last laugh in death, but then the tau were an altogether more sober species. Not that sobriety had done them much good here.

Fragments of tau armour and guns were buried amongst the bones like treasures in a defiled tomb, but the most wondrous relic had been given pride of place. Tethered to a coral totem piercing the heart of the ossuary was a towering suit of alien armour. Trussed up and defaced with primitive scrawls, the Crisis battlesuit had the look of a fallen star god. Under a patina of mould its plates were a mottled crimson and Iverson could still make out its heraldry – a five-flanged sunburst. He didn't recognise the symbol, but something told him that this dead warrior predated Commander Wintertide's rule. It was *old*, perhaps older than the war itself.

Who were you and what brought you to this doom?

Whatever the truth, the warrior's fate had been a grim one. The armour's breastplate had been cracked wide open, revealing the hero within. His skeleton was still intact, suspended almost tenderly in a cradle of fungal threads. There was something fleshy and infinitely unclean blossoming within his ruptured ribcage.

Phaedra loathes us all as equals. Human and tau, we're both just intruders to Her. Nothing but meat to be corrupted and devoured and turned...

Uneasily Iverson wondered what terrible alchemy Phaedra had worked on the kroot who haunted this village. The savage creatures believed they could steal the strength of an enemy by devouring its flesh. It seemed a far-fetched idea, but the kroot bloodline was known to be fluid and unpredictable. By all accounts the kroot hounds were a dead-end branch of the race that had overspecialised in hunting to the detriment of all else. Had their doom resulted from their choice of prey? And if that were true, what would happen to a kroot war band that glutted itself on tainted flesh? The flesh of a degenerate Saathlaa tribe for example...

Canker Eaters.

The name sprang into Iverson's mind with the clarity of a true vision. Suddenly he was sure that his guess about this place was correct: the village had fallen to the kroot and the kroot had in turn fallen to Phaedra.

And then the monsters had turned on their tau overlords and slaughtered them too.

'Burn it,' Iverson hissed at Modine. 'Burn it all.'

'Wait!' Vaskó said as the pyrotrooper raised his flamer. 'We cannot leave Zsolt in this tomb!'

'He's gone, zabaton,' Iverson said tightly. His head was pounding. 'And we have to be gone too. This place isn't a tomb. It's a larder.'

They wait for the flesh to putrefy before they feed...

The butchered Corsair wailed again. Everyone stared at the mutilated corpse. Its mouth was gummed up with clotted blood. Another cry came, soft and mocking this time, drawing their eyes upwards.

There was a xenos perched precariously at the tip of the totem. The creature was sitting back on its haunches, gripping the coral with clawed feet like a bird of prey. Its leathery skin was hairless, but a cascade of fungal coils sprouted from its throat and shoulders, draping the beast in a fibrous, fleshy cloak. The creature's limbs rippled with sinewy muscles and Iverson knew it would tower over most men when standing erect. Like the hounds it was evidently a predator, but the eyes shining above its flat beak regarded the intruders with sly amusement. Instinctively Iverson knew it was a leader – a *shaper*, the kroot called them.

The xenos tilted its head to one side in an unmistakably

avian gesture and spoke in a near perfect imitation of the commissar's voice: *'This place isn't a tomb. It's a lardeeeeer!'* The words trailed off into squawking laughter and a crest of quills flared out behind the beast's head in mockery. Recognising the deception, Iverson felt rage rising within him like a living thing. Or a long dead thing butchered by this foul species...

Suddenly Detlef Niemand was at his shoulder. 'Cleanse the xenos!' the mutilated commissar demanded, jabbing at the shaper with a raw stump.

Iverson and Vaskó opened fire at the same time, but both were too slow. Dodging ahead of their attacks with unnatural speed, the creature back-flipped from its perch and latched onto the ceiling with its talons. Chased by their fire it skittered away upside-down and disappeared among the rafters.

'Bring this charnel house down, Modine!' Iverson shouted.

The pyrotrooper's flamer burst into life, bathing the round-house in angry red light. A moment later a tide of purifying fire drenched the unclean bones. Iverson added his own salvo, punching round after round into the chest cavity of the infested battlesuit, ripping apart the fruiting body pulsing within. The dangling corpses of the Letheans dropped into the bonfire and Modine brushed them gently with promethium.

'Burn bitch, burn...' the diseased man muttered repeatedly and Iverson knew he was cursing Phaedra Herself.

The conflagration soon took on a life of its own and the intruders backed away. Except for Modine. The pyrotrooper kept up a steady stream of fire and hate, seemingly untroubled by the advancing flames. His ruined face looked rapturous.

'We're done here, soldier,' Iverson called, but the man paid him no heed. 'Modine, we're done!'

There was a warbling cry from outside, followed by a chorus

of angry hoots and squeals, then a thunderous squawk that sounded mercifully distant.

'Time to go!' Iverson yelled. For a moment he thought Modine planned on burning alive, but the Badlander nodded and turned his back on the inferno. Outside, the raindrops sizzled and popped against his cooling flamer like insects lured into an electric trap.

'Damn, that felt good,' Modine said.

'*Felt good...gooood...gooooood!*' His voice yodelled back from above.

They looked up and saw the shaper framed against the roiling sky, leering at them from the roof of the roundhouse. Its words spiralled up into a high war cry. A Corsair answered with a gurgling shriek as a spearhead erupted from his chest in a shower of blood and shattered flak plate. A kroot warrior sprang up behind him, hooting victoriously. It lifted the impaled man effortlessly by the haft of its spear and flung him over its shoulder. More of the monsters dived from the rooftops, landing amongst the away team like twisted angels of death. One ripped away a Mariner's face with its talons as it came down. Another was torn to ribbons by Vaskó's hellgun before it even touched the ground.

'Purge the unclean!' the zabaton roared. He leapt into the fray like a whirling dervish, lashing about with his whip as he fired his rifle one-handed.

'Sounds like a plan!' Modine hollered cheerily. He flicked his flamer back into life as Iverson backhanded a charging kroot with his metal fist. The xenos reeled away and Modine sent a chaser of flames after it, turning it into a wailing, flailing pyre of steam. The Badlander arched backwards, catching another savage in midair then spinning to intercept a pair of loping kroot hounds.

The booming squawk came again, much closer now.

'Fall back to the river!' Iverson shouted, ignoring dead Niemand's scowl.

This isn't worth dying for, he thought fiercely. *Only Wintertide matters. Wintertide and maybe the Sky Marshall. If there's still any difference between the two.*

Standing watch in the wheelhouse, Ysabel Reve saw the fire start up. It was only an orange smear against the darkness, but she knew it was the beginning. Scant seconds later her prediction was confirmed by the rattle of hellguns and the distant, desperate cries of dying men. It was the moment she had been waiting for.

'Lower the treads,' she said. 'We're going in.'

'Commissar, this we cannot do!' Gergo, the lanky helmsman protested.

'This is an amphibious vehicle is it not?' Reve said, giving him a withering look. 'We shall prove this.'

'But is not so easy, commissar,' Gergo whined, gesticulating vaguely. 'The machine spirit of the ship, it need *much* reverence for such big work.'

'We will revere it later. Right now you will do as I ask or I shall kill you.'

Gergo decided the machine spirit could wait after all.

'Fall back!' Iverson shouted as the Mariner beside him went down under a slavering kroot hound.

'A zabaton does not run!' Vaskó called back. The aquila tattooed across his face seemed to writhe with a life of its own in the dancing light of the inferno.

'*Ruuuuun!*' the shaper keened as it thudded down behind him.

Vaskó ducked the slash of its serrated knife and whirled into a low spinning kick, but the xenos hopped over his counter-attack and hacked downwards. The Lethean swung his rifle up into a two-handed block that shattered both weapons and threw him to the ground. As the shaper reached for him Iverson charged forwards, pumping rounds into the alien's chest as he came. The creature's spongy mantle absorbed the bullets, but the impact sent it careening backwards. With inhuman reflexes it twisted the imbalance to its advantage, flipping onto its back and kicking out with both talons like a spring-loaded trap. The blow took Iverson in the chest with the force of a pneumatic sledgehammer and hurled him through the building opposite. He hit the ground so hard a wave of oblivion came rushing in.

'On your feet!' Niemand sneered, reeling the fallen commissar back from the brink. In the darkness he was a jagged electric spectre haunting the green snow of Iverson's augmetic vision. 'For Emperor and Imperium!' Niemand demanded. For Hate and Vengeance, he meant, but right now either pair was just fine by Iverson.

He sat up, fighting the agony of his bruised ribs. Through the rent he'd made in the igloo he saw the shaper lift the struggling form of Vaskó above its head. It flicked its head round and looked right at the commissar, finding him unerringly in the darkness. Iverson couldn't read its expression, but he knew it was grinning in whatever way a kroot might grin. Then it hooted with mirth and cast its prize into the blazing roundhouse.

'Purge the xenos!' Iverson roared, stumbling back outside. The shaper waited for him, its mouldy quills rippling with excitement.

'*Purge the xenooooos…*' The alien's mimicry turned into a yowl of surprise as a cord lashed out and wrapped around its throat.

Iverson's eyes snapped to the blazing roundhouse. A burning man swayed at the threshold like a damned soul teetering at the gates of hell. Before the shaper could move, Vaskó sent a full charge rippling along his smouldering shockwhip. The kroot jerked about in a nerve-shredding, muscle-twitching spasm and gibbered in agony. Its quills blistered and its eyeballs exploded into blood-streaked geysers of steam. As his muscles melted away Vaskó lurched backwards, hauling his catch into the inferno after him. Niemand howled with rapture and spread his stunted arms wide.

'Like the man said, the Emperor condemns,' Modine smirked as he staggered up alongside Iverson. The big man was bleeding badly, but there was a madcap grin on his face. 'And sometimes He even gets it right!'

Then they were running, backtracking along the path of destruction Modine had ploughed on their way in. Only three Corsairs and one Mariner had survived the assault and Iverson himself was in bad shape. Bierce was waiting for him at every turn, his expression thunderous with disapproval, but Iverson paid him no heed.

It's duty that drives me to flight old man.

The kroot were relentless in their pursuit, taunting their prey with hoots and squawks as they sprang between the rooftops like manic acrobats. Iverson guessed they were enjoying the hunt too much to make a quick end of it.

Wintertide must die... Kircher must answer for his crimes...

The Corsair in the lead skidded to a halt and stumbled back with a frantic yell. Over his shoulder Iverson saw a hulking shape loping towards them on all fours, using its massive forearms to propel itself along like a hunched ape. Its head was a pugnacious caricature of a kroot, dominated by a slab-jawed beak jutting from beneath beady black eyes. A kroot warrior was perched between its shoulders, looking impossibly fragile beside its mount. Iverson had never seen one of the giants before, but he recognised it from the Tactica briefings. Like the hounds, the krootox was a dead-end branch of the kroot evolutionary tree. The creatures were dim-witted brutes, but their prodigious strength and resilience made them melee monsters on the battlefield. During his stint in the kroot-infested hell of Dolorosa Magenta he had been regaled with horror stories of the beasts. One veteran had sworn blind he'd seen a krootox tear a battle tank apart with its bare hands. Right now the commissar wasn't inclined to doubt him.

'Back up!' Iverson shouted, but the path behind them was swarming with kroot hounds.

'Keep 'em off me!' Modine snarled at the Corsairs behind him. As Mangled Helmet and his comrade raked the hounds with gunfire, Modine slammed a fist through the neighbouring igloo. Something lunged at him through the gap and he replied with a brief spurt of promethium. There was a howl from inside and a blazing kroot burst through the wall, groping blindly for him. He clubbed it aside and lashed out with a kick that sent it spinning into the baying hounds.

'Go! Go!' Iverson barked, firing vainly at the oncoming krootox as the others swept into the igloo. A heartbeat later he ducked under a lunging fist as the giant stampeded past. Moving too quickly to break its charge, it crashed headlong into the hounds and scattered them like yelping ninepins. Iverson saw that its hide was blotched with a lurid patchwork of toadstools and tendrils. The rider hung limp and shrivelled between its shoulder blades, seemingly welded to its mount in a cancerous saddle. The kroot turned at the waist, peering at him with cloudy white eyes.

This is Phaedra's heartland, Iverson realised. *The restless blood of the kroot was easy prey for Her here.*

Braying with frustration, the krootox swung round and Iverson hurried after the others. Modine was already breaking into the next igloo when he caught up. Somewhere in the medley of wind, rain and thunder Iverson thought he heard another, deeper rumbling. He listened, trying to make sense of the sound, but then the hovel behind them collapsed as the krootox waded in after them and the rumble wasn't important anymore.

'Clear!' Modine said as he peered through the rent he'd made.

Everyone dived through into the darkness and raced for the far side. The surviving Mariner shrieked as a sinewy arm shot down from above and hooked him by the scruff of the neck. Iverson glimpsed terrified eyes and wildly kicking legs, then the man was gone, yanked through a hole in the roof. Mangled Helmet sent a blind salvo after him, more in the hope of granting him a quick release than catching his attacker.

'Keep moving!' Iverson shouted. He heard more krootox bellowing nearby, sniffing them out in the ramshackle maze. Bierce was waiting on the roof outside, his hand extended in mute accusation. A kroot leapt right through the phantom and Iverson almost laughed as he blasted the xenos out of the air.

'Clear!' Modine called again as he tore open the next hut.

Halfway across the hovel one of the Corsairs tripped and clattered to the ground. Iverson turned to haul him up when their pursuer came barrelling through the wall. The commissar stumbled back as the beast lunged forward and snatched up the fallen Lethean. The man cursed in his native tongue as the krootox dangled him upside down and peered at him with dim curiosity. It rattled him about and pecked experimentally at his helmet, irritated by the noises he was making. The Corsair was still trying to level his hellgun when it grew bored and chewed off his head. It tossed the corpse aside, rose on its haunches and roared at Iverson. The challenge was cut short when a metal leviathan stormed over the hut and ground the beast into oblivion. Iverson dived back as a lethal wall of spinning wheels and churning treads passed just inches from his face.

'Reve!' Iverson shouted, but the gunboat's clatter drowned him out as it rolled past. He saw its hull was swaddled in enormous caterpillar tracks that suspended the deck high above the ground, transforming the gunboat into a gargantuan tank. The sponson-mounted autocannons on either side were blazing away, deterring attacks, but with only a skeleton crew the *Penance and Pain* was appallingly vulnerable.

She's heading for the fire at the roundhouse, he guessed.

'Back this way!' Iverson called to his companions as he hurried after the gunboat. It was moving fast, but not so fast a running man couldn't catch it.

Even a man with a chest like broken glass...

Iverson's breath was coming in harsh gasps now and his mashed ribs threatened to crush his lungs, but he pushed on. He shouted until he was hoarse, even though he knew the gunboat crew high above couldn't possibly hear him.

Wintertide... Kircher... Wintertide... Kircher... The names chased each other round Iverson's skull in a whirling mantra of loathing. He was riding high on hate the way some men soared on combat stimms. He felt a brief pang for the Glory he'd used against the Verzante deserters – so long ago now – but the narcotic was a tainted blessing. *Her blessing.* Hate was pure.

...Wintertide...

He looked back and saw his comrades behind him. There was a second krootox bounding after them, even bigger than the first. Blanking it out, Iverson locked his eyes on the receding stern of the boat and saw Bierce up there. The old man had his back to him, turning away in contempt as salvation raced away.

… *Kircher*…

Mangled Helmet hurtled past Iverson, twirling something around his head as he ran. The Corsair cast the grapple with a skill forged through years of ship-to-ship combat and it sailed over the gunwales like a guided missile and caught. The racing vessel yanked him forward violently, but he kept his balance and soared ahead. A moment later he was abseiling up the hull in leaps and bounds. Iverson heard the krootox squawking in fury at his escape.

…*Wintertide… We just need to stay ahead a little longer… Kircher*…

He glanced over his shoulder and saw the beast thrust itself into the air like a vaulting ape.

'Down!' he shouted, diving into the mud. Modine fell to his knees instantly, but the remaining Corsair made the mistake of looking back. The krootox tore through him like a cannonball, almost shearing him in half. It crashed down onto the path ahead, a rampaging barrier between its prey and the gunboat. The impact snapped its atrophied rider off at the waist like a dried twig, but the brute was unperturbed.

Phaedra is its true rider now, Iverson thought as he raised his pistol. There was nothing left now except the last stand. *Where are you Bierce? You should be here to see this, you old vulture!*

The krootox loomed over him, shrugging off the small calibre rounds like insect bites. Its beak snapped open as it reached out… and exploded into flames. Iverson dodged away from the squawking inferno as Modine advanced with his flamer. He was singing a bawdy Badlands ballad as he drove the beast back with a stream of fire.

'…and Lady Soozie, she ain't never looked so fine…' He winked at Iverson. His flamer sputtered and ran dry. 'Well shit…'

The krootox charged him like a raging bull. Its hide was a charred ruin that hissed and smoked in the rain, but the fire hadn't reached its muscles. A pile-driver punch sent Modine toppling to the ground. He kicked out but the brute caught him by the ankles and hoisted him into the air. Iverson opened fire as it began to whirl its catch round, but the bullets only irritated it further. At the corner of his eye he saw the gunboat brake to a halt and begin to crawl back.

Too late…

With a primal bellow the krootox smacked Modine against the ground like a human whip. The first impact shattered every bone in his body. The second left him hanging in its fist like a rag doll. By the time his legs came off he was a shapeless liquid ruin.

Too bad…

Iverson was already staggering for the gunboat when the beast came after him. He saw Mangled Helmet up on the deck, hollering for more speed. Reve appeared beside him, watching the chase through her magnoculars.

Too far… Wintertide… Too slow… Kircher…

He heard the krootox stomping just behind him. Felt its hot breath at his back. Felt his own breath tearing through him like razorwire. Some impulse told him to duck and he rolled away just as a claw swept over his head… and kept rolling as the beast pounded the ground with its fists, just one step behind him.

Winter…tide… Kir…cher…

Iverson's blind roll brought him up against something solid. He looked up and saw a metal giant towering over him. The thunder of the Sentinel's autocannon was deafening as it tore the krootox into steaming chunks of meat. The machine swivelled smoothly at the waist and raked the rooftops, obliterating a cluster of charging kroot. A second Sentinel clanked up alongside it, spewing fire from a gun that dwarfed Modine's flamer. Iverson froze as he recognised the Seven Stars stencilled across its barrel.

By Providence, they've found me!

After it was over and the town was silent, Iverson went looking for Modine. The Badlander's body was gone, but the rain hadn't quite erased the blood-smeared trail he'd left behind when he crawled away. Iverson followed it to a small hut at the edge of town and found his quarry curled up in the shadows like a shredded slug. The man was legless and liquescent, but hideously alive. For all its ravages, Modine's disease had turned him into one tough son-of-a-bitch.

'How are you doing, greyback?' Iverson asked from the threshold.

'I've had better days,' the Badlander wheezed through broken teeth. 'You here to give me the Emperor's Mercy then, Holt?'

'Do you want it?' Iverson asked, reaching for his pistol.

Modine shook his head. 'Nah, He ain't exactly been good to me so far. Why start now?'

'You know I should grant it anyway.'

'Sure, but you won't. Not unless I ask. And I ain't asking.' The Badlander chuckled wetly. 'Sorry chief, I ain't going to make it that easy for you.'

'Duty was never meant to be easy.'

Modine spat a gob of blood-flecked saliva. 'You toast all them freaks?'

'Most of them, but there will be survivors. There's no telling how many.'

'Well, I'll take my chances.' Modine raised a blubbery paw and grinned. 'Besides, they might even see me as kin now.'

'Why in the Hells would you want to live like this, man?'

Modine gave it some thought, then nodded slowly. 'I've never been much of a believer, Holt. The way I see it, when you're gone, you're done and there ain't nothing more.' He chuckled again. 'Anything's got to be better than that, right?'

'You're wrong, Modine.'

'Maybe so, but if it's all the same by you, I'll see this through.'

'What are you going to do?'

Modine shrugged vaguely. 'I guess I'll just sit here a while. See how things go.'

How things grow…

Iverson shook his head and turned away, but Modine stopped him with a sharp gesture. 'You won't forget what you promised me about that bastard Karjalan will you? You gave me your word back there, brother.'

'I did,' Iverson said.

'Well then, I reckon that's good enough for me.' Modine threw him a languid salute. 'I'll see you around, Holt.'

'I hope not.' Iverson walked out, leaving Kletus Modine to Phaedra. He suspected She wouldn't keep him waiting long.

CHAPTER
TEN

Day 67 – The Coil: A Silver Storm

My search is almost at an end. The Confederates came to our aid at the eleventh hour and we purged the kroot as brothers-in-arms. And by the Emperor the purging felt good! I've been chasing shadows for so long that I'd almost forgotten the taste of an honest battle. I admit there was little glory in it, but if Phaedra has taught me anything it's the value of truth over glory. This foe needed killing and my new-found allies obliged with thunder in their hearts!

True to their name the Sentinels of the 19th descended upon the kroot like a silver storm. There were only nine, but every one was a titan wrought in miniature. My kinfolk have always had an affinity for fighting machines, but these riders surpassed the old tales. Riders? Surely that does them an injustice, for each man's mastery of his machine was so perfect it moved like an extension of his own body. They raced and spun about with an agility that

I never imagined possible for such hulking machines. We prowled the town together, burning the tainted igloos and cleansing the savages in droves. Only one Sentinel fell, its legs torn from under it by a dying krootox.

Just one loss, yet even one was too many when they were already so few...

Iverson's Journal

Dawn was breaking over the village when Iverson returned from his tryst with Modine. He found the Arkan cavalrymen gathered around the fallen Sentinel, cutting their dead comrade from the wreckage with a dignity that belied their ragged appearance. Reve stood at the edge of the circle, aloof and watchful as ever.

'Modine?' she asked as Iverson approached.

'Gone,' he said. He nodded a greeting to the Sentinel commander. 'I believe we owe you our lives.'

'We'll take Boulter with us. Burn him downriver,' the man answered obliquely. 'There's not much of him left, but I won't leave one of my riders here.' He glared at Iverson as if expecting an objection.

He blames me for the death of his comrade, Iverson thought. *Or he blames himself for making one of his own pay for my salvation. Either way, he's wondering if I'll be worth the price.*

'Are you Cutler?' Reve asked the officer bluntly.

The man looked up from the wreckage with a scowl: 'Do you see any stars on my chest, lady?'

'I see no insignia of any kind,' Reve replied, glancing pointedly at the rider's fur-trimmed flying jacket. The garment was a gentleman's affectation, expensive and flamboyant, but it had weathered Phaedra better than its wearer. Haggard and wolfish, the man looked like a pirate dressed up in his victim's finery, yet there was a faded arrogance about him that betrayed his blue blood. There was blue in his eyes too – the lurid indigo stigma of a Glory addict.

'I may be a Throne-forsaken renegade, but I'm not Ensor bloody Cutler,' the commander said. 'The name's Vendrake.' He straightened up. 'Captain, 19th Arkan Confederates.' He made it sound like a challenge.

'Iverson,' the commissar said. 'And this is Cadet Reve. We've been looking for you – all of you – for quite some time.'

'Maybe we didn't want to be found.'

But that's a lie, Iverson thought. *After all, you came to us, Captain Vendrake.*

'That's unfortunate,' he said, 'because I'm here on the Emperor's business.'

Vendrake's eyes narrowed. 'And what would that be, commissar?'

Iverson hesitated. If he misread Vendrake these men would kill him where he stood. 'That would be justice, Captain Vendrake.' His words hung in the air like a whiplash waiting to fall. At the corner of his eye he saw Reve's hand inching towards her pistol. *Surely you're not such a fool, girl?*

Finally a sour smile touched Vendrake's lips.

'Justice?' He sighed with what might have been relief. 'Well then, say your piece and be done with it, commissar.'

Day 68 – The Coil: A Barbed Alliance

'You're no renegade, Hardin Vendrake,' I told him, 'and neither is the 19th.' They were simple words, but true – the right words for the moment.

Of course words won't be enough to win these men over, but they broke the ice and Vendrake agreed to take me to

Cutler. For all his hostile bravado I believe it's what he intended all along, so why the games? I sense there's more than brinkmanship going on here. It's almost as if Vendrake wants me to judge him. There's an edge of darkness to the man that runs deeper than his devotion to the Glory. Dead Niemand believes he is insane and I'm inclined to agree, but he's the only lead I have. Besides, he tells me his comrades are just two days upriver so I'll have my answers soon enough.

Iverson's Journal

'You won't like what you find, commissar,' Vendrake said. In the violet fungal light his features had a ghoulish cast. Iverson couldn't quite tell if he was grinning or not. 'Actually I think you'll want to shoot the lot of us.'

'Perhaps,' Iverson said, regarding the riders hunkered down around him on the banks of the river. Their Sentinels loomed over them like a second circle of judges. It was the first night of their journey together and the unspoken trial was in session once again. 'Do *you* think I should shoot you, Captain Vendrake?'

'Does it matter what I think?'

'Maybe not, but tell me anyway.'

'Well then…' Now Vendrake *was* grinning. 'What I think is this: we're not what you'd call heroes of the Imperium anymore. Not heroes of any stripe or colour in fact.'

'But you've been fighting the enemy,' Iverson said.

'Because they're here to fight.'

'The enemy will always be here to fight. It's the way of things.'

Vendrake snorted and took another swig from his canteen. He'd been working his way through it all night and Iverson guessed it wasn't filled with water.

'Sir, if I may?' The speaker was Silverstorm's second officer, Pericles Quint. 'Despite Captain Vendrake's misgivings, please rest assured that the 19th has not strayed from its tradition of courage and honour. We have harassed the rebels at every opportunity…'

'Oh quit whining, Quinto!' Vendrake snapped. He obviously despised his subordinate and Iverson could see why. Clear-eyed and clean-cut, Quint was his captain's opposite, the epitome of an Arkan noble confident of his place in the scheme of things. According to Vendrake the man had once been overweight, but there wasn't a trace of fat on him now. While Phaedra had sucked the vigour out of Vendrake, She had seemingly whipped Quint into shape.

'It needs to be said, sir.' To the commissar's trained ear there was the faintest tremor in Quint's voice. 'We have stayed true to Providence and the Imperium.'

There were murmurs of assent from the other riders and Iverson wondered if Quint was angling for a power play. If so, Vendrake seemed blind to the threat. Or perhaps he just didn't care.

'Do you really think an Imperial commissar will give a damn for anything you have to say, Quinto?' Vendrake scoffed.

He's speaking to Quint, but I'm the one he's really asking, Iverson realised. *Why are you so eager to be condemned, Captain Vendrake?*

'Tell us about Cutler,' Reve interjected. 'Is he at your camp?'

Vendrake squinted at her. 'You seem mighty keen to meet the Whitecrow, lady. Now why would that be?'

'He is your leader, is he not?' Reve said.

But is he your target, Reve? Iverson wondered.

'Colonel Cutler is…' Quint began.

'Quite dead,' Vendrake interrupted. Reve stared at him and he laughed, a harsh, humourless bark. Nobody joined in. 'No, don't worry girl, I'm just messing with you. As far as I know the Whitecrow is still breathing, but some things can wait. In fact *this…*' he swept his arm across the gathering, 'this can all wait. Let's see what the Raven makes of you.'

'The Raven?' Reve asked.

'Oh don't worry cadet, you're going to love her!' Vendrake hauled himself up. 'She's always full of questions too.' He turned towards his Sentinel. Out in the Mire all the riders slept in their machines. 'I'll see you at dawn.'

'Why don't you tell us about Trinity first, captain?' Iverson's words struck Vendrake like cold water. When he turned his grin was gone.

'What?'

'Trinity,' Iverson said. 'It's on the regimental records – a backwater town razed by the 19th. If I recall correctly it happened right at the tail end of the war.'

'What of it?'

'There were questions. A military tribunal.' Iverson was watching Vendrake closely. 'I thought it might be important.'

The captain swayed, looking unsteady on his feet. His men were silent. Even Pericles Quint kept his mouth shut.

'Captain?' Iverson pressed.

'That town died *after* the war, commissar,' Vendrake said. He paused, thinking about it. 'Or maybe long before. I'm still not sure which it was.'

'And was it important?'

'No,' Vendrake looked at him with eyes like broken windows into Hell. 'No, it wasn't important.'

But Iverson saw the lie. For Hardin Vendrake, Trinity was the most important thing of all.

* * *

'He is sick and almost certainly tainted,' Reve said when they were back aboard the *Penitence and Pain*.

'Perhaps,' Iverson said, 'but Vendrake is our only lead.'

'Why do you always retreat to "perhaps" or "maybe", sir?' She sounded exasperated. 'Doubt and you will falter, falter and you will fall.' It was a quotation from the Commissariat Primer.

Does that mean you're the real thing, Reve? Iverson wondered. *Or have you just done your homework? And does it matter either way?*

'Sometimes "maybe" is the best we can do, cadet. Sometimes there's no knowing the truth.'

She was indignant. 'Then we *act* regardless. Hesitation is a greater crime than error.' Another quotation. 'Your pardon, but you think too much for a commissar, sir.'

He was silent for a long time. 'Yes,' he replied finally and realised he meant it. 'Yes, I fear you're right.'

'Then you agree? You will act?'

'I believe I must,' he said sadly. 'Goodnight to you, Cadet Reve.'

That night, like most nights, Hardin Vendrake dreamt of murdering the town that was already dead. And yet again the nightmare began the same way.

His Sentinels reached the outskirts of Trinity at the head of an unravelling grey snake that stretched back almost a kilometre. Most of the men were so dazed with cold and starvation they could barely walk, let alone hold a formation together. The last of the Chimera sleds had given out four days ago, the last of the horses a day later. After that it had fallen to the Sentinels to haul along the wounded carts. It was an inglorious task that they rotated dutifully, but fuel had run as dry as blood by the time they reached the town.

Vendrake felt his heart leap at the sight. It almost made him forget the cold. He'd killed his Sentinel's heater days ago to save on power and the cabin had turned into an icebox. He was swathed in furs like a barbaric mummy, but his finger-less mittens left his hands vulnerable and the tips were blue with cold. Like any rider worth his salt he wouldn't sacrifice dexterity for comfort, but he guessed frostbite was just a hair's-breadth away. But the town was closer.

Then Vendrake spotted the major waiting by the side of the road like a grim gatekeeper and knew something was wrong. Of course Cutler wasn't the Whitecrow back then. His hair was still coal-black and he didn't wear misery like a mantle, but his fate was already closing in.

'Level the town, captain,' Cutler called over the wind. 'Bring it down and burn it.'

'Burn it...' Vendrake echoed hollowly.

'Except for the temple. Leave that to me.'

'And the people?' He was too tired for shock.

'Burn them too.'

'I don't understand.' And he was too tired to try.

'That's for the best, captain.'

Vendrake hesitated just once. 'Is this right?' he asked. But he must have been too tired to care, because he didn't remember Cutler's answer. Didn't even remember if Cutler had answered at all. What he did remember was leading the cavalry into Trin-ity and putting the town to the sword. And when the locals fell upon them, hacking at their metal steeds with axes and hatch-ets and even lesser weapons, he put them to the sword too. He was numb to their fury. The cold had made him invulnerable to doubt.

His invulnerability lasted until a putty-faced maniac leapt onto his steed from a collapsing rooftop. The attacker howled in futile outrage as he battered at the Sentinel's canopy, then pressed his molten features against the windshield. Pressed so hard it began to come apart.

Which, the face or the windshield?

Lost somewhere between the dream and the cold, Vendrake couldn't tell where flesh ended and glass began. He only knew he mustn't let that furious dissolution reach him. Desperately he tried to shake his attacker loose but the degenerate hung on like a leech, his wild eyes glaring hate and hope like dark-bright beacons in a whirlpool of vitreous flesh. And then the windshield began to bulge inwards...

'Belle du Morte signing in,' the vox crackled suddenly.

At those words the world ran down like a failing machine. The sounds of battle distended and faded to silence. The face outside/inside his windshield congealed into stillness, becoming a tortured sculpture framed against the frozen flames devouring the town.

'Leonora,' Vendrake croaked, dimly aware that this was a new twist on the nightmare. Something he hadn't seen before.

'Another night, another murdered town,' sang the voice of his dead protégé and lover. 'Tell me, which slaughter felt better, Hardin?'

'It had to be done,' he said. He was vaguely sure that was true. Hadn't someone important once said so? Cutler perhaps. Or maybe poor dead Elias Waite...

'That's not what I asked, Hardin.'

'You can't be here, Leonora. You joined us after the war ended. You weren't ever here.'

'But you're here. And that's all that matters, dear Hardin.'

'I don't understand,' Vendrake said. He couldn't take his eyes off the monstrosity carved into the windshield. There was hatred frozen in its eyes like an insect trapped in amber.

It was a voracious, crawling thing, eager to escape so it could make a nest of his skull. 'I don't understand...' he repeated in a whisper.

'That's because you're trying too hard, Hardin.' The dead voice giggled at the chance alliteration. 'It's like staring at the sun. Look right at it and you'll go blind, but catch it in the corner of your eye and you'll see the truth of things.'

'And what's that?'

'That you were blind all along and always will be!' Her laugh was like the swish of rotting velvet. 'The world is broken and there's no fixing it. The puzzle makes no sense and nonsense is our only hope.'

'You're not... Leonora.' He struggled to string the thoughts together, let alone the words. His hand fumbled for the service pistol taped to the dashboard.

'Don't be cruel, Hardin!' she chided. 'But no matter, you'll know me when we meet.'

'You're... lying.' His hand closed on the gun.

'Of course... I'm not!' She giggled again. 'Either way, I'm coming for you. Perhaps it was true love after all...'

He tore the pistol free and levelled it between the mad eyes petrified inside his windshield.

'Oh, you don't want to do that!' she exclaimed. 'Do you?'

Vendrake had no idea, but he did it anyway.

The two Sentinel riders keeping watch by the riverbank heard the pitiful shrieks coming from Vendrake's machine, but neither spoke up or moved to intervene. They were used to their captain's nightmares.

Day 69 – The Coil: Dead Men Sailing

Vendrake greeted me like a manic ghost this morning, his

eyes rancid with the Glory. He didn't mention Trinity, but waking or sleeping, I know that's where he spent his night. Without his narcotic fix I doubt he could walk straight let alone pilot a Sentinel. Reve was aghast at the sight of him, but I shrugged it off. There was a time when I would have berated or pitied his addiction, perhaps even shot him for it, but such things do not matter anymore. If Vendrake needs the Glory to lead me to Ensor Cutler then so be it. And lead he does...

The Sentinels guide my ship from the riverbank, flitting through the dark tangle of vegetation like bright shadows, navigating the weft and weave of the Coil without hesitation. Their riders have learnt to see hidden paths where lesser men – or men less damned – would see only chaos. And so we follow, sailing the Coil in a floating tomb, our numbers diminished and our supplies almost gone...

Iverson's Journal

Standing on the upper deck, watching the Mire drift by, Iverson caught sight of Bierce waiting at the river's bend. The phantom's finger was still jutting out in accusation. He was implacable and immovable, but the Sentinels waded through him as if he wasn't even there.

'You saw his eyes this morning,' Reve insisted. 'He is a degenerate.'

'Captain Vendrake will keep his word,' Iverson said.

'But he cannot be trusted.' She was whispering even though they were alone.

'You said the same thing about the Letheans. You're not the trusting type are you, cadet?'

'And you are?'

No, Ysabel Reve, I am not. But I've grown lax.

Before he could answer there was a heavy clanking on the steps below and the surviving Corsair climbed up to join them. He had discarded his mangled helmet after the battle, revealing a head like a craggy moon daubed with paint. His tattooed face was brutish, yet his pale green eyes were penetrating, suggesting a shrewd cunning. Iverson wasn't sure if that was going to be a problem, but so far the man had fallen into line and the Mariners had followed.

'Milosz's wounds claimed him this morning,' the Corsair said in surprisingly fluent Gothic. 'And Bencé will die before sunset. Six seadogs survive to serve.'

'This is a big ship. Can they keep it running?' Iverson asked.

'They are bred to sail,' the Lethean answered. 'They will be enough.'

The ship rounded a bend and Iverson watched Bierce drift by once again. He turned to face the Lethean. 'You understand that they are *your* men now, Corsair?'

The Lethean shrugged, seeming neither proud nor perturbed.

'And you are *my* man.' Iverson made it a statement.

'As you say, commissar,' the Corsair said flatly.

'I didn't get your name, soldier.'

'I am Tás Zsombor, tethered blood-brine of Underlocker 5.'

'You're proud of your lineage?'

'I am shamed. The Underlockers are sunken prisons where the scum of Lethea are cast down to brawl and drown and die,' Zsombor grinned like a shark, displaying his gem-studded teeth. 'But like all Corsairs I fought my way up to the land and the light.'

'To redemption?'

'To penitence and pain,' Zsombor growled. 'There is no redemption, commissar. There is only holy torment. Have you not heard the Lethean Revelation? The Emperor condemns.'

Iverson made no reply. Bierce was waiting for him at the next bend in the river.

Day 70 – The Coil: Redemption and Damnation

Vendrake says we will reach the Arkan camp tonight. I admit I am eager to meet Ensor Cutler at last. Whatever he has become, I am certain he will bring me a step closer to Wintertide and my salvation. Unlike the Letheans I will not accept that redemption is impossible. I'll willingly suffer and die for the God-Emperor, but I won't believe it's for nothing. Surely there must be a purpose to the misery we endure in His name?

But before I redeem myself I must fall a little further.

There's one final loose end to tie up before I reach Cutler. I've been putting it off because I've never been quite certain of my suspicions. By Providence, I'm still not certain, but with Cutler so close I can hesitate no longer. Too much hangs in the balance for doubt. Reve was right – I must act. And may the God-Emperor forgive me if I am wrong...

Iverson's Journal

Reve hacked through another curtain of creepers with her machete and pushed through into a narrow glade. The clearing was hemmed in on all sides by gargantuan toadstools whose caps melded into a knotted, mucilaginous canopy high above. Violet light drizzled down from the gills, transforming the space into a pocket nightscape.

'Surely this is far enough,' Reve said, scowling at the pale things scuttling amidst the fleshy rafters. 'We have been walking almost an hour, sir.'

'You're right,' Iverson said behind her. 'This place is as good as any.'

Something in his tone made her turn and she saw the pistol in his hand. It was levelled at her head. Iverson watched her face flit through a range of emotions until it settled on plain annoyance.

'You promised me the truth,' she said quietly.

Yes, I did, Reve…

Around midday Iverson had ordered a halt to their journey. Offering Vendrake no explanation for the delay, he'd asked Reve to follow him into the jungle. A little later he'd told her she'd earned the truth, but the truth was too dangerous to risk around the others. Later still he'd fallen behind and let her take the lead. And so they'd finally stumbled upon this twilight glade.

It seems a fitting place for our shadow play to end, Ysabel Reve.

'So you have decided not to trust me,' she challenged.

'I think you're working for the Sky Marshall,' he said.

'I am not.' There was no trace of fear in her voice. He had expected nothing less of her.

'You appeared out of nowhere and claimed Lomax sent you when I know she didn't. You pretended to be green when you were anything but and you've stuck to me like my own shadow, always prying for secrets.' He shook his head. 'You're a spy and an assassin, Ysabel Reve.'

'Then why did I come for you at the tainted village?'

'Because you needed me to reach Cutler.'

'You are wrong.'

'I might be,' he admitted sadly, 'but *you* were right: mistakes are smaller sins than doubts. I can't take the chance you'll kill Cutler.' The emotion slipped from his voice. 'Give me a reason not to shoot you.'

She sighed and opened her hands, palms upwards. 'High Commissar Lomax was my mother.'

'Too contrived. You can do better than that, Reve.'

'She kept my existence secret and trained me personally. I was raised to be her weapon against the Sky Marshall. I hate Zebasteyn Kircher more than you ever can. That bastard murdered my mother.'

'It's a good story.'

'It is a true story.'

'I don't believe it.' Iverson shook his head. 'I think *you* murdered Lomax. She was on to the Sky Marshall's game and you were sent to silence her, just as you'll silence anyone who threatens him.'

Reve sighed. 'Your mentor was correct. You are a fool, Holt Iverson.'

'What are you talking about?'

'I am talking about Commissar Nathaniel Bierce, the hero you betrayed in your youth. He was like a father to you, was he not?' She nodded, acknowledging the surprise on his face. 'Yes, I have seen your record, but that is the least of it.'

'You're not making any sense, Reve.'

'Then listen to me. Bierce never stopped looking for you. He followed your trail across the galaxy, but when he finally found you on Phaedra and saw what you had become he turned his back on you. I believe this was three or four years ago.'

'That's impossible. Nathaniel Bierce was murdered decades ago on a planet you've never even heard of.' The guilt tasted fresh on Iverson's tongue. 'An assassin got to him with a xenos neurotoxin – something the medicae couldn't begin to fight. I saw him die.'

And I've seen him dead every day of our journey through the Coil. In fact he's here now, hovering just over your shoulder. Turn around and maybe you'll see him too, Reve!

'You did *not* see Bierce die,' Reve said. 'You left him to rot, but he survived.' She gave him an icy smile – the first he'd ever seen on her face. 'The neurotoxin destroyed his flesh, but the Commissariat decreed his mind worthy of preservation so they gave him a new body. I never met him, but my mother thought him a remarkable man. Although *man* was no longer quite the right word for him.'

'You're lying, Reve.'

'Then how do I know all this?'

'Because the Sky Marshall has given you half-truths to work with.' He could feel the rage uncoiling in his chest like a burning snake aching to strike. He looked past her and met Bierce's eyes.

She's right of course. You were like a father to me, old man. And I'm sorry. I've never stopped being bloody sorry…

Iverson forced his gaze back to Reve. 'You're lying,' he repeated hollowly.

'Then shoot me.'

'Do it!' dead Niemand hissed in his ear. 'The bitch is playing mind games with you!'

Iverson's finger was tightening on the trigger when he saw Number 27. His third revenant was watching him from across the glade. Unlike her companions she was a rare and precious curse and weeks had passed since her last visitation. As always, she filled him with ineffable sorrow.

What do you want here? What are you trying to tell me?

Following his eye line, Reve glanced over her shoulder. She looked right through Bierce and saw nothing. She turned back to him, frowning. Iverson could almost hear her mind working, calculating her chances.

Yes, I'm distracted, Reve. Make a move! Force my hand and prove me right!

But Reve made no move. Doubtless she suspected a trick.

So be it, girl.

Iverson stepped back, widening the distance between them. Slowly he lowered his pistol and eased it back into its holster, but his hand hovered over the weapon.

'Back on Providence we have many old myths and customs,' he said. 'Most wouldn't make any sense to an off-worlder and truth to tell, many don't make much sense to me either.' He shook his head ruefully. 'But there's one I don't doubt. It dates right back to the first colonies and runs like firewater in the blood of every Arkan, noble and savage alike. We call it the Thunderground.'

Iverson noticed Bierce nodding in rare approval. The old vulture was Providence born. He was the one who'd taught Iverson the traditions and tales of their home world, weaving them into the Imperial creed with masterful logic.

'The Thunderground is a secret place waiting inside every one of us,' Iverson said. 'It's the needle in the eye in of the storm that's life, the testing point that'll make or break you in the God-Emperor's eyes. You'll only walk it once, but that walk will be forever. There's no turning back and no second chances so you'd better walk with fire in your heart and steel in your spine.'

'You sound more like a wordsmith than a commissar,' Reve said, sounding uncertain for the first time.

'All good commissars are wordsmiths, Reve. Words are our business as much as guns. When we get them right, our charges face death willingly.'

'Then you still believe you're a good commissar?'

He smiled bleakly. 'I know I'm a poor wordsmith.'

'Are you trying to tell me this is your Thunderground, Iverson?'

'No, Ysabel Reve, I'm telling you it's yours.'

The fingers of his augmetic hand twitched reflexively, but its human partner stayed rigid and perfectly poised over his holstered pistol.

'Go for your gun, Reve.'

Very slowly, very deliberately she raised her hands. 'No.'

'Then I'll kill you where you stand, assassin.'

'I will not humour your delusions of honour, Iverson.' She sounded angry now. 'I will not give you that comfort. If you kill me it is on you alone.'

They remained frozen for a long time, locked in a stale-mate while Iverson sought his bearings amongst his ghosts. Like a sailor navigating by black stars he floundered between Niemand's spite and Bierce's contempt and the dead girl's strange compassion, but in the end it was simple weariness that decided him.

'Throw aside your gun,' he said. She obeyed gingerly, careful not to offer any hint of a threat. He nodded. 'If you try to follow me I'll kill you.'

'I understand,' Reve said. As he turned to go she called after him. 'Iverson! You do realise you are insane, don't you?'

He stopped and looked back at his ghosts, lingering on Bierce. If she'd told the truth he was being haunted by the shade of a man who still lived. Was that worse than being haunted by the dead? He found he had no answers.

'Do you think it makes a difference?' he asked, but Reve had no answers either, so he turned away.

Have I just stepped back from the brink?

'She's going for her gun!' Niemand yelled.

Iverson swung round and his pistol seemed to leap into his hand with a will of its own. Number 27 rose up before him, her hands outstretched as if to beseech him or ward him off, but he was already firing. The bullets ripped through her in a splatter of ectoplasm and found Reve. She was standing motionless and…

What gun? I see no gun!

The first round punched through her right eye, the second and third sheared away half her face. Horribly she was still alive when she hit the ground.

'Reve!' Iverson knelt over her, already knowing there was nothing to be done. 'Ysabel, listen to me…'

Her surviving eye rolled in its socket, hunting for him. 'Ivaah…ssaah…' Her shattered jaw mangled the words into wet nonsense as she clutched at him. 'Yah… baahh…staaahh…' With a last shudder she was gone.

Iverson looked up at Niemand. The ghost was staring at the corpse avariciously.

'Why did you do it?' Iverson asked.

'It was the only way to be sure, Holt,' the dead commissar gloated.

Iverson opened fire on full auto and sundered the phantom into whirling ribbons of ectoplasm. His pistol clicked on an empty chamber and he slotted in a new clip mechanically. He kept on firing, going through clip after clip until the spectral gobbets had faded into nothing.

He never saw Detlef Niemand again.

'Where did your lady friend get to?' Vendrake asked when Iverson returned.

'She's gone,' Iverson said.

Just like Modine, he thought, knowing full well it wasn't. Unlike Kletus Modine, Ysabel Reve would certainly be coming back.

ACT 3
ASCENT

CHAPTER
ELEVEN

**PROVIDENCE MILITARY ARCHIVES,
CAPITOL HALL**

REPORT: GF067357

STATUS: *CLASSIFIED*

FROM: General Thaddeus Blackwood, Director (Internal Affairs)

ATT: Major Ranulph C. Kharter, Investigating Officer (Internal Affairs)

REF: War Crimes – 19th Arkan – Trinity Township, Vyrmont

SUM: Be advised that this town has been designated a *rebel affiliate*. While the ruthlessness of Major Cutler's purge is regrettable, such incidents are inevitable in times of war.

CON: You are ordered to desist all investigations of the Trinity site forthwith. The 19th Confederates will be disciplined by Internal Affairs in due course. This matter is *closed*.

Note: I want Cutler and the 19th gone within the month. Give the man his stars and ship him off-world. He did what needed doing, but he's a hothead and too unpredictable to trust with a secret like this. If the Inquisition gets wind of Trinity the consequences for Providence are unthinkable.

'You are an anomaly on Phaedra, Ensor Cutler,' Por'o Dal'yth Seishin observed from the pulpit of his throne drone, 'but you have always been an anomaly, have you not? Most especially to your superiors.'

The white haired prisoner behind the force barrier snorted. 'You're not telling me anything I don't already know, blueskin.'

'But I am offering you an opportunity you cannot deny,' the tau ambassador urged. 'Unlike your Imperium, the Tau Empire embraces creative leadership. A man such as yourself could be an invaluable asset to us.'

'Then let's see your cards.' Cutler leaned forward on his stool, his expression sly. He had grown lean and wolfish during his incarceration. 'Come clean with me, Si. What's your game on Phaedra?'

O'Seishin steepled his fingers, contemplating the question. This was his twenty-fifth 'interview' with Subject 11, yet the man's stubbornness was undiminished. Perhaps it was time to twist the blade a little deeper.

'Phaedra is worthless,' O'Seishin declared. 'It is a sinkhole for a war the Tau Empire has no intention of winning. The conflict serves the Greater Good where victory would not.'

'You're telling me the war is a sham?' Cutler said bitterly.

'Not so. The fighting is genuine, but there is no heart in it. A single company of your vaunted Space Marines would take this world within a week, a few regiments of seasoned Guardsmen within a year, but your Imperium *chooses* to send only the dregs of its military – the incompetent, the broken or the deranged – soldiers who have lost the will to win or the faith to care.'

'That sounds to me like a slur on the 19th,' Cutler snarled.

O'Seishin raised a placating hand. 'As I stated previously, anomalies sometimes slip through the net.'

'Real soldiers, you mean?' Cutler shook his head. 'No, I don't buy it. Why would the Imperium play to lose?'

'It does not play to lose. Like ourselves, it simply does not play to win.'

'Why fight a war nobody wants to win?'

O'Seishin twisted his face into an approximation of a human smile. He had been practising the manoeuvre rigorously and thought it rather good. 'I have a different question for you, Ensor Cutler. *Who* is your Imperium fighting on Phaedra?'

'I don't follow you.'

'Consider the facts. The Saathlaa indigenes are numerous, but primitive and militarily insignificant. Our mercenary auxiliaries are effective, but few. As to my own kind…' O'Seishin extended his hands, palms upwards. 'How many tau have you encountered on Phaedra, Ensor Cutler?'

'I'd say one too many, Si.'

'Then you are privileged, because I doubt there are more than two thousand of my kind remaining on the entire planet. Contrast that with nearly one hundred thousand of your Guardsmen.' O'Seishin paused to let the numbers sink in. 'I ask you again: who is the Imperium fighting on Phaedra?'

'Turncoats,' Cutler said bleakly, 'but the scale you're talking about…'

'Has been precisely balanced,' O'Seishin finished smoothly. 'Over the decades we have stripped back our own troops as yours have swelled our ranks. Your Imperium casts its people into oblivion and we offer them hope. You have been fighting each other, Ensor Cutler.'

'This really is just a game to you, isn't it?'

'On the contrary,' O'Seishin demurred, 'our purpose is serious and our message sincere. Phaedra is a feasibility study – a microcosm of a future happening as we speak. While your Imperium is diverted by this inconsequential war, our agents – *human agents* – are waging the true war beyond this gateway world, winning the hearts and minds of the subsector. Everywhere they go they find discontent and a desire for something better. Your species is not as unified as your Imperium pretends, my friend.'

'And you've got all the answers?'

'Not all,' O'Seishin admitted, 'but many. For example, the psychic malaise that plagues your race – you call it "the Chaos" I believe – this condition does not afflict the tau.'

Cutler stiffened visibly. 'It doesn't afflict you because you blueskins don't have souls.'

'Then perhaps the price of owning a soul is too high,' O'Seishin said seriously. 'I have more facts for you, Ensor Cutler. Your species is hardy, but riddled with the maladies of age. Mine is vigorous, but prone to the follies of youth. Separately we are vulnerable, but together we could become unbreakable. The tau are not your enemy.'

The ambassador sat back, awaiting the inevitable sarcasm, but Cutler was silent, his eyes glazed with thought. Surprised, O'Seishin pressed on.

'Phaedra is a sacrifice for the Greater Good of both our races, Ensor Cutler. In your heart you know your Imperium is in its death throes. Do not die with it. Do not let your men die *for* it.'

The haunted look on the prisoner's face was almost pitiful. In that moment O'Seishin was quite certain the gue'la were a doomed species. He leaned forward eagerly, sensing victory.

'Tell me, Ensor Cutler, does the name "Abel" mean anything to you?'

The blizzard had returned with a vengeance, but the fire raging through the murdered town had pushed the temperature right up. Skjoldis, the witch woman, remembered that she had been sweating inside her heavy robes that night. And suddenly the sweat was there.

Trinity burns cold…

She sighed, reluctant to walk this memory yet again, but once the nightmare began it always ran its course. Resigned, she picked her way across the field of charred limbs jutting from the snow, making for the hated temple that waited across the square. Her *weraldur* was at her back, his axe unsheathed lest some stray cultist had survived the massacre to threaten her. She recalled that a chasm-faced maniac was due to rise from the snow when they were halfway across the plaza and pointed him out to her guardian in good time. The cultist was duly despatched. Her *weraldur* would have caught him anyway, but the warning speeded matters along.

The Whitecrow and old Elias Waite were waiting for her by the heavy oak doors of the temple. Three squads of the regiment's finest were lined up alongside them, covering the entrance with lasrifles and bayonets while a pair of Sentinels prowled about, swivelling and tilting restlessly at the waist to scope the building. The rainbow light blazing from the stained glass window above transformed them all into torn shadows, insubstantial and fragile.

Which is nothing less than the truth, Skjoldis mused.

'You summoned me, Ensor Cutler,' she said, playing her part in the past once more.

'That I did, Mistress Raven.' It was the first time he had looked her in the eye, though he'd watched her covertly often enough, thinking she hadn't seen it. From the day she joined the regiment he'd been drawn to her strangeness, but sanity had kept him away. Now, in this twisted town she was irresistible. Inevitable.

He pointed towards the coruscating light streaming from the window above. 'As our sanctioned shaman, it occurred to me you might have some insights into this matter, lady.'

'The Great Wyrm has poisoned this place,' she answered. 'You were wise to clip its wings, but the heart of the beast still beats. You must find it and destroy it.'

'Well, I don't expect the finding will be troublesome,' Cutler said with forced lightness, 'but as to the other part...' He threw her a defiant grin. 'That might prove interesting.'

'I will come with you,' she said.

Did I ever have a choice or was the past as fated as this dream is now?

'I'll be glad to have you along, Raven.'

'That is not my name, Ensor Cutler.'

He nodded, weighing that up. 'Then perhaps you'll give me a better one when this is done, but right now...' Cutler turned to face the temple. 'I've a snake to crush under my boot.'

'Now hold fire there, Ensor!' Waite protested. 'I say we torch this heathen nest like the rest of the town. We ain't got no call to go in there...'

'I'm afraid we do,' Cutler said. 'Burning won't be enough, Elias. We have to be sure.' He glanced at Skjoldis, seeking her approval for the first time. 'Am I right, lady?'

'You are correct,' she said. 'If the evil slips away it will take root elsewhere.'

'Since when did her word hold any sway with you, Ensor?'

Waite looked at his friend askance. 'She's a witch in a town gone to the Hells with sorcery. For all we know the taint might be inside her too!'

'That's enough!' Cutler snapped, then his tone softened as he recognised the fear in his friend's eyes. 'I'm not asking you to come with us, Elias.'

'Now Ensor, you know that ain't what I meant…' But the relief in the old man's voice gave him away. He was almost sick with terror, just like the greybacks facing the temple. They were all veterans of untold carnage, but the horror haunting this town was worse than any flesh and blood enemy. They all sensed that a man risked losing much more than his life in Trinity.

'You know I'll back you to the hilt,' Waite finished weakly.

'Of course, old friend, but I need you right here, watching our backs in case anything gets past us.' Cutler turned to Skjoldis. 'Any idea what we're dealing with here?'

She sighed and spoke the litany of the nightmare: 'The Great Wyrm has many hues and poisons, Ensor Cutler. Some will turn hearts sour with black passions or rose-scented deliriums. Others will twist the mind with impossible despair or desperate possibility. Rage and lust, anguish and ambition, all are playthings of the Wyrm at the Heart of the World, but all corrupt the soul equally and warp the body like putty in the hands of a lunatic child.'

She saw him grasping for mockery or humour – anything to blunt the peril of her words. 'So tell me the really bad news?' he wanted to say, but her cold gaze wouldn't allow him the mercy.

The Great Wyrm is not a thing to be mocked, Ensor Cutler. Will you ever learn that lesson, I wonder?

And then the daemon bell chimed once again and any hope

of levity was gone. Terror congealed amongst the soldiers like bad blood. Skjoldis knew every one of them was praying he wouldn't be called upon to enter that desecrated temple. She also knew they had nothing to fear on that count because the burden had always fallen on Cutler, herself and her *weraldur* alone and always would.

'Psyker,' a voice buzzed in the wind, bone dry and impossibly distant. 'Are you there?'

The words sent a ripple of discord through the world. The swirling snow flickered into static and the memory of Trinity was swept away, carrying the men and the town back to limbo. Skjoldis sighed as a jagged shape twitched out of the chaos.

'Hello Abel,' she said.

Standing rigid on the riverbank like a rusting statue in his Zouave armour, Audie Joyce watched the returning Sentinels shepherd a gunboat into camp. A tall figure loomed at its prow, so still he might have been a statue himself. Though the newcomer's peaked cap was missing there could be no mistaking his calling. This was the commissar Captain Vendrake had gone chasing after.

'He's got a face to raise the Hells,' Audie Joyce muttered into the turgid waters where the murdered saint slept. He knew that Gurdy-Jeff had endured beyond death, as true heroes of the Imperium always did. The saint had followed his killers into the Coil, drifting along the silt bed and touching their dreams, but only Audie had been found worthy of his blessing. That blessing had carried him from green cap to knighthood and there was no telling where the path would end.

Blood… for… the God-Emperor…

'You say something, preacher?' a fellow Zouave asked over the vox.

Realising he'd left his armour's vox-channel open, Joyce smiled. For all their airs and graces, the Zouaves hung on his every word. The day was fast approaching when Audie would replace that fossil Machen at the head of the brotherhood. Sure, there weren't a whole lot of them left now, but it would still be a fine thing. The Emperor and Uncle Calhoun would be mighty proud of him.

'Penance just sailed into camp, brothers,' Joyce broadcast, reading the gunboat's insignia, 'and Pain won't be far behind.'

'What is this madness?' the shape hissed, oscillating wildly as it struggled to find a form in limbo. 'Where are you, psyker?'

'I am dreaming, Abel,' Skjoldis answered, 'and you are intruding.'

The spectre considered her reply. 'This is how you dream?'

Abel's confusion was telling. He – if indeed Abel was a *he* – did not possess the wyrd. He had little understanding of the immaterium and even less interest. His presence in her mind was facilitated by an astropath, a human relay station trained to channel telepathic messages across the void. The astropath's name had been eroded away by that corrosive flow of information long ago, along with everything else that had once made him human. He was a powerful psyker, yet he was also nothing. His mind was like a bright light shinning from an empty shell.

Abel was a remote ghost inside that shell, a shadow presence beyond Skjoldis's reach. She had often extended covert feelers through the astropath, hoping to taste Abel's mind, but had always met a blank. It was as if Abel had no psychic presence whatsoever. Forced to fall back on intuition, she had constructed a picture from his words alone, but that had proved equally frustrating. Abel did not talk like anyone she had ever encountered. His cadence was skewed and his expression stilted, his thoughts seemingly shaped by tactics and logistics alone, as if war was his sole concern.

'You are not welcome here,' Skjoldis said.

'I require the Counterweight,' Abel stated, dismissing the dream state as irrelevant, along with her reproach. 'The Pendulum must fall upon the Crown.'

She frowned. Abel's fondness for code words and allusions irritated her more than his coldness. 'That is impossible,' she replied. 'Our force has become divided.'

'Divided? How so? Why so?' he snapped. 'I instructed that you maintain cohesion of your assets at all times.'

Skjoldis bridled at his contempt. 'Our situation here is volatile. There is disquiet amongst the officers. We have been waiting too long...'

'And the waiting is over. A convoy of newly sworn janissaries is inbound for the Crown. They are due in three days time. I will divert them to your position.'

'We are not ready.'

'Another opportunity will not arise for many... months, psyker.'

'Give me a week.'

'I may not have a week,' Abel said. 'My position has become precarious. Certain of my agents have been exposed.'

'Will they betray you? Do they know your identity?'

'*Nobody* knows my identity,' Abel said. 'Not even this husk of a telepath who carries my voice.'

'Then why are you so frightened?'

'I am not frightened,' Abel hissed, displaying rare passion, 'but the Water Caste are subtle and clever. That ancient monster O'Seishin is getting too close.'

'Then why did you lure him to the Diadem?'

'To make him vulnerable! He is the true engineer of this stalemate and he is the key to ending it.'

'What of Wintertide and the Sky Marshall?'

The shape flickered, but said nothing.

'Who are you, Abel?' Skjoldis asked.

'You're a bloody fool, Vendrake!' Machen snarled, stomping forward as his fellow captain leapt from his Sentinel. 'You've brought a snake right into our camp!' He thrust an ironclad paw towards the scarred man watching from the gunboat. 'He'll betray us the first chance he gets.'

There were murmurs of assent from the greybacks crowding the riverbank.

'He's a commissar, but he's Providence born!' Vendrake shouted over the growing hubbub. 'He'll give us a fair hearing!' But there was no conviction in his voice.

'We murdered an Imperial confessor and his retinue!' Machen mocked. 'There's no going back from that!'

The greybacks roared their support and closed in on the gunboat like jackals.

'You're right,' the commissar called as he stepped onto the gangplank. 'There is no going back.' He didn't shout, yet his voice cut through the mob, snuffing out the clamour like a chill wind. None of them would meet his searching, glacial gaze. Even Machen looked away, blinking furiously.

The commissar nodded with infinite weariness, as if he had seen it all before. 'This far down the road to Hell you can only go forward.'

'Who are you, Abel?' Skjoldis repeated firmly. 'If you want my help you will tell me.'

'I have already answered this,' Abel said finally.

That was true, even if his answer had been a lie.

Abel professed to be a senior naval officer aboard the Sky Marshall's battleship, a man with connections that ran right to the nerve-centre of Kircher's inner cadre. He also claimed to lead a covert resistance movement dedicated to exposing the 'Phaedran Lie'. He was playing a long and dangerous game that required staunch allies and perfect timing. With access to the records of all inbound regiments, Abel had been quick to spot the potential of the 19th Arkan.

'You do not belong here,' Abel had said during that first, fleeting psychic contact in orbit almost a year ago. 'Your regiment has been betrayed.'

After the Arkan fled into the wilderness Abel had approached Skjoldis every night, wooing her with tantalising nuggets of information that offered a glimmer of hope. Finally she had told the Whitecrow and ever the gambler, he had taken a chance on Abel.

'What do we have to lose?' he'd said.

And so they'd listened and Abel's counsel had proven sound. He had outlined rebel patrol routes and supply lines, guided them to ammunition dumps and outposts, even revealed passwords that changed on a daily basis, always keeping them one step ahead of the enemy. But over the months his advice had grown more elaborate, his strategies bolder, and somewhere along the way their goal had changed from survival to striking back at the Sky Marshall.

You were right Hardin Vendrake, Skjoldis mused. *The regiment is being moved about like a piece on a regicide board, but the Whitecrow and I were never the players.*

'Tell me you hate them,' Skjoldis demanded. 'Tell me you hate the Sky Marshall and his puppet masters.'

Make me believe it…

She sharpened her senses to a razorwire edge, eager to taste every nuance of Abel's answer. It came without hesitation: 'I despise them.'

'Skjoldis!' called another voice. Then again and again...

An insistent pounding reverberated through the dream. Briefly she wondered if it was the daemon bell chiming from lost Trinity. Then she heard her *weraldur* bellow and her eyes flicked open. Dazed, she saw her guardian striding towards the cabin door just as it was flung open. Vendrake stood at the threshold, looking half-dead and all damned, but it was the face over his shoulder that tore her fully awake. One of its eyes was a lustreless black sun, the other a corroded augmetic rammed through the eye socket. Both were bound in a lattice of scars that glowed like seams of magma beneath parchment skin.

Worst of all, she recognised that face.

'He asked us to follow him into the heart of darkness,' Audie Joyce whispered to the still waters of the river. 'And then he promised he'd bring us out the other side if we had the guts for it.'

The Zouave was alone on the riverbank. While his comrades chewed over the commissar's revelations in noisy clusters he was communing with the drowned saint.

'He told us the Sky Marshall had broken faith with the Emperor and turned xenos lover,' Joyce went on. 'Told us the blueskins have been playing the Guard for fools, turning good men bad and chewing up the ones who stood tall.' He sighed. 'It's a helluva thing if it's true.'

Joyce glanced at the command boat moored further along the riverbank. The commissar had gone in there to talk with the witch. With a bit of luck he might even shoot her.

* * *

'The name's Iverson,' the dead man said, watching Skjoldis from across the table. His eyes were no longer monstrous – the left was a faded blue, the right a failing augmetic – and his scars no longer burned, but their geometry was unchanged. That tortured lattice held her gaze like a cage.

He looks younger, but it is him, Skjoldis decided. *And he is not dead.*

'It's an old wound,' he said, misunderstanding her fascination. 'Razorvine. I walked right into the bloody stuff. Strange to think it, but I was green to Phaedra once.' He smiled with bleak humour, distorting the mesh. She saw many things caught up in that net: determination and despair, broken faith and unbreakable hate, courage and the fear that courage was only a lie, murders old and new... but not a trace of recognition.

He does not know me. But how can that be? And how can he be younger?

'It was a lifetime ago,' he said.

She caught her breath, misunderstanding his statement.

'But are you still a fool?' Machen mocked from the doorway. 'It seems to me you must be, walking into a den of renegades.'

'I'm not here to judge you,' Iverson said, keeping his eyes on Skjoldis.

He does not know me, but he senses I am the authority here, she realised.

'You really expect us to believe that prattle about a pardon?' Machen snorted.

'No, I don't expect *you* to believe it, captain,' Iverson said. 'There'll be no pardon for any of us, but it's what your men needed to hear.'

Machen snorted. 'Then why would we help you?'

'Because we've all been betrayed,' Iverson said. 'And because we want the same thing.'

'Justice,' Vendrake said quietly. He was slouched in a chair, but his eyes were bright.

'To the Hells with justice!' Machen spat. 'I want to see those bastards burn!'

'Then let me help you,' Iverson said, talking to them all, but speaking to the witch. 'Trust me.'

I do, Skjoldis discovered to her surprise. *Against all sense and sanity, I do trust you, Iverson. Whatever you were in the past, you are untainted now.*

And finally, with the relief of one who has carried a burden too long, she told them about Abel and the Counterweight.

'The pendulum falls...' Verne Loomis stuttered. 'Three days... We have... three days...' His nose erupted in a welter of blood and his eyeballs rolled, showing the whites. Roach caught him before he hit the ground.

'Easy Verne,' the scout whispered, setting the trembling man down gently. 'We hear you. You just rest up now.'

Roach felt bad for his fellow greyback. Loomis hadn't been right in the head since he'd walked in on the warp-spawned nightmare in Dorm 31, way back in space. That horror had turned him into a wall-eyed scarecrow that saw things that nobody else could see. Sometimes those things made him giggle and sometimes they made him cry like a baby, but lately they mostly made him scream.

'It hurts,' Loomis moaned. 'Every time she talks to me it's like she turns my head inside out.'

'I know, but you done real good and she's gone now,' Roach said.

Unfortunately for Loomis his experience had left him sensitive to the wyrd, so he'd drawn the short straw of 'talking' to the witch long distance. He was the Arkan infiltrators' psychic vox-receiver and it was burning him out.

'Whenever she does it *they* can see me,' Loomis grabbed Roach's wrist in a vicelike claw. 'They can see right inside of me and I know they want to come in.'

Roach turned to the others. 'He can't take much more.'

'He won't need to,' said Klint Sandefur curtly. 'He's done his duty. The rest is down to us.'

The blandly handsome Arkan lieutenant cast a steely eye over the men gathered in the empty silo. They were deep in the bowels of the Diadem, well below the waterline. It was about as remote as they could get on the rebel refinery, but nowhere was really safe. They only gathered when Loomis got twitchy, which meant the witch had something to say.

'You all heard Loomis. We don't have much time,' Sandefur continued. He was the leader of the eight-man infiltration team who had 'betrayed' their colonel and signed up with the rebels. Roach couldn't fault his smarts, but he was a cold bastard and too heavy on the Creed by a long shot.

'Redemption Day is coming and I don't want any mistakes,' Sandefur finished sternly.

'Can't come soon enough for me, lieutenant.' Jakob Dix drawled. 'Another month hanging out with these xenos lovers and I'll start buying into their Greater Crud!'

'You do and I'll shoot you myself, Trooper Dix,' Sandefur said without a trace of humour. 'We've been sleeping with the enemy near on five months now. This isn't the time to fall for them.'

The man thinks he's the Whitecrow in waiting, Roach decided. He stifled a scowl as he weighed up his comrades. Mister Fish wore his usual serene smile, unmoved by Loomis's news. Dix was grinning like a ghoul in a graveyard and his buddy Tuggs was smirking along with him, showing buckteeth big enough to stop a bolt-round. The black crags of Pope's face were unreadable in the shadows, but then they were pretty much that way in any light. Guido Ortega's expression was only too easy to read. His eyes were wide and he was biting his flabby lips nervously. Roach guessed the Verzante pilot had given up on Sandefur's 'Redemption Day' ever coming and probably hadn't lost much sleep over it. Thinking it over, Roach realised he felt much the same way himself.

The rebs have treated us pretty good, he admitted. *Better than the Guard ever did. Even the blueskins ain't so bad once you get used to them…*

'I know this has been tough on all of you,' Sandefur was saying. 'We're soldiers, not filthy spies, but you'll get the chance for some payback.' He turned to Roach. 'You're certain you can breach the Eye, scout?'

'No problem,' Roach answered with a nod. 'See, we got this blueblood chump in our gang, name of Olim. He's got a regular shift up there. Man's the platoon punch-bag and I've become his best pal in the whole world. He'll get me in for a look-see.'

'Do you have a problem with that, Mister Roach?' Sandefur asked, catching the scout's sour tone.

'No sir, I'm just dandy,' Roach said, 'but things could get messy in there.'

'Nothing we can't clean up!' Dix quipped, raising a guffaw from Tuggs.

'Well let's make sure you've got the right tools for the job.' Sandefur turned to the dark skinned greyback. 'Pope, did you secure the devices?'

'I got 'em right here.' Pope, who'd wangled a stint guarding the tech-priests' arms laboratorium, slapped the satchel on his shoulder. 'Swiped four of 'em. Couldn't risk no more. The cog-boys watch their new toys like hawks.'

'Four it is then,' Sandefur said crisply. 'That's one per man taking a shot at the Eye. Pass them round, greyback.'

Pope pulled out a bundle of glassy, needle-like daggers with bulbous hilts and handed them over to the men chosen to strike at the comms centre: Roach, Fish, Dix and Tuggs. The two Badlanders eyed the fragile weapons dubiously.

'What d'you expect me to do with this here toothpick, lieutenant?' Dix snorted. 'It ain't fit to slice an owlskunk's hide. Won't do spit against an iron-plated zombie!'

'You got that wrong, Dixie,' Pope drawled. 'I seen these pig-stickers being tested out. One jab'll put down the biggest of the cogboys' freaks.'

'And one jab is all you'll get,' Sandefur warned. 'We got the word on this gear from the colonel's source. They're brand-new tech, something the cogboys have cooked up with their blue-skin pals…' He trailed off, looking uneasy at the blasphemy he was describing.

'It ain't right messing with stuff like that,' Dix said, sniffing his blade suspiciously. Tuggs nodded in vigorous agreement.

'Look, I won't pretend I like it any better than you,' Sandefur snapped, 'but we'll be turning the heretics' weapons against them. And you'll need every edge you can get in the Eye.'

'Go on,' Roach encouraged, genuinely curious now. 'Tell us what these things do.'

Sandefur straightened and nodded. 'Those blades are mods of EMP tech. They'll hit a target with an electromagnetic pulse that'll fry its machine spirit, but one charge is all they pack, so choose wisely.'

'We'll make 'em count,' Roach promised.

'See that you do, Dustsnake,' Sandefur said. 'Right, we're done here. You all know your parts, so let's make Providence and the Emperor proud.'

* * *

'It is done,' Skjoldis said. 'They have heard me.' She sank back into her chair, drained by her efforts.

'Good work,' Iverson said. He turned to the two captains. 'Brief your men then do it all over again. Hammer the plan home until they're breathing it. There will be no second chances. And find me a chainsword.'

They left without a word. All the words had already been said, all the arguments fought to a standstill. After Skjoldis's revelation Machen had raged and Vendrake had laughed, but Iverson had stuck to questions until the questions had become tactics and Abel's plan had become their plan.

He knows it is our only chance, Skjoldis observed. *He saw that from the beginning and embraced it with the fatalism of a drowning man.*

'Do you trust this Abel?' Iverson asked. He had asked before, but now they were alone he wanted the truth.

'No,' she said, 'but I trust his hatred for the Sky Marshall.'

He nodded, holding her gaze. 'Have we met before, witch?'

She froze, half expecting his scars to ignite with hellfire, but his expression was simply puzzled.

'That is not possible,' she answered cautiously. 'You said you were taken from Providence as a boy, while I have been away scarcely a year.'

'I know, but the look on your face when you first saw me…' Iverson faltered and she glimpsed something barbed shift beneath the black ice of his soul.

'I was sleeping,' she said. 'You walked in on a nightmare.'

'I see,' he said, but he obviously didn't.

And I hope you never do, Holt Iverson.

CHAPTER TWELVE

The Last Day: Counterweight

The witch knew me. Her veil couldn't hide the recognition in her eyes. Perhaps it was a consequence of her wyrd, some remote viewing or precognitive vision, yet neither would explain her dread of me. But I've no time to dwell on this mystery. Despite Raven's strangeness I must trust her as she trusts her shadowy benefactor, Abel. They are both enemies of my enemy and perhaps that's the best that friends can be in Hell. Besides, Abel's plan offers our only chance of ending this heresy.

Abel. He claims he's been building a network of dissidents for years, fomenting discord and preparing for a day of reckoning. Well, that day is today. In nine hours mutiny will break out on the Sky Marshall's battleship. The resistance doesn't have the muscle to take the ship, but that's where we come in. Abel calls us his 'Counterweight' – the secret weapon that will swing the balance of power. His mutiny will open a window for us to reach the Sky Marshall and end this. But first we have to get into space.

There aren't many ways off Phaedra, but the Diadem offers one of the few. The old refinery has its own shuttle, a rickety tanker used to ferry promethium into orbit. With its silos emptied the tug will easily take half a regiment – not a comfortable ride, but a short one at least. Unfortunately the Diadem is one of the most heavily defended enemy bastions on the entire planet. We can't hope to capture it, so we'll have to get in and out before the rebels know what's hit them. Once the assault begins there can be no hesitation and no mercy. We push on until the job is done – or until we're done.

Three hours from now a convoy of Concordance janissaries will pass through a choke point in the river, a narrow fjord overlooked by an escarpment…

Iverson's Journal

Howling with blissful rage, Audie Joyce leapt from the cliff top and plummeted towards the stalled convoy far below. The four ships looked like toys overrun with swarming ants. The gunboat in the lead was a blazing ruin and its three charges, all cumbersome hover barges, were in disarray. Rebel janissaries scurried about the decks, tormented by hidden snipers and heavy fire from the Sentinels lining the ridge. Iverson's gunboat was steaming up behind the convoy, packed with greybacks. Machen was clinging to the prow like an iron barnacle, excluded from the sky dive by his massive Thundersuit.

This glory is mine to lead, the young preacher thought.

'Flay the xenos lovers, brothers!' he shouted. As the ships raced closer he opened up with his heavy stubber, heralding his path with a hail of bullets. Plunging through the air alongside him, his fellow Zouaves followed suit and stitched the rebels with high velocity rounds. Together they were a coterie of armoured angels, falling into fiery atonement.

A beam of incandescent light flared up from an emplacement below and struck the man to Joyce's right, detonating him in a whirling nova of blood and steel. The preacher knight cursed, feeling the loss of his brother like a physical blow. He swivelled his aim and tore apart the rebels manning the lethal rail gun before it could fire again.

A flock of small saucers rose from the convoy to meet them, tilting awkwardly as they tried to aim their underslung weaponry towards the sky. Joyce whooped as he smashed through the strata of drones, scattering them like broken spinning tops.

'Thrusters!' he ordered, triggering the repulsion jet on his back. The Stormsuits didn't carry true jetpacks, but the single use rockets were enough to cushion their fall. As the Zouaves slowed, a stray blast from a drone ripped through another knight's rocket pack. Trailing puffs of steam he shot past Joyce and hit the leading barge like a missile, pulverising a gaggle of rebels and punching right through the deck. A second later the ship quaked as the human bomb ruptured something vital in its guts. Black smoke poured from the rent as Joyce crashed down into chaos. Grinning fiercely he fired up the buzz saws attached to his wrists and tore into the rebels, hacking a blind path through the choking, flailing mob. His heart soared as blood spattered his armour, lending it a crimson sheen.

'Blood for the God-Emperor!' the preacher bellowed, saying the words aloud for the first time.

'We're done here, Silverstorm,' Vendrake called into the vox. The Zouaves were down and Iverson's ship was seconds away from the convoy. 'You know the drill. Head for the rendezvous point, double time.'

Yanking levers expertly, he hauled his Sentinel away from the precipice and spun about. Up ahead the escarpment dipped sharply into the jungle, but Vendrake charged down the incline as if damnation was on his tail. And maybe she was. Lady Damnation, chasing him down in a rust-bitten Sentinel that reeked of the burial pit and ran on unclean truths.

I'm coming for you, my love, he heard her sing again, closer now, always closer. Vendrake's Glory-fired eyes tracked every dip and snarl in his path like violet lasers, triggering live wire reflexes that bound him to his machine. He'd given Iverson his word he wouldn't use the Glory today, knowing all along that his word was worthless.

I lost my honour at Trinity. I just didn't know it until I got to Phaedra.

As his gunboat bore down on the rearmost barge Iverson thumbed the activation stud of a borrowed chainsword. Angry tremors reverberated up through his metal fist, falling into harmony with the martial beats pounding from Machen's shoulder speakers. While his comrades crouched in cover the Zouave captain stood tall at the prow, suppressing the rebels with a constant stream of fire. He was like a tank and an orchestra combined, his music vying with the chatter of his heavy stubber. Sporadic ripostes flared back from the barge and scorched his iron hide, but he paid them no heed.

'Now!' Machen called, silencing his gun. His comrades surged to their feet and Zsombor, the last Corsair, cast his grappling hook. A wave of other grapples followed, launching from the gunboat like a shoal of barbed worms. They snarled in the gunwales of the barge and bound the ships a moment before they collided. There was a bone jarring impact and the grey-backs roared furiously, eager for the fight.

'For Providence and the Imperium!' Iverson shouted as he leapt over the narrow divide. His kinsmen followed like grey wolves, their lasrifles bristling with bayonets. They landed amongst a rabble of surprised janissaries who'd been crouching in cover. Before the rebels could level their guns Iverson was in close, slashing and stabbing and thinking of Reve.

She was a traitor... He sawed through an officer's breast-plate... *She would have turned on us...* Felt the teeth chew into the ribs beneath... *She'll answer me...* Thrust through the turn-coat's back, ripping away the face of the man behind... *When she comes back...* Yanked the blade free... *Why hasn't she come back?*

A withering fusillade rained down on the brawling mob, slicing indiscriminately through greybacks and janissaries alike. Iverson spun and saw a band of armoured xenos warriors perched on the upper deck. There were six of them, three kneeling and three standing behind, formed up in a classic defensive line. They fired their pulse rifles in disciplined, alternating bursts, cooperating to maintain an unbroken barrage. Iverson's bile rose at the sight of their backswept helmets and impassive lens-studded faceplates. Fire Warriors – the true enemy.

'Machen!' he yelled into his vox-bead. 'Upper deck – take them down!'

The Zouave acknowledged with a hail of bullets, but none found their mark. The air around the xenos squad crackled and scattered the rounds like sparking confetti. Iverson swore as he noticed a peculiar, tetrahedral machine hovering above the warriors. The thing must be some kind of shield drone, upgraded so it could throw a barrier around an entire squad.

There's no second guessing blueskin tech, Iverson thought bitterly. *It moves too fast for us.*

Machen threw up a gauntlet to protect his faceplate as the tau retaliated with a volley of pulse rounds. Even his tank-like Thundersuit could not withstand such punishment for long, so Machen launched himself across the divide and crashed down onto the barge. With his head bowed like a raging bull he charged the xenos squad, scattering soldiers of both camps while the Fire Warriors tracked him smoothly, chewing deep craters into his armour. His left knee guard ruptured and spurted steam, but he was moving too fast to stop. He smashed into the wall of the upper deck with a concussion that shook the whole barge and sent one of the tau tumbling towards him. He batted it overboard with his stubber and plunged the whirring bit of his drill attachment into the wall, tearing through the metal like paper.

'Wait! We need the ship!' Iverson shouted into his vox-bead, but Machen paid no heed. Cursing, the commissar fought his way towards him, hacking down rebels and shouldering aside greybacks. The battle was raging across the entire deck now, but the turncoats had little heart for it and were going down fast.

They don't know what's hit them, Iverson reflected grimly. *This deep inside the Coil they thought they were safe.*

With a shriek of tortured metal the upper deck lurched and canted downwards, spilling four of the tau from their perch. Machen caught one on his drill and stamped down on the others. The impaled alien spun about on the drill like a broken doll as its chest was liquidised. A moment later it whirled away in two pieces, trailing streamers of gore. The last Fire Warrior clung to the deck above, scrabbling for purchase. Machen tore him down and slung him to the mob. A dozen bayonets pierced the xenos before it could rise.

'We need the damn ship!' Iverson bawled into Machen's faceplate as he came up alongside.

The captain grinned, his face glistening with sweat behind the glass. 'And you have it!'

It was true. The fighting was over. Most of the rebels were dead and the survivors were on their knees with their hands over their heads.

'Move on to the second ship,' Iverson ordered.

'What about them?' Lieutenant Grayburn asked, indicating the prisoners. Bierce was standing by his side, watching his protégé expectantly. Iverson threw him a curt nod. 'Kill them,' he said.

'Please…' The rebel's plea was torn into a wet gurgle by Joyce's buzzsaws. His head spun away and his body slipped to its knees, offering up a fountain of blood. Joyce leaned forward, breathing deeply as he bathed his armour in the sacrificial spray.

'What in the Hells are you doing, boy?' Wade said as he marched out of the smoke. 'We're not bloody savages!'

Dripping gore, Joyce regarded his fellow Zouave. Wade was Machen's creature and an unbeliever to the core, but still… The boy hesitated, biting his lip uncertainly. Then he remembered how the saint had purged old Elias Waite and knew he had to be strong.

'You're a disgrace to the brotherhood,' Wade went on. 'When Captain Machen hears–'

Joyce thrust a buzzsaw into his fellow knight's visor. The glass shattered and Wade jerked about as his skull was bisected at the eye line. The preacher tugged his blade free and the heretic toppled over with a heavy clang.

'The Emperor condemns,' Joyce whispered reverently. He heard the other Zouaves approaching and turned to greet them as they emerged from the smoke. Together they had turned the barge into a floating abattoir.

But it won't float much longer, Joyce realised as another explosion rocked the deck. 'We need to move on,' he said. 'Brother Ellis gut-shot this tug good and proper when he came down.'

'The lieutenant…' Lascelles began, pointing at Wade's body.

'He died for the God-Emperor,' Joyce said. 'His penance is all done now.'

None of them questioned him.

The Last Day: Lake Amrythaa

The convoy is ours, what's left of it anyway. We lost one of the barges and that fool Machen almost wrecked another, so I've decided to take the Triton along. We need the capacity and the firepower. It's a gamble, but if Abel's clearance codes are good I doubt the rebels will question it. Certainly the codes have worked so far. We cancelled the convoy's distress calls and the rebels bought it. Of course they might be bluffing, hoping to lure us into a trap, but we'll have to take that chance.

We picked up the Sentinels an hour ago. Vendrake's burning Glory again, but at least he's got his squad running like clockwork, which is more than I can say for the Zouaves. There's an unspoken power struggle going on amongst them that makes me uneasy. I hope Machen can hold them together a little longer because we're going to need his knights on the Diadem. My kinsmen fought well this morning, but there's no telling what's waiting for them on that old rig. We're coming up on Lake Amrythaa now…

Iverson's Journal

The witch opened her eyes. 'It has begun,' she said. 'Abel has made his play and cast the Sky Marshall's dominion into disorder.'

'What about our infiltrators?' Iverson asked. He was standing at the porthole of his cabin, staring out at the mist wreathed lake.

'I have sent the signal. They will move within the hour.'

'Then we're set.' He shoved a battered journal into his pocket and turned. As she unravelled from her lotus position on the floor he stepped over to help her rise, but she flinched away.

'Why are you so afraid of me?' he asked.

Her green eyes narrowed. 'Now is not the time to talk of it.'

'It might be the only time we'll get.'

She got up stiffly. 'Do not go home, commissar.'

'What?'

'You must never return to Providence,' she urged.

'And how in the Hells would I ever manage such a thing?'

Perhaps only *through the Hells*, Skjoldis realised with a flash of insight. She shivered and backed towards the cabin door.

'You should seek a clean death today, Iverson,' she said gravely.

'Don't play games with me, witch.' Suddenly he seemed every inch the Imperial commissar. 'You're hiding something.'

'Your shadows are real, Iverson.' She turned then hesitated at the threshold. 'Even if they are not what you think they are.'

The blood drained from his face. 'What are you talking about?'

But she was already gone.

The door of the holding cell slid open and Ambassador O'Seishin glided in on his throne drone. As always, the prisoner was waiting for him behind the force barrier, his expression watchful.

'You asked to see me,' O'Seishin said, concealing the eagerness in his voice. He was certain the moment had finally come. The prisoner was going to turn.

'Here's how it's going to go down,' Cutler said. 'You give me the truth and I'll give you Abel.'

The doors of the turbolift hissed open and Cristobal Olim ushered his charges out into a dimly lit corridor. There wasn't much call for illumination on the upper levels of the Diadem; they were the domain of the tech-priests and their augmented servants, none of whom required light to see. Only a handful of rebel janissaries had any business up here: men with the aptitude to assist the tau engineers who monitored the Eye.

'Are you quite certain this is a good idea, Friend Roach?' Olim asked yet again. 'The Eye is the nerve centre of the Diadem and access is highly restricted. This information you have uncovered… perhaps I could pass it on to the tech-priests…'

Roach shook his head regretfully. 'That's real decent of you, Cristo, but it's ugly news. Trust me, you don't want to be the man telling it.'

And I don't want to be the man doing this, Roach thought bitterly. He felt like he'd signed up to a one-way voyage on a sinking ship.

Olim licked his lips nervously. 'Perhaps you are right. I would not wish to endanger my imminent elevation to the Eye.'

'Exactly!' Roach gave the chubby janissary a slap on the back. 'I just hope you won't forget your friends when you move on.'

Like I've forgotten Alvarez and Estrada and all the others in my cluster…

'A nobleman never neglects his allies,' Olim preened, 'but

my talents would be wasted in the Mire. I am a master con-joiner of communications.'

A halfway-decent vox-operator, Roach translated. Olim wasn't the dumbest blueblood he'd ever met, but he was mighty close. He was also so full of himself it was a miracle he didn't burst open at the seams. Someone with serious muscle had been pulling strings to get Olim a shift up in the Eye while keeping his feet down among the grunts – where he needed a buddy like Roach to look out for him. It was all part of The Plan.

And this is where The Plan really kicks in…

The infiltrators had received the go ahead from the witch a couple of hours ago and Roach had gone to Olim with 'The Story', saying he'd found out something so big they had to take it straight to the Eye. The rig's control room was located at its crown, right under the beacon tower. The whole level was locked down with security codes and patrolled by combat servitors, but Olim had the clearance. Whoever his mysterious backer was, he was certainly a major player.

I'd lay odds of ten-to-one we're talking the same *player who's backing the Whitecrow*, Roach guessed. *Whoever that sneaky son-of-a-bitch is, he's in deep.*

'You're doing the right thing here, Cristo,' he said cheerily, swallowing his own doubts. 'It might even speed up your pro-motion, but if you're worried I can always go through First Friend Alvarez.'

'No, no… that won't be necessary! But must these other gen-tlemen really accompany us?' Olim indicated Roach's three companions. 'Even one of you is a frightful breach of protocol.'

'I hear you, but they're part of the story,' Roach said. Dix and Tuggs nodded vigorously. Mister Fish smiled.

'Very well,' Olim said, sounding as if the weight of the war was on his shoulders, 'but I do hope this story of yours is a good one.'

'Hey, you got nothing to worry about, fatboy,' Dix said with a chuckle. 'It's gonna blow things wide open!'

'I have already told you the truth about the war,' O'Seishin said.

'Then tell me about Wintertide,' Cutler urged. 'If I'm going to sign up to your army I'll want to meet the general.'

O'Seishin's nostrils dilated in a smirk. 'You *have* met him, Ensor Cutler. Many times.'

'You.' Cutler nodded, unsurprised. 'You're Wintertide.'

'There is no Wintertide,' O'Seishin corrected. 'A mythical figurehead is infinitely more versatile than the reality could ever be. Wintertide is nowhere, so the enemy believes he is everywhere. Wintertide is nothing, so the enemy believes he is everything they fear.'

'But you're the man pulling the strings?'

'Following the lamentable fall of our revered Ethereal, Aun O'Hamaan, the honour of supreme administration has been mine, yes.'

'I thought war was Fire Warrior business.'

'Phaedra shall herald a new way of war that lies beyond the faculties of the Fire Caste,' O'Seishin crowed. 'The true craft of war lies in conquering your opponent without engaging him in battle.'

'You're telling me you're not up to the fight?'

'The Tau Empire is potent, but its enemies are legion. We cannot prosper through force of arms alone.'

'Like I said before, this is all a game to you.'

'Perhaps,' O'Seishin conceded, 'but if so, it is the noblest game of all.'

* * *

Olim brought his party to a halt outside a sealed metal hatch embossed with a stylised eye. The reinforced plasteel looked solid enough to stop a lascannon at close range. Nervously, the nobleman raised a podgy hand to the keypad by the door.

'Hold-up a moment, Friends,' said a familiar voice behind them. They turned and saw Ricardo Alvarez step from the shadows.

He's been following us all along, Roach realised with a start.

'Ah… Cluster Leader Alvarez,' Olim stuttered. 'I was just assisting…'

'Shut up, aristo.' The janissary commander's gaze bored into Roach. 'What's going on here, Friend Roach?'

Roach stared back dumbly, as if betrayal had strangled his words.

'Give me a good reason not to call this in, Claiborne,' Alvarez said quietly.

He's giving us a chance, Roach realised. *Maybe I can still turn this around…*

'I got plenty,' Dix blurted out. His friendly grin never slipped as he opened fire. Alvarez was thrown against the wall, leaking smoke from his scorched chest. An alarm blared into life before his corpse hit the ground.

The wail of the klaxon startled O'Seishin so badly he almost slipped from his perch. Flustered, he activated his drone's data array and began scouring for information.

'I'll save you the bother,' Cutler said. 'That will be our friend Abel.'

A moment later the muffled cacophony of gunfire exploded in the corridor outside. O'Seishin glanced up anxiously, but his fingers continued to flutter across his data array, as if with a life of their own. The door slid open and a pair of janissaries entered.

'Your report,' the ambassador demanded.

'Counterweight,' one of the newcomers said. He tapped a switch on the wall and the force barrier imprisoning Cutler vanished.

'Impeccable timing, Lieutenant Sandefur,' Cutler said as he loped forward. He threw O'Seishin a wolfish grin and yanked him from his throne. 'See, you're not the only player in this game, Si.'

Shas'vre Jhi'kaara was meditating in her quarters when the klaxon sounded. The tau veteran rose nimbly from her unity mat and activated her comms band.

'Fire Watch, status report?' she demanded.

'Unspecified security breach in the Watchtower, shas'vre,' the clipped voice of a Fire Warrior answered. 'Shas'ui Obihara's squad is en route now.'

Jhi'kaara paused, considering. A genuine breach in the eyrie of the tech-priests was doubtful. How could an enemy have penetrated to the highest levels of the Diadem? The duty officer had come to the same conclusion. 'I suspect a system error, shas'vre,' he ventured.

She frowned, knowing he was almost certainly correct. Despite the tech-priests devotions the refinery was in a state of decay and system errors were not uncommon. And yet...

'Prime the Crisis team,' she ordered.

'I don't understand,' Olim blubbered as Dix loomed over him.

'Open the door,' the Badlander said, 'or I'll open you.'

The terrified nobleman punched a code into the keypad and the hatch swivelled open with a whirr of hydraulics. A hulking combat servitor glided into their path from the chamber beyond, its bionic arms extended to cover them with a pair of burst cannons. Dix shoved Olim into its arms as Mister Fish leapt forward and rammed his EMP dagger between its jaws. The heretical blade pulsed and fried the cyborg's lobotomised brain with a surge of current. As the servitor jerked backwards Mister Fish vaulted onto its shoulders and opened fire on the surprised rebels beyond.

'Go!' Dix shouted as he stormed into the cavernous chamber. He and Tuggs blazed away with their carbines, gleefully mowing down charging skitarii guards and fleeing operators while Roach swung back to cover the corridor.

Chattering manically, the EMP scarred combat servitor began to whirl about on its hover skirt. Its arms flailed out and spat plasma around the room. Mister Fish leapt from its shoulders and Olim was flung away, catching several bursts of fire as he tumbled. Each one gouged a burning crater into his flesh and propelled him another step, keeping him on his feet by sheer kinetic force. When his corpse finally hit the ground it was little more than a charred husk.

'Hellfire, Dix! We needed him!' Roach yelled as he peered at the hatch mechanism. 'We got to lock this place down!'

'He had it coming,' Dix chuckled as he hurled a frag grenade across the chamber.

Roach's gaze drifted out to the access corridor and found Alvarez's corpse. The deserter's eyes were wide with the shock of betrayal and sudden death and they were staring straight at Claiborne Roach. The scout fought down the urge to go back and close them.

It won't make any difference. All my chances are used up. There's no getting off this ride now, even if it takes me all the way to the Hells.

* * *

The only thing going for the transport shuttle was its size, Guido Ortega decided as he approached the landing pad. To his pilot's eye the ship was a blocky, brutal monstrosity that looked like it had been patched up so many times there was nothing of the original left over. Still, he had no doubt it would fly well enough. The tech-priests might be blind to aesthetics, but they'd keep their precious machines ticking over.

He flinched as a squad of janissaries rushed past him. The whole rig was on alert now and the alarm was drawing security away from the outer platforms. Heading in the opposite direction, Ortega kept his pace swift and confident, trying to look like a man on official business. Unfortunately Verne Loomis wasn't doing so well. Ortega glanced back at his comrade and frowned at his blanched face and bloodshot eyes. The scraggy greyback had always been a strange one, but his last communion with the witch had really pushed him over the edge. He was muttering to himself as he jogged along at Ortega's heels, his lips twisting around the words as if they were broken glass. Ortega couldn't make out what he was saying and didn't want to know.

'You must get a grip, Señor Loomis,' he said as they reached the landing pad. 'With the alarm ringing the sentries will be watchful.'

Loomis gawped, showing black stubs of teeth. Neither of his skewed eyes met the pilot's gaze. 'Then they hear the bell too?' he asked eagerly. A trickle of drool oozed from his lips.

Ortega grimaced, wondering why he'd let Sandefur pair him up with this cretin. If Loomis was the only backup they could spare then Ortega would have preferred to do this alone. The fellow made him physically nauseous.

'Please follow my lead up there,' he said, indicating the

landing pad. Loomis nodded vaguely, bobbing his head up and down like a skull on a rubber stalk.

'It's an all-fired grox shoot!' Dix hollered as the last of the skitarii fell. There hadn't been many guards in the Eye and surprise had given the attackers an edge.

'They're coming up the corridor now!' Roach shouted from the hatch.

'So shut the fragging door, breed!' Dix called back cheerily. He and Tuggs were on the far side of the chamber now, chasing down the last of the operators. 'Hey, we got us some blueskins back here!'

A fusillade of plasma hissed down the corridor towards Roach. He ducked back from the threshold and peered at the strange sigils on the keypad, trying to make sense of it. More fire sizzled past him and he heard the hum of an approaching combat servitor. Crouched by the doorway across from him, Mister Fish frowned and gestured urgently.

'I know, man!' Roach snapped. 'I'm on it...'

To the Hells with this crap! He slammed his fist into the keypad and the hatch swung shut. That was usually the way with security – get things wrong and stuff just shut down. At least until somebody came along with the right codes...

'We've got to move fast...' Roach trailed off as he saw a pair of tech-priests sweep from a shadowed recess on the far side of the room. They glided across the floor like wraiths, their faces and limbs lost in billowing swathes of crimson fabric. Roach knew there was no telling what was under those robes. Some tech-priests were just human relics kept alive by augmetic implants, but others were souped-up killing machines packed full of nasty surprises. Something told him the Diadem's priests weren't going to be the easy kind.

'Take out the cogboys!' Roach shouted as he opened fire. Moving in perfect harmony the wraiths leapt away from his volley and latched onto the ceiling like shrouded bugs. As they scuttled overhead he caught a glimpse of chitinous metal tendrils swarming amongst the red robes.

'What you talking about?' Tuggs called as he gunned down a cowering blueskin tech. 'I don't see no–'

One of the priests dropped from above and engulfed him in a red swathe. His scream was cut short by a churning, cracking cacophony that made Roach's hair stand on end. Scant seconds later Tuggs was spewed out in a dozen glistening pieces. Some of them hit Dix, who'd been standing right beside him. With a snarl of hate the Badlander yanked his EMP dagger from his belt and plunged it into the priest. There was an electronic howl and the cyborg's robes erupted into a forest of spines as its tendrils went rigid with terminal shock. Caught in the priest's death throes, Dix was impaled a dozen times over.

Overhead, the second tech-priest raced towards Roach and Mister Fish, dodging past the frantic bursts of their carbines. Desperately the scout dived for the deranged combat servitor and swung a plasma-spitting arm towards the priest. As it leapt towards him three bursts found their mark and brought it crashing down in flames. The smouldering robes were still squirming with life when Roach and Mister Fish unloaded their carbines into it.

'Well, I guess that could have gone down a lot worse,' Roach said. His Saathlaa friend raised a quizzical eyebrow, for once unable to muster a smile. Roach figured he was finally getting cynical.

* * *

The landing pad was a massive platform built from moulded rockrete. Spiderwebs of scaffolding and fat metal feeder pipes formed a wall around it, broken by a ramp wide enough to take a tank. Ortega felt horribly vulnerable as he marched up the slope and the 'comrade' at his back wasn't helping his nerves at all. He could hear Loomis babbling away behind him, giggling occasionally, as if at some private joke. Pushing the idiot from his mind, Ortega waved at the janissaries waiting by the shuttle. There were six of them, all young and fired up by the distant alarm.

'How goes it, Friends?' he greeted them jovially.

'What's with th'alert?' the eldest janissary said in a low, liquid cant. Like his comrades, his swarthy face was riddled with tattoos and scars, betraying his ganger origins.

'They didn't tell you about the drill?' Ortega asked, feigning surprise.

'Didn't say no-t'ing to us, grandpa.'

'Well, take it from me, it's just an exercise.' Ortega stepped towards the cargo ramp, but the leader blocked his path.

'Where you t'ink you going, oldster?'

'Evidently they didn't tell you about us either!' Ortega sighed with exaggerated weariness. 'We're cover crew for–'

The janissary shoved him back. 'You t'ink we dumb fraks jus' 'cause we don't talk fancy like–' His lips were still moving when his head spun through the air, hacked clean off by Loomis's machete.

Snarling like a wolf the rangy greyback laid into the other janissaries, moving so fast Ortega could barely follow his lethal jig of chops and swipes. Half the men were dead before they knew what hit them, the other half died seconds after, their faces twisted with terror. Loomis was left standing over a pile of butchered corpses. He had his back to Ortega, but the pilot could tell he was shaking badly.

'Loomis...' the words dried up in Ortega's mouth as the maniac's head swung round to look at him. The pilot was sure a man's neck shouldn't swivel so far.

'They wasn't going to let us in,' Loomis said hoarsely. His eyes gleamed with delight. And they weren't skewed anymore.

'No...' Ortega agreed uncertainly.

'I guess we ought to stash 'em.' Loomis pointed at the cargo hatch.

'Yes...' But suddenly Guido Ortega was quite certain he didn't want to enter that dark space with Verne Loomis. In fact it was the very last thing in the world he wanted to do.

Jakob Dix was a mess. Skewered on the dead tech-priest's rigid, razor-sharp tendrils, he hung suspended in the air like a bug caught in a pincushion. Roach couldn't work out how he was still breathing.

'Wreck whatever you can,' Roach ordered Mister Fish. The Saathlaa nodded and hurried over to the nearest console while Roach stepped into Dix's field of vision. The Badlander's surviving eye rolled to fix on him. He gurgled around the spine piercing his throat, his breath coming in raw, wet rasps. Roach raised his carbine and Dix nodded, almost imperceptibly. Then Roach remembered Ricardo Alvarez and all the others Dix had killed so cheerily.

'Hey, you saying you're okay, man?' Roach said, slinging his carbine over his shoulder. Dix's eye widened and he groaned, pleading incoherently. Roach nodded. 'Well it's your call. You just hang in there then, brother.'

He turned away – just in time to see a blueskin engineer creeping up on him. Clad in a plain grey body stocking it was shorter and stouter than the Fire Warriors he'd seen, with a square-jawed face and big, workman's hands. *Big hands holding a laser cutter…* Roach flung himself aside as the xenos lunged at him. It was an awkward attack with a device intended as a tool rather than a weapon, but the beam was lethal at close range. He screamed as it sheared through his right hip and thigh, slicing and cauterising the flesh in the same instant. As he fell, the engineer loomed over him and jabbed at his face with the cutter. Desperately Roach lashed out and caught its wrist, knocking the beam off course. The tau hissed through its nostrils, its flat face puckered with hatred as it fought for control of the tool. Despite its size, the xenos was surprisingly strong, while Roach was in bad shape. The laser inched towards his head…

I thought these Earth Caste boys weren't meant to be fighters!

The engineer's head disappeared in a spray of purple mist. Roach threw the corpse aside as Mister Fish knelt beside him.

'You took your time,' Roach chided, then grinned at the Saathlaa's hurt expression. 'Hey, I'm just kidding, friend.'

Gingerly he examined his wounded leg and found there wasn't much of it left. When the Fish tried to haul him up, Roach shook him off.

'No, I ain't going nowhere. You finish up and get out if you can.' His comrade hesitated and Roach slapped him on the shoulder. 'They'll be through the hatch any time now. Go!'

The Fish nodded and rose. Roach watched him blast away at the remaining control panels, finishing up the job they'd come to do. He was pretty sure the rig's comms array would be down long enough for the 19th to make orbit without the Sky Marshall getting wind of things. Despite his doubts and the screaming pain in his leg, the thought felt good. This wasn't the path he'd have chosen, but at least he'd seen it through. He felt consciousness slipping away and hauled himself back with a brutal effort.

'You done enough,' he called to the Fish. 'Get out of here!'

His friend nodded and hurried over to the turbolift that served the beacon tower. Their exit strategy had always been hazy, Roach remembered. Just like his head was now… Something about abseiling down the outside of the tower…

Mister Fish paused at the lift doors and threw him a crisp salute. 'For Phaedra and the Imperium,' he said in perfect Gothic, grinning at Roach's incredulous expression. Then he was gone.

'Well sh–' Roach's words were cut short as the entrance hatch whooshed open and the first combat servitor glided in. Its cataract-filled eyes locked on him unerringly and it chattered something in harsh, nonsensical scrapcode.

'Yeah… and you too…' Roach answered with a grin. Offering up a prayer to a God-Emperor he didn't believe in, the scout drew his EMP dagger and prepared to walk his Thunderground. He figured it might be something worth seeing.

CHAPTER THIRTEEN

The Last Day: Diadem

Our convoy is almost halfway to the centre of the dead lake. I can't see the refinery yet, but its beacon light slices through the smog every minute or so, throwing the predatory shapes around us into stark brilliance. Devilfish and Piranhas – the tau vehicles could not have been more aptly named. They shadow us relentlessly, scenting for the blood of deceit. Though our passwords have been given and accepted I sense they do not trust us. Soon we shall fight. It is only a question of when. Bierce nods his agreement. Whatever he is, we are in concord now.

Iverson's Journal

Up in the gunboat's wheelhouse Iverson saw the Diadem rise through the mist like a titanic, scrap-metal octopus. The old rig was screeching – a wail of klaxons that told him the infiltrators had made their move. Some of them would be dead by now, perhaps all of them. Maybe they'd done what needed doing and maybe they hadn't. Either way, the Arkan were committed.

Wintertide will die. The Sky Marshall will die. Together we'll stand. Together they'll fall.

Iverson glanced to either side, appraising the captured transports chugging along beside the Triton. Both were badly battered and wouldn't take much more punishment. He'd packed as many men onto his own ship as possible, but the gunboat wasn't built for transport so most of the force was on the barges.

'How much further, Iverson?' Machen called over the vox. There was a strain in his voice that went beyond impatience.

'Not far,' Iverson replied. 'We're through the first wave of checkpoints. Maintain vox silence until I signal you, captain.'

Machen signed off with a grunt. Nominally he was in command of one barge, Vendrake the other, but neither captain was in a position to offer much leadership since both were sealed up inside their machines, playing dead along with the rest of the Arkan armour. Dispersed across the convoy, the Sentinels and Zouaves were powered down and sheathed in tarpaulin, as if in storage. It was a gamble, but the tau drones would have sniffed them out if they'd hidden below decks, so they'd hidden in plain sight instead. Likewise, the infantry were wearing the insignia of dead janissaries, giving them the appearance of rough and ready new recruits. The tau had bought the deception so far, but Iverson could almost taste their suspicion.

The blueskins don't know how to trust their instincts, Iverson decided. *They're too orderly and rational to go with a gut feeling. Maybe that will be the death of them.*

A Devilfish pulled up alongside the Triton and disgorged a pair of drones. The saucers flitted over to the gunboat and began to sniff inquisitively around the deck. It was the third search since they'd entered the lake.

But their instincts are screaming.

Machen felt like he was locked inside an iron coffin with a rabid dog chewing at his leg. The wound left by the Fire Warriors hadn't impaired his control of the Thundersuit, but the pain was shockingly insistent. For all he knew the limb might be gone from the knee down. Perhaps he was bleeding out inside his suit and he'd be dead before the battle even began. Hadn't something like that almost killed Wade once? Yes, a loxatl flechette to the femoral artery... in that ambush, so long ago now... but Wade had survived... only it hadn't made much difference in the end, because he was dead now. Daniel Wade, the last of *his* Zouaves. Machen would be damned if he didn't reap a measure of vengeance for the man.

Damned if you do or don't. Die if you will or won't. All's one in the love of hate...

'Get out of my head, Templeton!' Machen snarled, knowing full well the lost captain would shadow him to the end.

Vendrake sat in the lightless cockpit of his Sentinel with his eyes wide open. The darkness was preferable to the things he might see if he closed them. He'd taken another draught of the Glory and the need for action pulsed through his veins like liquid fire. He should have waited until the battle started, but this vigil in the dark had seemed intolerable without the drug. The nightmares were too close now. *She* was too close.

She isn't real. It's just this damned planet playing with my head – something in the air or the water. I know I'm not the only one who's haunted...

But he'd glimpsed Leonora's Sentinel stalking his barge from the riverbank, keeping to the shadows but never falling far behind. Perhaps he'd be safe on the lake. Surely she couldn't follow him onto the water without a ship?

She can't follow me anywhere because she's dead! But if she's dead how will water stop her? The thoughts spiralled around in his head, reason chasing away superstition, superstition chasing away reason. *Perhaps that's the curse of the Providence-born, he decided. We all think too bloody much.*

The waters around the convoy were seething with tau hover tanks and speeders now. Iverson could feel Bierce glaring at his back, urging him to commit. Almost unconsciously he reached for the ship's loudhailer.

'Wait,' the witch said at his shoulder. 'We must get closer.'

'The sentries are getting jumpy,' Iverson said. 'We have to strike before they do.' He noticed her eyes were locked on the rig and guessed she was thinking of Cutler. Vendrake had said that there was something between them.

'Wait a little longer,' she urged.

The convoy was about five hundred metres from the rig now. Iverson saw platoons of augmented skitarii warriors lined up along the iron promenade of the pier.

Waiting for us.

'Just a little closer…'

Somewhere nearby a buzz saw roared into life.

'What the…?' Iverson's face was thunderous as he yanked down the alarm lever and yelled into the loudhailer, 'Go! The Counterweight is go!'

Audie Joyce knew he was meant to hold fire until the commissar gave the order, but he'd waited and waited and nothing had come and all the while the xenos tanks had circled the

Triton like big, angry fish. The drone had been the last straw; it had circled him suspiciously, then stopped right in front of his hidden visor, trying to get a look inside. That was when the Emperor's righteous rage had lit Joyce up – and it must have lit up his armour too, because the next moment his buzz saws were screaming and the drone was falling out of the air in two pieces. Then the alarm went off and he heard the commissar hollering over the hailer, telling them the fight was on, so Joyce reckoned he'd done the right thing after all.

'Man the sides!' Lieutenant Hood bellowed and the grey-backs surged to the gunwales, blazing away with carbines and pulse rifles. They couldn't dent the tanks so they targeted the drones, swatting them from the air like flies. A moment later the ship's autocannons opened up on either side and battered the tau skimmers with armour piercing rounds. A Devilfish crumpled and a couple of Piranhas whirled away in flames. And then the lake caught fire. The scum of crude promethium coating the water sizzled and popped as it burned, turning grey smog to black smoke.

'Rebreathers!' Hood shouted. Choking men fumbled for their masks as the air turned caustic.

'Wake and burn, brothers!' Joyce voxed, knowing full well his knights were already powering up. He sang them a canticle of faith as he leapt to a firing platform and let rip with his heavy stubber. Behind him a Sentinel whirred into life and hopped over to the port side, firing intermittent bolts of energy from its lascannon. Its rate of fire was almost painfully slow, but the heavy weapon compensated with its sheer stopping power. Through the smoke Joyce saw a similar pattern playing out on the barges to either side of the gunboat, but the tau skimmers had been wary and many swept away untouched. Joyce longed to launch himself into the molten lake and give chase.

Yea, though I walk upon the Lake Infernal, my flesh shall not wither if my soul burns in His name!

He steadied himself as the Triton surged forward, steaming for the refinery at full tilt. It shamed Joyce to let the tau sentries go, but the plan was to stop for nothing until they reached the shuttle.

'Watch out to port!' someone yelled as a Devilfish darted up alongside the Triton. Spinning to face its prey, it strafed along sideways with its rotary gun blazing. Men screamed as they were raked from the gunwales. A blast grazed the edge of Joyce's shoulder pauldron and almost threw him from his perch. Cursing, he returned fire but his gun barely scratched the tank's white patina. As if irritated by the affront, it swivelled to target him. As its burst cannon spun up the Sentinel loomed over Joyce and spat incandescent light. The bolt from its lascannon punched through the Devilfish's nose and hurled it backwards. Long seconds later a second bolt struck an engine nacelle and the tank exploded.

'Stormchaser – second kill confirmed – Devilfish,' Vendrake's vox reported crisply. The captain nodded, recognising Beauregard Van Hal's call sign. It seemed Silverstorm's ace rider was already surging ahead in the kill stakes. Most cavalrymen lived for these fleeting, frantic moments when the world was distilled to the purity of the hunt.

Even a cesspit world like Phaedra...

Vendrake spotted a trio of T-shaped Piranhas bearing down on his barge. He skittered his Sentinel over to the stern and met them with a storm of bullets. The skimmer in the centre took the brunt of it and burst open, but its companions banked away to either side and kept coming, weaving a madcap pattern through his fire. Vendrake grinned and answered with a near random spray that clipped the skimmer to his left. It spun out of control and capsized, spilling both its riders into the burning water. He shredded them as he swerved after the remaining Piranha. It was dangerously close now.

'It's going for our engines!' someone yelled. Salvos of lighter gunfire erupted from the barge as greybacks crowded around Vendrake and sniped at the open-topped skimmer. Abruptly the Piranha abandoned its manoeuvring and sped straight for them, buzzing like a giant mosquito. Vendrake nailed the pilots in seconds, already knowing he was too late.

It has been too late for too long, if not forever…

To Vendrake's Glory-fried eyes time seemed to stretch taught, pinning the incoming Piranha just metres from its target, strung like an arrow in a bowstring of flames. And suddenly he knew he'd seen all this before, the same lethal hues painted across a different canvas – frozen flames and fate staring at him through his windshield.

'*Belle du Morte* signing in,' Leonora's spiteful voice sang from the vox.

Then the arrow was released and the skimmer smashed into the barge like a missile.

'Vendrake's in trouble,' Machen called over the vox. His voice sounded strained, as if he were struggling to stay awake.

'Confirmed,' Iverson said, watching the barge to starboard shake and stall. Within seconds Vendrake's ship had faded into the mist, left behind by its speeding companions.

'We cannot abandon them,' the witch said quietly.

'I'm going back,' Machen said. His ship was already turning about.

Iverson hesitated. Bierce shook his head. 'Negative,' Iverson ordered. 'We press on for the rig.'

'To the Hells with you, Iverson.' Machen cut the line.

Another explosion rippled through Vendrake's barge. This time the whole ship heaved, as if in the throes of a violent seizure. With a creak of tortured metal the stern plummeted towards the lake, sending scrabbling, screaming greybacks tumbling into the burning water. They burst into flames the moment they touched the lake, almost as if they'd combusted from within. Vendrake dug his Sentinel's claws into the deck and arched backwards, struggling for balance on the sheer slope. A third explosion rocked the barge and more men slid towards the brink. A lucky few found handholds on his machine's legs. Then a fellow Sentinel lurched over the lip, almost dislodging him.

Now we're only six, a distant, clinical part of Vendrake counted. *And Arness is on this tug too, somewhere up front. Once the ship goes down we'll be four. And I won't be one of them.*

With a throaty roar, Machen's barge pulled up alongside the dying ship and fired a barrage of grappling hooks. Desperate men abandoned their handholds and leapt for the lifelines. Coughing and cursing, they fought their way across the sloping deck towards the rescue ship. A Zouave who'd wedged himself behind a fuel pipe rocketed over with a greyback under each arm. Arness's Sentinel hopped across with men clinging to its cockpit. Balanced precariously over the lake, Vendrake didn't dare move, didn't see how he *could* move without falling.

'*Belle du Morte*, killed in action,' a sinuous voice whispered from his vox. '*Your* inaction, dear Hardin.'

Vendrake tried to blank her out. His entire body was taut with the effort of keeping his mount steady. He had never felt more at one with his machine.

'It's almost time, my love,' the wraith said.

'What do you want from me, you dead bitch?' Vendrake snarled, feeling his grip on sanity slipping along with his grip on the deck.

'Why, Hardin, that's no way to talk to a lady!' A broken glass giggle, then a death rattle sigh. 'I just want us to be together. Forever…'

He saw her dissolve from the smoke and come skittering across the fiery lake like a herald out of the Hells. Her Sentinel's hide was scorched black and encrusted with coral spines that flickered with unholy current.

'There's so much to see, Hardin. You just have to open your eyes.' Rainbow light oozed from her cockpit like prismatic pus, leaving swirling streamers of corruption in its wake.

'You aren't Leonora,' he hissed through gritted teeth. 'You aren't anything.'

'Then what does that make you, my love?'

'I…'

A trio of tau tanks stormed from the smog and swept the apparition away. Suddenly Leonora's challenge didn't matter anymore because Vendrake's focus had narrowed to another, more pressing question.

How do I stop them?

Two of the tanks were Devilfish, but the third was something much worse. It was built around the same sleek chassis, but sported a massive turret-mounted cannon that turned Vendrake's blood to ice. He'd never encountered one before, but he'd heard the descriptions: the third attacker was a Hammerhead, the main battle tank of the Tau Empire.

A couple of shots from that monster cannon will sink Machen's tug before he knows what's hit him.

Suddenly Vendrake saw the aliens' plan with dreadful clarity.

They could have finished his dying barge in seconds, but they'd been patient and used it to lure the others back into a trap. Wedged against the sinking barge, Machen's vessel was appallingly vulnerable. Vendrake's mind whirled, soaring on Glory as he sifted and discarded tactics, tearing through options in split seconds, hunting for an answer before it was too late. And somewhere in the desperate alchemy of Glory and guilt he found his answer.

I am the Silverstorm.

Vendrake let go and vaulted from the sloping deck. At the height of his arc he ignited his undercarriage thrusters and set the leap on fire. Pushing his customised machine to its limits he soared across the lake to intercept the leading Devilfish. It was an insane, outrageous move that was almost heretical in its abuse of the machine's tortured spirit, but then the machine itself was a heretical construct, twisted far beyond the sane limits of the Sentinel pattern by his obsessive tinkering. It was something more than a Sentinel, just as Vendrake himself had become something more than a man in this moment when the world had become something less than real.

This is my Thunderground.

His Sentinel came down hard on the tank, cracking its carapace and sending it into a wild spin. Calculating trajectories in a blur, Vendrake leapt across to its neighbour with his talons extended and his autocannon blazing. The landing raked deep grooves into the second Devilfish's canopy and the bullets tore it wide open. And then Vendrake was leaping again.

This is my redemption.

Intent on Machen's barge, the Hammerhead never saw him coming. Its gun was powering up to fire when the Sentinel slammed down onto its barrel. The ion cannon exploded like a miniature sun, disintegrating the tank's canopy and the

Sentinel's legs. Vendrake's burning cockpit was hurled into the air like a rocket. Thrust back into his couch by the propulsion, Vendrake watched the sickening clouds soaring towards him. His body was burning and his mind was almost burned out.

Maybe I'll see the stars, he thought fleetingly. *Maybe I'll escape Phaedra after all.*

'There is no escape, my love,' Leonora said, sounding peculiarly wistful. He could no longer tell if she was speaking through the vox or inside his head. 'But don't despair, Hardin. I'll always be with you.'

And then he jackknifed in the air and plummeted back towards the lake.

I'm a silver bullet that's going to punch right through to the heart of this sick world. Vendrake grinned. *Who knows, I might even kill the bitch.*

Spilling cascades of water, Iverson's gunboat surged from the lake and rolled onto the refinery pier. Combat servitors and skitarii were scattered or crushed as they tried to mount a defence against the armoured leviathan; more were mown down by the Triton's guns and the greybacks crouched behind its walls. The lascannon at the prow flared and rendered a chattering defence turret down to molten slag. The weapon was fully charged and eager to kill, its spirit restored to health by the ministrations of the Arkan tech-priests. It fired again, disintegrating a trio of skitarii as the gunboat rolled up the pier like a mobile fortress.

Iverson surveyed the scene from the wheelhouse, trying to marry up the reality of the rig with Abel's painstakingly transcribed maps. Up close, his first impression of an industrial octopus was reinforced. The Diadem was a city-sized sprawl built on a mosaic of interlocking platforms that were packed with manufactories, silos and hab-blocks linked by a network of roads and tunnels. The centre was occupied by the octopus's mantle, a cyclopean tower block crowned by the beacon light. A cascade of pipes and scaffolding splayed from the mantle like tentacles and enfolded the other buildings. Looking at that covetous tower, Iverson sensed the rig was somehow alive and even dimly aware of their presence.

'We have to get off this thing before it wakes up,' someone whispered at his ear. Iverson turned, half expecting Reve, but finding only the witch. He could feel the anger radiating from her in waves.

'I hope Abel's directions are as good as his codes,' he said. Their informer had plotted their path to the shuttle pad with meticulous care. It lay some two kilometres into the sprawl and the idea was to run the rig's gauntlet before it closed its grip.

'You should not have left the others behind,' she said coldly.

'I had no choice. We had to hit the pier hard and fast.' He activated the loudhailer. 'All armoured personnel disembark and assume flanking positions.'

'Armoured personnel,' she mocked. 'A handful of Sentinels and Zouaves! That's all we have left now.'

Something snapped inside him and he rounded on her. 'I don't know what your game is, but I won't tolerate insubordination during a combat operation.'

Standing beside her, Bierce nodded fierce approval.

'Do you intend to shoot me too, Holt Iverson?' she challenged.

Shoot you… too? How do you know about Reve?

Looking down, he saw his hand had strayed to his holster.

'Commissar,' Machen called over the vox, 'we're coming in now. I saved as many as I could.' The captain sounded worse than before, his voice a barely audible croak.

Iverson glanced out the window and saw Machen's barge pulling up alongside the pier. 'You disobeyed a direct order, captain.'

'Vendrake is dead,' Machen said. 'So are half the men who sailed with him.'

'Deploy around the Triton. We have to get moving.'

'Confirmed,' Machen said tightly over the vox. 'And Iverson – when this is done I'm going to kill you.'

'What do you hope to achieve with this insanity?' O'Seishin asked as Cutler's team crossed the deserted shuttle pad. The tau ambassador was back on his floating throne drone, but Obadiah Pope was right beside him with a carbine wedged discreetly into the small of his back. Most of the Diadem's forces had been drawn to the Watchtower and the handful of janissaries they'd encountered along the way hadn't questioned the ambassador and his 'retinue'.

'Just hang in there and you'll get the picture soon enough, Si,' Cutler said.

'emperor's blood!' Lieutenant Sandefur exclaimed from up front.

The party halted, staring at the scene ahead. There was indeed blood, a great deal of it, but Cutler doubted any of it belonged to the Emperor. It was pooled around the shuttle's cargo hatch in a semi-congealed swathe, black with swarming flies. A severed hand protruded from the ooze, its fingers extended almost apologetically. The shuttle's ramp was extended into the filth like a questing tongue, its length smeared with trails of blood.

'What in the Hells happened here?' Sandefur was pale with shock. Violence was nothing new to any of them, but there was an obscene quality to this carnage that went beyond honest killing. Almost a miasma…

It's back, Cutler sensed. Drawing his sabre, he stepped onto the ramp.

'I will not enter there,' O'Seishin said. He tried to pull back from the ship, but Pope shoved him forward. 'Ensor Cutler, I cannot!' the alien implored.

Cutler scowled at him. All the ambassador's arrogance had dissolved away, leaving behind an ancient, frightened relic.

'You can and you will,' Cutler said. 'You think you've got us gue'la monkeys worked out, don't you, Si? Well then, this is something you've just got to see.'

'Taking heavy fire!' Dryden shouted over the vox. 'Coming in from all sides!'

Lieutenant Pericles Quint peered through the windshield at his fellow rider. Fifty metres down the road ahead, Dryden's Sentinel was dancing about frantically, tormented by bright bursts of energy. Every strike bit deep into the machine's armour and drew a gush of smoke.

'I… I don't see them,' Quint blustered, hunting about for the attackers. The energy bursts seemed to be coming out of thin air. 'Initiate firing pattern Wolf 359…'

'Pull back!' Beauregard Van Hal cut in. 'Do it now, Dry!'

'I've lost my-' Dryden's Sentinel exploded with shocking suddenness.

'Dryden?' Quint asked dully, staring at the burning wreckage.

'Suppression fire, full auto,' Van Hal ordered. 'Purge the street.'

'But there's nothing…' Quint's whine was drowned in a barrage of gunfire as the other Sentinels followed Van Hal's lead. Almost against his will, the lieutenant followed suit. They battered the empty street ahead with bullets and las-fire for a full thirty seconds before Van Hal called a halt.

'You've got us shooting at ghosts,' Quint snapped, trying to regain the upper hand in the squadron. Now that Vendrake was gone, he was Silverstorm's commanding officer and Van Hal had no business undermining him.

'Not ghosts,' the veteran rider said, striding forward. 'But maybe something close.'

'What are you talking about, man?'

'They moved fast, but we got one.' Van Hal hopped over to a broken shape lying by the side of the road. It was a tau warrior in bulky black armour. The broken carapace was still phasing in and out of visibility erratically. 'It's some kind of cloaking system,' Van Hal said. 'Typical blueskin trickery.'

'What's the hold-up?' Iverson voxed. 'We've got a whole battalion of skitarii on our tails back here!'

The Sentinel squad had forged ahead, scouting out the path for the Triton and the infantry. It was dirty, dangerous work and they'd already lost Rees to a skitarii ambush. With Dryden gone they were down to just four machines.

'Bit of a tussle with the blueskins,' Quint said, 'but don't you worry, I've nailed them, commissar!'

'There'll be more,' Van Hal said. 'They were working as a squad.'

'Then perhaps you should take point,' Quint huffed, 'seeing as your eyes are so blasted sharp!'

'That man's an idiot,' Iverson snarled and flicked the vox over to Machen's channel. 'What's your status, captain?'

'We're holding, but there are hundreds of them now.' Machen's reply was framed by a relentless wash of gunfire. 'They've come crawling out of every bloody service tunnel along the way.'

The surviving Zouaves were arrayed around the Triton,

supporting the beleaguered infantry. At first resistance had been light and they'd made good speed, but then the Diadem had started to wake up and its guardians had massed around the intruders like antibodies. Iverson checked Abel's map: the shuttle pad was just a couple of blocks away, but the advance was in danger of stalling.

The infantry are too slow. We need to run for the shuttle.

Iverson wasn't sure if the thought was his or Bierce's… or perhaps even Reve's. His augmetic eye was playing up badly now, the electric wasp inside flittering about and painting sparks across his vision. He glanced down at the deck. There were some fifty greybacks manning the walls of the ship. Would they be enough?

'Don't do it,' the witch cautioned. 'Don't leave them behind again.'

But the mission is all that matters…

Machen mowed down another pair of charging skitarii. The Mechanicus warriors died as silently as they fought, their pallid Saathlaa faces untouched by pain or fear when they fell. All were clad in the same rust-red flak armour, but they sported a riot of customised augmetics. He saw glowing optics, bionic arms flush with blades, even spring-loaded legs, but every warrior moved with the same implacable purpose, as if controlled by an overarching mind. That mind had already ground down a score of greybacks on the road to the shuttle. There were less than a hundred men left on the ground now, every one of them battered and bleeding. Without the Zouaves they would have been overrun in minutes.

We forged our path in the blood and bones of our fallen, erecting squalid mortuary markers along the Crow Road…

'Shut up!' Machen screamed, berating the agony in his leg

as much as the ghost in his head. 'Let me think for a moment, Templeton!'

A squat skitarii warrior with piston-like legs sprang from the crowd, its arms extended to batter him with twin pneumatic hammers. Machen caught it on his drill, but the dying cyborg cracked him over the helmet so hard his visor shattered. Shards of glass licked his eyeballs like sandpaper. Half blind, he cast the corpse away and parried a jabbing blade. And suddenly he was vomiting inside his armour, his whole body wracked by spasms of agony. Phaedra's air was crowded with a billion tiny killers and he'd left the wound in his leg untreated too long.

'Make way!' Iverson yelled over the loudhailer and suddenly the Triton was rolling backwards. The Confederates leapt aside as it gathered speed and ploughed into the pursuing ranks of skitarii, steamrollering scores of the slow-moving cyborgs into a paste of meat and metal.

'Purge them, brothers!' Machen heard the boy preacher bellow.

With a cacophony of buzz saws and chainblades, Joyce and his Zouaves charged after the gunboat and tore into the skitarii stragglers who had escaped the onslaught. Squinting through a haze of blood the captain followed like a battered tank, trying in vain to blot out Templeton's endless saga.

And then the bell tolled thirteen and we knew all our granite-carved victories were but scribbles in the sands of time.

Cutler's torch found the words first:

'THE BELL TOLLS'

The phrase was smeared in blood above the gaping bulkhead to Silo Chamber 3. A headless corpse lay across the threshold with its arms folded neatly across its belly. Its wayward head was propped up inside the splayed ribcage, bloodshot eyes staring up at the colonel in mute outrage.

I guess you won't be flying us out of here after all, Señor Ortega, Cutler thought grimly as he recognised the corpse. *Which means none of us are getting off this mud ball. But that was a problem for later.*

Cutler shone his torch into the dark space beyond. The silo stank of promethium and blood, but all he could see was the blood and its sundered containers. Something had turned the chamber into an abattoir, garnishing it with a display of ragged limbs and yawning torsos, all bedecked with glistening streamers of entrails. There was a deranged order to the carnage, everything positioned and angled *just so*, the hideous parts hinting at some infinitely more hideous whole. It was a pattern Cutler had seen twice before, first in the hovels of Trinity, wrought in broken junk, then in Dorm 31, rendered in flesh.

'Who did this?' Sandefur asked weakly. He looked like he was going to be sick.

Loomis, Cutler decided. *It will be Loomis this time.*

'Nothing human,' Cutler answered. 'We have to kill it.'

They entered the silo one by one, with Pope taking the rear, still shepherding the tau ambassador. O'Seishin was almost apoplectic with terror, his deep-set eyes whirling about the butchery as if afraid to settle anywhere. He was muttering a mantra in his native tongue, speaking so fast he was almost tripping over his own words.

Welcome to our 'psychic malaise' you smug bastard, Cutler thought as he pushed on into the chamber. It was a hollow cylinder, about ten metres in diameter with a sloping ceiling that pinched into an intake duct high above their heads. He played his light around the aperture, but found nothing. Apart from the duct and the grilled vents in the floor the silo was featureless. There was nowhere to hide.

But you're in here somewhere. I can feel you…

A cackle came from behind them, fluid and feral and rancid with hate, then an awful cacophony of voices: *'Trinity in embers…'*

They whirled round and saw the daemon. It was plastered against the wall above the doorway with its arms splayed wide and its ebony talons buried in the metal. It wore Loomis's face like a flesh mask stretched across something *other*, but the bulging, terror-struck eyes were still his. His naked body had bulked out with muscles that rippled and writhed with a life of their own, as if searching for their true form. But worst of all were the faces. There were dozens of them suffocating under his skin, all screaming and snarling for a way out.

'Trinity remembers!' shrieked the faces drowning in Loomis's flesh.

Pope reacted first, but the daemon was faster. As the greyback raised his carbine it launched itself from the wall and landed right in front of him. Its jaws gaped impossibly wide, tearing the remnants of Loomis's face in half. A pink, leech-like maw surged forward and engulfed the horrified greyback's head before he could fire. The monster arched backwards at the waist with bone-snapping violence and hauled Pope into the air, swallowing him down to the waist. His flailing legs smacked O'Seishin from his perch and sent his drone spinning away. There was a violent burp and Pope was gone, compressed to a writhing bulge in the daemon's belly.

'Kill it!' Cutler roared and leapt forward with his sabre. A claw flashed out with inhuman speed and caught the blade mid-swing. The colonel fought to free it as that hungry, lamprey maw twisted to face him.

'Down!' Sandefur yelled, opening fire with his carbine. Cutler threw himself prone as the energy bolts seared across the chamber. The daemon screeched in pain and swung to face the new threat, letting Cutler's sabre clatter to the ground. The lieutenant was down on one knee, firing in rapid bursts that gouged smoking pits into the horror's churning flesh. The daemon belched and its entire body heaved as if wracked by a massive spasm.

'Look out!' Cutler yelled, but it was too late. The daemon spat Pope back out and the half-dissolved cadaver thudded into Sandefur, throwing him to the ground and spattering him with corrosive juices. He screamed, trying to throw the corpse off, but Pope's bony arms locked around his neck, animated by some hideous un-life. The corpse's mouth yawned wide and vomited into Sandefur's face. The lieutenant's shrieks trailed into ragged chokes as his flesh was eaten away by the smoking bile.

Cutler rammed his retrieved sabre into the daemon's belly and twisted. The beast roared in pain and lashed out, throwing him clear across the chamber. He hit the wall hard and sagged to the ground, blood spewing from deep gashes across his chest. Through a haze of pain he watched the abomination rear up towards its full height. It seemed to be uncoiling from within itself, erupting from the possessed man in a ravenous slurry of eyes and maws and tongues that blinked and gnawed and screamed their way into reality.

'He's coming home,' the drowned faces chorused. 'And you didn't kill him, Whitecrow. You never killed him!'

'What are you?' Cutler groaned through gritted teeth as he felt consciousness slipping away.

'What are we?' The faces cackled in disharmony. 'We are Trinity!'

Then they laughed like a winter wind, and through the wind Cutler heard the tolling of a bell. *The bell.*

And then he was back in the blighted town again, entering the heart of its darkness with the witch and her *weraldur*, who everyone called Mister Frost and whose true name was known only to her. They walked into the chapel of rainbow light and found the daemon bell hanging from a chain into nowhere. It was a black iron monstrosity tarnished by a cancer of coral nodules that pulsed with unholy vitality. The cone was easily big enough to accommodate several standing men, but Cutler doubted any man would last long if he attempted such a thing, for its mouth was the wellspring of the toxic light.

'What is it?' Cutler asked as he had asked so many times before.

'A rift into the Whispersea,' Skjoldis gave her eternal answer, 'a gateway to the warp. The taint flows from it like blood from an open wound.'

It's warp-forged, but it carries the blight of Phaedra, Cutler realised. And this was a new truth, something he hadn't known back then. *Someone's brought Phaedra to Providence...*

And then the bell tolled again and the world shimmered and twitched and the dark man was standing before them. His greatcoat seemed impossibly black in that place of many colours and his bowed head was swathed in the shadows of a wide-brimmed hat. He was taller than any man had a right to be, but agonisingly thin with it, as if every fibre of his body had been stretched to the breaking point, attenuating him into *otherness*.

'All the worlds unfold into one,' the stranger said, 'and so all the stains of corruption become one strain.' Its voice was an ephemeral whisper that rode the streamers of light. 'You know, it's taken forever and a day to find you, Colonel Ensor Cutler.

So long I've almost forgotten why I ever came looking.'

'How in the Hells do you know my name?' Cutler challenged, taking a step forward. 'Who are you?'

The stranger looked up, casting the shadows from its face. Its bloodless skin was incised with a lattice of smouldering, smoking scars that framed inhuman eyes: one was a dead black orb, the other a burning augmetic. It smiled and the seams of magma running through its flesh were routed into a fresh con-figuration. Reality seemed to shiver and shimmer before the new order.

'Me?' the stranger said. 'I'm just a man who found his way back home.'

And then the world exploded in a flash of pure white light.

CHAPTER FOURTEEN

The Last Day: The Shuttle Pad

The skitarii horde is broken for the time being, but the respite cost us heavily. We lost almost half our infantry in the struggle, together with a pair of Zouave knights. We must be gone from here before the tech-guard masses again, as they surely will. The Sentinel scouts are coming up on the shuttle pad now…

Iverson's Journal

'What do you mean you're not sure, Quint?' Iverson growled into the vox. 'Either you've found evidence of a skirmish or you haven't. Which is it?'

'Quite so, commissar, quite so,' Quint blustered. 'Indeed, *something* most certainly happened here, but it's…'

'Put Van Hal on the line.'

'Sir, I don't see…'

'Van Hal here,' the veteran broke in. 'We've got blood outside the shuttle – lots of it – but no bodies. Quint's right. Something's very wrong here.'

'Maybe Cutler's team hid the bodies,' Iverson suggested.

'Then they left Seven Hells of a mess behind,' Van Hal said. 'No, it doesn't add up.'

'And there's no sign of our infiltrators?' Iverson frowned. Without Cutler's pilot nobody was going anywhere.

'If they're here, they're inside the shuttle. Want me to check it out?'

'No, secure the pad and wait. We're only a block away.' Iverson cut the link and turned to the witch. To his surprise she was sitting cross-legged on the floor with her eyes closed. That was when he realised how cold the wheelhouse had grown despite the heat outside. The scrawny Lethean helmsman had noticed it too and was staring at the woman in abject terror.

'Is witchcraft,' the Mariner muttered in his broken Gothic. 'She carries the taint!'

'Keep your eyes on the road!' Iverson snapped. 'She is the Emperor's servant.' *At least I think she is.* Either way, he knew where her mind was wandering. *I just hope you find him alive...*

'Whitecrow!' the voice said again, growing more insistent. 'You must wake up!'

Skjoldis? Cutler stirred, struggling against the white oblivion that had swallowed him. *Is that you?* His eyes flicked open. He was still in the temple, but the unholy light was gone, leaving behind a washed-out façade of the reality. A jagged chasm yawned beneath the spot where the daemon bell had hung. The bell itself was gone, along with its master.

We fought, the dark man and I, Cutler remembered. *At least it felt like fighting.* He rose and hobbled over to the rift. It was an infinitely black gash in the greyscale murk of the temple. To fall in there would be to fall forever.

'Open your eyes, Whitecrow!' the voice nagged again.

I have, he thought. *Haven't I?*

'Skjoldis?' he said it aloud this time. 'We were wrong. We were wrong all along.'

More memories… Skjoldis with her arms spread wide, struggling to stem the tide of ghosts that came flooding from the bell in the dark man's wake. There were so many – angry ghosts and bitter ghosts and mournful ghosts – phantoms in every shade of misery and malice, all drawn to the dark man like moths to an unholy flame. He lured them with promises of redemption or vengeance or simple silence that radiated from him like black light. And while Skjoldis held them back with incantations and imprecations, Cutler duelled with their master, though they did not fight with guns or blades. He couldn't recall the way of it, but he knew his soul hung on the outcome, and perhaps the soul of his world too, so he fought with everything that he was, but in the end it was the *weraldur* who ended it. With an honest swing of his axe he sundered the chain suspending the bell and tore down the gate, casting out the dark man and his congregation.

But they never fell back into the Hells. They simply fell somewhere else.

'He's still on Providence,' Cutler said. 'We didn't kill him.'

'I know,' she sighed. 'I've always suspected it.'

'Then why didn't you tell me, woman?' he asked bitterly. 'Why didn't you tell me the bastard had us beat?'

'Because it was the best we could do, but it would not have been enough for you, Whitecrow.'

'The best we could do was lose him?' Cutler was staring into the rift as if he might jump. 'He'll come back, Skjoldis. Maybe he's the one sending the daemon after me.'

'The daemon was spawned by the death agonies of Trinity's damned.' She stood before him now, a hovering, hazy spectre. 'It shadows you through the warp because you are its father in murder, Whitecrow. It was your command that purged Trinity and conceived its malice.'

'And what am I supposed to do about it?'

'The only thing you can do: you fight.' She sighed, a long, soul-weary exhalation. 'Sometimes there is nothing more to be done. But now you must wake up…'

…Before it is too late.

Cutler opened his eyes. Again. He was back in the charnel house of Silo 3, slumped against the wall where the daemon had thrown him. *The daemon!* His eyes roved about frantically, but found nothing. *Why would it spare me?* Then he saw its legs. They were kneeling amongst the corpses, as if in prayer. Smoke was still pouring from the charred ridge of its waist and above the waist there was nothing at all.

What in the Hells? Cutler tried to rise and pain hit him in a raw red wave that almost washed him back to oblivion. He looked down and saw the shredded ruin of his jacket. Gingerly he pulled aside the rags and grimaced at the gouges in his chest. The daemon's slash had cut deep.

You have to get up, Whitecrow! Skjoldis urged.

'And do what, woman?' Cutler said. 'Our flyboy's dead. We're not going anywhere.'

A contemplative silence, then: *Is his head intact? Yes… I see from your thoughts it is.*

'His head? What's the poor bastard's head got to do with anything?

Bring it to the cockpit, Whitecrow. There may be a way.

He struggled to his feet, too exhausted to argue. His comrades were dead. Sandefur's skull had been hollowed out by the daemonic bile and what was left of Pope wasn't even recognisable as a man. O'Seishin was gone. Blackened shards of his throne drone were scattered around the chamber, a couple of them embedded in the metal walls like blades.

It was his drone that killed the daemon, Cutler realised. *There must have been a bomb built into it and O'Seishin triggered it when the beast went for him. But where's the sly son-of-a-bitch got to?*

He found the ambassador halfway down the access corridor. The ancient tau was breathing in ragged gasps as he pulled himself along, dragging his spindly legs behind him like dead things. He looked up in abject terror when the colonel loomed over him.

'Now where do you think you're going, Si?' Cutler chided.

'I was wrong,' the tau whispered, staring at the severed head hanging from the colonel's belt. 'We cannot work in concord. Your species is sick.'

'Well, I won't argue it.' Cutler bent painfully and heaved his quarry up and over his shoulders. 'But you and me, we're going to see this through together.'

'Then Cutler's alive?' Iverson asked as the witch got to her feet.

'He is dying,' she answered in a brittle monotone. 'We are running out of time.'

'I understand,' he said. 'We're coming up on the shuttle now.' He saw the Sentinels stalking about on the pad ahead, restless and distrustful of the lull. He appraised the witch thoughtfully.

I have to know. Whatever it is she's hiding about me, I have to know.

'Tell me,' he said quietly, certain she wouldn't mistake his meaning.

She didn't meet his eyes, but he could feel her coming to a decision.

'Iverson...'

Something hit the Triton so hard the whole world seemed to quake. There was an ear-splitting boom and a shriek of tortured metal. A bloom of orange fire spewed from the prow, detonating the lascannon and immolating everyone up front.

'Down!' Iverson yelled, throwing himself across the witch. The cabin windows exploded inwards, shredding the bewildered helmsman instantly. Fragments of glass and charred meat rained down on Iverson's back as he covered the witch.

Get up!

Iverson's greatcoat was smouldering as he rose to his knees. Bierce stood over him with his hands clasped behind his back, untouched by the fire storm.

War is the only truth, your will to fight the only virtue.

The witch's guardian burst through the door. His face went dark with fury as he took in the carnage. With a broken cry he hauled Iverson off his charge and lifted her in his arms.

'She's all right,' Iverson wheezed, coughing on the acrid smoke. 'Just dazed.'

That was when he heard the clamour from the deck below. He swung the door open and stared into a scene of abject chaos. The greybacks were milling about in disarray, trying to escape a searing hail of energy bolts that seemed to come out of nowhere. Men were going down fast, picked off by the unseen assailants amongst them.

'Follow their fire!' Iverson yelled, then ducked back inside as a burst of fire leapt towards him.

'They're on board!' someone in the crowd yelled. 'They're up here with us!'

'I don't see nothing!' old Cully swore. He was kneeling with the stock of his bulky rail rifle wedged into the crook of his shoulder. 'There ain't nothing here!' A bolt scorched away his left ear and he yelped, firing off a wild shot.

'Form up in your firing teams!' Lieutenant Grayburn was bawling from the stern. 'We need to establish–' Cully's hyper-velocity slug punched through his breastplate and exploded out of his back, almost decapitating the man behind. Grayburn staggered back, his lips working soundlessly, then toppled over the gunwales. Cully never even saw it happen. He had dropped his rifle and was on his knees, clawing at his ruined ear. Some-one snatched up the weapon.

Cort Toomy sighted down the long barrel of the xenos rifle and felt the old instincts kick in. The sniper had never recov-ered from the head wound he'd suffered on their first day in the Mire... so long ago... It was a kick, he remembered, from a knight... on a boat. After that the world had gone dim, like somebody had turned out the lights in his head, so he'd just tagged along with the other guys and done what he was told, never talking or even thinking much. Everyone figured he'd be dead within a week, but here he was, almost at the end of the road, still breathing when so many others were scrab meat. And now he knew why. A lopsided smile lit up his slack features as he felt the thrum of the rifle in his hands. This gun felt *right*.

'We got work to do, Eloise,' he told the rifle, marvelling at the sound of his own voice. He couldn't recall why he always called his guns Eloise, but he knew he always had, every one of them. Now he cradled her lovingly, careless of his own safety as he read the pattern of enemy fire, tracing the lethal threads back to their source, chasing a target...

Got you! The attacker was almost invisible, just a man-like shimmer on the starboard firing platform, but the flaring aperture of its gun was a beacon to the sniper. Toomy took the shot.

Iverson saw a burst of bright static through the crowd. A heart-beat later a headless body in bulky carapace armour toppled from one of the firing platforms, fizzling in and out of sight as its infiltration system went haywire.

Stealth suits, Iverson realised. Hadn't Van Hal mentioned running into them earlier? Alongside their invisibility the tau infiltrators were equipped with jetpacks so the Triton's open deck was an easy target for them. He scoured the deck for the others. According to reports their cloaking systems weren't *quite* perfect.

Where are you?

And then he had them – a pair of humanoid shapes, one crouching on the stern engine housing, the other on the port firing platform. The light seemed to slip around them, leaving behind colourless, quicksilver shadows that flickered wildly in the green-tinged field of his augmetic eye. Irritated, Iverson blocked the bionic with a hand and squinted with his good eye – and the shadows were gone.

It's the eye. Something about it lets me see them. Maybe there's more to this relic than I thought. Once again he wondered how many others had carried the optic before him. The thing was *old*. But this was no time for idle speculation. Men were dying out there. Firing up his chainsaw, he leapt to the deck below.

The Triton was a wreck. It was stalled some two hundred metres from the shuttle pad, its prow burning ferociously. To Machen it sounded like bedlam had broken out on the deck above, but that wasn't his battle. His heart pounded in fitful spurts as he raced across the platform housing the shuttle pad.

His body was rotting inside his carapace, just as his mind was rotting inside his skull, one eaten by microscopic vermin, the other by a dead poet's deliriums.

Weak meat inside an iron skin, kindred fates twinned too late...

The fever had him in its grip now and he was shivering and burning up all at once, but that didn't matter anymore. Nothing mattered except the fury that promised his Thunderground.

Racing fate for the final hour, chasing hate before hate turns sour...

He was loping towards the armoured giant that had killed the gunboat. The Broadside battlesuit had stepped into their path from a silo up ahead and fired its twin rail guns before anyone could react. That one shot had demolished the Triton's frontal armour as if it were the lightest flak plate. Squads of Fire Warriors had struck simultaneously, materialising from access tunnels and silos around the platform. There weren't many – no more than twenty or thirty troops – but they were lethal at long range. The surviving greybacks were crouched under the gunboat's treads, fighting back furiously, but the Fire Warriors' accuracy was terrifying. Once again, the Zouaves would have to turn back the tide.

'Engage them!' the boy preacher had commanded and the knights had obeyed without question, splitting up to charge the scattered aliens. Machen had gone straight for the Broadside and it had swivelled to face him, tracking him with those massive tank-killing cannons. As he closed in he stared into the impassive sensor cluster that passed for its face, trying to read the pilot's mind.

Burning rage before rage runs cold...

A pencil-thin ray of light touched Purcell when he was halfway to his foes. A moment later the Zouave was lit up with spectral blue light. As if following some unspoken edict, a dozen Fire Warriors focussed their attacks on the knight, pounding him with deadly accuracy. His archaic Stormsuit buckled under the barrage in seconds and he clattered to the ground. The marker light moved on from the melted wreckage, seeking another target.

Audie Joyce watched it happen from the other side of the square, where he was hacking apart a quartet of Fire Warriors. The tau were pathetically fragile in melee and there was no glory in killing them, but when he saw Purcell die he knew that was wrong. Cleansing the xenos – any xenos – was an Emperor-given gift!

Scowling, he followed the questing ray back to its source and spied a lightly armoured alien perched on a rooftop. The warrior's helmet bulged with enhanced optics and sensors that identified him as some kind of spotter. He was directing the marker light across the battlefield with a telescopic device in his hands. Joyce levelled his heavy stubber... and saw the ray drift towards Machen.

When every colour is just another shade of damnation...

Machen dodged a heartbeat before the battlesuit's rail guns fired. The killing bolts screamed past him, as if furious at his escape. He laughed triumphantly but heard only a brittle, dead man's cackle. It was only when he tried to fire that he noticed his gun was missing, along with his left arm. One of the hypervelocity slugs had sheared off the limb at the shoulder and he hadn't even noticed. He found he didn't care. One arm would suffice for his vengeance.

And the final fires have fallen into ash...

He ducked low and death streaked over his head, leaving twin contrails in its wake. Then he was upon his foe.

Shuddering with rage and fever, he thrust his drill into the battlesuit's chest. His entire body vibrated as the screeching bit bored through layers of tough carapace. It was agony, but he embraced it gladly.

And all hope's awash insensate fate…

The battlesuit's rail guns flailed about as the pilot tried to bring them to bear on an enemy that was too close. It tottered backwards, but Machen followed mercilessly, digging ever deeper as his own body tore itself apart in sympathy. Abruptly the drill surged forward, breaking through the final strata of plates into blood and bone. Machen held it there for several seconds, liquidising the xenos within, longing for the rapture and finding nothing.

'Are you my Thunderground?' he wheezed at the dead xenos, knowing it was not. He staggered back, leaving the suit standing mute witness to his failure. 'Templeton, if you know so much, then tell me…' his voice broke into a spasm of blood-flecked coughs, 'tell me what I need to do!'

Then heed the bell that tolls the end of always.

Dimly, Machen wondered why his fever had turned the world bright blue. Then the marker light fluttered through his broken visor and came to rest between his eyes, almost like a benediction.

For always was never a promise.

'Is this my–'

Joyce smiled wistfully as a score of pulse rounds hammered into Machen's visor. The captain's monstrous Thundersuit shuddered under the barrage, but did not fall.

'And yea, the old and the faithless were found wanting,' the boy preacher said, reciting truths the dead saint had shared with him. 'And the Emperor withdrew from them His grace and raised up the righteous so that they might carve His word across the galaxy in blood and fire!'

Then the murder light flitted away from Machen's iron tomb and Joyce opened fire, obliterating the spotter on the rooftop. Giving thanks to his god, he raced towards the nearest cluster of Fire Warriors. Doing the Emperor's work was good!

Shas've Jhi'kaara watched the battle unfold from a manufactory rooftop. She knew her comrades were impatient, but she waited until the Sentinels had charged into the fray before giving the order: 'Crisis team enable strike pattern Aoi'kais.'

Jhi'kaara launched herself into the air and rocketed towards the platform below, the blocky bulk of her battlesuit looking like some experimental flying machine. Her armoured companions, Kaorin and Asu'kai streaked after her on either flank, exhibiting a grace that humbled her own.

They despise my elevation to the Crisis team, Jhi'kaara thought.

The pair of veterans *were* the Diadem's Crisis team. They had served together for years and were Ta'lissera bonded, which made them closer than siblings. Jhi'kaara herself had never taken the warrior's oath of communion; the scars within and without had left her an outsider among her own kind, yet O'Seishin had elevated her over these bonded veterans. It was wrong, not least because the battlesuit didn't *feel* right to her. While she was familiar with the technology, it had been many years since she'd worn a Crisis battlesuit into combat. She knew she was no match for her subordinates and they knew it too.

O'Seishin, your power games have made a mockery of our ways, she thought bitterly. *The Water Caste has no reverence for the traditions.*

The canker had set in decades ago, when the Ethereal assigned to Phaedra, Aun'o Hamaan had been lost, along with Shas'o

Gheza, the commander of the Fire Warriors. As the most senior tau left on the planet, O'Seishin had assumed command and never relinquished it. For years Jhi'kaara had expected replacements from the Ethereal or Fire Castes to come, but nobody had and she'd finally accepted nobody would. Without a spiritual or martial figurehead the war had stagnated into something she no longer understood.

But here and now, I have a purity of purpose, Jhi'kaara decided. *Today my life or death shall serve the Greater Good. Whatever that is…*

That final dark thought disturbed her, but the time for thinking was done. Their fusion guns blazing, the battlesuits swooped on the Sentinels.

Van Hal was the only one who saw the attack coming, although 'saw' wasn't really the word for it. It was more the 'sense' of a shadow falling across the skin of his Sentinel. There was no logic to it, but the cavalryman had long ago learned that logic had nothing to do with survival. He didn't think, he just acted, swerving his machine aside so violently a lesser rider would have tripped. A barrage of powerful fusion blasts raked the air in his wake and chewed deep fissures into the metal floor. Arness's Sentinel took the full brunt of a parallel salvo and its cockpit exploded violently. The headless walker stumbled on a few paces before crashing to the ground. Mister Silver got lucky – his assailant, seemingly less skilled than its comrades, missed him completely. Quint hadn't been targeted at all. Doubtless the attackers had identified him as the poorest of the cavalrymen.

'Battlesuits,' Van Hal voxed, knowing it in his guts before the machines even touched the ground. Their splayed feet and piston-like legs absorbed the impact gracefully, but the one in the centre stumbled a little. *You sir, don't know your mount!* Van Hal observed wryly.

'I see fusion blasters and flamers!' Mister Silver yelled. He was a young Norlander who'd been drafted into Silverstorm as a mascot, but his talents had shone through and the captain himself had financed his walker. The move had riled the die-hard patricians like Quint, but Van Hal was proud to share the field with Silver.

'Pull back to the Triton!' Quint yelled and raced for the stranded gunboat. It was a fatal error. While Van Hal and Silver careered about in evasive loops, dancing through the battlesuits' sustained fire, Quint peeled away in a straight line. One of the suits spun and lanced his legs out from under him with derisory precision. His Sentinel toppled forward and the cockpit snapped off at the waist as it crashed to the ground. They heard Quint squealing in terror as his cabin skidded along like a runaway train. The squeals turned to screams as the wreckage caught fire.

Van Hal cut the lieutenant's vox-feed and weighed up his enemies as he danced around them. The blocky battlesuits had landed in a neat delta formation with the poorest pilot in the centre, presumably in command. 'Focus fire left,' he ordered.

The Sentinels spun violently at the waist and fired synchro-nously. Both made magnificent shots despite their wild evasive dance. Van Hal's lascannon took the Crisis battlesuit on the left square in the chest and Silver's autocannon battered its legs from under it.

'Split-kill: Battlesuit!' Van Hal called.

And just like that Kaorin was gone, all her years of training reduced to nothing. Jhi'kaara felt no grief, only a cold regret that they had underestimated these foes. With those perfect killing shots the surviving riders had proved themselves to be masters of their machines.

Which I am not...

She noticed that Asu'kai was hunting his comrade's killers furiously, his judgement clouded by the passion of her loss. His fire wasn't even coming close to the cavorting Sentinels. Any moment now they would turn and kill again...

I will not die so easily and I will not die a fool!

Jhi'kaara drew deep of the bitterness in her heart, struggling to bond with her unfamiliar machine. She chose a foe and focussed, studying his erratic manoeuvres, willing herself to find a pattern. And suddenly she had it.

Van Hal knew he was dead the moment he committed to attack the berserk battlesuit. It was the wrong target. The other one, the one that had missed them from the air and stumbled when it landed, *that one* was going to kill him. He saw it in a subtle shift of the machine's stance and weaponry and in the way its sensors locked onto him like they could see right into his soul. It had woken up to the game.

Stormchaser: 213 kills and counting.

There was no way out, so he completed his strike and blew apart the battlesuit on the right. A moment later the survivor hit him at precisely the right angle, just as he'd known it would. Van Hal didn't even try to dodge.

Stormchaser: 214 kills and we're all done.

Jhi'kaara growled with the joy of her kill, drinking in the burning Sentinel to feed her hate. Doubtless the Ethereals would not approve of such feelings, but the Ethereals had deserted them so what did it matter anymore? Perhaps the mystics were wrong about the Greater Good. If hate could bring such focus – such power – then perhaps it was the true path.

I will slay the gue'la and I will keep slaying them until they are nothing but dust and bitter memories!

She swung to track the remaining Sentinel. It was circling her warily, frightened by the loss of its brother. The rider was skilful – even more skilful than the one she had slain – but she could tell he didn't believe it and his uncertainty would be his undoing.

'Purge the blueskin plague!' a voice bellowed behind her.

With an agonised whine something crunched into her back plate. She lurched round and flailed out with her fusion blaster, but her attacker deflected the swipe with a spiky vambrace. He was wearing a baroque iron battlesuit that was the antithesis of her sleek, minimalist machine. The armour was spattered with blood and daubed with crude sigils that marked him out as a barbarian even by the standards of the gue'la.

'Look upon their heresies and reap!' the savage boomed through an amplifier as he pressed his attack, swinging the whirling buzz saws jutting from his wrists in wide, alternating arcs. Jhi'kaara blocked with the fusion blaster and felt the housing buckle. She could not bring her guns to bear. He was in too close…

If I am broken then I am stronger for it!

Snarling, she angled her flamer towards the ground and unleashed a deluge of fire. With a whoosh of tortured air the backwash surged up and engulfed them both. Warning indicators flashed across her vision, but she kept the stream flowing, confident her battlesuit would outlast her foe's relic.

Your species are the plague! Your time is done!

* * *

Joyce's armour was warming up like an oven, drenching him in sweat. He could hear the machine's archaic cooling systems wheezing and clattering as they struggled to dissipate the heat from the tau's flamer. Through the conflagration he saw the sensor module that served as his enemy's head regarding him with glacial detachment. He knew that detachment was a lie: the xenos inside the suit hated him, just as he hated it. It was how things were meant to be.

There isn't room for us both, not in all the Heavens and Hells of infinite space.

As his skin began to blister, Joyce swung at the battlesuit in a frenzy that drowned his pain. The xenos stood its ground, spewing fire and parrying clumsily with the fusion blaster clipped to its left arm. Finally the flames penetrated the gun's cracked housing and it exploded with a violence that tore away the battlesuit's arm and flung Joyce from the inferno.

'Hang back and I'll nail the bastard!' Mister Silver called over the vox, lining up his Sentinel for a shot, but Joyce paid no heed. Howling a psalm of castigation he threw himself back into the fray, but the respite had given his foe the chance to level its flamer…

Though you burn my flesh, my spirit shall not waver!

He took the full force of the fire head on. His armour whined in protest as its cooling systems overloaded and gave out. The breastplate turned red hot, scorching the flesh from his ribs and setting his skin alight. Joyce chewed up the pain and spat it out as sacred fury. With a burst of his rockets he leapt onto the Crisis battlesuit's broad shoulders and sawed into its stubby head. The machine clattered about, trying to dislodge him, but he sank a blade into its shoulder and clung on while he hacked away with the other.

'I am His will and His word made manifest!' Joyce sang

joyfully as his flesh bubbled inside its iron skin. 'I am the blade of His wrath…' The battlesuit's head came loose in a tangle of fizzing wires and he flung it aside. 'And I am the shield of His scorn!'

And then they were rocketing into the sky, propelled by the Crisis battlesuit's jetpack. With its sensor module gone the machine was flying blind, but it bucked and spun about as the pilot tried to dislodge him. Joyce hung on like a limpet, chopping away with his free hand, hunting for the tainted xenos flesh inside the shell. Something ruptured between the suit's shoulders and a cascade of small detonations rippled through it. Then the jetpack exploded with a sudden, terrible concussion that catapulted Joyce away like a kite caught in a tornado. Spiralling head-over-heels through the air, he glimpsed his nemesis plummeting towards the shuttle pad.

'Blood for the God-Emperor!' the preacher thundered, thinking how proud the saint and the Emperor and his old ma would be right now. As his momentum died and he began to fall he ignited his own rocket pack. The battered machinery squawked in protest, chugging impotently as it tried to engage. He cursed and thumped the ornery thing. It exploded like a krak grenade and Audie Joyce rained down from the sky in a thousand broiling pieces.

Jhi'kaara lay broken and blind inside the ruin of her Crisis battlesuit. The fall had shattered every bone in her body, but her hatred was undimmed, burning dark-bright at the core of her being, calling her back from the bliss of nothingness like a beacon.

I will… not… let go…

A crack of light appeared in the black vault above, almost painfully bright after the darkness, then the suit's chest plate was heaved away and the light became a flood. She tried to avert her gaze, but her neck wouldn't obey. A wrinkled gue'la appeared against the sky and peered down at her with a wolfish grin. He was missing an eye and an ear and most of his teeth.

'Hey, we got a blueskin alive in here!' he called to his unseen comrades. He licked his lips as he appraised her facial bionics. 'You got some real fancy gear going on there, sister,' he purred, 'and old Cully, he's what you'd call a collector, see.' A dagger appeared in his hand and he leaned inside. 'Hold still now, gal!'

He yelped with surprise as someone wrenched him away, then another face appeared above Jhi'kaara. All the gue'la looked alike to her, but this one wore scars like no other. Though it had been many *rotaa* since their encounter in the Mire she recognised him with shocking clarity.

'*Ko'miz'ar*,' she wheezed. His lattice of scars contorted and she knew he recognised her too. '*Ko'miz'ar...*'

'There's no such thing as chance, is there?' he said quietly. 'Or if there is, it's broken beyond repair.' She stared at him, uncertain of his meaning. Without a lexical module in play her grasp of the gue'la tongue was limited at best.

'Commissar!' someone called. 'Everyone's on board, sir. We're good to go!'

For the first time Jhi'kaara noticed the impatient rumble of the shuttle's engines. They hadn't seemed important before and they still didn't seem important to the scarred man. All his attention was on her.

'You should have killed me,' he told her, 'back when you had the chance.'

'Kill you...' she hissed, understanding this and trying to rise to it. 'Will... kill...'

'Yes. I think you're one of the few who still could.' He paused, as if puzzled by his own words. 'Next time perhaps.' And then he was gone.

Shortly afterwards the shuttle's rumble burst into brief, explosive thunder, then that too was gone and Jhi'kaara was alone with her hatred.

CHAPTER FIFTEEN

The Last Day: The Shuttle

Phaedra is behind us. She clung to our shuttle like a
spurned lover when we ascended, fighting our escape every
step of the way. I believe I felt the precise moment when we
broke free of Her atmosphere into the clean void of space.
I don't know what's waiting for us on the Sky Marshall's
ship, but at least we won't die in Her embrace.

There's a mystery to our escape because I'm not sure who's
actually flying the ship. I thought our pilot was dead or
missing, but the witch assured me he was waiting up in the
cockpit with Cutler. The edge in her voice told me this was
neither quite the truth nor a lie, but something I shouldn't
pursue. By tacit agreement I stayed in the cargo hold when
she headed up to the cockpit with her bodyguard. Shortly
afterwards we were in the air. For now that is enough.

We're due to dock with the Requiem of Virtue within the
hour, but we won't last long if Abel's revolt has faltered.

Truth to tell, we're not going to be much of a counterweight to the Sky Marshall's security forces. Our passage through the Diadem has left us battered and diminished.

Three Zouaves survived intact, but they're all shell-shocked by the loss of their leader, whoever that really was. I don't know if they're grieving for their captain or their adopted preacher, but I'll have to drum some spirit into them before we dock. Then there's the Norland cavalryman, 'Silver'. He's a skilled rider, but his Sentinel won't be much use to us on a battleship. Besides these four I have just sixty-three men left, ranging from fine soldiers to near vagabonds like the scum who tried to loot the Crisis battlesuit. The only officer amongst them is Lieutenant Hood, a dour veteran who's led the elite Burning Eagles for nearly a decade. He's a good man to have along, even if most of his Eagles have fallen.

There is another matter I must record. A scout called Valance found something in one of the silo chambers...

Iverson's Journal

'I figured you'd want to see it, commissar,' the black-bearded man said, 'so I came straight to you.'

He's too big to be a scout, Iverson reflected vaguely. His mind was trying to defer the carnage his eyes were sending its way. The precision mutilation in the silo defied comprehension, but it wasn't the horror that disturbed him so much as the sense that somewhere deep down he *did* comprehend it. It was nothing more than the tenebrous hint of an intuition, yet he couldn't shake it.

I know, or rather I will know what this madness means.

'You did the right thing, scout.' Iverson slammed the silo

hatch shut. 'Not a word of this to anyone else, you understand?'

'Whatever you say, sir.' Valance hesitated, looking troubled. Iverson could tell he wasn't a man much used to fear, but this… The scout spread his hands helplessly. 'What happened here, commissar?'

'The tau are degenerates,' Iverson said levelly. 'Don't let their superior airs and graces and all their techno heresies deceive you.'

'You're saying the blueskins did this?'

'Who else?' Iverson didn't intend it as a question, but it came out like one. Valance nodded, obviously unconvinced.

Which makes two of us, Iverson thought grimly.

'This is wrong,' O'Seishin said. It was the most direct thing Cutler had ever heard him say. The ambassador was huddled in a corner, shivering in the frigid electric air of the cockpit.

'Sometimes a few small wrongs can make a great big right,' Cutler drawled from the co-pilot's couch. His face was pale and drawn with the pain of the tainted wounds, but he'd managed to staunch the bleeding for the moment. 'Didn't your precious *Tau'va* ever teach you that, Si?'

'You think this is a *small wrong*?' the xenos hissed.

'I think we need to fly this Emperor-forsaken tug!' Cutler snapped, his bravado melting away in a moment. 'Now shut up and let the lady work.'

Cutler didn't believe his own bluster for a second. Watching the woman beside him he knew this was one 'Great Big Wrong' and then some. Skjoldis's hands were flitting expertly over the flight controls, but the eyes behind her veil were not her own. The dead pilot, Guido Ortega was in there, flying the shuttle while the witch steered him away from the memory of his recent death. Skjoldis's roving green eyes watched her body working from the sockets of Ortega's severed head, which was perched on the drive bay like a grisly totem.

Necromancy, the foulest of magicks...

Cutler recoiled from the truth of the woman. He'd come to accept and even respect her wyrd, but this was something darker and infinitely more dangerous than her scrying and telepathy. Something tainted.

'His spirit still lingers here,' Skjoldis had said, cradling Ortega's head in her hands and staring into his murder-stricken eyes. 'A bad death can chain a soul for days or years or even forever. We are fortunate – his death was very bad.'

Despite their long separation she'd offered Cutler no greeting. He'd watched her prepare the ritual and strap herself into the pilot's couch without a glance in his direction. Afterwards she'd appraised his wounds sombrely and spoken without meeting his eyes.

'The daemon's wrath has cut deep,' she'd said, as if he didn't know it already. 'Your wounds will not heal, Ensor Cutler.' Afterwards she'd relayed Abel's final instructions, barely leaving him time to think, let alone speak. Then without a word of warning she'd entered the trance and this new horror had begun.

She got us into space, Cutler told himself, *and she'll get us to Zebasteyn bloody Kircher. She knows what she's doing.* But he knew it wasn't that simple. Sorcery of this kind had consequences. *She was frightened. That's why she wouldn't look me in the eye. She thought I'd stop her.*

Cutler leaned towards the witch, but a restraining hand pulled him back. The *weraldur*, Frost, was looming over them both. The giant shook his head, though his watchful eyes never left his mistress. That was when Cutler noticed that Skjoldis's veil had slipped free, offering up her delicate, desiccated face to the stars.

Only it didn't slip. She's opened herself up to the warp.

Remembering her terror of the stars, Cutler tried to heave himself out of the couch, but Frost held him down.

It's too late, Cutler realised. *She's already committed. Whatever the price...*

Standing by a filthy porthole, Iverson watched the hulking battleship blot out the stars as the shuttle drew closer. The *Requiem of Virtue*: the name was redolent with irony, like almost every other name he'd encountered on his journey.

Nothing is chance or else chance is broken. The thought came to him again, trailing another: why hadn't he killed the scarred Fire Warrior on the landing pad? Yes, she had spared him once, but her act had been a mockery rather than a mercy. *And who's to say mine wasn't?* It was a pity Reve wasn't around to discuss the matter. She might have been a traitor and an assassin, but she'd had a logical mind.

Why hasn't she come back?

The battleship's hangar bay yawned ahead, black as an unanswerable question.

A clang reverberated through the shuttle as it touched down. The witch slid back in her couch with a shuddering sigh that seemed to ripple through her entire body.

'Skjoldis?' Cutler asked. 'Are you done?' He tried to get up, but the *weraldur* would not loosen his grip. 'Get your hands off me, man! Can't you see she needs my help?'

'Kill… it…' The psyker's voice was little more than a shrivelled exhalation. Cutler gawped at her convulsing body. She was breathing in harsh, rapid gasps, but her lips hadn't moved.

'I don't understand…'

'Kill it!' she hissed with sudden ferocity. Cutler looked round and met her outcast eyes, still glittering in Ortega's severed head. They were wide with horror and desperation. 'The pilot was not… the only one… who lingered here…' she croaked through dead lips.

She can't get back inside her body, Cutler realised with horror, *because something else is in there now.*

'*We see you, Whitecrow!*' a hateful chorus wheezed beside him. He swung round to the pilot's seat just as Skjoldis opened her eyes and looked right at him.

Black eyes leaking noxious rainbow light…

'*We taste you!*' A rictus grin tore the corners her mouth and the hairline fissures ran through her porcelain skin like fault lines, mirroring her tracery of tattoos. She raised an accusing hand and the fingers split open like overripe fruit, revealing black iron barbs. '*We will be you!*'

The *weraldur* howled with gut-wrenching grief and hefted his axe… and hesitated, staring at his mistress with tortured eyes.

'Kjordal!' Skjoldis shrieked from her dead prison. 'Do not betray me at the last!'

A new resolve hardened the giant's features, but it was too late. Cackling gleefully, the proto-daemon lashed out with razor blade claws and tore his throat open. The *weraldur* tottered on his feet, struggling to do his duty as his life gushed away. Inch by painful inch he raised the axe… and the abomination struck again, punching through his chest with splayed talons and digging deep, gouging and tearing. The giant screamed wordlessly as it wrenched his heart out in a welter of blood and bone. The weapon slipped from his numbed fingers and he pitched over.

Kjordal, Cutler thought feverishly. *His name was Kjordal…*

He dived aside as a claw slashed spastically across his couch. Laughing and chanting its endless litany of malice, the seething monstrosity tore free of its restraints. Cutler heard O'Seishin whimpering and Skjoldis screaming from the drive bay: 'Kill it before it grows too strong!'

How many times? How many times does the damned thing have to die? But Cutler already knew the answer, because the 'damned thing' was part of him. *It'll keep coming back as long as I live.*

His fingers found the haft of Kjordal's axe and the killing purity of the weapon thrilled through his body like wildfire. The daemon reared over him, dripping blood from the heart crammed into its lamprey maw, its swarming eyes weeping chromatic Chaos. *Laughing at me!* With a feral howl, Cutler swung from the ground and lopped off a leg at the knee. The beast screeched and toppled over, flailing out with its iron talons as it fell. Desperately he rammed the weapon's haft into its face and surged to his feet. The daemon reached after him, its arms dislocating and attenuating like thorny tentacles as it called his name.

You won't take me – not today, not ever! Cutler swore as he brought the axe chopping down with the full weight of his body and soul.

Iverson's vox-bead buzzed and someone spoke into his ear: 'Commissar.'

'Colonel,' Iverson answered, recognising the voice though he'd never spoken to the man before. It was a powerful voice used to command, but it was tight with pain. 'You've been a difficult man to find.'

There was a long pause, as if Cutler was disturbed by his words, then: 'I guess that's just the way it had to be, commissar.'

'I don't doubt it.' Iverson searched for something else to say to the man he'd been tracking for so long. 'Colonel–'

'Commissar,' Cutler interrupted. 'We don't have much time.

Here's what you've got to do.' He told Iverson the last part of
Abel's plan.

'Do you trust him?' Iverson asked afterwards.

'Like the Hells I do,' Cutler snorted. And then he explained
his own plan.

The Last Day: The Requiem of Virtue

I believe this will be my final entry. We have infiltrated
the Sky Marshall's eyrie and the remainder of my forces
are assembled. My forces? No, that's not quite correct
because I've returned command of the 19th to Colonel
Ensor Cutler. He will lead them on their final mission, as is
his right. Besides, our paths must diverge here. It's strange
that Cutler and I shall part without ever meeting, but he's
been delayed in the cockpit – 'attending to a personal
matter' – and I can wait no longer. Neither of us is likely
to survive this endeavour, yet I sense that Cutler and I will
meet someday.

I shall conceal this journal on the shuttle. If I fail to do
my duty today I trust you will find it and learn from my
mistakes. I don't know your name, your rank or even your
calling, yet you have followed me this far so I believe you
must be true. Whoever you are, I hope you are a better
soldier than I.

Iverson's Journal

'Counterweight,' Iverson said to the trio waiting for him in
the hangar bay. Two of them wore padded flak jackets over
blue jumpsuits and were armed with stubby shotguns. Their
uniforms marked them as naval security officers, but both had
torn away the Sky Marshall's insignia. The third was a cadaverous ancient swathed in a jade habit that arched up into a cowl.

His milky white eyes were almost luminous in the shadowed recess of his hood. He was blind, yet Iverson knew he could see further and deeper than any normal man. This was almost certainly Abel's astropath.

'You the 'sar?' the female officer growled in coarse Gothic. Her severe face was topped by a spiky, no-nonsense crewcut and her bare arms were corded with muscles. She was short but there was no mistaking her hard-bitten competence.

'Commissar Iverson,' he said and peered at her badge. 'Officer Privitera?'

'You don't look the part,' she said dubiously.

I know it, girl. His peaked cap was long gone and his great-coat had turned a stale grey that matched his lank hair – hair he hadn't cut since he'd departed the Antigone months ago. It hadn't seemed important.

'He is the Blade,' the hooded ancient said in a surprisingly resonant voice.

'Well that don't make no odds to me, astro.' Privitera scowled as she watched the Confederates disembarking from the shuttle. 'It's the muscle I'm after and I ain't seeing much of that right now.'

'These men have walked through the Seven Hells for your uprising,' Iverson said coldly. 'You will show them the respect they deserve.'

Privitera didn't flinch. 'Listen up 'sar, I've got people dying all over this fraggin' ship 'cause Abel told me the cavalry was on the way. He promised me an army.'

'So you've seen Abel?' Iverson asked with sudden interest.

'Me?' she snorted. 'Nobody gets to *see* Abel, except maybe his pet freak over there,' she jabbed a thumb at the astropath, 'and he ain't got no eyes.'

'But you trust him?' Always that same question, as if the

answer could make any difference so late in the game.

'Abel makes things happen. He's in so deep he can pull all the right strings and get people synced up. Our movement wasn't worth spit 'til he showed up.' She slung her shotgun over a shoulder. 'Look, I gotta shift, man. We nearly had the bridge cracked when a whole heap o' blueskins showed up.'

'He is the Blade,' repeated the astropath. 'He must come with me now.'

'Why didn't you want me to meet Iverson?' Cutler asked as he wiped the *weraldur*'s axe clean of daemonic ichor. The melee had reopened his wounds and he was running on raw willpower.

Because you would have tried to kill him, said the voice in his head, *and that is not possible, but he might have killed us.*

Us? Of course Skjoldis was right. She was a part of him now, her soul woven into the fabric of his own. After he'd killed the daemon she'd asked him to open up his mind and let her in. He hadn't hesitated for a moment. Without her guidance he was lost.

Cutler sighed and popped a couple of Furies. He hated using the combat stimms, but they were cleaner than Phaedra's narcotics and he wasn't going to last another hour without them.

'Why would I try to kill the commissar?' he asked.

Later. We must go now, Whitecrow. Your men are waiting for you.

A chorus of cheers greeted Ensor Cutler when he stepped from the shuttle. The honest joy of his men stopped him in his tracks. With O'Seishin slung across his shoulders and the axe in his hands he probably looked like some kind of barbarian king, but that didn't deter the Confederates. As they cheered him, Cutler felt a sadness bordering on despair. So many were gone and so few were left. What had happened to Vendrake and Machen and that promising young officer, Grayburn?

I did this, he realised. I brought the 19th to ruin.

Whitecrow, this is not the time for self-recrimination, urged Skjoldis. *Tell them what they need to hear. Let them believe in you.*

'Look, this is all real touching,' a woman in security officer's gear growled, 'but can we cut to the chase. My guys are dying up on A-Deck.'

Cutler looked at her with strange, mismatched eyes – one grey, the other green – and nodded. 'I think we can turn things round for you, officer.'

'And how d'you figure that exactly?' she challenged. 'The blueskins have got the bridge locked down.'

'Maybe so, but I've got one very special blueskin right here.' Cutler flung O'Seishin to the ground and grinned. 'Gentlemen – and lady – I'd like you to meet Commander Wintertide.'

Iverson had been following his eerie guide for almost an hour. Despite his blindness the astropath never hesitated or stumbled as he negotiated the vast, multi-tiered labyrinth of the battleship. Iverson had lost his bearings, but he sensed they were travelling into the bowels of the craft. Along the way he sometimes heard distant shouts and gunshots, but nobody crossed their path.

'Where are you taking me?' Iverson asked as they turned down another gloomy corridor.

'You are the Blade,' the astropath intoned. 'I am taking you to the Sky Marshall.'

'I understand that, but why would he be down here? Surely his place is on the bridge?'

'The bridge flies the ship and the ship does not fly,' his guide explained as if he were talking to a fool.

'But the engines must be fuelled and functional to maintain orbit,' Iverson pressed. 'So the ship *could* fly.'

'The ship does not fly,' the astropath repeated, letting Iverson's logic wash over him.

He's not wired to think, Iverson decided. *He's only a messenger. But he'd better be wrong about the ship.*

The doors of the turbolift slid open and Cutler's team swept into the corridor beyond. O'Seishin was strapped to the colonel's back, piggybacking like a withered child. Privitera was waiting with the forward team and a band of armsmen.

'Welcome to A-Deck,' she said. 'We're actually about midway up the ship, but this is officer country and "Deck 112" didn't cut it for 'em.'

'And the bridge?' Cutler asked as the turbolift descended for the next group.

'Up front, a few blocks along, but there's only one way in and it's crawling with blueskins. We've held on to this sector, but they've got the bridge access sewn up tight.'

'Show me.'

'Right, but stay sharp,' she said. 'The blueskins have got drones working the vents and those floaters pack a helluva punch.' As she turned away Cutler swallowed another Fury. He was already over the limit with the stimms, but that was the least of his worries right now.

'You all right, sir?' Valance asked, tagging along beside him.

'Never better, scout,' Cutler said as the angry glow lit up his blood. 'Let's go get us a bridge!'

Control the bridge and you control the ship, he reflected as he followed Privitera. It was the age-old logic of shipboard mutinies. The uprising had gravitated here like a force of nature, but it was just a distraction from Abel's real target. Cutler wondered how the armswoman would feel if she knew the truth. *She's just another pawn like all the rest of us sorry bastards…*

Along the way they passed scores of rebels. There were men and women from every strata of the ship's society: armoured security troops leading studious looking adepts, smartly dressed naval ratings paired with filthy galley dogs, even a tech-priest leading a trio of combat servitors, but shamefully no officers at all. According to Privitera nearly half the ship had risen up against the Sky Marshall and his xenos allies – far more than the rebels had anticipated. Cutler read the dissenters' faces as he swept by, clocking anger and fear, determination and desperation. And always hate.

Our loathing of the xenos runs deep. Kircher might have glossed over it for years, maybe even decades to keep his corrupt little empire ticking along, but the hatred was always there under the surface, waiting for this moment of truth.

To his surprise he wasn't sure how he felt about that truth. Trinity had shaken his faith in many things, including humanity's divine right to rule the stars, but that didn't make the tau any better. For all his fine talk of the Greater Good, O'Seishin was just another conniving son-of-a-bitch selling another flavour of oppression.

Better our evil empire than theirs…

'Hey, slow up!' Privitera cautioned as they came to a wide cross-junction. 'This cuts onto the main access corridor and trust me, you don't want to step out there.'

There were rebels positioned on either side of the junction, all well-armed and alert, doubtless the best of Privitera's men. There were also bodies – lots of them, scattered about in the random contortions of violent death. Most of them were human, but it was impossible to tell whether they'd been rebels or loyalists.

And of course the rebels are *the loyalists here*, Cutler mused with black humour. *Civil wars always play havoc with the rules.*

'Valance,' he said and signalled the scout forward.

The scout nodded and knelt by the junction. He fished a small mirror from his pouch and clipped it to the barrel of his lasrifle. Cautiously he angled the gun round the wall, reading the reflection with narrowed eyes.

'The whole corridor's packed with xenos soldiers,' Valance said. 'I've got at least fifty Fire Warriors and a Crisis battlesuit. Plenty of drones too.'

'Grenades?' Cutler suggested.

'You think we didn't try that?' Privitera gave him a dirty look. 'The blueskins know the game, man. They're too far back.'

'She's right,' Valance said. 'They've got the range and the firepower. Probably packing some shield drones too, just for insurance.'

'And there's no other way in?' Cutler asked the rebel leader.

'We tried the vents, but they're crawling with drones. I lost some good men that way.' Privitera shrugged. 'No man, there ain't no way in except through here.'

Cutler nodded and jabbed a thumb at the tau strapped to his back. 'Well then, I guess it's time to play Commander Wintertide.'

Iverson knew he was getting close to his quarry now. The dingy, corroded decrepitude of the lower deck had given way to pristine white corridors fashioned from some kind of moulded plastic that hummed softly and emitted its own light. This remote sector of the ship had been remodelled from the ground up by the tau, creating a secret world within the battleship.

How long has this been going on? Iverson wondered. *When did*

Kircher sell out the Imperium? Five years? Ten? Twenty? How long have we been fighting for a lie on Phaedra?

The scale of the betrayal was appalling and Iverson felt his fury catch fire with absolute conviction. It had been too long since he'd felt such pure contempt. Whatever else was true or false, right or wrong, one thing was certain: the Sky Marshall had cast countless lives into the meat grinder of this sham war. He had to die.

And I'll be the one to do it. This is what my life has been leading up to. This will be my redemption.

He wondered where Bierce had disappeared to; he hadn't seen the old ghost since he'd left Phaedra. It was almost as if his mentor had served his purpose.

'We are here,' the astropath said, coming to a stop outside an iris-like door.

Iverson stared at the sealed hatch. 'The Sky Marshall is through there?'

'Yes,' his guide said without inflection or interest.

'Where are the guards?' Iverson asked, indicating the brightly lit corridor. 'We're right in the heart of his territory, but we've seen nobody, not even a drone.'

'They are not here.' It was the most incontrovertible and pointless statement Iverson had ever heard.

'*Where* are they?' he asked through gritted teeth.

'They have been summoned to the bridge.'

'All of them?'

'Yes. Abel has arranged it.'

Iverson shook his head and turned his attention back to the hatch. 'And how do I get in there?'

'You are the Blade.' The astropath touched his palm to the sensor pad by the door and it spiralled open soundlessly. 'Abel has arranged it.' Without another word he turned and walked away.

Abel has arranged it. Why do I like that less and less?

Iverson walked through the door.

'I am Por'o Dal'yth Seishin,' the ambassador called out weakly. 'You will hold your fire, warriors.'

'You heard your boss,' Cutler shouted, 'none of us want any slip ups here so just take it easy.' He stepped out into the access corridor with the ambassador on his back and a grenade in each hand, the pins already depressed. 'If we do this right we might all make it through to tomorrow.'

Scores of dispassionate lenses stared back at him above a forest of pulse rifles and carbines. The Fire Warriors were lined up along the corridor in orderly formations, the foremost ranks lying prone, the next kneeling and the last standing. Gun drones hovered and flitted over the troops like miniaturised spacecraft and right at the back, looming by the bridge door, Cutler saw the blocky shape of a Crisis battlesuit.

Valance was right, Cutler decided. *This corridor is a killing ground.*

'See, what we've got here is a stalemate.' He advanced with his hands raised, making sure the tau got a good look at the grenades. 'Ain't that right, ambassador?'

'What do you hope to achieve with this?' O'Seishin asked wearily. 'They will not let you pass, Ensor Cutler.'

'Maybe I'll talk them round. Or make them see things differently.' Cutler stopped when he reached the first rank of Fire Warriors. 'Who's in charge here?' he called.

The Crisis battlesuit stomped forward. Fire Warriors slipped aside as it advanced to loom over Cutler. It tilted at the waist and regarded him impassively with its lens-studded head.

'I am Shas'vre Zen'kais,' a toneless voice boomed from the battlesuit's chest. 'You will release Por'o Dal'yth Seishin.'

'I could do that.' Cutler seemed to give it some thought. His mind was on fire with the Furies. He'd thrown caution to the wind and swallowed another couple before making his gambit. 'But then I wouldn't get to do this.' He threw the grenades over the battlesuit and dived against its bulk with a yell: 'Counterweight!'

One grenade exploded fiercely, tearing through the second rank of Fire Warriors. The other vented a cloud of smoke that billowed out to choke the corridor.

'Counterweight!' Lieutenant Hood bellowed back at the junction. 'Go!'

The sniper, Toomy, rolled out of cover, sighting down his rail rifle as he moved. The three Zouaves followed him on either side, allowing him just enough time for a single shot.

We got to make this one count, Eloise, he purred to his gun as he fired.

The Crisis battlesuit's sensor module disintegrated in a burst of light. Toomy managed a grin before a volley of return fire incinerated his face. Then the Zouaves were storming down the corridor like a moving shield, with greybacks and rebels racing along behind them. Intermittent pulse rounds battered their armour, melting away the heavy plates with frightening speed. Several stray bolts flashed past the knights, every one claiming a life in the packed corridor. If the xenos had a chance to rally and focus their fire the Zouaves would go down in seconds and it would all be over.

While the blinded Crisis battlesuit flailed about, Cutler tore the axe from his belt and leapt for the nearest Fire Warriors. The aliens hesitated a split second, unsure what to do about the ambassador. Then their chance was gone and he was in amongst them.

'For Providence and the Seven Stars!' he bellowed, swinging the axe like a madman as O'Seishin shrieked and swayed about on his back.

More tau rushed from the smoke to join the front ranks, adding their fire to the defence as drones zipped forwards. One of the Zouaves fell, his breastplate reduced to molten slag. Another barrage tore through the gap in the advancing shield wall and mowed down dozens of charging men.

'Put your backs into it you worthless dogs!' Hood shouted. A pulse round punched into his leg, another through his shoulder. The force spun him round, but he caught himself and limped on, trailing smoke.

And then the onslaught hit the xenos line like a hammer. One of the Zouaves crashed into the Crisis battlesuit and his momentum threw them both to the ground. His comrade dashed on into the smoke, hacking about blindly with his buzz saws. The Fire Warriors in the front ranks tried to fall back, but became entangled with others rushing forward to reinforce the line. A moment later the angry tide of humanity swept over them and any hope of cohesion was gone.

'Rip out their fraggin' blue hearts!' Privitera yelled as she rammed her shotgun into a Fire Warrior's faceplate and fired.

Cutler staggered from the melee, his head swimming in its own personal mire. The lacerations in his chest had opened right up and he was bleeding badly.

You must be strong, Whitecrow, Skjoldis insisted. *We have to finish this. Iverson must not be allowed to escape.*

'I still… don't get it,' Cutler murmured, trying to hold onto consciousness. 'Why does he matter? Who is he?'

* * *

'Commissar Holt Iverson,' the Sky Marshall said. 'I take it you've come for your Thunderground.'

CHAPTER SIXTEEN

My Thunderground?

'So you're familiar with our myths?' Iverson asked, keeping his pistol levelled on the pair standing inside the brightly lit chamber. One was a tau Fire Warrior, lightly armoured and bare headed. The other was a man in a plain grey uniform.

'You really think the Thunderground is just a myth?' The man seemed surprised. 'I would have thought that you of all people would be a true believer, Holt Iverson. Haven't you chased your destiny like a bloodhound?' He offered a smile that looked sincere. 'But to answer your question – yes, I've made a point of familiarising myself with all things Arkan.'

'Because we've been a thorn in your side?'

'Because your people intrigue me.' The smile became a frown. 'You most of all, Iverson.'

'How do you know my name?'

'Oh, I know rather more than that, though I admit you didn't catch my eye until Lomax singled you out for her mission. And then of course you vanished off the radar, but your record made for interesting reading.' He spread his hands magnanimously. 'So what do you make of my nerve centre?'

'It's impressive,' Iverson admitted.

The circular chamber was not particularly large, but it was alive with information. Banks of monitors and holo-screens tiled the walls all the way to the high, conical ceiling. Iverson saw live vid-feeds, topographical maps and tactical maps, psych reports and inventories... the density of intelligence was almost overwhelming. A huge photo-realistic hologram of Phaedra hovered above a dais at the centre of the room, revolving slowly. The image crawled with brightly coloured icons representing bases and troop movements, all appended with restless statistics.

'My window upon the world below,' the man said, approaching slowly. 'The science is all tau of course. We get most of our surveillance feeds from drones, although you wouldn't recognise them if you saw them. Drone tech is outstandingly flexible and a spy drone can be smaller than the human eye.' He smiled again. 'On occasion we've actually *replaced* the human eye with a drone and left the recipient none the wiser.'

Iverson touched his own optic uneasily, but the man shook his head. 'No, don't worry. Your augmetic is clean, Iverson.'

'You are Sky Marshall Zebasteyn Kircher?' Iverson asked, gathering his thoughts. He already knew the answer, but the question had to be aired. Protocol and the moment demanded it.

'I am.' Kircher stopped a couple of metres from Iverson and straightened up. 'I take it you're here to serve the Emperor's Justice?'

Iverson regarded the man he had come to kill. He had imagined his nemesis in many shades of corruption: a seedy, silk-tongued despot sagging with depravity, his uniform ripe with garish epaulettes and empty medals. Or a haggard ghost who kept to the shadows and whispered tormented riddles, all the while secretly longing for his own doom. Or perhaps a granite-faced egomaniac cut from the true military block, his eyes burning with fervour as he declaimed his creed. The galaxy was rife with tyrants, but their cancer always seemed to follow the same old strains of self-congratulation, self-loathing or self-deception.

Yet this man is none of those things.

Kircher was broad shouldered and muscular in the manner of a middle-aged soldier accustomed to hard exercise, although Iverson knew he must be over a century old. Doubtless he had availed himself of juvenat therapies to hold back the years, but there wasn't a trace of vanity about him. His square, businesslike face was free of wrinkles, but otherwise untouched by cosmetic enhancements. His nose had been broken and set askew, like an off-kilter sundial at the centre of his face. He wasn't particularly tall, but he was straight-backed and sturdy, lending him a quietly imposing air. The dignity ran through to his uniform – a modest tunic and cap devoid of any ornaments save the silver Skywatch badge. He looked more like an NCO than the governor of a world, yet there was a pervasive, muted authority about him.

You're not what I expected, Zebasteyn Kircher.

'Why?' Iverson asked. It was a simple question that encompassed so much. Like his first question it needed asking.

Kircher didn't show a trace of fear as he stared past the barrel of Iverson's gun and looked him in the eye. 'Because it was necessary.'

'That's not good enough.'

'No? I've just confessed that I've betrayed the Imperium.

Surely that's all the justification you need, *commissar*?' Iverson said nothing and Kircher nodded. 'No… no, of course it's not. For any other man of your creed it would be more than enough, but not for you, Holt Iverson. You see, you have become addicted to truth and you crave answers. Am I wrong?'

You think too much for a commissar. How many people have told me that down the years? How many of them have I failed?

'Furthermore you are incapable of denying a *manifest* truth, no matter how much it may torment you,' Kircher went on. 'I think it's your Arkan heritage showing through. For all your training and indoctrination, that troublesome, dissenting blood won't let you sleepwalk through life.'

'This isn't about me.'

'I disagree. At this particular moment in time it is *precisely* about you.' Kircher shrugged. 'After all, you're the man pointing a gun at my head. You have the power to end me if you so choose. I'd say that makes you very significant indeed.'

'Are you Abel?'

'What?' For the first time the Marshall seemed wrong-footed. He frowned, looking genuinely puzzled. 'No, I'm not Abel. Why would you think that?'

'It's the only answer that makes any sense,' Iverson said emphatically. 'Who else would have the authority to bring us this far? Who else could have cleared out the guards so I could walk right in here? Abel can only be you.'

Kircher nodded slowly. 'I see your logic and there is certainly a mystery here, but why would I assist my own assassin?'

'Because I am not your assassin – I am your judge. And you want to be judged.'

The Sky Marshall considered this, his wide-set eyes bright with thought. Finally he shook his head. 'You are mistaken, Iverson. I do not wish to be judged. I have already judged myself and continue to do so every day of my life.'

'So you think you're innocent?'

'No, not innocent, but simply necessary.' Kircher sighed. 'As I have already said, that's what this is all about – not honour or justice or any such rousing virtue – just plain necessity.'

'Betraying tens of thousands of Imperial lives was necessary?'

'To preserve hundreds of thousands, perhaps millions more? Absolutely.' Kircher waved a hand around the room, indicating the flow of information. 'The carnage on Phaedra is nothing beside the horrors to come if this war is allowed to spread across the subsector.'

'So you and your xenos friends decided to play us for fools and cap things here?' Iverson said bitterly. 'And never mind all the lives you threw into the meat grinder.'

'You still fail to grasp the wider picture, Iverson. This region is a buffer zone between two embattled giants. Neither the Imperium nor the Tau Empire can spare the resources to fight this war on a system-wide scale – not when there are so many greater threats elsewhere, but equally neither side can be seen to back down.'

'You're telling me the Imperium is party to this heresy?'

'My remit for the war came directly from the High Council of Terra,' Kircher said quietly. 'They tied my hands from the outset. I confess there was a time when that appalled me.' He searched Iverson's face. 'Don't tell me you're honestly surprised by this.'

No, I'm not surprised, Iverson realised sadly. *I'm not surprised by any of it.*

'But you decided to take things further,' he said with growing certainty.

* * *

Flanked by the two surviving Zouaves, Cutler stepped up to the bridge bulkhead. The massive hatch was sealed tight. 'Open it,' he snarled at the tau strapped to his back, 'or I'll throw you to the Hells after your lapdogs.'

'The tau do not have a concept of Hell,' O'Seishin said in a brittle voice. 'I have already explained this to you, Ensor Cutler.'

Lieutenant Hood limped up alongside them, smelling of burnt meat. 'A few of 'em slipped away in the chaos, but the corridor's ours, colonel.' He shook his head wearily. 'It cost us though.'

'Every step of this journey has cost us, Hood.' Cutler reeled against the hatch as another wave of nausea hit him. He was drenched in sweat and blood now – so much of both he couldn't tell where one ended and the other began. 'It's eaten us away… piece by piece…'

That is enough, Whitecrow! Skjoldis berated him.

'No, it's not enough. It's never going to be… nearly… enough,' he muttered through harsh gasps. Then he punched the hatch hard, drawing more blood. 'Open it!'

'You are correct,' the Sky Marshall said without hesitation. 'I took things *much* further. And I regret none of it.' He clenched his fists, as if to reinforce his thinking. 'The Imperium can't last, Iverson. It is a brutal, multi-headed leviathan forged for war, but despite the billions of souls that feed its engines, it is running down.' His voice rose with passion as he found his stride. 'Corruption and infighting have become endemic to its machinery. Ignorance and spite have become its orthodoxy. Shackled by fear, humanity tears itself apart from the inside out while it fights a thousand wars on a thousand fronts! Even the reprieve here is just a stopgap until the Imperium can spare the resources to prosecute *this* war to the full.' Kircher shook his head in disgust. 'I suspect the Imperium had a purpose once, but now it's nothing but a vicious relic.'

'What about the Emperor?' Iverson asked.

'The Emperor?' Kircher seemed surprised by the question. 'Who can say what He really stands for after all these millennia. Like His empire He might have meant something once, but now...' He snorted dismissively. 'Frankly I've had my fill of serving a corpse that won't die. Humanity needs a fresh perspective if it is to survive.'

'So you've bought into the tau and their Greater Good?' Iverson said tightly.

'I have not *bought* into anything,' Kircher snapped. 'I have *chosen* to use my intellect to find the best of all possible paths!' He calmed himself with a visible effort. 'But yes, the Greater Good has merit. It cultivates a mature humility in its followers, a rationality that puts our own fixations with honour and glory to shame. Mankind is an ancient race, yet we behave like feral infants beside the tau.' He shook his head. 'We have to grow up before the galaxy gives up on us.'

Iverson felt the electric wasp in his optic stirring awake and suddenly he remembered the most important question: 'What about Ysabel Reve?'

'Who?' The Sky Marshall seemed nonplussed.

'Commissar Cadet Ysabel Reve. Did you send her after me?'

'I don't know what you're talking about.' Kircher shook his head ruefully. 'Even I can't keep tabs on everyone. Who is Ysabel Reve?'

'She's dead,' Iverson said.

'I'm sorry,' Kircher said carefully. 'Was she was important to you?'

'I killed her.'

'And you regret this?'

'Should I?'

Kircher's eyes narrowed as he considered it. 'Was her killing necessary?'

Not right or wrong... The wasp in Iverson's skull was flitting about angrily... *Not just or unjust...* Hunting for a way out... *Merely necessary or not...*

'Is that all there is to it?' he asked hollowly.

'No, but everything else is suspect,' Kircher said, his eyes bright with conviction. 'To prosper we have to strip away the delusions of emotion and morality and work with the facts. That's the core philosophy of the Greater Good. It is a path focussed on hard reality rather than fluid ideals. A path we can build upon.'

'Why are you telling me all this?'

'Because you were right,' Kircher said with wonder, as if he had only just realised it himself. 'You *are* my judge, Iverson. I didn't seek you out, but here you are regardless – a sharp mind with a gun pointed in my face. Perhaps there's an opportunity in that.'

'You expect me to spare you?' Iverson's face twitched as the wasp burrowed through his brain, triggering strange synapses. 'You expect me to turn a blind eye to this heresy?'

'I expect you to *think*,' Kircher urged. 'Consider the horror you'll set loose if you end this stalemate.'

'I am an Imperial commissar.'

The Sky Marshall's eyes bored into him with an iron will. 'That is a lie, Holt Iverson. Whatever you are, you stopped being an Imperial commissar a long time ago.'

And I cannot deny a manifest truth.

* * *

The bridge crew didn't put up a fight. Fragile, pale-skinned men and women in smart naval uniforms, they backed away from the intruders with raised hands and lowered eyes.

'Where's the captain?' Cutler demanded. With his blood-drenched axe and rawhide jacket he knew he must look like the worst kind of pirate to them. Seeing their terrified expressions he wanted to laugh aloud, but if he did that something might break inside him before he was done here.

'I'll ask nicely one more time. After that I'll get mad.' Cutler hefted the axe meaningfully. 'Where in the Hells is the captain?'

'Kill me and millions more will die,' the Sky Marshall said. 'Justice demands it, so justice is blind.' He stepped forward so the barrel of Iverson's gun was touching his forehead. 'End this ugly lie and begin an infinitely uglier truth. Honour demands it, so honour is monstrous.'

Iverson held the gun rigid as thoughts flashed and faded across his mind like dancing fireflies. *Kill him and be damned? Spare him and be redeemed? Or is it the other way round? Redeemed or re-damned?* Where were his ghosts when he needed their counsel the most? He glanced past the Sky Marshall, searching for Bierce or Number 27 or even Niemand. Hoping for Reve… He saw the Fire Warrior. The tau hadn't moved at all during the confrontation, but he was watching them intently.

He's waiting for my choice.

And then the choice was taken away. Moving with a swiftness that belied his years, the Sky Marshall flung up an arm and caught Iverson's wrist in an iron grip. The gun fired, but Kircher had already sidestepped with the grace of a dancer. He twisted and the pistol slipped from Iverson's numbed hand. Kircher didn't pause for a moment. Using his fists like pistons he lashed out with almost inhuman speed, pummelling

Iverson's face and chest. The commissar staggered back, but Kircher followed remorselessly, battering him like a threshing machine until he fell.

'I'm sorry,' the Sky Marshall said as he stepped away from his prone opponent. 'I wish I could have let you choose, but there's too much at stake to gamble on your sanity.' He was breathing hard, as if the sudden violence had drained him. 'For what it's worth, I believe you would have done the right thing, Holt Iverson.'

The Fire Warrior appeared at his shoulder, holding Iverson's pistol. Kircher acknowledged the tau with a nod. 'Kill him, shas'el.'

The xenos shot Zebasteyn Kircher through the eye.

'The captain is gone,' a skinny naval lieutenant said. 'He disappeared decades ago. He never saw eye to eye with the Sky Marshall.'

'I like the man already,' Cutler said. 'Right, forget the captain. You boys can do the job, right?'

'The job?' the lieutenant stuttered. 'What are you asking me... sir?'

'Fire up the engines. We're leaving.'

'Leaving?' The officer's eyes goggled in confusion.

'Clearing out from Phaedra,' Cutler said. 'The way I see it, this ship's a symbol of everything that's wrong here, so I'm taking the symbol away.'

'But that's impossible,' the lieutenant was outraged. 'The *Requiem of Virtue* hasn't flown since the war started.' There were murmurs of support from his fellow officers. 'You've seen the state of her. She'll probably disintegrate before we break out of orbit.'

'I'm not telling you to break out of orbit, boy. I'm telling you to break out of space,' Cutler said cheerily. 'Let's do this like we mean it, eh?'

'You want us to enter the warp?' The officer's outrage had slipped into outright terror. 'That's suicide! I don't even know if the ship's Geller fields are still functioning. Without them we'll be eaten alive!'

'You are insane, Ensor Cutler,' O'Seishin said, but there was no strength in his protest. He sounded resigned to his fate.

Gunfire exploded somewhere outside.

'The blueskins are back!' Hood yelled from the doorway. 'And they've brought along a whole brigade of Skywatch cronies!'

'Well, I guess we're done talking,' Cutler said and shot the skinny lieutenant. He grinned at the man's shocked comrades. 'Now, who can fly this hellfired ship?'

'I am disappointed in you, human,' the Fire Warrior said, standing over Iverson. 'I chose you for this task because you are a commissar. I expected you to execute the traitor on sight.'

Iverson looked up from the Sky Marshall's crumpled body and met the alien's gaze. 'Who are you?'

'I am Shas'el Aabal, acting commander of the Fire Caste on this world,' the tau said proudly. 'I am also the one you know as "Abel".'

Iverson shook his head, trying to focus. 'I was sure it was Kircher. Why would you betray your own kind?'

'I have not,' the xenos said coldly. 'I am loyal to the Greater Good, but the Water Caste have made a mockery of this war. O'Seishin's "experiment" must not succeed.' He indicated the Sky Marshall. 'The chaos you have sown here will prove your species is too dangerous to be trusted. When reports of this mutiny reach the Tau Empire this travesty will be ended.'

'You want the war to spread,' Iverson said with growing understanding.

'I want the war to be prosecuted by warriors, as was decreed by the enlightened ones,' the tau said. 'The Greater Good will not prosper through conspiracies and lies.'

Iverson chuckled, low and bitter.

'This amuses you?' the tau asked coldly.

'Don't you see the irony?' Iverson smiled sourly. 'You're a schemer too, *Abel*. Maybe the biggest schemer of them all.'

'It was…'

'Necessary?' Iverson shook his head. 'You know, I don't think you blueskins are nearly as enlightened as you pretend to be. In fact I'd say you're much like us.' To his surprise Iverson found this casual heresy amusing.

'We are *nothing* like you, gue'la!' Abel spat. 'The *Tau'va* elevates and unites us.'

'Only when your precious Ethereals are around to keep you leashed,' Iverson mocked. 'When they're away things start to fall apart, don't they?' He frowned, intrigued by the idea. 'Why is that? What kind of a hold have the Ethereals got over the rest of you?'

'You know nothing about us.'

'And how much do you really know?' Iverson urged, following the shadowy intuition through. 'I'll wager you've actually enjoyed being free of them here.'

'Be silent.' Abel levelled the gun.

'It's a lie,' Iverson said with sudden certainty. 'The Greater Good, under all the fine talk and sparkle, it's just another lie.'

Abel fired just as the world was wrenched out from under them.

* * *

'We have to cut the engines!' a crewman yelled as the bridge quaked. 'The ship's tearing itself apart!' There were calls of agreement from his comrades so Cutler shot him, then shot the man next to him, just to be sure. The sounds of battle in the corridor were getting closer, the gunfire punctuated by desperate yells of fury and pain. Time was running out.

'Take us into the warp,' Cutler shouted. 'Or I'll put you all down!'

'We don't have a navigator.' The speaker was a tall, hairless woman in her autumn years. Unlike her comrades she seemed more angry than afraid. 'Even if the Geller field holds we'll never find our way back out of the warp.'

Perfect, Skjoldis whispered. *He must never escape.*

The quake threw Abel to the floor and sent his shot wide. The round punched through Iverson's left shoulder, but he barely registered the wound.

Cutler's done it! The thought filled him with fierce joy. *He's fired up the engines!*

Iverson surged to his feet, flooded by a reserve of strength that seemed to come out of nowhere. Tottering unsteadily he caught sight of his enemy. The xenos was lying prone, but it hadn't lost its hold on the gun. *You're no better than us, blueskin.* Fighting the tremors, he staggered towards the tau. Seeing him, it snarled and opened fire, gripping the bucking gun two-handed. Iverson threw up his metal hand to shield his face. *You're just like us!* He felt the bullets smacking into him like hammer blows as he advanced... and felt a dim pain in his legs... his gut... his chest... *You're just as lost and just as damned.* Heard the bullets pinging off the metal fist... saw the sparks as it took the punishment... *There's no way out for any of us.* Felt the scorching pain as a bullet slipped past and tore open his cheek.

'It's all a lie,' he wheezed as he fell upon the alien.

Abel had time for one last shot, then Iverson caught the autopistol in his augmetic and squeezed, crushing metal and flesh into a jagged aggregate pulp.

'Do you understand what I'm telling you?' the female officer said levelly. 'You're condemning us all to hell.' Despite her years, her eyes were a piercing blue.

Maybe that is where we belong, Skjoldis said.

'Maybe that's where we belong,' Cutler said. He found he didn't want to shoot the woman with the blue eyes. Whoever she was, she had more guts than all her comrades put together.

'There is no Hell,' O'Seishin muttered, sounding like he was trying to convince himself. 'It is just a primitive delusion.'

'Well, I guess we're going to find out together, Si.' Cutler levelled his gun at the woman he couldn't bring himself to shoot. 'Do it.'

'Your race… is dying!' Abel sneered as he wrestled hopelessly with Iverson. 'We are… the future!'

Iverson mashed his rigid augmetic eye into the tau's face and silenced its scorn. He struck again and again, ignoring the echoing agonies in his own skull as he hammered the bionic through flesh and bone.

We're all dying and there is no future. Perhaps there never was.

At last his enemy was still and Iverson slumped back, fighting for breath. Abel's final shot had pierced a lung and he could feel his chest filling up with liquid.

I'm drowning in my own blood. Perhaps I always was.

He stared at the alien's ruined features. One of its eyes had been ruptured, but the other stared back at him with lifeless spite. As he gazed into that black abyss the world seemed to stretch away from him, tearing him out of reality like a flat paper cut-out and leaving him behind at the wrong end of an infinitely extending telescope. Through its impossibly distant lens he glimpsed a seething maelstrom of rainbow light.

We've entered the warp and the Geller fields have failed and now the warp is in here with us. Perhaps it always was.

Nausea turned him inside out and he retched blood. The liquid whirled about his head in dark streamers as he slipped away from his enemy and fell backwards… and felt like he was falling forever… falling down the telescope towards that eager, prismatic oblivion.

I'm going to end here and that's for the best and there's no perhaps about it.

'You will not end here, Iverson.' The voice sounded like it had slithered from the bed of a polluted ocean, but the clipped accent was unmistakeable.

'Reve…' He closed his eyes and saw her kneeling beside him. The right side of her face was encrusted with iridescent fungi while the left was a bloodless alabaster. Pale things crawled about in the ragged cavity of her neck.

'Reve, you're wrong,' he whispered. 'You're too late. I'm already dead.'

She laughed, a low gurgle that scattered ephemeral parasites from her throat. 'That is just the beginning of the road, Holt Iverson.'

Somewhere across an immeasurable morass of space and time he heard a bell tolling and thought of home.

ABOUT THE AUTHOR

Peter Fehervari slipped into the parallel surreality of television almost twenty years ago and never quite escaped. As a rogue editor, his life is an eternity of cuts and mixes to quench the dreams of thirsting producers while actually getting things on air. He has cut promos for many well known television shows, but winning a place in a Black Library anthology eclipsed it all. Since then his short stories have appeared in *Heroes of the Space Marines* and *Xenos Hunters*. *Fire Caste* is his first novel.

He currently presides over a dormant Chaos Gate in London.

SHADOWSUN

THE LAST OF KIRU'S LINE

BRADEN CAMPBELL

WARHAMMER
40,000

An extract from Shadowsun,
a novella by Braden Campbell

The afternoon was waning by the time she drew near her destination. Shadowsun emerged into a wide strip of land where the forest had been snapped in half and knocked flat. It was like a road, rolled out before her to the horizon and paved with flattened logs. The Manta had carved this, she surmised. Easily, she imagined the flat, broad transport dropping lower and lower, at first shearing off the tops of the trees, and then eventually making itself a landing strip. Yo'uta hadn't been exaggerating. Even a species as technologically backward as the humans would have little difficulty following a trail like this.

Shadowsun decided that she was close enough now to risk reopening her comm channels. No sooner had she done so, then she was assaulted by a myriad of voices. Some were barking orders. Others were screaming. The background was punctuated by the sounds of weapons fire.

'Sabu'ro!' she yelled as she broke into a run. 'Sabu'ro, report!'

She wove out into the area of flattened trees where there was no longer anything to get in her way. She sprinted a few steps, kicked hard at the ground, and engaged the battlesuit's thrusters. She soared into the air in a long, bounding motion and landed a great distance away.

'Commander!' the young fire warrior responded, 'Commander, our position is under attack!'

'I'm almost there,' Shadowsun grunted as she leapt again. The ground blurred beneath her.

'Negative!' came the voice of Yo'uta. He was breathing heavily. 'We are surrounded and taking significant losses, Commander. Do not endanger yourself.'

Shadowsun landed hard atop a fallen trunk. Her hooves left deep imprints in the wood. She crouched, and leapt again. 'What did I tell you, Shas'vre?' she yelled.

The gruff voice gave no reply.

Shadowsun was close enough now to hear the battle through her external audio pick-ups. There came the familiar hiss of pulse rifle fire – a three round *chuffing* that she had known from childhood, and the reassuring sizzle of plasma rifles being fired from Crisis battlesuits. These were nearly drowned out though by the sounds of gue'la weapons. Their inefficient laser guns ejected hot air from their assemblies with a staccato cracking, and the large-calibre cannons they were so fond of thumped savagely. She took some hope in what she didn't hear. There was no rumble of ground tanks, no massive detonations from tracked artillery and no whine of hovering airships. This was an assault by large numbers of light infantry with little, if any, mechanised support. It would attack in waves, with no concern for casualties, until its enemy was eliminated. It was typically human and painfully predictable.

Shadowsun crested a ridge of dirt ploughed up by the Manta's landing. As she had done on countless battlefields before, she catalogued the details of the scene in a heartbeat. The Manta was tilted slightly to one side with its nose in the air, a deep sea creature dragged up onto a wooded shore and left to die. Its hull looked crumpled and charred. The topmost of its two rear hatches was open, and a long boarding plank extended to the ground. Around the base of the transport, the warriors had erected a perimeter of four staggered barricades.

The ground in front of them was littered with dead humans. They were dressed in knee-length, dark-green coats with bright yellow armoured plates along the front and back. Their boots and gloves were made of light-brown leather. Their discarded rifles appeared to have wooden frames. Shadowsun could instantly tell that they had indeed tried to storm the Manta en masse only to be cut to pieces by the superiority of tau technology. Having sent the equivalent of eight fire warrior teams to a pointless doom, the remaining humans had evidently now decided to withdraw to the tree line where they too could have some protective cover. Volleys of laser fire continued to pour down onto her men, but they weren't doing much damage.

The walking machines, on the other hand, were.

Six of them were holding place just outside the woods. Their main body was little more than an open-topped, reinforced cage large enough to hold a single gue'la pilot. They had two back-bent legs and pipes on their rear quarters that belched black smoke. They looked pathetic to Shadowsun, a child's interpretation of a battlesuit. There was nothing laughable about their armaments though. Four of them had been mounted with projectile cannons; the other two had racks of missiles slung beneath them.

Shadowsun engaged her booster pack and arced high over the carnage. At the apex of her flight, she deactivated the suit's camouflage systems and landed in a crouch behind the barricades. Heavy shells whistled over her head, exploding into shrapnel as they impacted the Manta hull. Several tau soldiers, huddled down as low as they could, whirled around to face her. She raised her hands and retracted her helmet. Upon seeing her face, they quickly lowered their weapons.